DISTORTION

GAUTAM MALKANI

HarperCollins *Publishers* India

First published in India by
HarperCollins *Publishers* in 2019
Building 10, Tower A, 4th Floor, DLF Cyber City, Phase II,
Gurugram Haryana – 122002, India
www.harpercollins.co.in

2 4 6 8 10 9 7 5 3 1

First published in Great Britain in 2018 by Unbound

P-ISBN: 978-93-5357-103-0
E-ISBN: 978-93-5357-104-7

Text design by PDQ Digital Media Solutions, Bungay UK

Printed and bound at
MicroPrints India, New Delhi

To the hidden army of young carers.
Even if you do your worst, you're still doing your best.

For Bharat Malkani.

DISTORTION

Praise for *Distortion*

"An ambitious tale . . . Part post-truth nightmare, part social commentary, *Distortion* is an involved, complex book that rewards the close attention it deserves."

Financial Times

"Written with verve and dark humour."

Telegraph

"Interesting and thought-provoking analogies between the role of fate and prophecy in Greek myth, and search engines' predictions about out lives, likes and desires."

The Spectator

"This book is fearless – no one writes like Gautam Malkani."

Mona Arshi, Forward Prize-winning author of *Small Hands*

"Through a life lived in triplicate, Malkani's timely novel, in all its beguiling, addictive and emotive glory, shines a light onto our increasingly fractured lives and in doing so, makes clear the ongoing tensions and contradictions between the care we must give to ourselves and others over our desire for freedom in the digital world."

Niven Govinden, author of *This Brutal House*

"Gautam Malkani, the man behind one of the seminal books on the British-Asian experience, does something original and important once again, this time on the crucial issue of young carers. *Distortion* is essential reading."

Sathnam Sanghera, author of *The Boy with the Topknot*

"A taut and timely return for Gautam Malkani, *Distortion* is a brilliant exploration of social media, code-switching and toxic masculinity."

Nikesh Shukla, editor of *The Good Immigrant*

Praise for *Londonstani*

"Breathless, hilarious and convincing."

New York Times

"Gripping stuff . . . both disturbing and compelling. Malkani skilfully highlights the intersection of machismo and consumerism."

Guardian

"Malkani's debut novel displays all the bravado of his swaggering young protagonists . . . His writing achieves moments of real verve and power."

Washington Post

"Artful, thought-provoking and strikingly inventive. An impressive, in some respects brilliant, first novel."

Los Angeles Times

"A *bhuna* of gang-fights, inter-faith romance and organised crime, and the dizzying humour that underpins his voice is sharp, clever and convincing."

Independent

"Malkani has some interesting observations about identity and the way in which the culturally oppressed can take strength from their exclusion."

Sunday Telegraph

"*Londonstani* is a bold debut, brimming with energy and authenticity."

Observer

"The incessant blend of boyish patois and text-message speak is captivating."

The New Yorker

The misrepresentation succeeds to the point of making possible the appearance of the progenitor.

– Lou Reed, LP liner notes for
Metal Machine Music

1

MAMA'S DYING AGAIN. We're talking actual end-of-story dying. When she texts to tell me, she sounds like as if I owe her a fiver to settle a bet. Always texts when I silence her calls. Thinks I'm geeking it up in the library. Hiding in some late-night lecture. If I answered then for dead cert she'd start crying.

In the taxi, I delete Mum's texts, stash my fone in the backseat. Ramona next to me, not noticing – ain't even looking. Her streetlit silhouette. Strobe effect. Pulsing with the passing lamp posts. Each red traffic light a chance for me to stop all the shit that'll happen later. *Turn around. Turn around. Don't wait for some next signal, just ask the driver to turn the fuck around. Go geek in some library for real. Go read textbooks by her latest deathbed.* If you know you gonna regret something in the future, does that mean you already regret it?

She's on her blue velvet shoes tonight – four-inch heels, plunging top-lines, straps like padlocks across her insteps and ankles. Curls her toes before opening her mouth: "Okay, look Dillon, I don't know what's worse – completely ignoring me to check your fones or just fading me out while you check out my feet."

Coulda called off this evening – even though fuck knows what "rain check" actually means. Coulda just told her about Mum, I guess. That she got rushed into A&E earlier. That her cocktail of chemo's too strong for her. After collapsing again on the crapper. And the shit ain't even working.

Ramona now fixing her eyeliner without no need of make-up mirror or front-lens smartfone. Cab driver flipping on a light for her. Not to leer at her in the rear-view. Tonight our driver is a woman.

Happened in our downstairs, disabled-access toilet. Various assorted bodily fluids. Broken hand-towel holder.

Tonight, I remembered to hold open the door for Ramona. Held a brolly over her head, made sure her backless dress only flashed her back. Some slit in her dress that giggled as she stepped outta student halls. My fingers on her pencil heels as she climbed inside the cab, just trying to hold shit steady. First time I ever took Ramona out, was on budget so tight I pretended like I was fasting.

They keeping Mum in a separate room cos her white blood count is in the red. Charing Cross Hospital this time, not Ealing, West Middlesex or Hammersmith – i.e. visiting hours end at eight. Shoulda told Ramona I could meet her after, just couldn't join her for this gig or whatever.

Single-lane standstill means our driver breaks left, sharp left. Kerb-crawling the homeless hanging round Holborn. One of the homeless makes eye contact with me and starts shouting. Ramona opens handbag then window then gives him cigarettes and multivitamins.

Be good to go hold Mama's hand. One last grasp before the final croak. Ain't necessary to describe a dying woman's hand.

Ramona's feet now crossed just above her ankle straps, sinews stretched, heels puncturing the carpet.

I mean a dying woman's hand trying its hand at tapping or swiping or just feeble-style fingering a touchscreen.

Her heels the reason for this dipshit taxi; me the dipshit reason for her heels. Gig we headed to is some secret album launch in some poncey West End theatre. Sit-down only, no latecomers, strictly limited capacity to enhance the experience of the live web-stream. Can't just tell her I gotta go see my mum – ain't even told her Mum's got the C-bomb. I tell other people, though – other girls, other women. Do women hold it against you if you don't make them come when they fucking you outta sympathy? Asking for a friend.

Got all dressed up for the gig and that. Her special trainers – the left sole elevated.

Wouldn't ever actually do that to Ramona, though. Wish I could say I wouldn't even know how to. Just thinking random rebound options for when she wises up and dumps me.

Ear plugs and Kleenex. *Check.* Live music as opposed to what? Digital content ain't dead. Don't never dies. Ain't dying or dead or dying. Only other time I been to a gig, I went with Mummy. Her long-lost denim jacket. Her secret Google mission to school up on John Legend. Stage-side, Row A – for people with special access requirements. Told Ramona I was on some Economics homework that evening. Even texted her questions.

A short first gear, a long second. Tarmac and puddles become a mashup of brake lights, rear lights, red traffic lights. Glow from some blood-red backlit billboard. Slashing through wetness – tyres making toilet sounds. Pull out my fone, my *other* fone – my other fones plural. Different login and password combos permanently stored in my fingers.

> @DILLON: HEADING TO John Legend's new album launch tonight – gig being streamed live if you wanna join

> @DHILAN: MUM SICK again. Gonna spend evening and night by her hospital bedside

> @DYLAN: TUESDAY NITE is student start-up nite. And we got a private-equity guest speaker

Ramona being too busy to eavesread my touchscreens. Or she just wants to trust me. When the fuck was it? That time it first hit me how trustworthy and truthful ain't always the same?

Allow that bullshit – can't just tell her I gotta go see Mama. Can't tell her about the cancer and the caregiving and the mornings. That I ain't really got conjunctivitis. To begin with,

I didn't tell no one. We're talking just the first five or so years. Classified. Need-to-know only. Access-restricted content. Not cos Mum was shamed or nothing – weren't like she'd got crabs or herpes. And not cos she knew how much other kids'd rinse you if your parent was even vaguely disabled. Most probly it was cos of them three bearded aunties – the ones who'd said her sickness was her karma for being so cleverclogs and carefree and divorced.

When she's done with her eyeliner, Ramona straightens then outstretches her toes. Ankles undulating like my mother's Adam's apple – like an ankle got lodged like a tumour in her throat. And what the fuck am I meant to tell her anycase? By the way, Ramona, you know how we always given each other the full friggin download since way back in Year Eight? Well, I totally forgot to mention that for the past ten years my mum's been battle-axing breast cancer. That for the past six of them years, she's been dying from it. Guess it just slipped my mind. Didn't really go to some family wedding in the middle of school term that time. Didn't really lose that T-shirt.

Roadworks, so our cabbie floors it in reverse, spins the steering wheel left, then forward in first. One of the roadworkers makes eye contact with me and starts shouting. Told Ramona about Mum's divorce, though. All the violin shit about how she worked three different jobs just to make sure I didn't get no scurvy. That her loneliness was why I spent Fresher's year still living at home in Acton. If I'd known she'd get readmitted to hospital today, I'd have ducked back to Acton to borrow her car for tonight. Her disabled person's parking permit. The cold window massaging my head as we pass by Covent Garden.

Was a time I couldn't even go chip shop without worrying so much I'd peg it back home. Allow this fuckness – I don't even *like* John Legend. Don't like R&B, don't like grime, don't like hip-hop, don't like rock, don't like rhymes, don't like *songs*.

Taxi pulls up beside a bunch of drunk-and-derogatory posh boys. Doing their whole beige trousers and self-belief thing. One of the posh boys makes eye contact with me and starts shouting. Consider telling our cabbie to keep the change, but cos she's a woman it feels cheesy. Still, I don't think twice about umbrella-walking Ramona five feet from taxi to foyer. My dry hand taking her raincoat as we queue at some ticket collection counter. My student discount card, my booking reference. And they say chivalry is just for sex.

At counter, check pockets to make sure "Dhilan" handset was left dead and buried in the back of the taxi. *Check.* But despite remembering to forget it, I can still hear its dumbfuck ringtone. Even though it's wedged deep in the backseat. Even though I switched it to silent. Even though I powered off. Even though I told Mum to not even think about foning me this evening. Shoulda just buried the thing in some desert someplace. Let future archaeologists get hard-ons over how humans evolved a wireless umbilical cord.

Twenty-four missed fone calls.

Twenty-fucking-four.

Probly now nearer thirty.

Forty and still counting.

Tell Ramona I'm sorry but I gotta go. I tell her I'm feeling sick. Sinuses, stomach, eye ducts, brain – various assorted bodily fluids. "But you should watch the gig without me, Ramona – ain't no sense both of us missing it." Hand her the tickets, raincoat, umbrella. Tenner for a taxi home.

"What the actual fuck?" Ramona calls out behind me. "Dillon, you can't keep treating me like this."

Tell her again that I'm sorry. Tell her again that I'm sick.

Outside the theatre, you push past the queues of tourists and ponces-who-probly-had-tennis-lessons. Piano tutors, even. Textured toilet roll and cricket practice. Pardon yourself politely for swearing in their faces, but no apologising for your pro-style push and shove. Cos like a child in some school play, your mum's just *dying* for you to watch her dying. One of the ponces makes eye contact with you and starts shouting. Doorman telling them to dash inside and take their seats.

Try hailing another taxi but ain't easy when acting like some police-chased crack addict. Telling tourists and posh boys to get outta your way, hair dripping through all your tears and your snot like you been fucking about with some facial warping app. Yelling, "Stop," at any taxi that passes, then screaming, "Take me to the fucking hospital." Shouldn't be rolling in no taxi anyway – not when not with Ramona. Tube cheaper, better, faster, stronger. Posh boys and tourists still walking too slowly; you quit the pavement to run on the road. Ain't sprinting, though. Ain't even running, really. But walking too quick to just call it just walking. Breathing in car exhaust fumes to try and warm your chest and your heart. At 7.30pm, all the West End theatres start sounding their buzzers and beeps and bells in sync, i.e. half an hour to get there – before the nurses become bouncers who won't let you in. Half an hour would probly be excess if Charing Cross Hospital was actually in Charing Cross, but it's actually five miles away in Hammersmith. Meanwhile, Hammersmith Hospital's in Acton. Slam-dunk excuse for turning up too late, but you already used it last year.

Man walks outta some restaurant with a foto of his meal stuck to his forehead. Woman walks outta some cinema and starts telling random people what she thought of the film. Hammersmith Station's on the Piccadilly Line; can pick it up from Leicester Square or Covent Garden. Journey Planner app says Covent Garden.

Sorry it took me so long. My fone got lost.

I got here quicker than I could.

Before you went uni, you thought all West End theatres were strictly for tourists or ponces brought up in private schools. Musicals and operas, grown-ups dropping nursery rhymes; making a song and a dance. Your mum wanted to celebrate being back in remission and was like, "*Fuck the* Phantom of the *Poncey* Opera." Pulled out her fone and started scrolling through random R&B concerts. Said that night was the only night she could get tickets and time off work at the same time. While booking the special Valentine's-rate intimate-dinner-and-concert deal, she asked you to pick which restaurant. *"Be my big man, Dhilan, and make decisions. Whisk me off my feet."* You decided to pack her painkillers and tranquilators in her pill pouch.

You cross a street dodging more taxis, more minicabs. More women on foot, more waiters putting out rubbish. Cobbled Covent Garden roads strictly for pedestrians, but still you get honked at twice. One of the drivers makes eye contact with you and starts shouting. One of the waiters makes eye contact with you and starts shouting. One of the women makes eye contact with you and starts shouting. Gap in the crowd opens, Tube station ticket barriers open, doors to the lift open. Somewhere between all the openings, you fixed up your hair and dried your eyes. And bought her a bunch of flowers. The fuck did you just buy flowers from? Some woman in backbone-friendly flat-heeled shoes smiles at them as if you bought the bunch for her. Then she makes eye contact with you and starts shouting.

Day before the John Legend gig, your mum made you fone to confirm the table reservation, her appointment at the hairdresser's and her special elevated trainers. Soon as you replaced the receiver, phone started ringing again – like there was one more thing you forgot to confirm. Ramona smiling down the landline, telling you she was throwing a last-minute blowout for her birthday tomorrow – her fourteenth on the fourteenth. At first, you was relieved to tell her your butt was busy – that you were sorry, but you really needed to be on your Economics homework tomorrow night.

Next morning, you weren't no longer feeling relieved. Some follow-up Facebook invite from Ramona, a bump on your forehead, a dent in your laptop. And so you told your mum you were feeling sick, real sick – so sick that she should do her Valentine's thing with someone else tonight. After all, ain't no sense both of you missing out. So sick and feverish and sick that, look, you even bumped your head. Your mum felt your bump, rubbed it, kissed it. Mixed up some honey and turmeric in boiling-hot milk. *"Down it, Dhilan. Turmeric always does the trick."* Made you neck the exact same stuff whenever you coughed, sneezed or sniffled. Even when you got asthma. Even when some fucktard from Year Eleven tore your shirt collar.

Tube station platform already a playground. Grown men waving scarves, chanting football-team nursery rhymes. One of the chanters makes eye contact with you, stops chanting and starts shouting. When a train pulls in, you head to the carriage furthest away from them.

Later that morning, your mum started with the whole ice-water-forehead routine. Sudden role-reversal making your brain hurt. Counterfeit fever and fake face flannels made from her no-longer-needed sanitary towels – the same ones you'd repurposed for her just three months earlier. Cold water dripping down your scalp; you remembered her hair appointment – first since her hair had started growing again. *"Don't sweat it,"* she told you. *"I already cancelled everything while I was boiling the milk."* Way too wet about the prospect of nursing you – like she couldn't wait to even shit out, settle some kinda caregiving scorecard. Next thing you knew, you were telling her not to cry – that she hadn't failed as a single mother just cos you'd caught a fever. That she didn't need to score evenings out that bust her federal budget, she didn't need to buy you a Nintendo DS, she didn't need hair and she definitely didn't need no left breast. Told her she just needed to smile. (Fuck it – it sounded good at the time.)

Tube driver says we gotta "wait here a few minutes" – you clock her exact words cos she's a she. You check the time on your Dillon handset: eighteen minutes. Double-check it on your Dylan handset: eighteen minutes. Should probly check yourself even. Use your fone as a mirror even though none of your handsets frown or smile or smell like your mum's face. You sit your butt down and switch off. Shield your flowers from the droplets of coughs, colds and flu.

After lowering your phoney fever, your mum combed your wet fringe. Kisses rubbed in like hair wax. *"I know what, Dhilan, let's watch a DVD tonight instead. Just like we did when I was sick.*

It'll be fun, darling – we'll take your duvet down to the sofa. We'll snuggle up tight and warm together."

You told her that, boom, you were cured. That your warp-speed full recovery must've been down to the miracle of milk and turmeric.

During something called the "support act", she took you to this place called the Upper Circle Bar, clutching a dealer's ounce of turmeric powder in a plastic Ziploc bag. She'd even scored a single-serve sachet of formula milk.

As I leg it through the ticket barriers and outta the Tube station, I for serious still reckon I might actually make it. Dillon handset says 19:55. No point hailing no taxi or hopping a bus – ain't even one stop. But as soon as straight away, I can tell from the sound of the place that most probly I'm too late. My flowers like they been in some nuclear hurricane. Still, I run up the stairs – to go through the motions at least; at least just to say I came. And, sure as shedding eyebrows, when I knock at the door, they won't even think about letting me in. When I wave the flowers through small square window, they still won't. Finally, I convince them to give her a note from me, but the only lame crap I can come up with is: "I'm here. I'm right outside." They read the note, change their minds, let my ass in.

Hand her what's left of the flowers then sit down beside her. The seat comfortably uncomfortable – like as if even the furniture's been waiting for me. "I knew you'd come," she whispers as she leans in close. "I knew you'd be back." As she looks back towards the stage, Ramona slips me a copy of some booklet/programme thing and slowly uncurls her toes. Cos fuck what the doctors say, there's always tomorrow. I'll go say bye to Mummy tomorrow.

2

AIN'T MY FAULT that being Mama's carer has been sweet for my career. Kept me off streets, made me school up for my GCSEs, got me into this big boss uni. Today's lecture about some BS I already taught myself – bossed the whole reading list the last time she was rotting in hospital. My brain like a Tampax for textbooks and the side effects of her Tamoxifen tablets. *Cos whatever it takes, okay?* Whatever grades I needed to attain for her to carry on smiling and fighting and live-blogging parents' evening. My positive exam results = her negative test results = forget fucking chemo, just intravenously administer my academic accomplishments. *Well, good for me, yeh.* Guess all this shit's been good for me.

Sermon going on up front is just some seminar, not a full-on lecture. Minor, modular, mid-term summary. Still, I told my family weren't no way I could skip it, that it was critical like sitting the final paper of my final-year finals. *Good luck, Dhilan. Good for you and good, good luck. Do whatever you bloody want.* To them all my bullshit's just academic. The lecturer reciting her twenty-page checklist to the beat of us typing it up.

Ain't never told Mum this, but I even tried getting my dumb ass into Cambridge – figured that'd be one way to justify going to uni outside London. One way to justify going to dorms and draft-dodge having to hold her tighter than Spandex every morning-sickness morning. And, check this: I even got accepted by Cambridge. But then Ramona decides to do her degree right here, at the London School of Economics.

Proper sleepstipated today. Chasing back Pro-Plus tablets with Red Bull. Ain't nothing wrong with planting them little candy love hearts inside her pillbox.

Ten minutes in, the trolling starts. All my tinkling and twinkling touchscreens laid out in line formation like they waiting to whip me. Kicks off with just gentle, early-morning bants. For instance: *"Go suck shit out of a drainpipe."* For instance: *"You've got blowjob-vomit in your brain."* For instance: *"You dirty stinking shitlump of a boy, how you could do like this?"* Only this time, the trolls are on some kinda different vibe – instead of stepping up the abuse, they start getting anal:

"There's a split infinitive in your Facebook profile."

"Would it kill you to iron your T-shirt?"

"Stop slouching like a sack of liposuction."

"I hope you've at least steam-ironed your scrotum."

I sit up and type: "wait – who is this? how the hell you know I'm slouching?"

"Much better," the troll comes back. *"Now try to keep your vertebrae straight."*

"thanks v much for the ergonomic advice but I'll sit however I want."

"But why are you sitting here in the first place, kid? Why are you even in this lecture?"

"get myself educated. who is this?"

"Good for you. After all, to be ignorant is to bend over and spread your ass cheeks for the forces of darkness."

"er. ok. who is this?"

"Which is why the first thing the forces of darkness attack is the educated. The experts, the complex explanations, all those cumbersome facts and inconvenient truths. So it's good you're here to get educated."

"well then educate me by telling me who the fuck you are."

"Only that isn't really the reason you're here, is it kid?"

Start scoping the whole lecture hall to see which of these dipshits is fucking with me. All the posh boys with their posture and opinions; all us state-school kids sitting like we on a train without a ticket. Don't take no time to clock them – two random geriatric dudes geeking it up in the front row. We're talking aged out and played out, sticking out like skin tags. And, yeh, I know it ain't right to generaltype – not every old white dude is a dirty-assed evil-doer. But even from nine rows behind, can tell that this troll action is coming from them. Banging the crap outta their keypads and slap-swiping their touchscreens. Soon as I spot them, both men turn around, stare dead-eyed in my direction like we on some psychic sixth-sense type shit. Mama calls it "animal magnetism". More like electromagnets with these dudes – eyes like MRI scanners. Kinda eyes that distract you from what someone actually looks like. Only shit I register proper is wardrobe-related: one of the old men is on some classic double-breasted biker jacket look; the other one's rocking a grey off-the-peg suit. But it's the biker jacket dude looks more dapper.

Get enough openings to back off. Best way to deal with trolls is to just click the fuck away. Lecturer now giving it some serious data visualisation action – her laptop linked up to three separate projectors. Guy sat beside me highlighting the whole fucking everything – shoulda just printed the handout on day-glo yellow paper. Auditorium radiators randomly bleeding and sniffling – and so I message home to check that she's okay.

Some girl to my left starts crying on the quiet.

And so I message home to check she's okay.

After all, ain't in primary school no more: no one's gonna confiscate my fones. Now an ad for pre-bereavement bereavement counselling. Story about a miracle mud cure. Twenty-four-hour flash sale on post-surgical lingerie. My fones hit me up with different ads depending on whether I'm logged on as Dillon or Dylan or Dhilan. Different ads, different Facebook stories, Google results and YouTube videos, different solutions for dealing with different kinds of bodily fluid. You know how all the ads, stories and search results are custom-tailorised according to your own individual search history and click history and personal info? Well, trust me, yeh, you got no idea how proper fucked this can get – not unless you constantly compare your Facebook feed and your most top-secret Google results with an identical search or scroll by someone else. I do this on the regular for Dillon, Dylan and Dhilan to help me school up on the differences between them.

Actually, scrap that – ain't just simply *schooling up* on each of them. More like stepping up to some next-level version of them.

One time when I grabbed my Dylan handset and googled with franticness the words "Female, Body, Unresponsive", I got hit with ads and articles about erectile dysfunction. As for when I log on as Dhilan – well, that shit's between me and Google.

Don't even ask what happens when I google what gift to get Mummy for Christmas. Or more like what gift *not* to get in case it's once again her last-ever Christmas. Or her latest last-ever birthday. Or her last Mother's Day or Valentine's Day – or Monday or Tuesday or Wednesday. Got me a different gift, game plan and Topman T-shirt for each different prognosis. Mum trusting Google and Facebook more than she trusts the doctors and specialists and experts. Me trusting Google more than I trust my mum. And, yeh, I do know that probly means we just end up confirming our own shit – our fears and prejudgements and shit. I know it means our most deep-down secret thoughts get reinforced. I know the apps and websites try and keep our eyeballs locked on by showing us more of the stories, videos and info we wanna be shown and by telling us more of what we wanna hear. I know that's how shit with Mum and me got so messed up. Now an ad for a memory foam bed wedge. A story about conjoined urns. Special offer on long-sleeved latex gloves.

Those two old ancientquated dudes are still checking me. Fuck knows whether to show them my finger or the most photogenic side of my face. One of Mum's most lame-ass excuses when I've caught her staring at me is to claim she thought we was playing a game of that goofball blink-and-you-lose bullshit. Even when my eyes are closed on account of me being asleep and her staring had woken me up. Try returning the two men's exact same gawkward gaze but it's like trying to stare out a fish. A dead fish. Corpse of a fish that died of shock. Swipe back to my Dhilan handset. An ad for an all-night pharmacy. Lymphatic drainage massage techniques. YouTube videos for teaching myself advanced paramedic driving skills. But the two old men keep carjacking my attention. Man in the suit's on some neck-length has-been hairstyle; dude in the biker jacket, some crew-cut combover combo. You'd think a guy in his seventies or eighties would look dickish rocking a biker jacket, but this coffin-dodger carries it off like it's some second-skin cashmere cardigan. Deffo ain't ever seen them before, but clearly they reckon they know me. Ten minutes later, they still shooting me evils. I lay down my Dhilan fone, duck my head down and give them the back of my laptop – with this 'I ♥ Mom' sticker across it to block all that ambient advertising for Apple.

Soon as I type the words "my late beloved mother", I bang on the backspace.

Even though I know "late" is the technical term for it. I know that if I don't use the word "late", it'll imply she's alive.

Still though – "late" sounds proper ridickulous. Like she got held up in traffic on her way to heaven. Like her organs were so corrupted they had to get rerouted over even broader-band bandwidth.

Like I been waiting for her to hurry the fuck up and check out.

Anyway, allow that shit – people who use the word "late" are the same ponces who call the crapper a "water closet" and then still need to abbreviate it. Saps who use words like "splendid".

Late. (But then what if some thickshit idiot thinks it means she was pregnant?)

When I'm done with the website I've set up in Mum's memory, I answer another email of condolence then upload the funeral service playlist. We're talking Bono. We're talking John Lennon. We're talking every single track from her bi-monthly funeral service prep talks. Her horrible-adorable angstipating about whether I'd need copyright-holder permissions to play them. Next, I upload fotos, videos, sound clips. Metadata for the message forum. The digital version of the guestbook that got passed round like a spliff at the crematorium. Cos digital content ain't dead, doesn't die, etc. Been keeping Mum's Facebook page alive ever since she first got sick. And I been downloading every available Ouija board app but I'm staying the fuck away from actual Ouija boards, actual séances, actual psychics. Anyshit that might actually work. When bereavement fatigue kicks in, I click on other tabs, open other windows. Ramona wants to know if I'm up for going bowling this evening. Anjali wants to know if I'm scattering Mum's ashes in the Ganges. Two girls whose real names I don't know ask if I'll meet them after so they can copy my lecture notes. Sonya asks me if I'm happy now then carries on walking past me.

Okay, allow this gimpness. Hold up my fone now and snap a selfie to see if there's a reason why those two old dudes keep scoping me. Bruises on my face, vomit stains; anything that might pass for a male equivalent of a woman's messed-up mascara. Ain't nothing out of place, though – not a hair, not some standing-ovation lapel. Flip from front lens to back lens and then pinch-to-zoom on the two old men. Seems they on some proper dopple-twin shit – stick them in the same haircut and stubble and they'd pass for identikit clones. Too age-gapped to be twins, too alike to be just brothers, too brother-like to be father and son. It's more as if they in a before-and-after ad for some backstreet Botox clinic. When the before-Botox dude leans in to chat to the after-Botox dude, it's like a mashup of a man and his younger self.

Take a foto of them on the sly. This is when my fone starts randomly swiping all on its own. With a quickness – like as if train carriages covered in ads are dashing across my home screens. Special offers on Kleenex, discounts on disinfectant, Horlicks, ear plugs, some hand-carved prayer for hanging on the wall above my bed. Apparently Google's stock exchange filings state that ads are basically answers. But I ain't even asked any questions.

Power off my fone, switch back to my laptop.

Now my cursor's moving by itself. Typing up random comebacks to all the trolling I been ignoring. Clicking open tabs and windows – like when you allow remote access to someone from tech support. The cursor flies up to the task bar, starts opening up my search history. The young carers' networks and online support forums, an eBay listing for a hazard button and baby monitor, fishnets, *body fresh*, nasal cannula, the chemical composition of the scent of her night sweats. Should probly hide my screen from the guy sat beside me, but allow it – dude seems busy enough eating up the lecturer's latest pie charts. Anycase, fuck knows why I ain't ever just wiped my browsing and search histories. Takes a couple minutes to clean out your shit and then it's laters to embarrassing ads. That's like travelling back in time and fixing up the past but with no need to bust out a time machine. And fuck it, maybe that time-travel shit works the other way round? Maybe I can fix what went down in the past by straightening out stuff in the present?

Now an app for checking Mama's oxygen levels. One-click replacement cylinders. An online virtual confession booth. An interactive karma calculator.

Ain't no big mystery what dumbfuckness is going on here – must've accidentally clicked open some malware sent by those two doddery old men. Look up to sneak a peek and sure as shitfits all my windows are synced up on their own laptop screen. One laptop, two old codgers, four shaky hands fighting over the keyboard like they playing some geriatric mobility scooter version of *Grand Theft Auto*.

Next come all the scare stories. Or the scary headlines that don't reflect the actual stories. Articles about side effects, step-by-step instructions for cleaning radioactive secretions, silicone prosthetics that won't harm the environment when they finally cremated.

Try clicking back to an article about mammary scar tissue. A manual for deep-tissue massaging. Wait, *what?* Now all my fones flickering back to backlit – start vomiting up post-surgical image searches directly onto my laptop. We're talking pictures from all four corners of the worldwide world cos this kinda porn, it ain't mono-racial. Oh, and diversity of textures as well as skin colours: bumps, lumps, abscesses, scarring, inversions, nodules, bombed-out and burnt out, respectfully blurred out. From outside the lecture theatre, ambulance sirens sound like some maniac life-support machine. Accelerating then silent.

Thing is, though, I didn't feel much in control back when I actually clicked on all this shit in the first place. Not even for those first drafts of my search history.

Couple minutes later, I finally think to run an anti-malware program so I can kick the old men outta my laptop, retake control of my cursor.

Done and done.

Still, though: the fuck don't I just delete my search history?

This time, allow all that clicking and weeping and whining and dying on my mummy's memorial website. This time, I log on as Dylan, click open my side-hustle. Spreadsheet stretches out across my screen with rows of client billings and columns of net margins before interest, tax, depreciation and amortisation. We're talking entrepreneurial windows, not bereavement windows. Business shit, not gormless doormat degree shit. I call my start-up 'Company A' cos that's what we call companies in our Business Studies module – i.e. it ain't the name of my company, it's just what I call the thing while I think of a name. Technically, it's just a data-entry business – I'm a jumped-up freelance data temp. Figured this'd be how I'd put food on the table so Mama wouldn't have to work and die and struggle. Figured this'd keep me so busy I wouldn't have to sit at the table with her. My corporate bank account is basically the mother–son joint account for doing the housekeeping finance and admin. Well, good for me, yeh. Told you all this young carer shit's been good for me. Now an ad for a brand-new brand of lavender massage oil. *Special non-sticky formula can also be used as lubricant – ideal for seamless transitioning between massage and intimate play.*

The two old men have split. After nailing my fifth invoice of the morning, I peep over my laptop screen and it's like both dudes been deleted.

Then I turn around.

Up close, both men look even more like clones, even though the differences are now more blatant. The creases and the wrinkles, the clean shaves, the white stubble, the skin so smooth it reflects the light, the sharkskin-grey suit, the battered double-breasted biker jacket. Their four legs stretched the fuck out in the row right behind me. Fart smell, leather and old-school cologne. Was wrong about their faces, though – we ain't talking *before-and-after* Botox, we're talking botched Botox and proper, blankpage Botox. Both of them scoping over my shoulder old-school style cos I blocked them from remote-accessing my laptop. Eating from some greasy bag of choc-chip cookies. Nodding at my spreadsheets and bank statements like as if they tagging me with their approval. Smiling, scoffing, sprinkling blessings of cookie crumbs. I turn back round and face the front like some non-confrontational goth.

Then what I do is I try and make the men quit snooping by deliberately clicking on upsetting content. Proper gastric teargas trigger-warning content. The fotos, the videos, the sound clips, the digital version of the guestbook, the metadata on the message forum, the funeral service playlist, the online coffin catalogue with the pop-up 3D images and combustion-rate data tables. The T&Cs of corporate bridge financing deals while I wait for her life insurance to clear. The fourteenth draft of my eulogy for her, even though I'm now on draft sixty-seven. Even load up an earlier version of Mama's memorial website – version 6.0 that I built one time when she was technically in remission. Because her code-red A&E action plan became her detailed blueprint for her funeral service programme. And cos her *stop-being-in-denial* sermons became dry-run dress rehearsals. And cos Dylan, not Dhilan or Dillon.

And check this: my randomly worked-out plan ends up actually working out. Next time I turn round, both old men are stood up, heads bowed on some condolence-type shit as they start shuffling out the lecture theatre. Packet of chocolate chip cookies left behind like lilies where they just been sitting. Ten minutes later, though, I lose control of my cursor again. And up comes another sick-bag bout of my search history. This time, my laptop flashing up a proper alert prompt – telling me it's "remotely reconnecting to another device".

And then the lecturer starts cursing cos something's gone wrong with the overhead projector.

3

FOOLS THOUGHT YOU was asleep. That night you found out your mummy and daddy had decided to live separately. Even though it was a school night, your parents had gone to your uncle's house and your aunties had come over to yours. You was seven years old but still they called it babysitting. *Babysitting.* You were sitting at the top of the stairs listening to every friggin word they said. One aunty, two aunties, three – a three-way combo of cousins and sisters-in-law, but still they called each other sisters. *Bhanjis.* Laughing in sync with the laughter on TV. Or was the live studio audience laughing in sync with them? The light from the living room like thumping moonlight, a floodlight hooked up to life support. Why – why was you already on thoughts of medical equipment when this was two years before her sickness? Rubbing your eyes cos you actually *had* been sleeping – something had woke you open and dragged you to the top of the steps. Like that time you peeped through the crack in your mum and dad's bedroom doorway – TV switched on back then as well, the volume upped to hush out your mama's *sigh-squeal-repeat.*

But with the three bearded aunties, the TV was different. Weren't just the sound from the speakers, was also the light it pumped outta the living room. Flickering, beating, breathing through the banisters and up the stairs, then settling straight-line style, like a beam from a torch. Like as if the light was showing you how far down the steps you could sit without them spotting your Batman bed-socks. Stench of whatever they was eating like some sweated palm on your face, forcing you to stay sitting. Outside, the wind and the rain twisting the satellite signal – the TV trying to untune itself. The picture jumping. Ad breaks skipping. Aunties talking in riddles. *I tell you, always I knew she'd get herself into trouble.* Always too clever she was. *Yes.* Yes, yes, yes. How she thinks she can break up her marriage? *She's got the selfishness, yes. WHAT SHE THINKS SHE IS?* You also – try the mango chutney. Is so shameful, yes. *Hahn-ji, hahn-ji.* To throw a good husband in the street. *No – the mango one. WHAT SHE THINKS SHE IS? SHE THINKS SHE'S A MAN OR WHAT?* Or is it she thinks she's English? *Yes. Yes, yes, yes.* AND SO WHAT IF HER HUSBAND HE WORKS ALL THE TIME? Theek hai, theek hai, that's plenty-plenty for me. *One day she will get her punishment. When her karma it catches her, it will kill her.*

You tried to quit listening, but instead you found yourself listening *and* looking. Sight of the aunties through the gap in the doorway, pakora-filling spilling from the gaps in their teeth. None of them realising they'd got mint chutney on their chins. Or that their chins were in need of waxing. They'd brought ice-cream tubs full of green-chilli pakoras that looked more like ready-fried reptiles. Some big black cooking pot the size of a toilet. All three of them strictly vegetarian but consuming more meat than most meat-eaters do cos they bought all their veg with income from a kebab shop. Wetness of whistling as they cooled down their mouths by sucking air through clenched teeth. *Me, I only feel sorry for the son. THIS IS NOT A THING TO DO. TO DO LIKE THIS. I MEAN, WHAT IS THIS? Hahn-ji,* I tell you divorce is always worse for the child. *Yes. Yes, yes, yes, this is what it said on the* Daily Mail *– the mother will live off the welfare and the son will go to the jail.* Yes, either he will go around with the ruffians, or he will stay at home and become the weirdo. *HE WILL GO OFF THE RUFFIAN RAILS.*

All of them making it all about you – as if you'd already done what you were gonna do.

JUST YOU WAIT AND SEE. *Close the light and come and see.* WHAT WILL HAPPEN IS THIS: HE WILL TAKE THE FATHER'S PLACE. *Yes. Yes, yes, yes* – he will take the father's place. *The pundit told her no matter if her marriage breaks – no matter because her son is her soulmate. That in the last life they were husband and wife. HA! YES, YES, YES, HA, HA, HA!* Don't laugh, *Bhanji*. This is not something to laugh. *Her son will take the father's place.* BUT FROM WHERE YOU HAVE HEARD THIS DISGUSTING THING? *It says so on the line. The Googly-engine told me when I looked it on the line: the son will take the father's place.* YOU MEAN *ONLINE*, STUPID – *ONLINE.* Wait – just you wait and see. *Close the light and come and see.*

Jewellery jangling, make-up bubbling, forks scraping empty plates. All three of them still sitting on some slaughtered-cow sofa, but now each of them with one arm outstretched. First aunty's hand placed flat against the TV, second aunty's hand against the PC monitor, third aunty touching a laptop screen. Couldn't see which screen the laughter was coming from, though, cos your focus was on staying the fuck outta their sight. Avoid being caught by their eyes. Your mum had told you how she'd seen your various assorted aunties' powers in play. The broken engagements, the birthmarks, the business bankruptcies, the blotches of acne, the broken-down Audis, the bad bloodline marriages, the malware, the maladies, the miscarriages. She'd told you the word for what they did was "*nazar*". *Nazar* weren't like voodoo or black magic – it didn't need no potions or dolls or photographs. Just ill-will and a belief in the power of bad vibes. Your mum told you that people put *nazar* on others cos they couldn't help themselves – they just got too easily offended or too easily jealous. But they also too easily forget the golden-but-unspoken rule: *if you put* nazar *on someone, your own children or grandchildren will suffer more than the person you put* nazar *on.*

Your mum told you don't be afraid, though. Told you that men invented scary women just to keep women down. Brainful, knowledgeful women in particular – the women who'd got all the dirt and all the info. Told you fear leads to hatred.

If my daughter did a thing like this I would thapar her – I'm telling you, one hard slap across her face. Then she would understand. She would know she's done a wrong thing. *THE OTHER DAY SHE TELLS ME THAT HER SON IS HER LIFE.* Well, let's just see; let's all just watch and see what kind of a life it is he leads. *Not fit. I tell you; not fit.* The Facebook story says she will lose him to the ruffians – he will go off the broken rails. BUT THE THREE OF US, WE'VE AGREED, NO? HE WILL TAKE THE FATHER'S PLACE. *Yes. Yes, yes, yes.* The Googly-engine has said it: *he will take the father's place.*

4

RAMONA. THE LIBRARY. Refuge. Sanctuary. General-purpose hiding place. No ID, no entry – we're talking bag checks and bouncers. The library. All private study rooms already booked out. But, hey, who the fuck ever goes to the Institutional Archives section?

"Relax, Dillon – this is fine?" Ramona always whispers like she's asking you a question. "I'll lean against this?"

Ain't my fault that being Mama's carer has been sweet for my sex life. Gave me a higher-charged late start, saved me from teeny boppers in chain bars, forced me to seek out alternatives to intercourse and most forms of actual bodily contact. And, no, we ain't talking cybersex or phone-sex or dry-humping or any other dropdown category of interactive wanking – I mean proper, full-on, contactless sex. And I ain't mean no sympathy sex either – after all, Ramona don't even know about my mum. Each time I do tell someone, I swear the girl in question to top-secret secrecy. Next thing, they start thinking they my one-and-only confidant. Start turning up at my student halls with freshly home-baked baked stuff. Feel touched by my fear of touching them – their hands or their coat or their fone or whatever. Nicole, Neena and Nadine know my mum to be permanently terminally ill; Anjali, Amelia and Aarti know my mum to already be dead. Ain't looking to cheat on Ramona or nothing – ain't trying to be like one of them masculinity assholes. I just needed to tell a couple of peeps in order to keep Dhilan and Dylan for real and fully realised and just generally in touch with reality. Besides, way I see it, there's basically one key common denominating link between sympathy, non-sympathy and with-deepest-sympathy sex and that's the actual act of actual sex. Remember how back in the day, boys got told that if they wanked too much they'd go blind? Yeh, well, after Mum got even more ill, I told myself that if I ever yanked the plank again, her eyes would shut for good. Her sickness keeping my fists in check. Skip forward six years of cold showers and bedtime prayers and I finally figured out the only sure-fire way not to masturbate was to keep having real actual sex – with or without all that teenage titty-twiddling. Or intercourse. Or bodily contact. Ditto from the geek angle: I've schooled up about Oedipus and Hamlet and Norman Bates and how it's bad news to even *think* about marital relations with your mum and how apparently real actual sex can offset the "inevitability of proximal Oedipal inclinations" – i.e. I don't wanna wind up some lonely celibate psycho who dresses up in his dead mother's clothes and caresses her prosthetic breasts while wanking off to her favourite Celine Dion album. So you see, all things weighed and done, there really ain't much choice for me.

Today we talking proper toe cleavage – only the top of the slit, just a tiny bit; but part of it. Also, her shoes show off her arches more than most shoes with similar shank, girth and depth of throat. This ain't no miracle of shoe design. Or clever counter-structural engineering. This is the miracle of Ramona's tarsal and metatarsal, ligaments and tendons. The stretch along her instep whenever she spreads her toes open. All them times I bullshitted myself, thinking I weren't objectifising her just cos I weren't zooming in on her sex organs. Proper shamefulness. Still, I carry on checking out her feet arches as she shifts into some less painless position. No flatness, no puffiness. Her whole body bearing down on them now. No folded lip of man-flab. Two-hundred thousand sweat glands secreting a sweeter brand of bodily fluid. The thing about mummy/sex issues that most people don't get is that it ain't got fuck all to do with your actual mum. And it deffo ain't your mummy's fault. The mother complex is *you* – it's your own shit. So when I pass up a feel of Ramona's Achilles tendon, she don't get why I'm now acting all Kentucky Fried Chickenshit. Starts offering the usual reassurances – her chafing has healed, she ain't got warts or verrucas or fungal issues. Can't tell her the truth about all my various issues so I just start scoping over her shoulder. And this is when I clock that those two old men from lectures have been watching us. Lurking like a file of malware behind a rack of shelves. Ramona don't notice them, though, and I figure probly best I don't tell her. Besides, she ain't even taken her headphones off, never mind any of her clothes. Which means she's grabbed all her shit and gone before I can tell her there ain't nothing wrong with her.

Sign on the wall tells you to disable electronic camera sounds when copying library content. Should hang out here more often for the smell of this place. Ain't no restrictions yet on memorising smells. I mean hang out here for real. You know how libraries always got that special library aroma? I'm thinking maybe that ain't the scent of old books, more like it's the vibe of essay deadlines and exam stress. Cold sweat and sweet milky tea. Crisis and cosiness. Panic and comfort becoming the exact same thing. Maybe if I hung here more often I'd feel less of a freak.

Somewhere to my left, some book slams shut. Might even be a laptop or a door. You know that feeling when you ain't sure whether to click on something? Yeh, *that.* Next thing, I'm legging it down some big-ass spiral staircase beneath some bigger-ass atrium in the centre of the library. My run looks more dickless than dramafied, though, cos it's the most longed-out staircase you ever saw. Steps so far apart you gotta keep checking your stride. Halfway down, I actually forget if I'm running away from the two old men or running after them. Or if I'm running after Ramona. Whatever the fuck I'm doing, everyone in here can hear me if not see me, so I try and take the librarian's bollocking like a man.

*

Those two aged-out goons crash my next lecture and then some bullshit web-based workshop after that. They in Tesco Metro when I go there for cashback, they in Café Amici when I roll there for lunch. Baiting me to look back at them. Stare-out version of a Mexican stand-off. Them sitting by the window, me by the counter. And we ain't talking blank-document stares – more like the opposite. Soap-opera emotional overload. Both men maxed out on anger and sadness and every emoji in between. As if I'm already meant to know what their problem is. Behind them, the traffic round Aldwych like some freeze-frame car chase; my laptop decides I've forgotten my password. Slam it shut and bail before the men can pay their bill.

Holborn is basically this buffer zone between the City and West End. Stuck in some kinda fuckness between work and play. Try texting Ramona but she's on some voicemail bullshit. Try emailing her, she still on voicemail. Now a story about ankle tattoos. Register before December and get twelve weeks' free subscription. Herbal remedies for swollen feet. Fluid-filled balloon feet. Pictures of pustulating ulcerated ankles. The smell of vomit in my mind's nostrils. Don't need to be paranoid about suffering from paranoia to start wondering if maybe all these ads, stories and search results are trying to tell me something. I been wondering that shit for years. But seeing as how all the ads and stories are custom-tailorised by my own search history, by my fone soaking up all my thoughtstains, does that mean that *I'm* the one who's telling me something?

Swipe back to the ad-free blankness of the Google home page. But now I just get dicked about by some autocomplete/predictive-text type fuckery. When the system decides what you're typing soon as you start to type it. Finishing your sentences for you like you're stuck in some happily married couple situation. Crunching and recrunching all your data with each letter you type. Like your fone is fucking psychic. Like it knows your ass better than you know yourself. Knows what you gonna do next. My autocompleted sentences start making me nauseated; I switch to my Dylan handset. Allow this bullshit. My mum been reading my mind long before any of my fones could.

5

NEXT TIME I clock those two old men, I man the fuck up and go full-on confrontational. All goes down around 3pm in the King's College student bar. King's College is just round the way from the London School of Economics, but unlike LSE, place ain't crawling with my course-mates, co-students and future LinkedIn contacts. Cos right from the first day of Fresher's Week, I been having my own personalised university motto: *When she's finally dead I'll have to ditch all my uni friends to help me forget how much I'd wished she was dead so that I could hang out with them.* (Yeh, okay, probly sounds better in Latin.)

The KC student bar is way up on the top floor, windows scoping out across the Thames like we in some river-view safety-deposit penthouse. Apart from the two old men, only people up here are a bunch of seven or eight guys all trying to listen to some same pair of headphones, various well-read culturally rich kids having their usual bullshit convos about hip-hop and that, plus the man behind the by-now empty sandwich counter. One of the girls is fronting with her holiday fotos printed on her clothes. Man in the biker jacket – the botched-Botox man – takes a sip from some half-empty glass of beer that was already there when they showed up. His fist making the pint glass look more like a shot. Dodgy Botox giving him chipmunk cheeks that don't even move none when he swallows.

In my head, I start scrolling through ways to out-psyche them. Like, if this place was a proper bar and not some pimped-up student common room that reckons it's a bar, then I'd maybe buy them a bottle of Hennessy and have a waiter take it over. Buy one for myself too, then raise my glass to them like some Bentley-driving badass. Or just Jack Daniels if they don't have any Hennessy. Instead, I stride right up to them and ask the men straight out what the fuck they think they doing by following me the fuck around all day. Only I don't actually use the word fuck.

"Horseshit. Little man." The botched-Botox one talking like he got problems on the breathing front – like his lungs are letting in liquid. Some stateside accent mixed in with the liquid. "Nobody's been following you anywhere, kid. Matter of fact, I think you'll find that *you've* been following *us*." Dude coughs into my space to respond, before hitting me with: "We were even contemplating calling the cops. Tell them how you've been stalking us. The whole day long. In fact, we even thought about calling the cops." And again with that combo of old-school aftershave and old-man flatulence.

"Nah, you must be mistaken, old man. I weren't following you nowhere. I study here. Well, not here in King's, I mean at LSE."

Younger-looking old man now starts up with his own OTT coughing routine, like they having some sorta bronchial congestion contest. "Oh, you study." He turns to talk to the man who looks like his older self: "He studies." And then back to me: "You're a student."

Botched-Botox man raises his shot-sized pint glass – fingers so obese they entering proper obscenity territory. "Good for you, kid. Good to get educated. Challenge your own thinking. That way you won't get duped into cutting off your own face as an anti-wrinkle remedy. I'm speaking metaphorically, of course – about voters and consumers and so on." Touches his botched-Botoxed forehead. Upturned eyebrows and swollen thoughts. "I mean, I'm speaking metaphorically, not literally."

Start telling them they already gave me their pro-educational public-service sermon when they was trolling me during lectures this morning, but the younger-looking man cuts me off. "And now here you are once again. What are the chances, eh? What a coincidence. What a small and fucking wonderful world."

Can't puzzle out whether all this fuckery calls for angstipating and adrenal-gland action, so what I do is, I end up angstipating about whether or not I should be angstipating. That kinda dicklessness actually happens to me on the regular – even when it just comes to feeling up or down. Ain't gonna go all *open-process* here or nothing, but apparently it's cos I've spent way too long "mirroring my mother's feelings" instead of growing my own. Turns out this is why some dogs end up looking like their owner – all them years of aping their owner's moods, vibes and facial expressions. Fuck knows if I look like my mum, though, cos even Mum don't look like Mum.

I tell the men ain't no effing way I coulda been following them – whether to lectures or the library or any other obligationary day-in-the-life-of-a-student destination. For starts, wherever the men had gone, my ass had been sat there way before they showed. While the botched-Botox man hears me out, his right eye starts twitching. White lashes that match his stubble. He scratches his stubble and it's like as if salt is falling from his face – this neat line of it across their table. They carry on listening from behind the salt. Meantime, the other man – Mister Clean-Shaven Blankpage-Botox man – is some perfect picture of airline-pilot healthiness, fixed up and double-filtered on Instagram. Skin so shiny and silky smooth, my focus keeps slipping off his face and onto the noticeboard beside them. Ads seeking co-founders for student tech start-ups instead of lead guitarists. And all those Student Union slogans: *A short dress is not a yes. A yes is not a yes if she's intoxicated. Consent means asking every time.*

"So tell me something," goes the botched-Botox one. "Your withdrawal in the library today – that was because of us, yes?"

Tell them I didn't withdraw diddly jack from the library – that I already bossed this term's reading list.

"Oh, for the sake of your own self-respect, don't play all geek and innocent. I'm talking about the withdrawal of your fingers from the soft and warming flesh of that fetching young girl. Because, you know, you could have just ignored us and continued – honestly, we wouldn't have minded."

"Yeh, and you won't mind if I report you to the feds for being a pair of dirty old pervs."

"Though I gotta say, kid, it was damn decent of you to clip and scrub your fingernails in the bathroom beforehand. I don't think I've ever witnessed such creepy considerateness before. Presume that means you intended to progress further up her legs than her feet?"

Fuck's sake. Now I'll probly spend the next three hours wondering why every guy doesn't clean their fingernails beforehand. That shit's just basic hygiene, right? Like dressing a woman's wound. Or rubbing iodine into her surgical scars. Surely you can't just use antibac handgel – the alcohol would sting her.

"Although, I suppose you could always first cleanse your fingers with antibacterial handgel," goes the older-looking old man. "But then of course that would dry her out. *Bad, bad,* skanky and crusty. Because you did intend to move your fingers further up her legs, didn't you? Please don't tell us you were just planning on fumbling at the foot of the garden. I mean this metaphorically, of course." His smile flexing a vein across his temples like he got some extra blood supply for his eyes. "Trouble is, it isn't just diversion or distraction for you, is it, kid? No. And nor is it a plain and simple pain reliever to block out all those years of icky feelings."

I look to the other man to help clue me in a little here, but his blankpage-Botox face is completely cleaned out of everything – no smirk action, no frown action, not even them tiny changes in expression that anyone with a pain-managed mum learns to trust more than what she says.

"No, you just do it to feel independent, don't you? Reclaim your body for yourself. You see the irony in this, don't you? That the act of coupling should make you feel autonomous. I mean, you see the irony in this?"

Tell him I dunno what he's talking about.

That I don't give a fuck what he's talking about.

Then I ask him what he's talking about.

"Of course you know. You know everything there is to know. You have a smartphone with Google access, don't you? In fact, it seems you have several. So you know. Just tap in the entry passcode on the keypad and, hey sesame, open presto: all the world's knowledge on tap. Anticipating your every informational need. But let me help you scroll straight through the bullshit: I'm talking about antiperspirant. Disinfectant. Latex barrier protection. I'm talking about boundaries. Hard border controls. I'm trying to tell you that it isn't about all that fingering and sucking and fake fucking, it's just about that thrilling hit of independence. And do you know what this means?"

"Means y'all a pair of dirty old men who need serious psychiatric help, is what it means."

"It means that you'd do a lot less damage all round if you just played with yourself, kiddo. Buff your own banana. I mean this metaphorically, of course. Don't go around breaking young girls' hearts, hymens and shoe heels – just burp your worm by yourself. Revert back to a ten-year-old boy who barricades himself in his bedroom with a box of Kleenex and a copy of the *Sun*. Use Vaseline if your dick chafes, take ibuprofen for tennis elbow. And one, two, three: wank yourself free."

Before I can even think how the fuck to respond, the old man nods towards the men's room. "In fact, why not beat off in the bathroom right now? Go on – go in there and choke the chicken. Don't worry, we'll still be here when you return."

"Er, no thanks. I'm fine."

"But you're a teenager – you're supposed to masturbate. Go on, go squirt out a cupful of boy milk."

Man carries on like this for another three minutes, but problem is I'm too weirded-out by this whole concept of officially sanctioned wanking to just get up and walk. Every time he offers a practical pro tip (his pun, not mine), I just sit there giving it: "No thanks, I'm fine."

"You sure?" The veins bulging across his temples finally shrink back into his Botox. "Okay then, well maybe later. Maybe you'll sauté your sausage in the shower this evening – with one of your brochures for underfloor heating solutions. All those naked and splayed and stockinged feet."

That feeling when your mum walks in on you.

How the fuck did you forget to lock the door?

That feeling when you walk in on your mum.

Older man puckers his lips and blows like he's trying to wolf whistle. "If only you could have stuck with all those underfloor heating brochures, heh? Instead of moving on to harder stuff. But as with all the extremities, it's an easy slope to slip down. I'm speaking metaphorically, of course – you don't literally slip down a slope. Otherwise there'd be a helluva lot of perverts and terrorists and far-right neo-Nazis walking around with twisted ankles. But you know how it is, kid: once you've clicked on one link, you keep stumbling into others. The way they just keep magically appearing on your screens. Your search results. Your social media feeds. *Up next* on YouTube. One minute you're googling strappy stilettos and then sooner or later you're looking at pink furry ankle cuffs. Next, a sponsored story about how to safely use manacles and shackles. Autoplay. A targeted Facebook post. And before you know it, nothing can save you from the bright-red rope. In fact, it's an easy slope to slip down. Of course, I mean this metaphorically."

I tell him I'm still on strappy stilettos but thanks very much for the *Fifty Shades* plot spoiler.

And now an ad for an amputee porn app.

"The personalisation of your digital experience"– the botched-Botox man now sounding like some greasy TV ad – "No more coming across any pesky content you find boring or confusing or at odds with your own made-up mind. And the more you click on the links, the more your dirty stinking twistedness is validated rather than challenged. Slowly, you start to feel a little less ashamed. You take strength from seeing like-minded people sharing like-minded content and from the sheer assortment of targeted products."

The two old men carry on mansplaining how the fucking internet works like as if I don't already know that shit. Like as if blaming Facebook and Google is the new blaming your mother.

Allow that fuckery. It's just basicness, standardness business. The websites and apps figured out way back that showing you hardercore versions of stuff you already like or agree with will keep your ass logged on for longer. Meaning more advertising bucks for them. And the more you click and share and scroll, the more custom-tailored the shit that appears on your fone, and so the more you click and share and scroll. Ain't exactly gonna keep you logged on and clicking/sharing/scrolling if they start sticking stories about green veggies in your feed.

Blankpage-Botox man tags himself back in: "So you see, it's not your fault, kid."

I cut him a look like as if to say give me a break – or, actualtruth, more like: *don't* give me a break. All them kerb-kicked therapists who wanted me to blame my mother or someshit. And now these two goons telling me to blame Silicon Valley. Bollocks to that – I done all my messed-up fuckery. *Me.*

"After all, people are biologically hardwired to feel all warm and fuzzy and fired up inside whenever their own inclinations are backed up by what they watch or hear or read. It's why we like to underline passages in books that we strongly agree with. Makes us feel better about ourselves – shores up our fragile egos. Confirms our good standing within our respective tribes. Underline, highlight, retweet, share . . ."

". . . Click, click, click," goes the older-looking man, "Slip and slide. Big juicy dopamine hit. Whatever supports your deepest beliefs or triggers your darkest desires."

Some ashtray appears from a more smoking-friendly decade. Fones laid out like empty coasters. Blankpage-Botox man now giving it some more about people's inbuilt guidance system for seeking out info that backs up what we already think while dumping any info that contradicts us. I step up and tell them that I already know this – that the technical term for that shit is "confirmation bias". That I was in the same bloody lecture as them this morning for our Behavioural Economics module. "Or have you two grandpas already forgot?"

"I seem to recall a number of technical terms from that lecture," goes the botched-Botox man. "I particularly liked the Dunning-Kruger Effect – the dumber you are, the more confident you'll be that you aren't actually dumb. Makes people believe that their ignorance is somehow equal to an expert's actual knowledge. In fact, I lost count of how many design flaws the human mind can hold. All those cognitive biases. But there are things that your lecturer failed to explain, kid. Things that perhaps you should know."

Other man cuts him off: "So you see, we're just trying to help you here. Offer you some kind of solution."

"Exactly, a solution to all your problems, Dylan."

"Yeh, well my problems ain't need no solving."

"Then don't call it a solution, call it a proposition."

"Yeh – you want me to go and jerk off so that you can proposition me in the men's room."

"Maybe you should hear us out before mocking us," goes the botched-Botox man. "And, no, we do not intend to follow you to the washroom – we're quite content to wait here and keep our eyes on our drinks. You may masturbate in private, Dylan. Download your dongle. Milk your own memory stick. But be careful while you back up your hard drive or you might upload all over your clothes. Metaphorically speaking, I mean." He throws me some paper napkins and like some doughnut-fucker I actually catch them. "Oh, and by the way, did you know you can expand your bandwidth by using a wire to restrict your windpipe? That's actually one of my favourite tricks. So please, stop dithering and delaying and go and be done with it, kid. Don't worry, we'll wait right here and keep our eyeballs on the table – I'm speaking metaphorically, of course. We're not actually going to gouge our eyes out."

Men's room. Vomit in the toilet cubicle. Try not to take too long about it in case the two men actually think I'm actually wanking. When I'm done, wash out my mouth with Red Bull, then paper towel my shirt collar. Normally I'd brush my teeth, pop a breath mint, chase it down with Listerine. Light a match to sulphurise the stench, clean the bowl and basin for the next occupant. Cos you can redecorate your home with sick bowls and commodes, but you should never forget basic bathroom etiquette. Mama was proper specific on this even before she got sick: *"Dhilan, don't sprinkle when you tinkle." "Be sweet and wipe the seat."* Actualtruth, before they finally split the sheets, she and my dad first tried out separate bathroom sinks, then separate toilets. None of that marriage therapy bullshit – Mama used to say "analysis is paralysis". Might as well say that cats are fucking hats. Still, when Mum went for chemo in the Nuclear Medicine Unit, I agreed to go get counselled in the Patient and Family Support Unit. Technical term for that shit was "anticipatory grief counselling", but I prefer calling it pre-bereavement bereavement counselling. Place for me to work through my pre-mourning mourning. Next, I agreed to go for counselling *with* Mum. Technical term for that shit was family therapy, but we called it mother–son marriage guidance. Place for us to work through our bathroom and bedroom and headspace etiquette. But when that shit broke down, we settled on separate counselling sessions, but at the same time and in side-by-side rooms. Like we was shitting in adjacent toilet cubicles.

"Well, that didn't take you very long."

I walk outta the men's room and into some music. When the fuck they start playing music?

"Here, have one of these chocolate chip cookies. They'll help you reload your pistol."

Before I can clarify that I ain't been wanking, the younger old man tells me the cookies are *mint* chocolate chip – "Mint for oral freshness, Dylan."

Music's some proper playtime/funtime bullshit – Daft Punk or Beyoncé or Barney the Dinosaur. And also people – there's now more people. Sound system in the corner; I shoulda stayed in the men's room.

"You know the other great thing about masturbation?" – older-man has to amp up his voice to level nine – "It's much more time-efficient. You can masturbate while you check your emails or even while you eat. So, all in all, a perfect addition to all those time-saving strategies you've already deployed to make your life more manageable."

By this, he means studying in the toilet. He means shaving in the waiting room. He means online grocery shopping during school lessons. Teleconferencing for my tech start-up during lectures. Eating sandwiches for dinner while showering.

"In fact, with enough practice, you can even wank while you puke."

So, yeh, I shoulda stayed in the friggin men's room.

"By the way, you can purchase a handy wrist support by clicking on this link."

Shoulda stayed put in the library.

"Another product we'd recommend for you is a lubricated Fleshlight."

Shoulda gone to some client's office.

"It comes in a variety of skin tones, textures and orifice styles."

Shoulda gone to the library/hospital/necropolis/hospice/office/library/hospital/temple/chapel/office. I had this place pegged as some quiet Student Union joint, but now it's morphed into a real-life music promo. Press play for cleavage. Press play for vigour and vitality. Press play for toned-and-waxed six-packs loaded with actual Corona. The two men continue shouting out the benefits of various masturbation aids; I blank them, down a double Red Bull. Pop a Pro-Plus caffeine pill. Pack up my shit. Leave. Everyone getting ready to get frisky, talk bullshit, get more frisky, talk louder bullshit, feel good about themselves. I pack up my shit and leave. And what the hell is with that whole rugby-team recreational vomiting thing? I pack up my shit. And leave.

6

USUALLY IT STARTS around 5pm. She thinks it's still the 1960s or something when people actually stopped work at 5pm. Make sure the webcam's switched on, then plug in my headphones so my co-workers can't hear her shouting at me. Type my replies as instant messages so they can't hear me shouting back at her. Except I don't even get to reply. Every time I start to type something, she shuts me down with more shouting.

"DAMN TO YOU." That's her opening shot this evening. "DAMN TO YOU, DAMN TO YOU, ALL THE DAMNS AND DAMNING TO YOU."

Some slowass high-speed connection means the image on my screen is two or three seconds delayed. Hear her screaming into my earholes before she actually opens her cakehole. This technical hitch means I don't get that early warning signal before each time Masi starts to speak – all them minor earthquakes in the folds of her face.

"WHAT KIND OF MAN YOU ARE," she says instead of asks. Her skinny, bleached face; her blood-clot-coloured lipstick. The webcam making the whole package appear even more bleached and blood-clotted. "DON'T YOU DID LIKE THIS, DHILAN. DON'T YOU BLOODY DID LIKE THIS."

To the left, some guy shouts, "Piece of crap!" cos some brand-new laser printer has jammed. Fluorescent tube in a ceiling panel starts flickering. All these things happen in this client's office all the time, not just when Masi's bollocking me. But they *always* happen when she's bollocking me.

"GO TO THE HELL," she says. "YOU'RE THE SHAMED, YOU'RE THE SHAMED, YOU SHOULD BE THE SHAMED."

Check the totally unnecessary uses of the word "the". And when she *should* use the word "the", she doesn't – as in: "WHO HELL YOU THINK YOU ARE?"

And, yep, I *am* making fun of her Indian accent. That's cos I can't argue with the sentiment.

"HUH? WHO HELL YOU THINK YOU ARE?"

And I'm glad this whole webcam-and-instant-messenger arrangement makes it difficult to defend myself. But, fact is, the set-up suits Masi even more than it suits me. Instead of being annoyed that I ain't responding, she feels all honoured and butt-licked by it. Reckons I'm being respectful.

"DON'T YOU DID LIKE THIS," she gives it again. Like as if whatever I'm gonna do is such a bad thing to have already done.

Should probly try to Gaviscon the situation. Ask her if Mama needs anything. If I should head home to help Mum with her diaphragm and her general will to live. Or collect that copy of her death certificate for council-tax transferral purposes. Or help her with her will to live. When Masi starts name-dropping the devil, I remind myself this is just an audio and video live-feed. Her words and her face, just bits of digital data. Besides, I got my amulets. My protective trinkets. My close-by co-workers and the strip lighting still holding back the night outside.

"IT'S DISGUSTING, DHILAN – YOU ABSOLUTELY, YOU DISGUST ME." She screams this last line so loud my laptop freezes, my eyes twitch, my kidneys twinge, her bleached face disintegrates. But the audio stream carries on breathing – "DISGUST-GUST-GUSTING. DISGUST-GUST-GUSTING."

Standard practice on any large-scale data-entry project: everyone here has to hot-desk. Don't matter if you're a consultant, a contractor, a subcontractor, a data-enterer, a digitiser or a typist.

We connect our laptops to a full-size monitor and keyboard at one of the work stations set aside for us. First come, first pick; no cockfights over who sits where. If you roll into the office early enough you can nab a desk with better privacy settings – where the only thing peeping over your shoulder at your screen is some ancientquated filing cabinet. When Masi's face starts slowly returning, I check ain't no one behind me is watching her. We're talking some old-school analogue ghosting image. We're talking the buzzing and fuzzing and fury of an untuned, old-school television. Then the hardware catches up with the correct century and Masi's just this pixelated digital scramble – like her face is having a fight with my screensaver. Masi has beef on the regular with anything and anyone. Her whole life story timelined by intercontinental blood feuds. But these days I don't need to play that game where you gotta guess what the hell it was upset her.

Soon as Masi's face is back, fully formed and restored on my screen, my iPad announces someone's trying to hit me up on FaceTime. I place the iPad outta the desktop webcam's line of sight. Turns out it's Aunty Rachna – i.e. Aunty Number Five. As if her and Masi have coordinated this. (Though of course if they had done, Aunty Five would've made sure she got in first.) Doesn't say hello or nothing, just cuts straight to her question: "WHAT KIND OF BLOODY ASSHOLE OF A BOY YOU ARE?"

Hope she don't mean it literally when she keeps dropping the words "bloody asshole". Hope for her sake that her image is just imaginary. That's she's just conjunctivating the worst two swear words in her vocab. And, yep, I *am* making fun of her diction or whatever. That's cos I can't argue with her opinion.

"EH? HUH? HEH? WHAT SORT OF BLOODY ASSHOLE BOY DOES LIKE THIS?"

Try to look away from my iPad and like a dumbass I stare straight at my webcam. Masi, i.e. Aunty Number Three, sees this as some cue to come at me with more of her backlit bad vibes:

"I DON'T EVEN WANT TO SEE YOUR FACE NOW – NOW THAT I SEE WHAT YOUR FACE HAS DONE."

Don't need to tell her I ain't a fan of her face either. The way her cheekbones still poke out despite the LCD flat-screen. In my fantasy office environment, we'd downgrade from flat-screens to them proper bulky old-school monitors. The ones you couldn't spill coffee on cos they'd short and explode. Shards of jagged glass imploding into the image of her jugular.

". . . LIKE A COCKROACH," screams Aunty Number Five.

". . . IN THE MOUTH," goes Aunty Number Three, "IN THE BLOODY IDIOT MOUTH!"

Usually around this point in our Skype convo, I remind myself what a lucky bloke Masi's husband is. You see, the dude don't even exist. Somewhere out there in the world there's some non-existent husband who just sits around shaking his right hand and wiping it across his forehead while repeating the word "phew".

"EH? HUH? HEH?" goes Aunty Number Five, "WHAT THE HELL YOU HAVE TO SAY?"

Next comes a text message from Aunty Number Six, but before I can read it Aunty Number Five hits me up with another "EH? HUH? HEH?"

Then back to Aunty Number Three: "YOU'RE THE SHAMED, YOU'RE THE SHAMED, YOU SHOULD BE THE SHAMED."

And now let's bring back Aunty Number Five: "HEH? WHAT KIND OF A MAN YOU ARE?"

(Aunty Number Six still seems to be stuck on emojis so fuck knows what she's saying.)

"AND WHAT THE BLOODY ASSHOLE IS THIS MUSIC YOU'RE NOW PLAYING, HEH? I THOUGHT YOU TOLD US YOU WERE WORKING."

I start typing that I ain't playing no music – that that's the sound of my mobile ringing. But I stop typing halfway so I can answer the fone. It's Uncle Deepak – aka Uncle Number Eight: "OKAY, WHERE YOU ARE, DHILAN? WHERE IN THE HELL YOU HAVE GONE? ALWAYS YOU'RE WITH YOUR STUDIES

AND YOUR BUSINESS AND NOW YOU'RE BUSY RUNNING AWAY FROM THIS SICK, SICK THING YOU'VE DONE."

Don't respond – so long as your lips stay zipped, he'll just assume he's gone straight through to voicemail. And, yep, I *am* making fun of his weirdass combo of technophilia and tech-incompetence. That's cos I can't argue with his argument.

"AND WHAT THE HELL KIND OF IDIOT BUSINESS IS IT TO BE TYPING UP ALL THIS TYPIST BUSINESS ANYWAY? YOU SHOULD BE TYPING GOD A LETTER OF APOLOGIES."

Next, my twelve-year-old coloured-contacts and two-parents cousin starts hitting me on WhatsApp telling me to straighten the fuck up. Then a home video of my nana who died five years before I was even conceived, telling me, "Dhilan, you've been a very naughty boy."

Aunty Number Three now screaming at me from the monitor: "DON'T LOOK OVER THERE, LOOK AT ME! LOOK AT ME WHEN I'M TALKING TO YOU, DHILAN."

"WHAT YOU HAVE TO SAY FOR YOURSELF?" screams Aunty Number Six in some weirdly unabbreviated text.

"LOOK – LOOK AT HOW YOU CAN'T EVEN LOOK AT MY FACE," says Aunty Number Five. "EH? HUH? HEH?"

"JUST STOP YOUR SILLY IDIOT TYPING BUSINESS AND COME AND FUCKING HELL FACE ALL THIS."

Each of the carpet floor tiles in this client's office is worn out to a different shade of grey. I seen the maintenance men lift them up sometimes when everyone's gone home to their recharging ports.

I ear-check my fone: Uncle Number Eight is still leaving what he reckons is a voicemail. "WE KNOW WHERE YOU LIVE," he says. "WE'VE RUNG THE UNIVERSITY, DHILAN. WE HAVE YOUR STUDENT HALL ADDRESS."

Beneath the carpet tiles, there's this mashup of metal beams, plastic tubing and rubber-coated cables – fibre-optic worms twisting and squirming to deliver each desk five plug sockets and two connections for telecoms and internet. The actual floor a foot lower than the carpet tiles we walk on.

Next thing I know, Uncle Number Eight has already hung up. But I only notice this cos he rings right back to add a sequel to what he thought was his earlier voicemail. While he's doing that, the phone starts ringing – the other phone, the deskphone, the actual fucking landline.

Okay, now this is just getting weird.

Firstly, ain't told no one in my family knows the names of my clients, so how the fuck can they be trying to loop my neck with the landline? Secondly, all the workstations on this floor are for hot-desking so the landlines hardly ever ring. Maybe you'll hear one once a month, but it's always a wrong number or, if it's an internal call, a sloppily dialled extension. Should probly just let it ring out, but my left hand picks it up on some ancient human instinct. Slip the receiver beneath my headset, hoping Aunty Number Three won't notice.

Some woman on the other end starts giving it: "I'd like to speak to someone about Mr Deckardas."

"Yep, this is me," I say – figuring that this latest caller is safer to actually speak to seeing as she don't sound blood-related.

"WHAT YOU SAID?" screams Aunty Number Three.

"WHAT YOU SAID?" screams Uncle Number Eight. "BUT I THOUGHT THIS WAS YOUR VOICEMAIL?"

"What – but, wait," goes the woman on the other end. "I mean, excuse me, pardon me . . . But, no. No."

"Hello?" I go, though whispering this time so that my various assorted screens can't hear me. I ask the non-blood-related woman how I can help her but she's already hung up. Ain't no number on the caller-display screen – meaning that she came through via the switchboard. Keep staring at the dead plastic deskphone like it's some lump of bad bodefulness. Then back once again at my other screens. Everyone except for Masi has hung up as well. Masi's now shouting something about hell and insects and carrot juice. I grow the balls to just pull my headset clean off. Grow a second pair to minimise the size of Masi's window.

Just me and my screensaver now.

Thirty seconds later, Masi breaks my concentration by stepping-up her screaming to max volume. "WHAT YOU HAVE TO SAY FOR YOURSELF? WHAT'S THE USE OF ALL THE YEARS AGO?" After that, she starts grunting – just grunting, though, not groaning or moaning or the kung-fu sound of Mummy puking. Click the tab to reopen Masi's Skype screen. Somehow her face is even skinnier than Mama's size-zero junkie anaemic look. Narrower chin, longer nose. Baggy, candle-drip cheeks. Click back to my screensaver: only bagginess on Mama's face is beneath her eyes. We're talking crumpled plastic carrier bag eyes – even before our carrier bags became sick bags. Fuck's sake, even with this screensaver of her right in front of me I still can't properly picture her. Been like that since my GCSEs. Every time I try and think of my mummy I can't hardly even see her, can only see her sickness. Click between Mama and Masi. Masi's skinniness telling you that she's the older sister; Mama's eyes making it seem like it's the other way round. Start wondering whether to tell Masi to just go fuck herself but bail when I realise she's been spitting at her webcam. Either that, or once again she's crying.

7

FIRST TIME YOUR mum told you she had the C-bomb was the first time you changed the TV channel without first asking permission. She'd turned the sound down before telling you, so what difference did it make? Weren't even facing the stupid TV, so what difference?

In the car on the way home from school: "So tell me all about all your lessons today."

In the hallway as she took off her shoes: "What did Ms Feldman think of your spelling homework?"

In the living room – placing a dining chair in front of you as you sat down to watch those dumbass after-school cartoons: "Dhilan, we have to have a talk about something."

Exact same opening line, exact same timing, exact same furniture set-up as two years earlier when she'd told you that she and your dad had "decided not to live in the same house". Then she hit you up with the exact same laugh – her non-laughing laugh. Short blast of vocal cord like she was clearing her soul in order to properly laugh.

"Darling, I went to see the doctor today."

You realised she weren't wearing her work clothes. Instead rocking some peach summertime dress.

"Don't worry, it's nothing serious, sweetheart. It's nothing to worry about at all. But, the thing is, they've found something called a lump." And then once again with her non-laughing laugh. "I'm not sure if you understand, Dhilan – do you understand what that means?"

The difference between the height of the dining chair and the height of the sofa meant that you replied to her neck instead of her face. Just below her neck, so more like her chest. "Yes, Mum – it means that you've got cancer."

Instead of being impressed, she seemed kinda pissed at you: "Well, a lump doesn't always mean someone has cancer, Dhilan. But in my case, yes, it seems it does."

In your hand you found the TV remote. Couldn't properly hug her without first laying it down and you couldn't lay it down without first hugging her. You started rubbing your fingers across its rubbery buttons. Looking at the remoteness of it. Looking for a button to press that would make you start crying. Instead you just nodded. Once. Then twice – in case your nod weren't clear enough the first time.

"I went straight for a scan this afternoon – the GP, she sent me straight to the hospital for a scan. But there's nothing for either of us to worry about – we're both going to be fine. We'll both need to be strong. I'll have maybe one or two bad months – and you'll need to be extra good at being the man of the house – but afterwards we'll be completely fine."

You nodded. Twice. Thrice. Fuck it, four nods.

"Dhilan, don't you have any questions? Questions about what type of cancer it is?" Her hands to the remote for the DVD player. Her next words directed to the remote – like it was a fone set to loudspeaker mode. "It's what's known as breast cancer, son."

You nodded more quickly this time, as if to say, *Duh, well obviously.* After all, while the ads telling people to quit smoking were all about lung cancer, it was always breast cancer in all the other cancer ads.

"So you understand, then, Dhilan? That's what I meant when I said they'd found a lump."

Fuck it, maybe that's what the word "lump" already meant back then. Definitely from that day on – you knew straight away that from that day on, that's what the word lump would now mean. Whenever someone asked you "one lump or two?" your first thought would no longer be about sugar cubes. You'd just think they were offering to put tumours in your tea.

"That means they've found that there's cancer growing in my breast – not in my chest, Dhilan, in one of my boobies."

And that's when you accidently pressed down on one of the buttons, somehow changing the channel from ITV cartoons to CNN. Soon as she clocked this, she stood up and straightened her peach summertime dress. Said something about needing to hit the kitchen – some special Tesco cherry and raspberry mousse. Instead of bailing, though, she stayed put in the doorway. "Actually, Dhilan, to tell you the truth, there isn't really a lump." Then turning towards the kitchen, but then turning back. "Actually, it's more like the opposite of a lump – it's what some doctors call an inverted nipple, although other doctors still call it a lump. But it's still the same thing, it's still breast cancer."

When she went to the kitchen for real this time, you just sat there on the sofa, watching the wrong channel with the sound still turned down. Wondering why she hadn't just told you in the first place that it wasn't a lump, it was an inverted nipple.

8

YOU KNOW HOW sometimes some basic words and phrases just keep on passing you by? Hear the word all the time, but either you don't never find out what it actually means or you just get stuck in some groove with some completely wrong meaning. I used to think "homesick" meant that feeling you get when you walk up to your front door. Didn't learn the dictionary definition till I was twelve. I was crying out of nowhere in my school canteen and these idiotfucks started rinsing me, asking me if I was homesick. So I go to them: "The fuck can I be homesick when I ain't even at my home?" The conversation didn't go well.

Tonight, even the welcome-home smell of fabric conditioner doesn't soften the retch reflex. Laundry and Lynx deodorant. Green glow from a fire exit. Condoms stretched over the extinguishers. Ever since my home become these dorms, my misdefinition of homesick and the dictionary definition been meaning the same thing. You return to your room and it's like you need to do your mum's deep-breathing drills. Return to your room like you been kicked in the guts – people thinking you just drunk too much vodka or whatever. Return to your room at six in the a.m. for a shower and change of clothing, and it ain't cos you got lucky. And ain't no point psychotherapising this shit. Don't matter if it's cos of guilt or cos I wanna bounce back to Acton to tuck her in. Ain't like different reasons will make the puke stains in my gullet taste different. Anycase. Tonight as I turn the corridor and head to my room, my main reason for feeling sick is cos I get slapped in the stomach by the two doddery old Botox men.

"Still following us, then?" goes the younger-looking old man.

Takes me a sec or so to get my shit back together. Dillon-ness, manliness and Mummy's diaphragm drills. Cos fuck it, this round is gonna be different. Tell the two old men I'm flattered by this whole stalking thing, but I'm a little too old for paedophiles. Tell em to go suck each other's haemorrhoids. That faeces will be kinder on their dentures.

"Depends on dietary fibre, Dylan." Botched-Botox man offers me an oatmeal cookie like he's busting out some magic trick. "Or is it *Dillon* this evening? Or maybe *Dhilan*?"

I tell them they can call me Dildo for all the high-in-fibre shits I give – anyway, they can't for serious expect to scare me just by knowing all my usernames. "So you been scoping me out on social media. So what? You, the NSA and every self-respecting digital business." This basic entry-level bollocks actually seems to throw them, so I try coming out with more of it. Tell em that with the amount of time I spend online, it'd actually be weirder if they *didn't* know everything about me. Tell em if they're trying to shit me up by telling me things I already revealed to Facebook, then I'm afraid they picked the wrong bloke. That privacy is for pussies. That ain't no such thing as the "cloud", it's just some big corporate's computer. Crunching up all the data from my clicking and searching and posting and sharing and recording and screenshotting and liking and emailing and hovering and hesitating and whatever the opposite of hesitating is. Tell em I actually feel more privacy when I'm online cos the biggest infringencies ain't coming from no tech companies but from my mum being all up in my shit. I tell em every idiot knows that social media's just some Trojan soap opera – a gateway opiate for turning all us dopeheads into hard data. That surveillance is the digital economy's basic business model. Fuck knows why I'm now busting out word-for-word lines from our Advanced Data

Analytics module – I just get psyched by the need to shut the old men down, take the initiative, control the situation. Show em that I know someshit. *"Data is the new oil and so on." "We get to use the websites and apps for free cos we're the product being sold."* Ain't even just fronting now – this shit's fully immersive, 360° interactive exam revision. Start dropping some Economic Science about ad-funded digital businesses. How scoping out your customers is the whole point of online ads – allows you to micro-target the ads better. Deeper and deeper you scope, the more personal info you can suck out, the more valuable the ads. *"Anything less than total surveillance is a missed opportunity to generate more revenues."* I tell them reason ad revenues are the default digital business model is cos it's piss-easy – *"You just focus on maxing your user base and the ads will take care of your cashflow."* And the more I shoot my mouth, the more the corridor we're standing in seems to get emptier and quieter and longer – and so the more space I got to shoot my mouth. Older-looking man has to hold up his hand mid-flow to stop me chatting about data-mining optimisation techniques.

"Dylan, shut the heck up. Please, for just a minute. Just hush up for one minute. Why would you think we'd even *want* to know everything about you, let alone claim to?"

"I ain't give a shit what you claim to know. End of the day, any idiot with a fone can do basic due diligence on anyone."

"Due diligence, eh?" His eyeballs stay locked on me while he turns his head a little to the right. Exact same head-neck-and-eye position I slip into whenever I watch TV. (Mum used to worry there was maybe something wrong with me but the doc said it was just a default position from when I was a baby being breastfed.) "Dylan, did someone warn you we'd be talking to you? I mean, were you tipped off about this?"

"I ain't even know what *this* is."

He holds out his flabby forefinger, leaves it juddering in my direction. "Might as well just fart the beans, kid. Won't be hard for us to find out ourselves. I'm speaking metaphorically, of course. I mean, you might as well just fart the beans."

I tell him I ain't farting nothing – firstly cos ain't nobody told me nothing and, second, cos I ain't some gassy old man like him with flatulence problems.

"Well, if nobody told you nothing, it follows that they must've told you something. You see that, don't you, Dylan? Not nothing, so something."

Figure this is probly my one window to bail. Could outrun these fogeys, easy. All them times I hear alarm bells in my head and I reckon it's just a ringtone. Or when I clock the beat of the countdown and reckon it's just the beep of an alarm. Be as easy as changing the channel. Easy as clicking or swiping away.

"No one's warned him about anything," goes the other man. "The kid's just trying to cut out the foreplay. After all, he does have more urgent things to attend to. Back in west London."

And, boom – shit finally clicks into place. Problem with my different definitions of homesickness is that the cure is the cause of it.

"For fuck's sake. My family sent you guys here, didn't they? My masi?"

"Your what?"

"My aunt, my mother's sister." Just like Eskimos got different names for different kinds of snow, we got stackloads of names for different categories of aunt. "So what's the play here, then? You gonna escort me back to Acton? Is that what she told you to do? Or was it someone else in my family sent you?"

"Your family?" goes the blankpage-Botox man. "Now why would you want to bring your family into this?" Offering me another biscuit or cookie or cracker or whatever – like as if boosting my blood sugar's gonna help me answer.

"Dylan, we don't give a constipated geriatric crap whether you go back to west London or if you stay exiled here in your student halls. We don't care what you do with your mother's remains or with what remains of your mother's time." He lays some proper heavy hand on my shoulder – ain't running nowhere now. "As far as I'm concerned, you're just ahead of the curve. All children end up mopping up their parents' mess. Even before they go senile, they need to be weaned off greasy fats and xenophobic nationalism. Prevented from walking into polling booths and crapping all over the country – I'm speaking metaphorically, of course. Even before they go senile. So, no, we don't care about your mommy issues. We don't care about your mommy's son issues. Would you like to know what we do care about?"

As a general rule, I try not to respond to rhetorical questions. If you actually met my family, you'd understand why.

"What we care about is this: you have no business with your business." And in case I didn't clock the pun, he then comes out with another: "It's time to stop your start-up, Dylan."

The silence is shot by a bunch of those loudly-proudly posh boys approaching from the top of the corridor. Just the sound of them, though, cos ain't nobody actually appears – like as if the corridor's been blocked off with one of them "Cleaning in progress" traffic cones. Or that police tape that says "Crime scene: Do not enter".

"What's wrong, kid?" goes the younger-looking old man. "This isn't the fight you thought you were in? Even though apparently you're a budding young tech entrepreneur."

The botched-Botox man drops a snort then sparks up an old-school cigarette – keeps fat-fingering the whole procedure, though, cos of his sumo-sized hands. I tell him there ain't no smoking allowed.

"Seriously? Not aloud? Well, then I'll smoke it silently." Reaches into his double-breasted biker jacket all slowmo and badass like he's gonna pull a gun silencer. Turns out he's packing a small plastic thermos flask. Uses the lid for an ashtray. I look for the "No Smoking" signs along the corridor, but it's like they all on loan somewhere.

The old men then tell me they know my corporate net cashflow is positive and so I'll have no trouble returning the upfront payments some of my clients have already made to me: "And then you can fold your silly little student start-up without any outstanding accounts."

This is when I clock that all the noticeboards along the corridor are empty. No jokes – not even them ads for student debt problems.

"It isn't as if your fledgling little business will be missed, Dylan."

Not even them ads for Class-A drug addiction.

"After all, you're more a consultant than an actual company."

Not even them ads for STDs.

"Just a jumped-up freelance data-enterer."

Not even them ads for self-harm, sexual assault, suicidal thoughts.

"So you understand what we're asking of you?" goes the blankpage-Botox man. "We'd like you to fold up your business."

"We mean your start-up," adds the botched-Botox man.

"Your enterprise."

"Your wholly owned venture."

While all three of us wait for my dumb ass to respond, there's a thud from somewhere behind us. The noise coming from inside a shower room – like some jumbo bog roll just dropped off the wall, dead magpie-style.

"Oh come on, Dylan, here we are presenting you with a serious business proposition and you want to go chasing after things that go bump in the bathroom." Blankpage-Botox man LOLing as he says this. Laughter without the lines.

The botched-Botox man tags himself back in: "Little man, look, if you think we've come all the way here just to deliver comeuppance or reset your moral compass then, frankly, I don't know whether you need a little more imagination or a lot less. Our business with you, it's just business." His eyes locked double-latched on mine like he's trying to figure out if I'm buying this. "Besides, if you people could actually see your moral compasses you wouldn't call it a compass, you'd call it a clock – I mean if you could actually see it."

And then another big-ass thud from the shower room. Only this time I'm like, allow it, it's just a thud. Not a crack. Not a fracture, or a rupture. Probly weren't even the shower room – more like the laundry room two doors down. Or the photocopier room. The X-ray department or intensive care unit. Anycase, most rooms along here are en suite.

"Dylan, how the pigfuck are we supposed to do business if you act as if we've come here to punish you? You won't appreciate the deal we're offering you. Either you'll think you don't deserve this windfall or you'll assume it's some sort of penalty – as if we've come here to punish you. And apparently we can't even disabuse you of that assumption because in your own little twisted head, not being punished is a punishment in itself."

He stubs out his cigarette in the lid of his thermos flask then pours out the capful of ash onto the floor. The ash is white, bright white, whiter than crushed-up paracetamol. And just like the man's dandruff earlier today, it falls neatly between us like some line of salt.

"You know, kid, it's actually been pitiful having to watch you. All your sillyfuck self-chastisement. As if you'd rather have remained a little boy with a clear conscience. In fact, it's actually been pitiful having to watch you. Trying to be a diligent and well-behaved schoolboy but always secretly hoping for class detention. Staying in the office late even when you don't even need to. And all those evenings at your desk doing Google searches about Oedipus just because you attended a few relationship counselling sessions with your mommy. I mean what the hellfuck were you hoping to find?"

Starts fiddling his fingers like he needs another cigarette. Goes for his trouser pocket and pulls out a string of wooden beads. I'm guessing they for meditating and mindfulating rather than post-surgery massaging. (Pro tip: never, ever, ever order massage beads online if you're squeamish about anal stimulation safety manuals.)

My eyes to the floor while he fat-fingers his stress beads, like as if I'm giving him privacy to pray or something. Even the plug sockets along this corridor have buggered off somewhere.

"Listen," he says when he's done with his beads. "I mean, really listen to what I'm going to tell you, Dylan. A few moments ago you stood there trying to impress us with some spiel about social media and search engines turning their users into data. Well, as a professional data-enterer, surely you appreciate that all that data is neutral. It doesn't matter if one person clicks on the vilest pornography and another person clicks on a saintly charity. Both actions generate equally valuable data and therefore their data is equal. Same goes for the actions of Dhilan and Dylan and Dillon. I mean, surely as a professional data-enterer, you appreciate this."

My nod stops midway so once again I end up gormless-like, looking at the floor. Protein stains on the carpet again. Mainly by the laundry room.

"So if all those clever algorithms that power the social media feeds and search engines haven't cared all that much about whether or not something is moral – or even truthful – if they've only cared about whether something gets clicked on or liked or shared, then how the hell would we care? So, you see, the things that you've done, Dylan – we really couldn't give a dry or dribbling fart about them. Same goes for all the twisted poop that's been running through your brain since you were, what, nine years old? We don't care. We don't care a damn. You see that now, don't you? You know this now. It's known that you know this. You know it in the marrow of your morally decayed bones."

Forget my bones – this is the sound of my brain untwisting.

The sound of headfucks slowly starting to unfuck.

Cos, thing is, I way back lost track of all the times those quick-fix counsellors and therapists tried telling me something similar – how you shouldn't feel guilty cos you was just *"Being Yourself"*, *"Being Truthful To Your Own Emotions"*, *"All Emotions Are Valuable"*.

"Just Acting According to Your Own Internal Reality."

"Because Feelings Are Never False – how you feel about something is as real as the things that are actually happening."

"Emotions Have the Same Weight as Facts."

"You Can Change a Situation Just by Interpreting Things Differently."

That kinda thing.

Problem was, it always sounded like a mashup of bollocks and bullshit. Until right now.

All your clicks are valuable cos they're clicks.

Clicks = emotional data.

Emotional data = truth.

The botched-Botox man grins like he's just pumped out a gallon of water to butt-cleanse my conscience. You can water down paint and eventually it'll switch from cloudy to crystal clear. Trouble is, you can't do that shit with milk or other protein-based fluids. Not even if you use holy water made from Evian.

"So now you fully understand we haven't come here to punish you, you'll also understand that what we've offered you here is a brilliant business deal."

"The hell you chatting about? You ain't actually offered me jack."

"Are you high on your mother's morphine again? We've offered you a fantastic deal. We're proposing that you fold up your upstart start-up. Just fold it up, wash your hands and walk away."

Botched-Botox man somehow nods without actually moving his neck. "And what's more, when we met you earlier today we also proposed that you switch from having pseudo-sexual relations to masturbation. You can treat that piece of advice as a kind of divestiture bonus."

"Besides, kid, like we said before, you're more of a contractor than entrepreneur. I believe the correct term is a 'data temp'. Little boy stuck somewhere between start-up culture and the gig economy."

"Start-up founder, my wrinkly ass," goes the botched-Botox man. "More like floundering fucking foundling. You lack the one key ingredient for launching a start-up – thick, creamy lashings of self-belief."

"What's more, your business doesn't even have a proper name – you still call it 'Company A.'"

"And just because you operate at the manual end of the data-entry market, that doesn't mean you have a unique niche."

"So why not do yourself a favour, kid, and just focus on finishing your studies. On being a student. No more mad antics from client to campus to Acton fuelled by caffeinated drinks and wasted cunni-juice."

"And then afterwards you can find yourself something more lucrative in a less crowded market."

The old men carry on like this for another ten minutes. Busting out lines from my balance sheet to prove they really have been running their slide rule. Also some broader sectoral analysis that's pretty much bang-on about the wider market. Cos the data-entry business ain't no longer just about entering shit into databases. It's now part of the whole digitising game – which means everyone wants a piece of this pie. *Executive summary:* when clients with shelf-loads of printed stuff wanna convert it into online archives, they gotta digitise the originals. We're talking every single species of dead tree: documents, journals, libraries, filing systems, ledgers, deeds, books, newspapers, magazines – plus enough rolls of microfilm to bandage the planet. To put all that crap up online, clients normally hire specialist digitising firms that got these superfast, superfat scanning machines. But sometimes those machines make mistakes – either cos of the speed, smudged printing or crap handwriting. That's when those scanning companies subcontract to data-entry plankton like Yours Truly – so I can correct the mistakes manually and type up all the unscannable crap from scratch.

"Something amusing you, Dylan?"

I tell them I just figured out what's really going down here. And now that it's finally hit me, I feel like the dumbest dumbfuck in the classroom for not wising up before. After all, I'm supposed to know how this shit works – "Dylan" is the founding friggin president of this London students' entrepreneur society (though, full disclosure, there's probly, like, 2,000 different student entrepreneur societies so that everyone can stick "founding president" on their CV). Sooner or later, all big bad corporates realise they ain't nimble and creative enough to keep having new ideas and new breakthroughs. So what do these big, badass corporates do? They go round strangling start-ups at birth, is what they do. And when they can't strangle them, they try to scare them or sue their asses for patent infringement – or they just open their big sweaty arms and buy them. My dopey, dipshit stupidness notwithstanding, I know exactly how to play this. Fuck knows I've organised enough networking events with self-stroking scumbuckets invited as keynote speakers – and we ain't just talking tech entrepreneurs, we've also hosted angel investors, early-stage venture capitalists, start-up incubators, expansion-stage venture capitalists, private equity ponces, strategic-stage venture capitalists, plus this one slicked-back dickwad who called himself a Disruptive Value Creator. Handing out copies of some bullshit business book he'd wrote like as if books were the new business cards. Right now, I basically do my own mashup of all these keynote speeches – kicking off with some bog-standard stand-up-for-yourself stuff. For instance, I tell them I'm very flattered by their efforts to snuff out the competitive threat that I will one day pose to them or whatever the hell big corporate they work for, but if they want to influence my business then they'll have to invest in it. And if they want to full-on alter my strategic direction, then they'll just have to buy me out outright.

Botched-Botox man raises his hand to stop the blankpage-Botox man ROFLing. "Money? That all you want, Dylan? We've tried to ask you nicely, but if you'd rather just have money then, sure, why the hell not. How about £500,000 for the whole poxy enterprise? I can have it for you in cash in an hour."

Doesn't take me long to do the sums. £500K = nearly thirty times my mum's full-time salary back when she was well enough to work full-time. But as every self-stroking keynote speaker will tell you, you don't never, ever accept the opening offer. "Don't insult me," I tell them.

"Oh please, we should be offering you £500, not £500,000," says the blankpage-Botox man. "Would you like us to remind you what your revenues are?"

"Fuck my revenues – what century are you from?" I tell them that, at this stage in my start-up's development phase, they're s'posed to consider my projected future cash flows based on my estimated critical mass. "Frankly, fellas, I'd have expected better due diligence from a potential suitor than all your bully-boy corporate scare tactics." Next, I find myself giving them some idiot sales pitch I got nailed for all the fucktard funding competitions on the student entrepreneurial society circuit. Start with the projected size of the digitising market given how much data and stuff still only exists on paper – in libraries, filing cabinets, museums, notebooks. All of it still waiting to be scanned or typed or just generally uploaded. I tell them that even the largest search engines still know only a cut of everything publicly printed to know – though, again in the interests of SEC-style full disclosure, I fess up that the number of as-yet-undigitised books and documents is actually getting smaller every minute. Then I close out by dropping my big business idea – cos, after all, every budding tech tycoon needs their very own Big Idea. Some big, hairy bollocks about the "sharing economy" and shifting social norms around privacy or whatever just to hype up their own corporate growth projections. Here's the PowerPoint script: *"The definitive version of something is now the digital version, not the paper version. Whereas, before, the paper copy was seen as permanent and the electronic versions were just fly-by formats – like the analogue waves carrying old-school broadcast signals."* (Sometimes, depending on the audience, I'll even go full poshboy and drop in some word like "*ephemeral*".)

The botched-Botox man seems to sigh through his eyes– like a man already burnt by life and earlier tech-market bubbles. "You really want to play it like this, don't you, Dylan? Fine, but you're not in a pitch meeting now, so how about we stop bullshitting. We may not be privy to your 'projected future critical mass', but we know about your current clients – all piddling three of them. We know about the dissertations you're digitising for your university's soon-to-be-shut-down Faculty of Irrelevant Studies. We know about the little import–export company that's hired you to type twenty years of invoices into a basic database – and the only reason they hired you instead of a proper outfit is because their whole company's just a front for selling fake vitamins. Not even fake Viagra, mind, fake vitamins. And then let's not forget the dying newspaper that's got you manually correcting all the scanning mistakes in an online archive of back issues that they're ten years too late to compile in the first place. We know that your corporate bank account is actually the joint marital account your mother set up when you were ten so that you could sign cheques on her behalf. And we know that your debt–equity ratio is still modelled on the same high-street remortgaging terms you found online when you were twelve. Now, granted, that's not much of a childhood, Dylan, but neither is it an MBA."

The botched-Botox man zips up his double-breasted biker jacket and coughs like he's closing up his lungs.

"Wait up," I go. "How can you—"

"How can you get a higher pension income?" the younger-looking old man cuts me off. "How can you play the lottery while abroad? How can you open a link in a new window? How can you mend a broken heart?"

"We do realise what you've been doing here, Dylan. Acting dumb, trying to distract us with information about your projected future cash flows. We're proposing that you wind up your start-up and instead of agreeing to do so, you puke out your company prospectus. Which means I was right the first time: someone warned you we'd be speaking to you, didn't they? That's why you're so well-prepped."

And, just like that, they close out our business meeting. Before I can issue some cleverly worded denial.

@DYLAN: JUST BOSSED a business meet with some guys who wanna buy my start-up. Could donate proceeds to charity in memory of my late mum. Told em I'm holding out for a Nasdaq listing. #NotForSale #RIPMum

@DHILAN: CHECKING IN on Mum again. Need to step up my monitoring/surveillance/psychic connection. The way she knows how to push my buttons & dig out my most embarrassful info. As if our privacy infringencies = public displays of affection. #YoungCarers

@DILLON: TURNS OUT the student film society is holding a marathon screening of all the 'Alien' films – the ones where the alien foetuses have to infect/rot/disintegrate/liquidate whoever's giving birth to them in order to be born. #BirthPangs

9

DESKPHONE'S GOT SOME caller-display screen but it only does its thing if they dial you direct. If they come through the switchboard, they basically wearing a balaclava beneath a burqa. Meaning I can't just phone that woman back. I just sit at the exact same workstation as I done earlier. Lay my fones on the desk, just me and my fones. And together we wait. And I'll bail on Ramona. And I'll munch dinner in the staff canteen like some lonely dickless loser. And I'll work or I'll try or I'll pretend to work.

Cos, fuck it, this is how it is – this is what I do. While the others are flexing their biceps and their books.

This is what I do.

Or farting around playing rugby.

This is what I do.

Except, tonight, ain't even lying when I text Mama to say I'm sorry but I'm working late. And ain't lying when I text Ramona to say I'm sorry but I'm working late. Instead of running from one to the other. Downing duplicate dinners or lunches, duplicate birthday cakes. Checking the timestamp printed on the Starbucks receipt so she don't clock me checking my watch. Heading eastbound instead of westbound to corroborate my story about broken down Tubes. Switching my fone to airplane mode to make it sound like I'm still underground. And tonight I'll stay in the office till I get to the bottom of all this fuckery. And then tomorrow I can go back to lying.

She might've just been telesales.

Cold-calling to sell compensation for mis-selling something.

Might've had diddly-fuck to do with those two aged-out Botox men.

Try replaying the woman's voice in my head. Can't hardly even remember it, though – was too busy being multimedia-bollocked by my aunties and aunties and uncles. All I know for definite is that the two old men were proper certain someone had tipped me off about them. Just cos I managed to front with them as if I'd been properly prepped or someshit. Spitting lines straight outta some student start-up forum and my Advanced Data Analytics module. Dropping all them obviousness bombs about online privacy, personal-data mining, ad-targeting, digital surveillance. Was just stock-standard basicness, though. They call it "data mining" instead of snooping to sound less creepy but, fact is, all the easy-to-reach data lying close to the surface has already been extracted and crunched. Digital businesses can't just scrape it out no more, they gotta dig deeper and deeper into all your shit just to keep their profits on the upward. Mostly they do this by keeping you logged on for longer and by monitoring your actual behaviour – your lingering and hovering and hesitating. Scoping out your personality by measuring shit like how long you typically take to click. Whether you're easily addictable. Whether you're scared of whatever you're searching for. The algorithms learning more from the way you behave than from the data you intentionally disclose. We're talking known and unknown info. Sharing shit you don't even know about yourself. I look once again at the dead plastic deskphone and realise how doubtful it is the woman will call back.

Big tech corporations got other tools for digging deeper. Analysing your friends' foto uploads. Selling you some voice-activated digital assistant to stick inside your home. Even used to eavesread your emails to help tailorise your ads. The algorithms constantly reconfiguring themselves by learning from their own success rates. Success = whether you stay logged on and under watch. I reach for a pack of antibac wipes and start cleaning my fones. She ain't gonna call me back.

Main reason I was so well prepped on this shit ain't just cos of my student start-up forums – it's cos sometimes I reckon maybe I'm *glad* all my shit's being monitored. Like as if I wanna be measured and evaluationed – under the scope of some great big watchful dataflow up in the clouds. Just to know that someone or something is keeping the score. Clocking that my bad clicks are outgunned by my good clicks. That I gave money to a beggar in the street. That I'm sorry – that I'm so, so sleepstipated and sorry. And once I get going with this thinking, I feel like some official suspect of something even darker and wronger and dirtier. Start getting properly suspicious of myself, even. And then I wanna fall under even more surveillance. Maybe she'll call me back if I walk away from the phone?

What goes down next happens when I leave my post to trigger the motion-sensor ceiling lights. Check me striding up and down like some Jedi electrician. Even though I'm the only gimp holed up on this floor, the open-plan office feels smaller. Surely it should be the opposite? Ditto the late-night lecture theatres. Ditto every unlocked classroom in my secondary school. Down on this deck, it's usually just data-enterers, the IT helpdesk and the Website Functionality Enablers. All the ad people, journalists and Other Assorted Media Professionals sit on the floors above us – bagging not just the best views but also better kitchenettes and vending machines. So ain't no reason for someone who ain't in this department to be using our food facilities.

The woman is squeezing some kinda melting plastic pasta thing into a plastic bowl. Green pesto that matches her dress. Beside her, the rows of microwave ovens lined up like gym lockers – each oven reflecting her face at a slightly different angle. I hit up the coin-op for a can of Red Bull.

"Burning the midnight caffeine, are we?" Her voice tells me loud and clear that she ain't the woman who'd phoned me earlier. There's way too much subwoof on it – like an old woman moaning for pain relief. Though she can't be more than forty-five, tops. "Still, I suppose it's high time the IT helpdesk had a late shift."

I tell her I don't work in tech support. That I'm a consultant. A contractor. A freelance data-enterer. Okay, a typist.

She sniffs her plastic pasta thing like she's taking an extra-long toke. "What rot that the staff canteen's shut. I loathe these vending-machine dinners."

I start asking one of her various microwave oven reflections if she eats dinner in the office often, but then stop in case it sounds like I'm on some kinda cougar-type shit.

"Still, nice to meet you, young man. I suppose that's one good thing about dining à la vending machine. After all, it isn't as if I have someone at home to eat with. All by my lonesome self."

Trust me to find the only posh person in the building who doesn't have that whole stiff-upper-lip thing going on.

Then she tells me that I'm missing something. Her exact words are, "Aren't *we* missing something," but it's obvious she's doing that thing where the word "we" just refers to you.

"I am?"

Starts pointing to the left of her chest. Tapping it like it's some touchscreen.

"Oh," I give it. "Yeh, sorry – I keep forgetting we're meant to wear these all the time now." Pull out my office security pass and clip it to my left lapel.

"That's better. I hang mine around my neck, you see. Along with my press card. Like a necklace – you see?"

I go back to interacting with the vending machine. Foto of my mummy tucked behind my student card. The woman looks at my wallet then turns to face the microwaves.

"Well, not much point showing me your ID, was there? Not if it bears the wrong name."

"I'm sorry?"

"The security pass on your lapel says that your name is Dylan. But that student card there in your wallet says your name is Dillon."

Slide my vending card back in my wallet.

"*Well*? Which is it?"

I ask her if I'm making her nervous. This happens to be one of them news publications that keeps shit easy and simple by blaming immigrants and skin pigments for every explosion or economic downturn or earthquake or whatever.

"Which is it?" Her reflections all look up at me in sync. "Is it Dillon? Or is it Dylan?"

Should tell her that either will do. That Mummy and Daddy spell it differently. That I ain't a terrorist or welfare tourist or crack dealer – that I ain't even doing retakes. Instead I tell her my real name is "Dhilan" but everyone misspells it.

After that, the one-minute wait for her pasta to ping feels like a whole fucking hour. She actually starts pulling faces at me in her reflection in the microwave ovens – puffing her cheeks, narrowing her eyes, even doing some buck-teeth baring like she's showing off her gum disease. At one point, it looks like she's simultaneously pulling completely different faces in each different microwave – though obviously she ain't; that'd just be weird.

These kinds of slip-ups over my name don't actually happen all that often. Can't be arsed to go into how I manage to juggle my different IDs – end of the day, everyone fronts differently when they're in fonespace. Everyone's like some rock star juggling different stage personas. Different vibes for different apps – different usernames/profiles/filters. I just take it to some next level is all. Ain't anything deep and meaningful and sociologicalful, it's just functional– lets me keep shit real for me while at the same time lying to Ramona about my mum. It ain't as if I wear different facial expressions for each of them. Or think in different voices. Ain't even some cleverly designed system; it's just a strategy that works on the fly. And so long as I keep strictly separate fones for Dillon, Dhilan and Dylan, I hardly ever fuck things up. But, yeh – I do realise that there's a pretty big-ass design flaw in trying to use social media to keep shit secret. Sometimes I reckon the tech actually makes it *harder* to run double lives.

"Well, Mr So-and-So" – her make-up less pancake than it had looked in all the microwaves – "Perhaps it's easier when people just refer to you by your surname?"

And so I go back to the exact same workstation. Lay my fones on the desk, just me and my fones. But this time ain't no need to wait around for jack. I click open the client's internal staff directory and scroll down the list of four-digit phone extensions, searching for my surname. That woman who'd phoned here earlier didn't ask to speak to no Dillon or Dylan or Dhilan, she'd asked for *Mr Deckardas*. I deffo shouldn't be listed, though, cos everyone on this project is a temp – even the Digital Archive Project Manager ain't on the payroll of permanent, pensioned-and-share-optioned-and-phone-extensioned staff. Soon as I start tapping in my surname, I get hit by some fucking plot-spoiler before I even finish typing. No shitting: I'm literally typing the letters "DECK" on my keyboard when the full word DECKARDAS pops up on my Dhilan fone – like as if my different devices are doing each other's autocomplete. The full text of the text message is this: "DAMN YOU DECKARDAS, WHEN ARE YOU COMING BACK HERE TO FUCKING HELL FACE ALL THIS?" You see, Masi often calls me Deckardas instead of Dhilan or Dillon or Dylan – i.e. my father's family name. Subtext's so unsubtle it takes dipshit-idiotness to the next level. And it don't even mean nothing, seeing as how I know next to fuck all about my dad. Just childhood memories that feel like someone else's (his eyebrows, his voice, his hairy hands, the fact that he worked loads and that his work was selling insurance). Mum once said he's one of them blokes who couldn't ever piss without ripping out a fart – that was basically her filler for the holes in the family fotos. Oh, and apparently he used to shoot his load too quick. And so I hate it when Masi calls me Deckardas. And I love it that she calls me something that means she and I ain't the same. My mum changed her surname to Gital – her maiden name and probly the only surname Masi'll ever have – but, still, Mum kept the name Deckardas as her middle name. He can't be such a useless, loner, loser, wanker, workaholic shitface if she kept it as her middle name.

When I'm done typing my surname into the directory, I know in my head that it makes fuck all sense for my father's full name to pop up. Like I said, I'm for definite the man's always worked in insurance and, anyway, I know for a fact he can't have been no journalist or nothing – cos, let's face it, it ain't as if I haven't tried looking him up on the internet over the years. I mean, whenever I been bored enough to bother to google him. I ain't gonna milk the violins here by telling you how the last time I tried to fone him was from the hospital waiting room during the removal of tumour number four. How he didn't turn up at the hospital that day, that week, that year – ten years since she was first diagnosed and he never friggin showed up once. No big deal, though. Done and done. No drama, no obligatory obligations. Ain't like it's in some custody contract – an "In Case Mum Gets Cancer" clause.

Next to my father's name is an old-school phone symbol. Click on it, but it's password-protected. Only shit I can read is this: *Name: Ramnik Deckardas; Job Title: General Reporter; Active Dates: 2001–2001.*

We've already digitised all the back issues from 2001 so I click open the live digital archive and start searching for stories under his authorship. But there ain't diddly nothing. So next I load up the work-in-progress digital archive, but once again zero: none of the archives contain any stories written by my dad. Surely I shoulda been clued in that the man had been some journalist one time? It's the kinda stuff that'd come up in everyday convo – after all, newspapers are always in the news: "Oh, by the way, Dhilan, your daddy once wrote stories for a newspaper." Maybe nothing more than that, but that much at least: your dad once wrote for a newspaper. End of story. Anyway, allow that, surely it would've come up on Google?

10

DORMS LIKE SOME hourly rate hotel. Cash machine by the lifts. Also Diet Coke, confectionary, birth control, exact change only. Sound of her shoes against the cold hard floor, meaning the rubber pads beneath her heels have worn down. Probly the metal pegs are mashed up too. Time to start dropping some pseudoness technical mansplaining: the rubber pads are called top-lifts, the steel pegs are called spigots – we're talking actual fucking crutches inside the shells of women's heels. Sometimes Ramona ditches the rubber pads on purpose so that the spigots can make that sound while her soles are still new and making their own sound.

This ain't the sound of the beat when you breastfeeding.

This ain't her heartbeat before you was born.

It's the sound of your mama's forehead. When she began banging it against the wall.

Later, the sound of my dysfunction going full-on malfunction, i.e. avoidance of even contactless sex just to avoid Ramona's breasts. That stupidass sound of me failing to apologise – just a wounded-dog whimper somewhere in the space between us. Me standing there like some dickless idiot, wondering if maybe dogs woof each other apologies when they reject a friendly genital sniff. Ramona starts taking it all on herself again. And so I tell her again there ain't nothing wrong with her. And then telling her once again – telling her till her sadness upgrades to anger.

"Well then, thanks a lot," she goes. "Thanks for getting me wetter than a pregnant woman with breaking waters and then turning into a wussy wet blanket."

"I ain't being a wet blanket," I say like some whining wet blanket. "It's just that it's cold in your flat. How about you put on a sweater and we try again?"

But Ramona doesn't put on no sweater.

She puts on a pair of shoes.

Now another pair. Then another. Like we're in a lock-in at some Christian Louboutin boutique. Sliding and slipping in and out of each shoe with the same skilfulness I use to stay inside my self-bought boxer shorts. Inserting herself into each insole like she's plugging herself in. We're talking box-fresh – me fetching each pair with a quickness from their original packaging. Her red patent pumps from their black velvet shoebox. Her violet strappy sandals from their grey cardboard shoebox. Her green buckled ankle boots from their white plastic shoebox. Tissue paper and silica-gel sachets spilling all over the floor. Ramona hitting me up with rolling-news-style running commentary: "Silica-gel for moisture absorption, polystyrene balls for stiffness and shape retention, tissue paper for protection." Her black stacked-heel slingbacks from their purple cardboard shoebox; her purple open-toe pumps from their black cardboard shoebox. Ten minutes later, we hit that sweet spot in relationships when selfishness and selflessness become the exact same thing – like as if she's got actual G-spots along her ankle straps. "Well, go on, touch them then, Dillon," she sighs. "Finger me in the highest part beneath them" – she means that corner where the shoe's heel ends and the sole's descent begins. Her blue wedge-heel pumps from their pale-yellow shoebox; her black open-toe slingbacks from their clear plastic shoebox. Her unworn pairs placed tight together so that their arches touch and form little love caverns. The white pair, the knee-length boots, the pumps I once accidentally shot my load into (she was safe about it, though – she'd stuffed them with newspaper to keep their shape). Next, the blue velvet pair that pushes her centre of gravity even further forward than her other shoes do. Their alignments, their angles, their badass Shard-ness. The light from her floor lamp splashing into each pursed-together arch-cavern. Google told me that, with standard-issue Oedipal problems, the more a guy loves his girlfriend, the more she starts repping his mother, the less able he is to have standard sexual relations with her. Meanwhile, the more he lusts after a woman, the less able he is to actually love her. Hence this hang-up that sexperts call "Madonna/whore". Well, you can fuck that game for starters – I'd rather be turned into a frog or an insect or a fucking pumpkin. Anycase, I've schooled myself up on this shit: King Oedipus didn't even have an Oedipal complex – if anything, he had the opposite. Dude wanted to get as far away from his mum as possible. So fuck off with all that blaming-your-mother bollocks. All those theories and psychoprobabilities. Those astrology columns and health-insurance models. Those prophecies we studied in English Lit. – *You will murder your father and marry your mother. You will become Thane and then become King. You will marry and then bone your mother.* "Well, slide in then," Ramona sighs. "Slide your finger in and touch my toe cleavage."

After we're done, we line up her shoes at the foot of her bed – in descending height order like some perfect toe cascade. Their leather more wet-look in the moonlight. Her toenails only leather-like at the cuticles. Ramona says high heels make her feet look perfect. But would she still torture herself with all this fuckery if guys like me didn't click on all the images – didn't reinforce her heels with our attention? The fuck is wrong with me I can't even get my dick straight unless she misaligns her vertebrae? Ramona tells me to stop making it all about myself. Tells me high heels make her feet look perfect.

Back when Mum booted my dad out, most girls just wore blunt-toed trainers to school but Ramona was already sticking her feet into more grown-up stuff. Didn't really know her from Adam back then, though – and even when we both moved up to the same secondary school, we still had separate lessons, separate friends, separate sets of friend requests. And obviously by then my mum had got sick so I had that whole cellfone-and-secret-existence situation going on. Mum yanking on my Vodafone umbilical cord even before the home-time bell. My SMS set to auto-reply: *I'm still in school, I love you too, did you manage to go to the loo?* Everyone pegging me as some psycho weirdo just cos I cried a couple times during lessons. And cos I could never pull off all that Disneyfied playtime/fun-time/party-time fuckery. Ramona never cussed me, though – Ramona just ignored me. Rest of this movie happened with a slowness. Truth is, I thought I was just stalling instead of stalking. Just another random reason to delay going home. Every day after school, Ramona's grown-up shoes would take her in the direction of this nearby newsagent's. First, sweets, then magazines; later, low-tar Marlboro. For real, though, I didn't even trust all that tingling crap – I just figured that thinking about Ramona was just a way of not thinking. Like as if I was on some extreme-sports-type shit. By the time I hit twelve, the newsagent knew me by name, what part of India my family was from and whether I wanted to be a doctor or dentist or pharmacist. Dude started chatting to me when I upgraded from superhero comics to *The Economist*. Next step was to enter the shop while Ramona was still in there and then let this random Shaadi.com newsagent do the intro I was too chickenshit to do myself. After that, she'd shoot me a smile whenever we passed each other in the school corridor. *"Just some guy called Dillon,"* she told one of her friends. Some random local kid who gets milk from the same corner shop. A boy who lived nearer her than I actually did. And pretty soon it became impossible for me to carry on stalking her. Can't stalk someone as they walk home from school if they wanna walk with you and invite you in.

Ramona swaps her slingbacks for bed-socks and hits her en-suite bathroom. Starts doing all that open-door weirdness. (Stay in a honeymoon suite with your mum and you'll know what I'm chatting about). When she's done brushing her teeth and flossing between her toes, I wait for the scent of Sudocrem. Ramona says it's just a pro tip anti-acne hack, but we both know how Sudocrem is basically her perfume. Dettol is basically my mum's. The difference when I'm lying beside her is the difference between hugging and cuddling. For a sec or so, I swear down I can hear Ramona sniffling. Like I'm ten years old again, trying to figure out whether to go and hold her or just lie there listening, counting her sobs as if they sheep. Back when I could still get some kinda rush from being able to make Mummy stop crying. Turn her tears into smiles like as if I was flexing some special magic skills. My whole body locked and ready for the wetness of her face. But Ramona ain't crying. Ain't never even seen her cry. Sometimes I worry that maybe it's the same shit as the high-heel-torture thing – like as if maybe I'm actually attracted to her tear duct drought. That long-term overexposure has left me with some kinda allergy – breaks me out in, like, the headache equivalent of hives. And cos I know just how deeply fucked-up this is, if Ramona ever actually *did* cry in front of me, I'd probly end up doing all that compensatory caring crap – and, trust me, that shit's even more fucked-up.

Even though Ramona ain't even crying, some kinda autopilot kicks in. I start randomly telling her how my day was. This means I now gotta data-sift what I can and cannot share with her. For instance, I can tell her about those two doddery old men who'd offered to buy my start-up, but I can't tell her how they were all clued up about my mother. Can tell her I missed my meeting with that potential new client, but I can't tell her they think I missed it cos of my mother. Can tell her about my latest bollocking from various assorted aunties and uncles, so long as I pretend the bollocking was about some minor shit and not about my mother.

All started when Ramona would fone me on Thursday evenings to cross-check her Economics homework. And like some idiotfuck I'd tell her I was out at the Park Royal bowling alley – the one with the underage video-games arcade. My whole week spent waiting for her Thursday-evening fone call and then I'd pretend like as if I was out with my imaginary mates. Still helped her, of course – after simulating stepping away from all the simulated fun. Only reason I started up with that shit was cos Mum started playing her stereo loud – like, proper loudness; so loud so that you couldn't hear her crying in her bedroom. By the time we got to A levels, I'd even tell Ramona that I was in a pub or a bar or the Broadway-bloody-Boulevard in Ealing – that I'd talk her through her Economics essay while drinking and chilling and LOLing, actual out-loud LOLing. One time, I even told her I was in some gym. If only Mum had blasted out her bhajans or gazals on her stereo – or even her calm-forest-mood meditations – then maybe I might not have lied. Might even've broken the Official Secrets Act and told Ramona about Mum's sickness. But instead Mum would drop some muthafuckin big-beat hip-hop tunes cos she figured that's what I was probly into. And by the time Ramona and I were bouncing out somewhere beyond best-friend territory, I weren't about to hit the self-destruct button by letting her know how I'd been lying to her on the regular. Not just them big lies about being on holiday when I'd actually been sitting with Mum in hospital. And not just the lies about her not being allowed to my house cos of renovations/Rottweiler/possible underground radiation leak. Also all them little lies to cover up the big lies and the later lies to cover up the earlier ones. Them lies about the Rottweiler eating the T-shirt she got me for my birthday cos I couldn't tell her how it really got trashed. Them lies about me being hungover, them lies about being stoned, them lies about me having a rare form of hay fever in the middle of friggin winter. And, during all this time, Ramona was telling me everything about her own complicated family-related shit. About her mother's epic fail on the Valium dosage front that nearly required a stomach pump. About how much she couldn't stand this one guy who her mum was dating cos he tried so hard to be such a stand-up substitute dad. About how she thought he was up to some no-good shadyness and so asked me to tag along with her on some crazyass toy-binoculars espionage mission. She even told me about her mum's yeast infections, like as if I'd have any advice about yoghurt-based routines for feminine hygiene. Meanwhile, by then my own bullshit was flowing so freestyle, I'd end up lying to her even when I didn't even need to. Been lying about movies I seen cos I didn't want her knowing I'd seen them on some date night with my mum. Next thing, I started lying about watching shit on TV. About the Saturday nights of DIY, the pipework, the plumbing and U-bends. I lied about my lunch-hour bag of bathroom-tile grout. Total tally of lies told to Ramona has now bust through the 5,000 mark – I know this cos once when Mum got really sick I hit a batting average of 73.8 lies a day. Probly be a lot less lies if I weren't always having some urge to call Ramona whenever Mum's been taken into hospital. To see her straight after visiting hours. The fuck did I always do that for? And, yeh, I know that lots of young carers keep their real shit hidden from their closest friends, but still though, surely there's a line somewhere?

Tonight, I try and keep my bullshit in check by just keeping my trap shut. Holding her tighter than tender while we lay on her bedding of shoeboxes, tissue paper, whatever, the mattress and duvet. Never claiming her but still clinging to her – keeping her from having a better life with some better guy. Both of us knowing it's some crime against the laws of chemistry that we're basically just casual fuck-buddies who don't even actually fuck. Best-friends-with-benefits but without the full-disclosure friendship benefit. But the even bigger crime going on here is that Ramona reckons it's cos I don't *want* a full-on relationship. Truth is, in order for us to go there, I'd first have to come clean about all my lies. And then, if she's got any self-respect, there won't be no relationship left to lie in.

11

SECOND TIME YOUR mum told you she had the C-bomb, you guessed it was in her remaining breast. Even though you'd been geeking up about axillary nodes and lymph nodes and how the other common place for it to spread was to a woman's bones.

She'd been parked up by the school gates for you since three o'clock. Could see her stillness from your classroom window. Like as if she was a part of the car. Fixed into position like some human child-seat.

You thought to yourself: *So it had been too good, then.* Technical term for it was "in remission". Maybe even the non-good days had been too good? Also: *Will she still let me rent out* Batman Begins, *even though it's rated 12?*

"It's spread," she said before hitting the ignition. The engine cut out. "It's in my second breast." Way she said the word "second" was like she had a third, a fourth, a fifth. Just junctions you pass on some motorway – them elevated interchange roundabouts. "They only picked it up in the mammogram – you can barely even feel a lump. But, listen to me, there's nothing for you to worry about, okay, Dhilan? Together we'll beat this one too."

You told her "spread" weren't the right word for it – that the correct term was "metastasise". Google had told you the technical term for it.

Later, staring straight ahead at a red traffic light. Tick-tock of the turn-left indicator. School bag sulking between your seats where the handbrake used to be.

Plus points of being told of new tumours in the car:

1) You didn't need to be told to sit down.
2) Didn't have to worry about a facial expression fail.
3) You didn't have to hug her – i.e. you didn't have to calibrate hugging her. *Hold her too tightly and you'd cause her physical pain; hold her too lightly and you'd cause her emotional pain.*

All those dictums to fall back on for whenever you couldn't think clear. Why did the physical caring and the emotional caring have to get so interlinked?

She'd picked you up from school cos she'd taken the day off work. Always took the whole day off for test results. You'd suggested you could skip school and go with her, but she'd vetoed it. All that compassionate truancy wouldn't start till a year or so later. Lying to your teachers. Lying to your mum about teacher-training days. Least if you went with her you wouldn't worry yourself to stupidness. Rule was, she'd let you tag along for her scans or treatments, but never to her routine annual check-ups and results and stuff. Never needing to beg her boss for time off, though, cos of all them years she'd been Employee of the Month. The sick-pay pages of her contract spread out across your floor like a safety net.

Should probly mention her jobs and stuff. Should probly mention her childhood and her whole immigrant experience. The poverty, the racism, the bedsit. The mangoes and the saris. But your mum had told you that only *"pishy posh people"* wanna know about all that motherland malarkey – *"rest of us are trying to run away from it".* Besides, you already figured out in primary school that a second-gen immigrant ain't technically even an immigrant.

And you already figured out in primary school that she'd be dying for longer than her childhood.

Your mum wiped it off the steering wheel. Wiped the windscreen, even, as if that would clear her eyes. "And just like last time, Dhilan, I don't want you telling anyone about my illness yet . . ."

Eyes, nose, mouth, ears.

Between four and five feet tall.

There's this scene in the film *Blade Runner* where a guy in some kinda interview situation is asked to describe his mother. Instead of doing so, he shoots the interviewer.

". . . You know what those people are like, Dhilan. They think that if a person's sick it's because they deserve it. Either because of something bad they've done in this life or something bad they've done in a previous life. They'll say I'm being punished for divorcing your dad. That's how these people actually think, Dhilan – they actually have the time and the energy to think these things."

Kept telling you that her sickness weren't a punishment like as if she was trying to tell it to herself. Told you how some religions even saw women's periods as a punishment for bad things they were supposed to have done. And always worrying about what the "other people" thought of her. The ones with the husbands and the handbags that matched their saris. Like as if she was some cokehead straight outta rehab and they'd all placed bets on how long she'd take to fall apart again. Or for her poor, fatherless son to fall from the proper path.

Anycase, you didn't even want to tell anyone. Didn't want to talk. Kids would just make fun of you; grown-ups would probly just feel sorry for you. They wouldn't be able to do nothing about all the things you was worrying about, so nothing to talk about. Truth is, you actually *wanted* to close ranks.

"Or at least just for now," she said as you stopped outside the house – dead slowly but always parking like she'd pulled up after a car chase. "Let's just keep this to ourselves for the next few weeks.

Then I'll start by telling the immediate family. But for now just you and me."

. . . Because, just because, Dhilan. Because I'm asking you not to tell anyone yet . . .

. . . No, not even your cousins in Birmingham, Dhilan – they might tell your cousins in London . . .

. . . Because people will think it's my karma and they think karma means punishment instead of destiny . . .

. . . No, not even people at school – not even the white people . . .

. . . Yes, I know we told everyone that Uncle Ashok had cancer – but that was because he didn't really have cancer. Instead he was dying of a different disease . . .

. . . Because I'm asking you to keep it a secret, Dhilan. Haven't we always had our secrets? I wish I could keep it a secret from you, but I already know that would be impossible.

After that, you tried to make her calm.

Made her watch some TV.

Didn't let her use her fone.

Okay – but voice calls only. No getting baited by all them scare stories.

Stop clicking on the links.

Took you a full two hours to bring the subject of her sickness back up. Did it by asking her how she was feeling. The takeaway dinner. The Tesco cherry and raspberry mousse that seemed to become your after-news-of-new-tumour tradition.

"Well, you tell me," she pushed away her bowl. "How the hell do you think I'm feeling?"

Oh gimpfuck. You hadn't meant to upset her. Started scrambling explanations like fighter jets. Told her she'd misheard you. Told her you'd asked if you could *feel it.*

"What do you mean 'feel it', Dhilan? Feel what?"

You followed through the dumbfuck logic of what you'd just said and realised you'd now have to follow through with your fingers.

"Feel what, Dhilan?"

Couldn't tell her you meant her boobs or her breasts. If anything, you'd have to say it singular. But if you said it singular, you might offend her. And you couldn't exactly say you meant her lump in case she thought you were dissing her singular boob by calling it a lump. In the end, you just called it "it" – told her you wanted to make sure "it" didn't hurt her.

"It doesn't hurt me, sweetheart. Not even a teeny bit. The doctor says breast cancer lumps hardly ever hurt."

Still, her hand to your hand; then both hands to the side of her breast – i.e. her right breast, i.e. the only breast she had left. The new lump impossible to distinguish from the surrounding flesh. Her probly bra-less beneath her peach summertime dress. Soft at the touch of your fingers; hardening at the brush of your wrist. You stood up, cleared away the dessert, the plates. Told her again that you wouldn't tell no one.

12

"WAKE UP, DILLON."

In theory, Ramona's mattress ain't no more soft than my own student hall mattress.

"Dillon, wake the fuck up."

In practice, mornings are easier when I can't sleep through the night.

"Some people are here to speak with you – they say it's about your mother."

Before the invention of spine-supporting memory foam, mattresses made of foam were mostly for brothels. No bed-springs, no noise.

"My mother?"

Brothels and hospitals.

"Yeh. Your mother."

Ramona's student room is L-shaped, the bed tucked outta sight. Now another voice – some bloke's voice – rolls in round the corner from the doorway: "We should've brought you two lovebirds breakfast in bed. Some McDonald's Egg McMuffins, maybe. Dipped in boiling Big Mac *jus de boeuf.*" Sound of her room door closing – latch like a slow handclap. "Still, how about one of these instead – they've been sweating through the paper bag like my ass cheeks in a sauna." The two aged-out Botox men join Ramona at the foot of her bed with an offering of Starbucks oatmeal cookies.

"Er, *excuse* me," Ramona tries drawing her already-drawn dressing gown, "I told you two to wait at the door for him."

Can't recall if I'm butt naked under her duvet so stay under it just in case. Sitting up in bed like I'm sick. One of them flips on the light switch, killing off the sunlight behind the curtains.

"You realise you weren't in lectures this morning, Dylan?" Botched-Botox man is still on his whole biker jacket thing, but today the leather is cracked and faded. "Nor were you at your client's office doing your do-do-da-da data entry. And also you weren't in lectures."

Display on my Dylan handset gives me the damage report. Three missed client meetings, forty-nine reminders and an already-rescheduled conference call. I know my fones ain't actually part of me but, thing is, they also ain't not-me. Oh, and there are bloodstains on my touchscreen again. That ouching below my left shoulder blade from the cleansed-and-dressed stab wound (or graze or scratch or, whatever, some minor abrasion).

"And you also weren't in your dorm room. And of course neither were you somewhere else."

Beside me, Ramona's broken three-inch pencil heel – staining her bedsheets like some amputated finger. Pointing and laughing in the general direction of my dick.

Younger-looking old man cuts me a look to see if I'm gonna play along with this bullshit. If we've agreed the basic groundhog rules. If we on the same wank-stained webpage. Then he starts backing away till he's out of frame again cos of the whole L-shaped room situation. Fiver says he's gone to stand by the door. Can always tell when someone's blocking the door.

Breath mint. Eye bogey. Leave fones switched to silent. I ask the men what the hell they doing here.

"They started banging on my door ten minutes ago," Ramona says, stepping away from them to stand beside me at her bedside. "Well?" she goes to the older-looking old man.

"Tell us, then. You said you wanted to talk to Dillon about his mother – well, what's happened to his mother?" Squeezing my hand like as if she's prepping me for the worst – or more like for whatever she imagines could be worst. Ain't got no clue how I've always had me a drill for that day. All them times during lessons sitting there waiting for the knock on the classroom door.

"Don't be talking 'bout my mother," I give it at max volume before either man can speak.

"We don't want to talk about your mother," goes the botched-Botox man.

Ramona does that thing where she scrunches her nose. "Wait, what? But a minute ago – when you were beating the crap out of my door – you said you needed to speak to him about his mother."

"You clearly misheard. We said we needed to speak about his baby. Not his mother, his *baby*."

"What baby?" I ask this without freaking out like other guys might. Let's face it, my jism rarely travels further up a girl's anatomy than her ankles.

"Your tech start-up, Dylan. What other baby could we be talking about?" And then to Ramona: "Perhaps you could give us a few minutes."

The lack of a question mark is a big bulging mistake. Ramona puts up with so much shit from me, ain't no room left for her to take it from anyone else. "Or how about you guys go hold your business meeting somewhere more suitable? Like, for instance, the 1950s" – slam-shutting her laptop even though it ain't even powered on. "Besides, I need my room this morning. I've got a degree to study for so that I can be underemployed and forced to live in perpetual pre-adulthood with my mum."

Keep my arms under the duvet like as if I'm shamed of my hairy knuckles or something.

"And, anyway," Ramona presses on, "who the hell actually stands with their hands on their hips like that? You fellas been taking body-language lessons from ITV police dramas?"

The botched-Botox man starts scoping out the Pinterest situation going on across Ramona's opposite wall. The fotos, the poems and the pizza flyers. A laminated copy of her Blu Tack permit. Leaning in closer like he's doing that pinch-to-zoom thing. Postcards, leaflets, ticket stubs – random shit from random things round London we've somehow managed to do together. A gig, a film, Somerset House ice rink. Fridge magnet of a book we read for GCSE English. Nando's, Tate Modern, selfishness, Wagamama, subterfuge and deception, a flyer for the LSE Ideas Fest. Tapping his foot in time with the gig ticket. Nodding at each post like it's firing up memories. Hands behind his back, fingers working his string of meditation beads.

"Well, go on then, Dillon, tell your two bum-chum business buddies to get out my room."

Some new flyer up on her wall I ain't ever noticed before – some famous music person she hasn't schooled me up on yet. Some grime or hip-hop or rock or roadworks or sirens or life support. Never thinks any less of me, though, just corrects me and moves on: *"No Dillon, Kanye West and Yeezy are the same person. And Kafka was a novelist not an Organisational Management theorist."*

I'm hitting some whole new level of limpdick gimpery today, though. Problem is I just woke up. Ain't that I'm not a morning person or nothing, it's just I only ever dream as Dhilan.

"Well? Tell them, Dillon."

Her mouth like when she hates posing for Instagram pics. Arms too open to fold, too closed to plead. Then inadvertently drawing attention to her underwear by snatching it off the radiator rack and shoving it in a desk drawer. She scrolls through her facial expressions – from sad to angry to nothing. But ain't neither of the men even notices her face. Or the way her dressing gown barely even encryptionates her body as she grabs some clothes, slips on some heels, tells the younger old man to move away from her door, clicks out of her own room.

*

Now an ad for a detachable lumbar support. A story about jellyfish. The Big Tech firms sucking enough data from my fingers to know when I feel spineless or insecure or just in need of a self-esteem signal-boost. Anyways, fuck my fones – the pain below my shoulder blade gives me the clarity of backbone to tell the men to leave, go, get the fuck out of Ramona's room: "*Please*, I think it would be better if both of you left."

"Little bit late for chivalry, kid." Blankpage-Botox man leans against Ramona's desk, hands touching her drawers. Same necktie he wore yesterday but he's swapped out his sharkskin blue suit for a three-button charcoal-grey. Some scar on the sleeve that needs stitching.

Take a swig from last night's Red Bull then jack up my voice so that Ramona'll hear me if she's hanging in the corridor: "So I take it you two fellas still wanna buy my start-up, then?"

"Only because you still want to sell it to us," goes the blankpage-Botox man. "How much did you want for it again, Dylan?"

"Ain't want nothing from you two."

"Well that's not very much, is it?"

I tell them ain't got time for all this beating-around-the-bullshit. Even try milking the fact that today I got me a stage-prop to back me up, lowering the duvet a little and jabbing at the dressing across my general breast area: "See? Can you grandpas see this? I got an injury problem here. I need to go get me a tetanus injection before the doctor's surgery shuts."

"You had a ten-year tetanus booster two years ago," goes the botched-Botox man.

"I told you guys yesterday: you can't scare me by knowing everything about me. I run a tech start-up, remember – I know how the digital economy works."

"And as we told you yesterday, we'd very much like to buy your little typing business."

"But if that's what all this bullshit's really about, then why the hell you just tell Ramona to leave?"

"We didn't." The botched-Botox man now sitting at the other end of the mattress – embedded smell of Ramona's Sudocrem doing hand-to-hand combat with his cologne. "We simply asked her to give us a minute. *You* were the one who told her to go – by not asking her to stay. In fact, all we did was ask her to give us a minute."

Other man picks up one of Ramona's stray TV-watching slipper-socks, sniffs the sock, then stuffs it in his pocket. Starts fucking about with her make-up kit, which basically just consists of lip balm and a spare tub of Sudocrem – i.e. the smell of her smiling. The way that she smiles sometimes. And that ouching in my chest right now? It's just the shoe injury thing, okay? I just need a better technique for kissing her feet from a supine position.

The two aged-out men continue longing out their General-Purpose Threatening Behaviour while I weigh up whether to just level with them. Voluntary disclosure. After all, I ain't some gimpshit idiot who takes a whole week and five scenes to figure out that maybe there might be a link between two separate up-the-arse headfucks. Ain't got that kinda time. All I'd have to do is just ask the old men a straight question – the obvious question, the honest question, the question that jumped me last night while I was walking back from work. Does all this bully-boy badassery of theirs have something to do with the fact that apparently my dad once worked for one of my data-entry clients? I'd have to cut out the vagueness – tell em straight out that he wrote for the newspaper where I'm helping fix up up some digital archive. How I'd stumbled into his name in an old version of the staff directory, even though there's diddly-fuck all info about him on Google. Even though I'm for sure the man's always worked in insurance. Problem is, with these two goons, best probable outcome would be a trick answer to my straight question. Allow it – if there's one thing I'm good at, it's keeping shit on the sly.

"Listen, fellas, why don't—"

"Why don't cats like being held?" the blankpage-Botox man cuts me off. "Why don't cellphones have thermometers? Why don't men ever listen to women?"

Botched-Botox man holds his finger to his mouth like as if to say mute the fuck up. Then he leans in and sniffs the mattress. "Seems that you've rejected our masturbating advice. That's a pity, kid. Our advice was freely given. You've no idea how excruciating it is to watch you fuck up your love life for the rest of your life." Pats the bed like he wants me to shift down next to him. I do practically the opposite. "Dylan, you realise your mother isn't like Google or Facebook, right? Which means she won't even know that you don't actually fuck Ramona. So she won't be any more inclined to approve. Or any less inclined."

"I thought you guys wanted me to leave her alone and masturbate?"

He hands me a Volvic instead of the Red Bull. I pop a painkiller instead of a Pro-Plus. "Just pick a path and commit to it, kid. Otherwise all this mother–son madness of yours will become hardwired instead of merely being your default setting. And I'm not just referring to your phobias and perversions, I mean this whole damn thing, Dylan – the whole tiresome hating-whatever-you-love shtick."

Bothers me that he thinks I'd be so easily taken in by his whole kind-and-caring Uncle Phil routine. Not cos it means he reckons I'm an idiot, but cos it's exactly how I'd want him to roll. I mean if I were tripping. Delusionating. Okay, if I were just making these dudes up. Kinda blatant this time – them showing up while I'm lying in bed, like one of my mummy's lucid dreams.

"You guys ain't for real, are you?"

"You doubt our seriousness, Dylan?"

"No, I doubt your existence. When I say you ain't for real, I mean as in you ain't actually there. I don't need to be in an

M. Night Shyamalan film to have already wised up and worked that shit out."

I watch both men closely for any signs of panic, mayhem and meltdown caused by my devastating powers of deduction.

"Oh, for fuck's sake, don't be so insipid," goes the botched-Botox man. "The clock is ticking and you're wasting time looking for a humdrum plot twist to get you out of this. Meanwhile the clock is ticking."

Blankpage-Botox man has to scrunch up a pair of Ramona's knickers just to stop himself from facepalming. Then he face-palms anyway – sneaking a sniff as he does so. And, yeh, I know I should probly stand up for Ramona's honour or something. Do that whole gallantry thing. But who the fuck would I be kidding?

"Well, I'm sorry to disappoint you, Dylan, but my associate and I are both men of flesh and blood. Well, perhaps also a bit of Botox, but then you guessed that much the first time you saw us. In any case, follow the logic of your laughable suggestion. Even if you seriously think we're just some figment of one of your fictional online personas, you're forgetting that your fictional personas are real. They even have real-life girlfriends made of flesh and menstrual blood."

"Look, just stop talking about my girlfriend, yeh? And while you're at it, please don't sniff her panties – it ain't polite."

Wanna change the word "panties" to "underwear" to be more respectful, but the botched-Botox man gets his clarification in first: "Of course, it's debatable whether she's even really your girlfriend. After all, if you're going to lose her then you've already lost her, right? Did I say that correctly, kiddo?"

Ain't no slack in the bedcover to pull it up over my face so I just close my eyes and head under my breath to ask them how much they'd told her – i.e. the fuck did they say about my mother before Ramona had woke me up?

"How much do you want us to have told her?" The botched-Botox man stands up from the bed – hands like two giant car jacks flattening the foam mattress. "All that hard work, kid. All that running around and deception. All those years you were besotted with her – duping her into falling for Dillon, keeping her blissfully ignorant of Dhilan. And the fact is, you did it, kid – all your cack-handed amorous antics actually paid off. Because despite all your underlying dishonesty and false advertising, Ramona still somehow gets you. I mean she truly seems to *get* you. That isn't the kind of connection a man should just let slip away."

Great. Now they got me stuck here butt naked and basically bed-ridden, I gotta listen to more longed-out relationship advice.

"Of course, these days it's common practice to *get* people – to truly and deeply understand them. Guess their feelings, predict their behaviours, how they'll respond to x, y and z. You just monitor their digital activity and then crunch all the data through algorithms. Who will like this, who will buy that, who will fall sick, who will ejaculate too quick, who'll wake up crying in the middle of their miserable excuse for sleep. You people keep secreting your secret thoughts and feelings like plants fart out oxygen. Touching your cellphones thousands of times a day. But the fact is Ramona can't possibly be doing any intuitive form of this kind of data-harvesting, can she, Dylan? After all, she has no idea about all your mother-related clicking and browsing and searching. If she did, her connection with you wouldn't be so special; it would just be computation."

I ask him if that's meant to sound romantic or something. If so, I take it he's single.

"I'm with Dylan on this one," goes the blankpage-Botox man. "Why the hell are you giving him relationship tips?"

Older man just presses on: "I mean, sure, she knows what you like to eat and what music you like to listen to – in part, because she recommends it to you. But she doesn't know what you *read*, does she? What you feed your mind. For instance, how you click on every recommended article and book about Oedipus."

"Sorry, but am I meant to be triggered or something by the way you guys keep dropping drive-by references to Oedipus?"

"Just trying to connect with you, Dylan. After all, if your search history serves me correctly, then that's the one cultural reference I know you're familiar with. After all, you did actually *read* all those articles and books, didn't you? You are familiar with the story? Yes, you know it. It's known that you know it."

I tell him everyone knows the story of Oedipus – or they can google it, so same thing. Ain't even gotta scroll all the way back to Ancient Greece. Oedipus goes to an oracle to score some knowledge and gets given this prophecy that he'll do a bunch of bad shit, including marrying his own mum. So he gets the fuck out of Dodge and never calls or texts or smoke-signals his mum again. Problem is, dude doesn't know he was actually adopted. And the woman he ends up marrying – this queen of this city called Thebes – turns out to be his real actual mum. Only reason he finds out the truth is cos he tries to hunt down and punish the perpetrator of some other bad shit he's unknowingly done. Anyway, it's really fucked. Skip forward nearly 3,000 years and every therapist and student-counselling service uses the word "Oedipal" to describe messed-up mother–son stuff. You know, like acrimonious driving lessons. Shit like that.

"No need to look so anxious, Dylan. Just because we know lots of things about you, that doesn't mean we know what you'll do next. That isn't how this works. Technically speaking, that isn't even how it works with your smartphone – with Google and Amazon and Facebook." The botched-Botox man starts flicking through a pile of old Tesco Clubcard statements. "They can monitor your activity and purchases and drill deep into all your data, but that by itself doesn't give them the best possible predictions about what you'll do, buy, click, or read and think next week. For that, their algorithms have to crunch their data for all the *other people* – people with similar preferences and responses and behaviours to you. To learn what those other people actually bought or did or clicked on next. Instead of calculating what you *will* do, they're calculating what millions of similar people *did* do."

He knows I already know this. Anyone trying to build a digital business knows this shit. Any business that taps into your personal info and monitors your digital behaviour. Data crunching leads to patterns, patterns lead to predictions, predictions lead to personalised recommendations, recommendations lead to reality – and therefore more revenues. That's why anything less than total surveillance is a missed opportunity to generate more revenues/reality.

Memories now rush me like some kinda backchannel data flow. Shit I always known but just hadn't properly puzzled out. My brain swiping all the way back to those three bearded aunties. As if whatever I was gonna do was such a bad thing to have already done.

Wait. Just you wait and see.

Close the light and come and see.

The Googly-engine says he will take the father's place.

But, anycase, what the fuck could Google and Facebook have even known about me back then? I had a fone, but it weren't a smartfone. We had a home PC, but we was still on some ancientquated AOL-type shit. Matterfact, Mum and me even shared the same user profile. We had the same user profile for years. And, anyway, if you wanna be flexing some proper predictive data analytics – if you want patterns and prophecies and product recommendations – then you'll be needing the kinda patterns you could only spot by ramming millions of terabytes of digital data through supercomputer algorithms.

For instance, vegetarians will miss fewer flights.

For instance, people with lower credit ratings will have more accidents.

For instance, people who use more exclamation marks will have more car crashes.

For instance, that Scottish bloke we studied in GCSE English Lit. who became Thane of Cawdor.

For instance, that motherfucker who became King of Thebes.

First time I read the story of Oedipus I just wanted to file that shit under Disgusting Dirtyass Bollocks. For one thing, all them oracles and prophets who'd predicted Oedipus would marry his mum had been outgunned by modern science. Outgunned, outsmarted, debunked – same way science had debunked astrology, Flat Earthery, studies funded by the tobacco industry and masturbation-induced blindness. Problem is, these days the science has gone and shifted once again. These days, prophecies and oracles have become proper scientific. Happens every millisecond of every single day: digital data, patterns, predictions, recommendations, reality. No more crash barrier between tech and Mystic Meg. These days, you couldn't just tell old Oedipus to just allow all them prophecies and take a fucking tranquilator.

"Fuck's sake, fellas," I tell the two old men. "Give me some cred, yeh? I get it, okay – reckon maybe I even got it years ago. So don't treat me like some idiot and make me spell it out to you. But what I don't get, though, is how and why it's any of your business."

"Kid, we have no idea what you're getting at." The botched-Botox man sounding more pissed than rumbled.

"Yes you do. Because it's the same thing you been talking about. Just like how Oedipus got fucked up by the knowledge and prophecies he got from the oracle, I been fucked by all knowledge and predictions and ads and videos and recommended reading material about Oedipus that I got from Google and Facebook and YouTube and Amazon. This is not some bolt from a breaking-news flash to me. But how the fuck's it got anything to do with you guys?"

Should probly also mention my three bearded aunties. But I know how guys invent scary women just to keep women down. Fuck it, this shit's ridiculous enough without throwing my aunties into the mix – me lying naked in my sort-of-girlfriend's bed, chatting about Oedipus to two old men who want me to masturbate.

"Dylan, your Oedipus obsession should have taught you that knowledge without understanding is worse than no knowledge at all." Even as the blankpage-Botox man starts giving it some sniggering action, his face muscles still don't budge a fraction of a millimetre. I even try hitting him up with a smile – aka *Young*

Carer's Playbook #23 – but the dude doesn't mimic it. This means his face ain't sending his brain signals to tap into how I'm feeling. Why do I know this shit? Cos micro-facial mimicry with our mums is how we learn all that "emotional interaction" crap. Learn how to make Mummy happy.

"Truth be told, though, we did actually think about Oedipus," goes the older-looking old man. "Thought about him a lot. Many, many years ago. Back when we first started to wonder what the hell would happen as search engines and social media platforms became more and more sophisticated and more and more personalised. More predictive, more prophetic, more prone to giving people access to their own data-crunched destinies. We started to wonder what would happen. How would people respond to having their own little touchscreen Delphic oracles in their pocket? Would they try to avoid the predictions and prophecies or would they instead try to accelerate them? – I believe the technical phrase is to try and 'catch the nearest way'." Starts examining a box of Ramona's feminine hygiene products like as if he's scared of it or something. Even wipes his hands after putting it back down. "You'd think it would simply depend on whether the prophecy in question bodes good or ill for the person. But, Dylan, you'd be amazed at how many people actually *choose* to run away from positive predictions and accelerate the fulfilment of negative ones. Now, of course, obviously all this predictive digital data has been good for tech giants and insurers and credit agencies and security services, but is it good for *people*, Dylan? After all, humans have been debating these questions with respect to Oedipus for more than two-and-a-half-thousand years. Was the horror worse for the fact that Oedipus knew the prophecy and tried so hard to escape it? Would it have even happened if it hadn't been prophesied? In short, was the prophetic knowledge a net benefit or net liability? That's more than two millennia of literary, philosophical and psychoanalytical enquiry. And still not even the greatest human minds have come up with a completely satisfactory answer. So tell me, kiddo. How *do* everyday people cope with that kind of knowledge? Come on, you can tell me."

While my dumb ass gets ready to drop some kinda brainful response, the two old men start LOLing like as if they just told me some funniest joke in the worldwide world. Next, they just swipe all the way back to the buyout bullshit they pulled on me yesterday. Some same-old argument about how exiting my start-up will be good for my studies and my love life. I start for serious considering whether maybe I should just swallow what they saying when I realise I'm now munching one of their oatmeal cookies. Some dodgy download deep in my gullet making me think it's maybe better if we just chat about business instead of Oedipus.

Then, from fuck knows where, the younger old man in the charcoal-grey suit conjures up some matching rucksack – not just the same shade of charcoal, the same fabric. "Like we said yesterday, kid, we'd really like to buy your start-up. Inside this bag is £10,000 in cash. All you've got to do is hand over your fledgling little typing business to us." He raises the rucksack higher like he's some tribal warrior holding aloft a still-bleeding severed head, entrails dropping out with its brains because, fuck it, why not, there's neurons in people's bowels.

"Ten grand? Yesterday your opening offer to me was £500,000."

"Just take the rucksack," goes the botched-Botox man. "Don't be a dick-fuck about this, Dylan. It's ten grand in cash."

"I can't fucking believe this kid," goes the other man. "He's still trying to play this game." The rucksack now dangling madness-style from his hand like as if the severed head's just woke up from the dead and doesn't like the whole being-decapitated thing.

I tell em I ain't the one playing games. "You're the ones trying to spook me, buy my start-up on the cheap so that you can strangle it at birth." Sniffling as I say this, though, which kinda ruins the effect.

13

WE DON'T ACTUALLY talk about it till after some 3pm seminar or webinar about interbank interest rates. All my standard avoidance strategies: the men's room, the vending machine, customising my Google search bar to disable predictive autocomplete. Ramona trying to corner me like as if she's on some live chat window. Telling me how dare I treat her bedroom like it was my company boardroom. "I was still in my dressing gown, for fuck's sake. And I've no burning desire to burn images into the wank banks of men too old to use them."

Start telling her I'm sorry, but then the following fuckery happens: from someplace deep in some ancestor's testicles, I start fronting like some masculinity asshole – beasting out and turning shit round so that *I'm* the one having a go at *her.* "Why the hell you let two total strangers into your room like that in the first place? Why not get dressed before getting the door?" But then the caps lock on my voice shocks me into shutting the hush up. My plug-in for shouting still disabled.

"I *didn't* let them in," goes Ramona. "I told them to wait at the door." We walk into Café Amici. Some quick scanning action to check the two old Botox men ain't sitting at some next table. "Anyway, for a couple of supposed 'total strangers' they seemed pretty clued up about *us* – and it isn't as if I have our headfuck of a relationship as my Facebook status."

Dunno whether it'll make shit better or worse to tell Ramona that I don't even know their names. Don't even know if they're for real about buying my start-up. Don't even know if they for real.

"Ramona, you definitely saw those old men, right? I mean, it weren't just, like, you know, a lucid dream or something?"

"Don't do that, Dillon. Don't try and smooth things out again by pretending to flake out. I'm so tired of that bullshit. Besides, how the hell are you and I meant to dream the same dream together? We can't even watch a whole movie together without you bailing out."

Of course Ramona wouldn't wanna be having the same dreams as me, even if that shit *was* possible. Even with Mum and me – it ain't about dreaming the *same* dreams. Most likely we just been *flipping* each other's dreams. Me flipping her nightmares into happy dreams by intervening in my own lucid dreams.

"Actually, Dillon, those two men knew something else about us." She rests her elbows on the table like as if they're on her knees – like she's sitting up in bed, switching on some lamp cos she can't sleep.

"What?" I go. "What is it they told you?"

"Something that I haven't told you. Something about myself. But let me just explain it properly before you jump to any judgements, okay?"

Turns out Ramona ain't actually her real name. Or rather it is, but it ain't the name her parents gave her and ain't the name she had when she was in primary school, way back before we met. Her parents had named her Rona. She'd got them to change it by deed poll when she was ten. "The thing is, though, I didn't change my name because I didn't like it or anything. I changed it because I felt like I had to. And this is the bit that's tricky to explain. You see, when I was nine, I had to have my appendix removed. Routine operation, no big deal. Only problem was that the surgeons went for keyhole surgery so as not to give me a scar on my midriff." She holds her belly like as if she's gonna be sick. "Not sure how much you know about surgical procedures, but basically, Dillon, that meant two tiny keyhole incisions in my belly and then a third through my belly button." She explains how they opened up her belly button and then retied it. But she can't explain why it upset her so much. Says they tied it back so tightly, it looks more like a dimple than a knot. "I don't know why it bothered me, but I got in this really weird funk about it. I actually think maybe I'd have been less upset if they'd just slashed some Caesarean-style scar across my midriff. Next thing, I decided that, seeing as I'd had my umbilical cord re-cut, I wanted to do the whole maternity-ward routine and give myself a brand-new name as well. Of course my mum just thought it was some crazy reaction to the fact that she and my dad had just got divorced. And, truth is, it was actually easier to let people think that was the reason rather than try to explain that I did it because I was mourning my belly button."

Then Ramona says just for jokes that ain't as if I ever shown any interest in her midriff anyway. Starts telling the me ABCs of women's anatomy. But then she stops joking. "It really fruck me out the way those two old men kept calling me Rona even after I'd told them my name's Ramona. Maybe they were just deaf or senile, but they were so insistent. Anyway, the point is that I should have told you all this years ago, Dillon. I feel like I've been keeping some whole other identity a secret from you. And you know what Mark Zuckerberg says about that, right?"

Ramona collects quotations from tech tycoons. Even used to stick them up on her wall. But then one day she decided it was literary pretentiousness or someshit and tore them all down. But, yeh, I know the Mark Zuckerberg quote she's chatting about: *"You have one identity. Having two identities for yourself is an example of a lack of integrity."*

I start scoping the road outside the window like as if I'm figuring out the best route for outrunning Mark Zuckerberg's words. Tell Ramona something about how the traffic ain't budged since we come in here.

"But of course that's complete bullshit," she goes.

"My traffic report?"

"No – what Mark Zuckerberg said. I mean, just because someone's got different identities for when they're on LinkedIn and when they're on Facebook, doesn't mean they lack integrity. It's basically just like me acting differently when I'm at uni and when I'm at my nan's – doesn't mean I'm being sneaky or being two different people. It isn't as if my nan wants to have a six-way convo about Deepika's missing underwear problems."

Next thing, Ramona's telling me she reckons that either Mark Zuckerberg's so bloody privileged that he ain't never had to check himself in different social situations, or he's just deliberately chatting shit cos it's in Facebook's interests for everyone to only have one identity and to always front the same way with everyone: "After all, he'll make more billions for himself if he can sell 100 per cent of you to advertisers instead of just 30 per cent of you, right?"

Some draught from the doorway signal-boosts my sigh of relief. Like, how the fuck did I just dodge another truth bullet here? "Wait a sec," I tell her. "So despite having that Mark Zuckerberg quote stuck up on your bedroom wall, you're now saying it's actually fine for someone to front with different IDs?"

"Well, yeh, otherwise how the hell else could people function? It's like everyday code-switching. You choose which bit of yourself is the most appropriate bit for each situation. I tore that quote down from my wall because I realised it was just another case of another Silicon Valley squillionaire trying to base an entire philosophy of living on whatever will make more money for their tech company." She tells me to think of all the shit we do cos we tell ourselves that the technology makes it possible when, in actual fact, we ain't really doing it cos of the tech, we're doing it cos that's what's best for the tech companies' profits. Says this means we ain't just like cavemen flexing the latest tools no more; we're now flexing the business models of the companies that control the tools. "So, yeh, of course it's fine to have different identities, Dillon. And it's also okay not to share everything about yourself."

Check my smile as she says this.

"A person's content is different because the app or platform or context is different, not because the person themself is different. Otherwise it'd be like saying that Dillon-the-student is a different person to Dillon-the-start-up-founder. Only thing that matters is that you're all still Dillon – that there's no other Dillons knocking around."

14

DIDN'T ONLY ASK Google. Not cos I'm going for a more varied and balanced diet or something like as if to improve my bowel movements. It's cos Google didn't have an answer. Proper scoped everywhere – using different combos of different search tools, different search words, different search engines.

And obviously different search histories.

Always get me different results when logged on as Dhilan and Dylan and so on. Different search results, stories, ads – sometimes even different weather reports, even though all my IDs live in the same city.

This time, though, all three spellings of me got the exact same diddly-zero answers.

So now there's just one place left to look.

Walk into a shop and walk out with some brand-new, top-of-the-range torch. Batteries and replacement bulbs included. Fuck knows why I bought it, though – ain't like it'll be dark.

Reason search results are custom-tailorised is cos they gotta narrow shit down somehow. Can't just be hitting you back with every piece of fuckery on the internet containing your specific searched-for keywords – i.e. if they didn't have some kinda filter/slant/bias, there wouldn't hardly be no point to them. Next thing, the search engine's got more data on you than you could ever hold in your brain. Knows all your unknowns. Cuts through all your self-illusions – the stories you gotta tell yourself to boost your self-respect. The goal according to Google is for search engines to one day get so custom-tailorised and Jedi, they'll be able to give you the correct, data-crunched answer to questions of a higher headfuck order, such as: "What uni should I go to?" "Should I even go to uni?" "Should I stay or should I administer a lethal dose?" Cut to a quote from Eric Schmidt, Google's former executive chairman: *"Most people don't want Google to answer their questions . . . They want Google to tell them what they should be doing next."*

i.e. those two aged-out Botox men weren't just fronting about this stuff. It's time to start junking all the old-school jargon: ain't about search engines no more – we're talking badass prophesising prediction engines. In which the shit you're searching for is also searching for you. But did any of this searching-the-minds-of-psychic-search-engines using different combos of different search words and IDs and search histories tell me anyshit about my dad being a journalist? Did it, fuck. Each combo just threw up a bunch of random square roots of irrelevance. People are only supposed to be invisible to search engines if their name or surname is some proper commonspread word – like "Who" or "What" or "Why".

After that, I tried me a more direct approach: I foned home. Asked straight up whether my dad had ever been a journalist and, if so, how come I weren't ever told about it? And more to the point of the story, why weren't there no record of it anywhere on the internet?

"Dhilan? Is this some sort of a joke?"

"No. I just wanna know."

Shoulda asked how everything was, of course. If things were getting better again or if things were again getting worse. Some diplomatic opening gambit to kick the chit-chat off. Shoulda offered to show up.

To demo Mum's new diaphragm exercises and that mindfulness munching-and-swallowing technique.

To help them clear out all her emails and belongings – maybe play us one more round of Donate, Bin or Burn. Fun for all the family.

To make her some soup and hold the spoon like a lollipop to her polka-dot lips.

To polish the urn that contains her ashes while we figure out where to scatter her – all the years of false alarms and dry-run dress rehearsals and she ain't never told me where she should be sprinkled.

To crush up her tablets and sprinkle them into her soup like the district nurse had shown me to.

To tell her that I love her or whatever. That I got 91 per cent in some multiple-choice test.

I breathed, bone-crushed the fone and said it again: "No, this ain't a joke, Uncle, I just wanna know. There's nothing on Google about him ever being a journalist – not that Google knows everything yet, but I also tried Bing and Yahoo! and Ask.com. I even tried Yandex and Baidu. Even tried Facebook and YouTube . . ." And when the line went dead as well, I tried calling back, but this time ain't nobody bothered picking up.

When the line went dead *instead.*

When the line went dead *as well.*

When the line went dead, I tried calling back, but this time ain't nobody bothered picking up.

Flick the switch to make sure my brand-new, randomly bought top-of-the-range torch actually works. Even though still dunno why I even need a torch. Even though I've already made sure. *Torch or binoculars or magnifying glass?* – who the hell decides that stuff? And, once again, turns out that today I ain't lying when I fone home to say I'm sorry but I'll be working late. And I ain't lying when I fone Ramona to say I'm sorry but I'll be working late. Eat my dinner in the queue to pay for it then pay for an empty sandwich wrapper and hop on the 59 bus. Because I cannot stop this shit. Cos how can you stop doing what you already done? Her fucking lipstick-stained surgical mask. Can't even manage to miss my stop.

My co-workers call this shit "dungeon duty". Other people call it the bunker. The project's Project Manager prefers "The Client's Offsite Site". Whatever you call it, I'm the only data temp to go down there voluntarily, i.e. ain't even asked permission. The Stockwell Deep-Level Shelter used to be this big-ass World War Two air-raid shelter. Wouldn't recognise it for shit from street level, though – just looks like some concrete public toilet. Big blank stare of a big steel door that opens before I can fat-finger the passcode on the touchscreen keypad. Ain't no buttons to push for the lift – security guard's already got it waiting for me. Tapping her left foot. Regulation rounded-toe work-boots. It's a cage lift. Only way is down. First time I came here, I was with the Online Archive Project Manager and three fellow Project Inductees. But this place creeps her out so she gave some of us clearance to head down here by ourselves. One level beneath the sewers and the disused Tube stations.

Didn't *want* to do it this way, of course. Didn't wanna be so extra about it – just wanted to call it just browsing. Just pissing about in some searchbox. Like when you're sitting on the shitter and you start randomly looking up the name of the actor who played the dog in some cartoon you watched when you was seven. Surely a magnifying glass should be for zooming in?

Lift hits the bottom and clicks into place like a plug being jacked in. This other security woman full-bodies the door open, then starts walking me through the tunnel. It's one of two parallel tunnels connected crossbar-style by smaller tunnels. Steel-panelled walls – painted white, but with bright neon strip lighting making them look even more metal than if they'd just been left the colour of steel. Each section bolted together like some ribcage made of steel ridges. Smell of fresh paint job even though the paintwork is rusted and faded and blistered and ulcerated.

We press on through the tunnel. Strip lighting amping up like floodlights, motion-sensor style. Talk about wasted bucks on my deadweight torch. Ain't passed a single other body, even. Other times I been down here, there at least been a couple of legal clerks.

That woman who was singing to herself. That bloke who sold vintage pornos on eBay. We press on through the tunnel. Security guard now moaning about the weather being crap like as if we ain't 120 feet underground. Looking like she dug the 120 feet all by herself – shoulders broader than daylight and arms that could probly carve out shortcuts with just a penknife for a pickaxe. Next, she comes out with some autoplay tour-guide routine that takes five whole minutes to get across two facts: turns out 8,000 people could be staying down here during the war, and there are seven other deep-level shelters like this beneath London.

But now it's all for paperwork.

The mother of all storage facilities.

Also known as the largest filing cabinet in London.

"We're not a storage facility," the security woman says. "We're an Information Management Facility."

Jumbo shelving jutting out from the wall like we in some long-ass library. Mostly corporate documents – records, papers, dossiers, reports, notebooks, catalogues, back issues. *Actual folders.* Actual padlocks on actual files. Except they ain't actually shelves, though – they're bomb-shelter bunk beds. Minus the mattresses, so just the original metal bed frames. "During the war, six people could sleep on each of these," goes the security woman. This is fact number three – the final fact of her guided tour. After that just the *Robocop* sound of her work-boots. The underground Tube trains above us.

"Dhilan, please son, let's change the conversation. Why to spoil your birthday by talking about your father? Please – just for today – let's don't even mention the F-word."

Okay – done and done, Mum.

And so you quit asking her questions about him.

"Didn't you hear what I said yesterday? Can we, please, can we just talk about something else."

And so you quit asking questions about him.

"I thought I told you last week: I don't want to talk about that man."

And so you quit asking questions about him.

Kept your head down.

Allow that fucked-up feeling when you weren't sure if she was pissed at you or pissed at him.

And then a couple of years after that – or maybe even a couple of years before: *"Because I don't want to see that man when I look at you, Dhilan. When the time comes for me to look at you for the final time, I want to see you, not that man."*

Kept your head down and trimmed your eyebrows and your knuckle hair to cut back any resemblance.

And then a year or so later or a year or so earlier: *"Don't you want me to die in peace? If you don't want me to die in peace then bloody just leave me to bloody die alone."*

Two-thirds of the way along the first tunnel, the metal bed-frames-cum-shelves are spaced even more further apart. Inside one of the spaces, this cast-iron table and a green plastic chair – aka the offsite office for the newspaper's Online Archive Project. Boxes of back issues I need are all lying on the lower bunks. Security woman prying as we open them up: "I thought you were all finished with the papers from 2001? I'm sure one of your colleagues said you'd put that whole decade up on the internet."

I tell her we'd found a batch of stories from 2001 that were full of scanning mistakes. "So what I'm gonna do is set up my laptop here, check the scans against the original papers, then type up all the corrections."

"I have a scanner at home. It never makes mistakes." Her eyes staying locked on me – though ain't no telling if she's wise to my bullshit or just making convo. I tell her how it ain't so easy to scan an old newspaper – you can usually get a good image of each page, either from the original newspaper itself or from the microfilm version of it, but sometimes there's smudged newsprint or warped microfilm.

Seems this ain't enough for her. Usually when I wanna be left alone, I just start dropping some dial-tone dullness. But today I go with geekery. Tell her how a proper online archive has gotta allow readers to search for specific keywords, names, phrases. You can't do that with just a scanned image of the words – you gotta break shit down, apply some Optical Character Recognition Software so that a computer can read it and search it. Every block of text becoming a searchable index of itself.

The security woman doesn't back off or get bored, though. Just side-eyes like she's getting sus. So what I do next is I step up with some proper desperate mansplaining to pretend like I'm legit. Tell her that it ain't like digitising a book: if you scan a book, all the words look roughly the same – same size, same font – which makes it piss-easy for software and computers to trawl the text for a specific searched-for keyword. But the words in newspapers get printed in different sizes, styles and fonts – captions and headlines and that. Different kinds of articles, different kinds of page layouts with different kinds of shit going on. You can get special software specifically for digitising newspapers that can figure out where one kind of story or layout ends and another begins. But, again, even the slickest software can make mistakes when there's creases and smudges and other fingertip-related fuck-ups. When that happens, the digital version of the story can get all mashed up. Worst case: a reader searching for some specific keyword might end up downloading not just the text of a story but also the small print of some random competition the story was printed next to.

"That's interesting," she says instead of goes. My laptop long ago set up and started up on the cast-iron table. "Could I find all these stories just by searching on Google or do I have to search on your newspaper's website? I mean, does every single story appear on Google?"

I duck the question. Change tactics. Try spooking her out with some spiel about search engines being more like prediction engines – how it's more like trying to search the mind of a psychic.

"A psychic, you say? I once went to see one of those – my brother recommended him to me and I—"

"Well, actually, it's more like searching the mind of a psychic while they're mindreading a clairvoyant while she's reading her crystal ball."

"Well, excuse me for showing an interest in your work."

After she's gone, I wanna call her back. Carry on chatting or someshit. Maybe she was just one of them people who gets proper interested in stuff? And I didn't even tell her the most interesting thing about digitising stories: that she's probly done it herself without even realising it. You know how sometimes when a website wants to check that you're a human and not some spam bot, it asks you to type in the letters of some murky or smudged or scrambled-up word? Some of those words are actually taken from printed newspaper stories that the scanning software couldn't read – and so they basically draft you in to help them digitise it. No shitting – this crowd-sourced project is how hundreds of thousands of random everyday people have helped digitise decades of back issues in just a couple months, tops. Each story becoming an index of itself. Each publication becoming an archive of itself. Each person building an archive of themselves every time they click or swipe or like or type some search query.

Didn't take you long to just grow the fuck out of asking your mum random stuff about your dad. What the hell difference would knowing his exam grades make? Anycase, everyone's parents got divorced. Done and done, no big drama, no big deal at all. Ain't even like your mum and dad had some big-ass soap-opera bust-up or nothing – they just did that gradual growing-apart thing. End of convo, no biggie, done and done and logout. Only reason other people like getting all deep and drama-queen about their dads is cos *nobody* knows much about their dad – not even those people you read about who still got two whole parents. And, anyway, besides, ain't like you needed some father figure. Your own dumbfuck Homer Simpson. Ain't nobody needs no male role model when their mum's been popping anti-oestrogen pills since her son was in Year Four. And, anyway, lots of fathers failed their families and fucked off – or more like *got told* to fuck off for being wife-beaters or gamblers or alcoholics or cheaters or workaholics or just plain old useless losers. And before fathers started fucking off, they used to go and die someplace. On a battlefield. In a dockyard. Down a mineshaft. Even if they weren't from up north. Even if there weren't no war.

The boxes protect the stacks of newspapers inside them. The stacks inside them strengthen the boxes. Flick each page of each edition from the year my dad was down in the staff directory. Ain't diddly-fuck in the first box. Diddly-squat in the second. Pressing inky fingerprints into my forehead like as if to save the feds some time. Smudging. Swiping. Dripping like her mascara. Supposed to be wearing latex gloves. Apparently the air down here actually sucks the moisture out of paper. Apparently this is a big draw for people who store second-hand vintage porn. Diddly-nothing in the third box. Ain't angstipating about it, though – like as if I already know for definite I'm gonna find something down here. Or that something's gonna find me. And so I don't even feel no surprise when I finally hit a bunch of stories that clearly couldn't have been scanned in the first place cos they been blacked out with marker pen. Neat black blocks made up of messed-up madman streaks. Total tally: thirty-six blacked-out stories. Some Post-it note glued and taped to each of them, shouting, "DO NOT INCLUDE IN LEXIS NEXIS OR ANY FUTURE DIGITAL OR ELECTRONIC ARCHIVE."

Whoever'd got busy with the marker pen had got twice as busy blacking out the headlines. Only shit that looks like maybe it could be readable are the bold-font bylines at the top of each story. Even if I can't read the stories, least I can try and read the name of whoever it was who wrote them. Just for formal confirmation and so on. Next thing, I'm standing up on this cast-iron table giving it some crazyass yoga pose or someshit, trying not crease up the pages as I hold them up to the strip lighting. Problem is, the lights give off that reflective diffusion shit like they got in hospital wards instead of just focusing on one spot. Allow it – ain't as if some black-and-white confirmation of his name is gonna help me feel surprised. Just like I don't feel no surprise even though I nearly fall the fuck off the table when some ear-bleeding clang rips out from the cast iron beneath me. My brand-new top-of-the-range torch dropped outta my pocket to tell me why I bought it.

15

THIRD TIME YOUR mum told you she had the C-bomb was the first time she mentioned dying. No drama, just theatrics. Jumped you on your own doorstep to deliver the news.

You'd bussed it back from school rocking some sense of relief that she hadn't come to pick you up. No fone call to tell you her test results. No texts, no telepathy. You thought about what people said about no news being good news. You thought of her out there in the all-clear. Maybe even celebrating. One of them swanky places where they randomly give you olives. Problem was, you'd forgotten your house keys. Soon as you hit the doorbell, you turned round and she was standing right behind you. Like as if she was already rehearsing for the role of ghost or guardian angel. "You really need to start remembering your own set of keys, sweetheart. Because it looks like the cancer's going to kill me."

She was wearing her beige bucket cap. Allow all them cut-and-blow-dried wigs – the headgear your mum liked rocking the most was that adorkable beige bucket cap. (Later you'd call it her fisherman's cap.) (You'd learn to hate the word "bucket".)

"Dhilan?"

Couldn't remember why you hadn't just foned her yourself to find out the test results. Some days you foned or texted her during every single school break. Reminded her to take her meds and that. Fresh fruit and vegetables. Her state of mind while she was driving.

You stepped up and hugged her.

Could feel the endorphins release into her bloodstream.

Back then, the path to that doorstep was the only part of your front yard made of concrete. Some special cement paving stones your mum had shaped and laid and levelled by herself. Borrowed a circular wet saw from work. (She did back-office stock control for a DIY chain.) (And shift work at a paper and packaging plant.) Beside the path, this patch of dead grass she liked to call the "lawn". Said it was more of a lawn than all them other single mums had. You'd tried to wean her off all those bullshit stories – the ones about single mothers and welfare scroungers. Could see how the stories were making her hate herself. And work way too hard at both her jobs. And hate herself. You told her people only attacked single mothers on welfare cos they were easy targets for government cutbacks. Told her people only hated on single mums cos they made them feel insecure about themselves. A year later, your mum would finally have to accept one of the welfare benefits she was entitled to when the council covered the dead grass in concrete to turn it into a drive. That was the deal for residents who got injured or sick or just generally incapacitated: *"The provision where feasible of driveways rather than on-street disabled parking spaces."* You couldn't tell if she was crying cos of the lawn or cos of the handout.

Right now, your mum started going through her diagnosis right there on the doorstep. Dropping words like "glands" and "armpit", even though you both knew she meant her axillary lymph nodes. Skipping past the usual reassurances. Couldn't figure out why she suddenly had this thing about chatting on the front doorstep.

"Dhilan, why can't Indians have bar mitzvahs?"

"I don't know, Mama. Why?" You thought she was dropping some joke or something – take the edge off the fact she was dying.

"I don't know, sweetheart – that's why I'm asking. You remember Suzanne from the HR department? She was telling me about her son's bar mitzvah last week. And so I was just thinking it would be good to have something like that in our culture. Just something to say that something's happened. That something has changed."

You told her you didn't think having a party would be very appropriate now. Started thinking how bar mitzvahs were about taking moral responsibility. Owning your own shit. What you really wanted was something to mark this whole young carer thing. Even the label 'young carer' didn't hardly even exist back then, meaning you weren't just keeping it hidden from other people, it was like as if you were keeping it hidden from yourself. Weren't just that you couldn't tag yourself on social media or whatever, you couldn't even tag yourself in your own head. You wondered what it would be like to be a Muslim or something in a world where there weren't no label for "Muslim" or "Islam" – where you had to explain the whole thing from scratch every single time. Allow it – weren't even about the caring anyway; it was about worrying about getting the caring right.

"Of course, it would give me an excuse to wear one of my good dresses again" – her key now finally in the front door – "Okay, now, let's go and rerun the laundry load I already ran but forgot to dry."

Inside, the house looking like some last florist on earth. "Get Well Soon" straight through to "Thinking of You". All of them dumped by the foot of the stairs that your mum had sanded and painted after removing the carpet and grippers with just a chisel and a pair of pliers.

"Mama, how did all these bunches of flowers show up so fast? You ain't even started treatment yet."

"Just because I haven't started treatment, doesn't mean I'm not sick."

Then you clocked that all the Get Well Soon pap was from the last time she had the C-bomb. Plastic bouquets, artificial roses, a bonsai, a cactus, the cardboard George Clooney. Cluster of pot plants still hanging on like the cells they was meant to have wished away. Not some Eng. Lit. symbol of her sickness, though. Not some poetry lesson thing about her clinging onto life or of how alive she was before staying alive was even an issue. Truth was, your mum didn't give a crap about all that botanical bullshit back then – said flowers were for pansies. Only reason they were out in the hallway was cos she needed to make space in the shed for her brand-new Black & Decker workbench. Her Mother's Day bouquets of power tools.

She'd got into fixing stuff up around the house cos, after the divorce, she was scared of letting workmen in. Landing that stock-control job at a DIY chain was just one of them weird coincid-flukes. Taught herself from YouTube videos. "Chores" too small a word for her (later, too small for both of you). That time she had to go back into hospital and you tried painting her bedroom to make her less depressed or less sleepstipated, whatever, impress her. She fixed up your fuck-ups and finished the other two walls in less than three hours, tops. You couldn't figure out who it was *she* was trying to impress.

And even when you didn't jump in and try and help her, you remember how you kept checking and rechecking the ladder, the safety catches, the blades, the cables, the electrical trip-switch. Her seatbelt. All them rituals you followed and prayers you said to protect her. Switching the lights on with your left hand only. Avoiding physical contact with this orphan in your class called Amjad in case Dead Mummy Disease was somehow contagious. You remember doing all this stuff even before she got sick. But then, after the C-bomb dropped, your rituals started slipping. That day after school, you didn't even read the results of her sentinel node biopsy – propped up on her self-sanded mantelpiece, beneath the fotos from various mother–son weekend wellness breaks and holidays. Her with her straw hats and this random Ryanair captain's cap; you with your smiles that she knew were fake. All along the wall in self-made A4 frames, like *Excellence in Single Motherhood* certificates. That time – the third time she told you she had the C-bomb and the first time she told you she was dying – was the first time you forgot to check the trip-switches and the general safety features of whatever the fuck she was fixing.

16

IF YOU DON'T want them suspecting you of doing something you know you shouldn't've done, best thing is to tell them straight up that you did it.

Not cos you wanna be some man about it.

Not cos a quick-time confession can buy you lenienceness.

You fess up to create the impression you didn't even know what you done was wrong.

I walk into the Online Archive Project Manager's office and tell her about the blacked-out stories I found in the Stockwell Deep-Level Shelter. Don't tell her that all thirty-six stories were written by my dad. Don't tell her how I'd managed to make out my dad's byline with the help of some randomly bought torch. Or how seems like my dad hadn't written a single story that *hadn't* been blacked out. Matterfact, I don't even mention my dad – a trick that, let's face it, I already got pretty well nailed.

She asks what I was doing rechecking the "dead tree editions" in the first place. I bust out some bullshit about wanting to be thorough.

Seems she's on some kinda paperless office look – so far on it, ain't no point in her even having her own office. Empty desktop even though she's the only one of us who don't have to hot-desk. Shelves cleared of actual shelves.

"So what exactly are you asking me, Dylan?"

Sameshit goes for her wardrobe – she's rocking some white mandarin-style jacket with no buttons, no zips, no stitching, no nothing – like it's moulded from surgical latex.

"I was just wondering whether those stories should be digitised?"

"How are we supposed to digitise them if you can't even read them?"

Fuck – this point is actually legit. Even with my brand-new top-of-the-range torch, only words I could make out beneath all the black marker pen were my dad's bold-font bylines.

"And more to the point, Dylan, you said they were covered in Post-it notes stating they mustn't be included in future electronic archives. Seems pretty clear instructions to me." She looks out her floor-to-ceiling window. Do you call an internal glass wall a window?

"Yeh, but those Post-it notes must've been written way back in 2001. A lot of stuff has happened since then . . ."

For instance, the first time Mum told you she had the C-bomb.

For instance, the second time Mum told you she had the C-bomb.

For instance, the third, the fourth, the fifth and all the fuckugly shit that followed.

". . . For instance, these days the definitive version of something is the digital version of it, not the paper version – if there even *is* a paper version." My eyes like a yellow highlighter pen across her paperless office.

"Definitive?" she asks.

"I mean permanent."

"Much like the ink of the black marker pen, then."

Boss my whole day's data entry in two hours, tops. Like as if I knew I should clear me some calendar space and headspace for the crapfuckery still to come. Clock an essay for uni, even. Even email my mummy. Don't need no work ethic or nothing, you just need a steady take of energy drinks, caffeine pills, carbohydrate gels and isotonic sports supplements. Barley water to flush your kidneys. Plus it also helps that I'm a very fast typist. And I mean, like, proper fast – so fast, I prefer doing it in private. Might even be it's a superpower or something, though fuck knows how you check this. In the films, Clark Kent only got a job as a journalist cos the editor spotted that he was a fuck-off fast typist. In this place they'd probly stick him in tech support. Technically, it's more like some self-taught skill set than a natural-born talent, but either way, it's a good skill set to have if your start-up's a subcontractor or sub-subcontractor in the market for manual data entry. That's how I got the idea for this gig in the first place – way back in Year Eleven when Ramona needed to type up one of her essays that was still in someone else's handwriting. After aiding and betting on her plagiarism, I branched out into turbo-typing essays for other people – also their coursework, CVs, cover letters. All them bullshit personal statements on uni application forms. And with all the shit going down with Mum, I didn't exactly need no do-gooding energy-saving light bulb to flash above my head to figure out it could help us if I took things further. Expand, diversify, strategically reposition. Get a temping job as a typist. Subcontract my fingers to help companies compile databases and digital archives.

Two hours after I fessed up to the Online Archive Project Manager, another woman rocks up to my desk. Reading glasses on her nose; Diet Coke; ears that understand classical music.

"You must be Dylan? Dylan Deckardas?"

Doesn't wait for Dillon to say something smartass like, "Guilty as charged." Doesn't wait for Dhilan to say something dickless like, "Yup."

"I work in the editorial department. I'm the Managing Editor of this news organisation."

Fuck knows why, but I stand up and give it some kinda half-nod, half-bow – even though I ain't even clued in on what a Managing Editor even is. A shit-ton of people in this place got the word Editor in their job title – there's even some dude called the TV Listings Editor. Surely you ain't meant to bow your dipshit head to each and every Whatever Editor.

"Do please drop the theatrics and come with me to my office. We need to have a chat."

Lift doors open straight into the newsroom and straight up we get ambushed by some lanky posh dude who looks like he got breastfed into his teens. Starts telling the boss person some kind of opinion and that. Her gif-like talk-to-the-hand face is too quick for him – she's gotta follow through with old-fashioned audio.

After that it's just her footsteps. Each step signal-boosting the background beat of typing, like as if the whole office is now jamming to the sound of some countdown.

"So, Dylan Deckardas." We're talking proper wood-panelled office. We're talking polarised opposite of paperless. "This is the part where you tell me what you're doing asking questions about blacked-out stories."

I tell her I didn't wanna leave anything out of the digital archive. That I was just trying to be thorough. That it was just a one-time thing.

"Do you think we're bloody idiots? That we wouldn't realise the stories you're asking about were written by an ex-employee who just happens to share your surname. So, tell me then, how are you related to him?"

"To who?"

"To Deckardas. Ramnik Dickfuck Deckardas. Who the hell else are we talking about?"

"I don't even know no Ramnik Deckardas." I stay standing up. She doesn't ask me to sit down.

"What's your business here, mister?"

"But I couldn't even read the name of whoever it was wrote them stories. They were all blacked-out with marker pen – that's kind of the point."

Ain't gonna get another straight shot at this, though, so, fuck it, I just go for it. Proper klutz style. Ask her why all them stories had been blacked out and what they was all about – trying to sound like I'm just asking in passing (if you can ram-raid something in passing).

"They're blacked-out because they're meant to be left out – and left well alone." Some box of tissues by her sofa – like she expects all her visitors to bust out crying or someshit. "So you're telling me that your shared surname is just a coincidence? Well in that case, Dylan, my mistake. So sorry. You may leave now."

Breathe in like as if to stand up, even though I'm already standing.

"But please use a plastic bag to clean up the shit you've just crapped onto my carpet. Because I've been working in journalism for twenty-five years – so I know damn well there's no such thing as a coincidence. Certainly not with a name as uncommon as Deckardas."

Tell her again I ain't never even heard of no Ramnik Deckardas. I swear down I'm being on the level with her. Then I double down – tell her that Deckardas is actually a trending Indian surname, that it's just a couple of chart positions down from Patel. And even though I ain't exactly planned this, the bullshit now flows faster than even Clark Kent could type it. "That's cos it's usually shortened," I tell her. "To Das. It's usually shortened to the word Das, which is pronounced D-U-S and is a very common Indian surname. Sometimes it's even bolted onto the end of other names so you get things like Devdas and Shukdas and Shankardas." I give her time to google this shit as the part about Das being common is actually true – only the part about it being short for Deckardas is bollocks. Next thing, I'm standing in this big boss office, dropping a list of random Indian names and tagging on the word Das, before finally playing a card that I should probly hate myself for playing: "Not all Asians are related, you know."

Even though I'm hoping she'll feel shamed of her ignorance, I ain't banking my chickens. After all, this is one of them politely pro-deportation newspapers, so maybe she won't give a flying Febreze-scented fart.

"You're implying I'm being a bigot?"

"I'm just pointing out that my surname is common, is all."

"Well, given our content, I suppose it wouldn't be much of a mental leap." She starts scoping out these front pages she's got hung up and framed, like as if they just appeared on her wall right now. *Migrants Fuel Housing Crisis; Migrants Bleed National Health Service; Prime Minister Warns of "Swarm" of Migrants.* One of the stories about "parasite" immigrant single mothers on benefits. Headline doesn't say what kind of benefits, though – incapacity or disability living allowance.

"Just because we publish xenophobic stories that doesn't mean the people who work here are xenophobic. Would you like me to show you our diversity awards? Or our campaigns against racism?"

"It's okay, I can see you're very diverse."

"If you're referring to the ethnic make-up of the newsroom, that isn't about racism, it's about self-confidence – our section chiefs just can't relate to people who aren't cocksure of themselves. Race has nothing to do with it."

She does that thing where they just wait you out till you nod in agreement.

"And as for our editorial content, we're just responding to the concerns of our readers. Our readers want something straightforward to blame – they don't want to be told that the world is actually very complicated. So we respond to their concerns by simplifying things and telling them that immigrants are to blame. Or people on welfare. Or single mothers. And the more we make them feel angry and outraged and hateful, the more they'll click on our stories and share our content on social media. That means more ad revenues for us, more fame and followers for our columnists – and the more I get to go on nice holidays. It isn't a complicated business model."

I ask her why the hell she's fessing up all this.

"To demonstrate that I'm not racist." She looks at me like, wake the fuck up. "This isn't about racism, it's about economics. We have an economic imperative to make our readers angry and outraged and hateful."

I cut a look at the tissue box again, like as if I'm waiting for the crying part to start.

"In fact, strictly speaking, we aren't actually hate-mongering, we're now more focused on fear-mongering. Generating fear is a much more sustainable way of fuelling anger and hatred – and therefore reader engagement." She starts busting out some next-level buck-pass about the cutthroat market for people's eyeballs: "We didn't design this new world, my friend. Didn't invent the attention economy – the compulsion to keep smartphone users hooked on compulsive content. The financial incentivisation of virality and reader engagement, which in practice obviously means a system that rewards misinformation and hatred. Novelty. Stronger emotional responses. I mean, do you have any idea how many of our readers only reach our stories via social media and search engines? Last year, Facebook was basically our biggest distributor – sometimes I think they might as well just own us."

Fuck's sake, not again. Everyone trying to blame Facebook and Google for their own fucked-upness. I tell her I already know how the digital economy works. Tell her I also know that her newspaper was hate-baiting way back before the internet was even invented. That immigrant single mothers on benefits been getting fucked over by fake news stories for years. Fuck knows where my front is coming from – maybe it's just cos I'm standing up or something. Like as if I'm taking my posture too literally and trying to stand up for my mum or something. So then what I do is, I try and broaden away from her paper's hate-baiting and talk about story distortion more generally. Tell her that stories been getting distorted for time – from way back in once-upon-a-time. Even drop some beard-stroking brainfulness about how Freud distorted the story of Oedipus – how he even distorted *Hamlet* by giving Hamlet an Oedipus complex. I tell her that even the guy who wrote the famous play about Oedipus distorted the original myth.

She looks at me like as if she reckons I'm on some sarcasm or something. Comes back at me with more of her *I'm not racist, but* bullshit: "This isn't about whether we published bias and distortion in the pre-Facebook-and-Twitter days, it's about the scale and the speed of all the bullshit and bile we've had to compete with more recently." She talks about how all the crap spreads faster and further than she ever thought thinkable. How there's no time for the clunky old truth to catch up. "And if we don't play by the rules of the game and work harder and faster to make people feel outraged or righteous or fearful or hateful, then we'll keep on haemorrhaging readers to all those crackpot fringe sites and fake news merchants. And the big tech Data Lords will take even more of our audiences and ad revenues until there's nothing left for them to take from us. So, you see, you mustn't judge us by the stories we put on our home page or on the front of our paper. We're not racist, Dylan. Nobody's looking to lynch you."

Scope out all her cardboard folders while I weigh up how the hell to respond to that shit. Start wondering gormless-style if they'd still look so strange if computer drives and directories hadn't been organised into folders and files? If the original designers of operating systems chose some different structure for arranging shit – envelopes or pockets or cardboard boxes? Would real boxes start looking proper weirdness?

The boss person rests her head in her hands, elbows on her desk. "Well, now that I've reclaimed the moral high ground, Dylan, we can move on to the rest of this conversation. And I'm afraid that for this next part, you'll probably need to sit down."

Fuck knows why I take the sofa by the wood-panelled wall instead of the obvious chair facing her wooden desk. But now it'd look even more dickless to get up and move.

"Before coming to speak to you, I had our IT geeks review your web activity from this office. As your employer, this is something we're perfectly entitled to do. I wanted to know if you'd been emailing that man who shares the long-form of your surname – the man you aren't related to."

Start mentally scrolling through my office-based web activity. Minor infractions, mostly – my cache a catalogue of women's shoe catalogues. Can always just say I was just buying them as a present for my mum.

Or maybe not.

The Managing Editor chucks some fileful of printouts from her desk to the coffee table. Hard copies of my search history. The swollen, the fluid-filled, the ankle fetish manifesto. The blog posts. The post-surgical images. The bombed-out. The burnt-out. The respectfully blurred-out. The silicone prosthetics that won't harm the environment when they finally cremated. The supposed-to-be Oedipal support forum that actually turned out to be just dickhead guys posting on-the-sly fotos of everyday MILFs.

Ain't got no choice here now but to tell this boss person the truth.

I mean the actual truth.

I mean, no choice but to say it. Tell her how things got proper intense between us cos it was just me and her and her illness and whatever. Tell her how Mum trusted Google and Facebook more than the doctors and experts and how I trusted Google more than I trusted my mum. Tell her how we ended up having to go see this couples therapist who told us to try and see things from inside each other's shoes. Tell her how I decided to blog from Mum's perspective instead – proper multimedia blog with interactive graphic images. (Anycase, Mummy wrote stuff by me back when I was a baby.) (Letters in my voice – thank-you notes to my nani and that.) Figured a blog would basically be the same thing as a diary. But because blogs can be organised by subject rather than date, I ended up just maxing out on each subject. Even once wrote a blog from the perspective of some online alter-ego I developed for Mum – you know, like how amputees sometimes create an alternate online persona? I tell her how even back in Year Nine, I was getting proper worried that I weren't hardly able to even *see* my mum – could only see her illness. And I didn't want Mummy to see me not seeing her – didn't want her to catch me hesitating or flinching or looking away. I tell her the most sickening stuff in my search history is cos I didn't want be fearful or phobic or nothing.

Tell her that fearfulness fuels anger and hatred.

The boss person slides her reading glasses back into position. Looks up at the ceiling like she's praying to the HR department. "Why does it always have to be more complicated than just simple gross misconduct?"

Then I start hitting her with some next info – not just the sob stories with their violin strings. Also start dropping some theoretical underpinnings: the stuff I read about how the internet can help women transcend dehumanisation, body dysmorphia, bodily objectification, or just generally being defined by their body parts. I tell her I know the digital world doesn't work like that in practice because men, etc., but it had the potential. Tell her how I tried to help Mummy with her digital living. And the more times I mention the word "digital", the more she seems to buy what I'm saying, like some bubble-eyed tech investor.

"So you're a carer, then?"

I tell her I prefer the word "son".

She scopes out some foto on their desk. "It's awful when they realise that their child is now their parent." Then she asks me if Mum and I are still seeing the couples therapist. Doesn't think to ask how Mum is. Or even *if* Mum is. Just asks how *I* am. This is another reason I sometimes feel proper constipated about telling people.

"Listen, Dylan, even though you're just a freelance data temp, we'd still like to extend to you the support that we'd normally offer our permanent staff. We have a part-time occupational health consultant you might find helpful to talk to. Or if you just want some work experience in the newsroom during the holidays – just to get you out of the house."

Try and dodge eye contact. Try not reach for some dipshit tissue. Try counting all the cardboard folders all over her floor space.

"There's just one small problem, however. Not with you – with the whole digital archiving project. Even though there evidently wasn't a security breach in this particular instance, the incident nonetheless highlights the potential. To be honest, the whole hotchpotch of freelancers, temps and subcontractors really isn't working for us – it was only set up that way to keep the costs down. So we'll be looking to wind up those freelance arrangements over the next few weeks and then we'll bring the whole archiving project in-house. We'll obviously have to hire more permanent staff, but that'll come out of the IT department's budget, not mine. I'm sorry about this, Dylan. It's not my decision. As I said, technically it isn't even my department – although why the archive is being completely governed by IT and not editorial still defeats me. I mean, what happens when we cease publishing a print edition altogether – surely the archive and the live edition become the same thing? And to make things even more confusing for us, they've just this morning parachuted in a new Acting Head of IT. Though 'parachute' is probably not the right word, mind, as he was pulled out of retirement – and I don't mean early retirement. Speaking of whom, if you'll excuse me . . ." She nods towards her door as the botched-Botox man walks in, apologising for being early for some meet they meant to be having. Shooting me this shit-eating grin and offering me a chocolate chip cookie. Thing that weirds me out the most, though, ain't the fact that he's here, it's the fact that the man's still donning his dickhead biker jacket for his first day in some top job.

17

SCROLL BACK TO a time when you was little and your parents had a bust-up. What would it teach you about fighting if they never made up again? And what'd it teach you if, every time you had a row with your mum, you thought she'd hit the deck and never wake up?

Botox man clearly ain't never got taught these lessons. Comes out the gate sparking with his new colleague like it don't matter for nothing.

"Of course I don't read this publication," he goes to the boss person Managing Editor. "For the same reason I don't eat out of the toilet." Hobbling around her office like he's looking for some weak spot. Architectural vulnerability. "You see, just because I'm old and decrepit and I've never worked in the media before, that doesn't mean that I'm clueless. For one thing, I know not to even read your publication. By which I mean both your paper edition and digital edition. The object and the subject."

"Well, I can see we're going to have a *wonderful* working relationship." Boss person cuts me a look as she says this. Can tell she hears this stuff on the regular. Haters gonna be hated.

Move to make my exit, but the Botox man's hand on my shoulder keeps me in check. Then, to make shit proper awkward, he takes a pass on the chair opposite her desk and parks down on the sofa beside me. Feet on the coffee table goes without saying. "But I have to hand it to you people, you're onto a lucrative business model with all this hatred and division. Give your readers a festering scab to pick at and they'll keep on picking. And clicking. Should apply the business strategy more laterally – start spreading measles and smallpox just for clicks. I hear those things always go viral."

"Oh, for the sake of your sanctimony I hope that accent of yours is Canadian." Sticks her feet up too now – on the corner of her desk, like the two of them are playing some kinda furniture-dissing game. Black patent four-inch skyscrapers with solid earthquake-proof foundations.

Botox man's comeback to this is some advanced-grade childishness. Pulls out a pack of cigarettes – no branding, just fotos of cancer. Doesn't light up or nothing, though, just flips open the box and pours ash straight out onto the coffee table.

"Excuse me, what do think you're doing?" She tries fronting with anger but the fear scans more clearly.

He dips his hand in the ash, rubs it between his fat fingers. "Pixel dust," he goes. "Hundreds of thousands of tiny black-and-white pixels. You and I clearly need to have words. Well, you can't have words without pixels."

"Look, I don't know what you've been smoking, mister, but if you've got a problem with our content, you're welcome to take it up with the Editor. My remit is managing editorial resources – hence the title *Managing* Editor. And it appears no one's told you yet that *your* remit's confined to IT."

He rubs some more ash between his finger and thumb. "You know what I love about the media business? The way that everything's a story. A celebrity overdoses and it isn't simply a death, it's a story. A local council compiles density studies for different grades of tarmac and, again, it isn't just a planning inquiry, it's a story. The same goes for stock-market bubbles and cryptocurrencies – but, then again, even the money in your wallet is a story. The state declares that this piece of paper is worth twenty pounds sterling and their story becomes true. Then they say that the on-screen digital digits are worth the same as the paper notes and then *that* story becomes true. Same applies to nation states themselves, of course. And of course the same applies to a person. But it's only in the media business that people talk openly about these things – every little thing and every big thing – in terms of their story-ness."

She locks her eyes onto mine like as if to stop hers from rolling.

Botox man starts giving her some next-level sermon about how stories and storytelling are the basic motherboard building-blocks of all societies – how no one can trust in anything if the thing in question doesn't have a story behind it. Says the first thing you gotta be able to trust in is the truth of a story's claim to be true.

Managing Editor shifts her chair to change to a more comfortable topic of convo. "Before you hobbled into my office, I was telling this young typist here how we'll be bringing the digital archive project in-house now and restricting access to the storage depot."

"Storage device?"

"*Depot* – rhymes with deafo. The external storage facility in Stockwell where we keep all our back issues."

"Won't be necessary," he goes.

"A U-turn on your first day? Not a very good look."

"Don't you read your own publication? Breaking news on your website this morning. Terrible accident over there – seems that a whole section of the tunnel has collapsed. So I guess nobody will be heading down there for some time." He nods at her PC. "Go on – click on your own story. It includes lots of shaky cellphone footage of sirens and traffic chaos. Oh, and of course your newsdesk has been duly insinuating terrorism to get maximum clicks. Go on, don't be shy – read your own story."

The Managing Editor does as she's told, shaking her head as she reads or watches or listens or whatever. "But that's *awful*. A woman down there has been critically injured. How is such a thing even possible?"

"I can't imagine," goes the Botox man. "Apparently she's a security guard. Six foot, built like a rugby player. That said, she's also a Polish immigrant and a single mother so I'm sure you'll find a way to demonise her."

The boss person blanks him so he takes another shot at triggering her. Takes my dumb ass a whole minute to realise the man's actually trying to trigger me. "Such a pity, really. Poor woman was just a bystander in all this. And she wasn't even bystanding in the part of tunnel that collapsed. My guess is that she was roughly about, say, 83.7 feet away."

The Managing Editor grabs a pen like she's on some kinda reporting instinct.

"My understanding is that the tunnel collapse caused the shelves to topple like dominoes and the woman was crushed under the weight of paper. Can you imagine?"

Boss person's still jotting down notes.

"Of course, your reporters will need to verify all that info before you can publish it. Though I appreciate that fact-checking might be a bit novel for them."

Botox man carries on dropping laser-guided truth bombs like he's trying to burn her in some rap battle. Feel like maybe I should try and liquefy the tension or something, but I'm too busy sitting here praying that the paper-crushed security woman story is just another fake news story. That tomorrow they'll publish a correction – maybe even later this pm. Like all those 180° corrections they dress up as minor story updates. *Madonna is Fine: Fury as Pop Star's Twitter Account Hacked for Death Hoax.*

Managing Editor takes her time with her comeback. "Well, I wouldn't expect a bumbling geriatric to understand this, but stories get shared on social media faster than we could verify the facts even if we *could* afford to hire proper fact-checkers. And if you don't publish fast enough, you don't get any shares and if you don't get any shares, you don't get any clicks. Even our Luddite film critic appreciates this new reality – last week she helpfully filed her review of the new *Star Wars* movie before the end of the press screening."

"I'm up to speed with your speed problem," he says. "The tech firms call it 'sharing' instead of 'spreading' so that it sounds less virulent. But I guess I *am* too geriatric in one respect: you see, I always thought reporting and fact-checking were the same thing."

Boss person just starts casual-style checking her emails.

The Botox man presses on. "If our publication can't survive as a business without undermining the sanctity of our stories, then surely it's better we don't survive."

Can't see her screen from the sofa – I just know she's checking her emails cos of the way she types her replies. The rhythm of it. Like she's talking in Morse code. Then she stops. And she asks the Botox man to hit repeat.

"I said if our publication can't survive as a business without undermining the sanctity of our stories, then better that we don't survive."

She switches back to emailing or messaging or tweeting or whatever.

The Botox man leans forward on the sofa. "You sure you got that?"

"Yep," she nods. "Just typing it up now."

He throat-clears. Starts speaking at a lower speed-setting. "Which means the value of our stories must no longer be measured by likes, shares and clicks."

Again the tapping of her typing this up. We're talking proper old-school dictation action. Followed by her firing out a question – though just the starting gun of a question. "Why shouldn't—"

"Why shouldn't stories be measured by clicks?" he cuts her off. "Because stories shouldn't be clickbait. They should just be the stories they're meant to be."

Now mouthing the words while she types them. Cracking her knuckles like it's punctuation. Looking up from her screen when she's done: "But we—"

And again he cuts her off. "But we shall also stop publishing clickbait headlines that don't reflect the stories beneath them. Even though Facebook has been designed so that people can share or like stories without actually reading them."

Can feel her keyboard flinching. Her deskphones start ringing and her ceiling lights are flickering. She just presses on typing.

"And even though cleverly optimised headlines have often got our stories ranked higher in Google's search results."

A guy with more balls or backbone or whatever would just ask these jokers straight up what the fuck is going on here. Me, I just offer to help her type. She looks at me like as if to say, what the hell am I still doing here? Stares at her hands, like why the fuck are they held out in front of her?

"And we shall preserve the sanctity of storytelling by ensuring our writers don't even *know* how many clicks their stories get."

They carry on rocking back and forth like this, each line of dictation getting more and more technical. (Technical term for that shit is "inside baseball".) Start chatting about the old days, the pre-click days, when all the "toxic lunatic fringe bullshit" stayed on the fringes. When no self-respectable news organisation would dare give space to hate preachers just for clicks – even if the hate preacher was running for some highest public office or something. Then he starts busting out some dictation about ad-free business models – even though Google and Facebook have tended to crap on content that users have to pay for. Wait, *what?* Botox man's now holding up some random megaphone. "And our stories shall cease to give more weight to emotionally charged anecdotes rather than actual evidence – even though anecdotes get more likes, shares and clicks."

Her eyes wincing and watering as if the pace is getting painful. Looking down at her deskphones but just letting them ring – like she doesn't actually know how to stop the ringing sound.

Allow all this fuckery. So what if some serious weirdness is going down? Probly be weirder if there wasn't. But there's also some proper wrongness here. Messed-up power relations. *Young Carer's*

Playbook #242: No matter the role reversal, always remember who's the boss – let them run the shots and call the show.

Whatever's wrong with this picture, though, I ain't even sure it'd make a pixel of difference if the woman was doing the dictating and the man was being some secretary. Ain't about male dominationating. The wrongness is coming from something else.

"Even though being quick instead of first checking whether we're correct has often got our stories ranked higher on Google and therefore got us even more clicks."

And whatever the hell is happening here, it ain't some clever Jedi mind trick. Ain't hypnotism or faith healing or neuro-linguistic programming. Can tell this from the way the Managing Editor eye-rolls whenever the Botox man says something she reckons is stupidness. Even cuts me a look like as if she's apologising for all this dipshit dumbfuckulousness.

"Even though slanted and sensationalist stories have effectively been favoured by Facebook because they get more shares, more engagement, more clicks."

Her deskphones are still ringing and the lights are still flickering.

"Because if *we* don't differentiate between proper stories and crapfuck bullshit, why the hell should readers?"

She picks up and hangs up and carries on typing. Tries asking another question but, once again, the Botox man cuts her off soon as she starts asking.

This is when I clock that I been getting the timing all wrong. The Managing Editor ain't simply typing up what he says. *First,* she starts typing up her own question, *then* he interrupts her – and *then* she types up what he says. I scope them more closely just to be sure. Yep, we're talking proper autocomplete action – even stronger than my mum's. And right now that shit feels even creepier than some creepy old boss man giving dictation.

"Because if all stories look equally credible, then of course readers will disregard anything they disagree with."

He closes out by saying that clearly they'll lose a shit-ton of readers if they don't focus on maxing their clicks and engagement.

"But better to lose people than to bullshit them" – gut-nudging me as he says this.

The boss person stops typing. Fingers seizing up all the way up to her face. "Okay, now you're just living in fucking La La Land."

18

FOURTH TIME YOUR mum told you she had the C-bomb, you figured it was best not to mention the deadline for your GCSE Business Studies coursework. Best not to mention deadlines full stop. When you headed out to school that morning, she'd told you she was positive the results of her bone scan would turn out negative. When she followed you to your room in the afternoon, she was already walking with a limp. Standing in your doorway, asking you to guess where it had spread to, like you was playing pin the dying donkey. Part of you thinking if you just picked the right spot, you might change things, make shit okay. Pin the *voodoo-doll* donkey. Your mummy still hanging in your doorway while you tried coming up with some least-critical location on her body. Her little toenail. A thumbnail. Cancer of the earrings. Didn't just tell her your final answer, you decided to write it down. Make shit more official. Her shakes as she limped up to your laptop to read what you'd just typed.

"My tear ducts?"

Told her you were trying to think of the smallest organ of the body.

"Well, I can see why you dropped Biology." Could practically hear levers and pulleys and chains in her face as she made her eyes smile in sync with her mouth. "Hey, it's just another challenge for us both to beat, Dhilan. Just one more push and we can be happy again."

You cut to the safe question, the straight-down-to-business question. The turnaround strategy – the net-net.

Plan was to hit her hip with post-surgery radiotherapy before a second-line chemo regime. Probly a shot of docetaxel laced with carboplatin. Steroids as a chaser, anti-vomiting drugs for the morning after.

And then the answer to the question you couldn't ask. The doctor had said she could still live a good few years – would depend on how she responded to the new kind of chemo they gave her. Apparently the exact word he'd used was "maybe". Weren't sure of the exact wording of his exact words, though – whether he'd said your mum would "maybe still live a good few years" or whether he'd just said the word "maybe" when she'd asked if she could still live a good few years.

Soon as she hit the bathroom to fix some plumbing and stuff – some leaky tap or some busted hinge – you shut your bedroom door and pulled out your fone.

Because knowledge and so on.

Because you needed to know.

Her oncologist had given you his mobile number a couple years back to stop you crying in his consulting room. You'd never dialled it of course – never dialled any of them numbers people gave you. But you dialled it that afternoon. Didn't actually expect to get through, though. The fuck did you manage to get through?

Her doctor told you that if she didn't respond well to the chemo, she might only have a few more months. Told you it was impossible to predict "the aggression of its progression". Talking like some hip-hop artist who reckoned having their name on a clothing range made them a bona fide businessman. That they'd "realign their outlook in response to various variables". That they "couldn't determine their strategic direction till in possession of more visible projections".

You asked him how long before they knew whether she'd have a few years or a few months.

"Dhilan, you know how this works by now," he said. "It'll take a few months to know how she responds to the chemo."

And then you was alone again in your bedroom. Just you and your fone. Would there be any after-recovery surgery? Google said any long-term wrecking of her hip bone would be fixed up with surgical pin-and-plating. What kinds of things could go wrong with hip surgery? Google told you some patients lost lots of blood during hip surgery so there might be "complications".

You had a special set of rituals for whenever your mummy went under the knife. Specific OCD routines, specific trinkets. Whenever the surgery was longed out, you worried it meant something had gone wrong. But when the surgery *wasn't* longed out, you worried that maybe the docs had done shit on the quick. Hadn't been concentrating while slicing or scraping or splicing her.

You searched for another opinion. Another link. Another person's personal experience. A cure. Was like the search engine was sparking the questions instead of the other way round. You scrolled all the way down to the risks. You scrolled straight to the worse-case scenarios. You clicked on the risks. You clicked on the worst-case scenarios. An even riskier risk. The outside chances slowly moving to the centre of your screen.

Sound of hammering from the bathroom. Or just hitting the walls with her fists. Hitting herself, even – smacking herself on her forehead again.

You called out to ask if she was okay. If she needed any help.

Then Facebook stories – using social media like as if it was a search engine, same way search engines now tap into social media. Then YouTube videos. YouTube is now the world's second-largest search engine; YouTube is owned by Google. How to do in-home physio on her hip. How to fart on a blowtorch. How to build a nail bomb. How to insert a cannula. Fix a leaky catheter. How to give her those weekly injections without fucking up her veins again. How to sedate her with aromatherapy. How to do the surgery yourself.

You knew it was batfuck crazy to think some next man's opinions about medical science should have the same weightage as a qualified doctor's, but that's how shit seemed to work on your fone. Like as if having some strong opinion about someshit was the same thing as actually knowing shit. As if equal rights somehow meant everyone was equally qualified. Just bypass the doctors and experts and ask some neighbour to perform the op. Like diagnosing your own hypochondria. Evicting the pilot and letting the passengers fly the plane. Blanking the mosque or the church for some online hate preacher. Telling your mummy that everything's gonna be okay.

And then more sounds from your mother – sound of the shower head dropping into the bathtub.

You stood outside the bathroom and asked if she was okay, if she was managing.

How to pick the lock on a bathroom door.

How to remove the lock altogether.

Her behind the shower curtain. *Peek-a-boo. Hide-and-seek.* Mummy both there and not there. *Click on, click off.* (You didn't realise that all them childhood peek-a-boo games were basically just rehearsals.) (Didn't realise it till a year later, when she first fell unconscious.)

Later, clicking away from your coursework again to ask Google for the lowdown on hip-op blood loss.

Turned out that some hospitals would squirt a bag of blood into her arm right there and then in the operating theatre.

Turned out other hospitals waited till after surgery to see if the patient needed a pint of the red stuff.

Turned out he was a typical mummy's boy.

Turned out some guy from your school called Dave was having some family holiday in some family foto.

Turned out that another serial killer was blaming it all on his mother.

Turned out that Anjali had ordered the salad . . . And so on and so what. Not to pretend it wasn't happening; to *prepare yourself.* Not to prepare yourself; to *pretend it wasn't happening.* Till in the end just doing both – clicking and swiping and scrolling so quickly that, in the end, everything you read and watched and thought and did was both. Your coursework slowly dying of link-rot while Google morphed into some kinda helpdesk for your soul. Facebook still schooling itself to profile your psyche, micro-target your desires, troll your inner demons. Both of them hitting you with even more answers. Stories to your questions. Shouting down your own thoughts. Even shouting down those dicks from school who randomly wrote shit on your wall. And even if the babble of bullshit fake stories started with health stories, who else was gonna show you how to find the right fucking vein?

Google told you her bone scan had involved injecting her with this radioactive liquid that would joyride through her bloodstream and then park up in her bones.

"Your mum's so thick that when they told her the drinks were on the house, she went and got a ladder."

YouTube showed you the kinds of fotos they'd taken of her bones with some high-tech bad-boy called a gamma camera. The places where lots of liquid collected were called "hot spots".

"Tell your mum to stick with one shade of lipstick – my dick looks like a rainbow."

Facebook told you the odds of survival after working out the odds that you wanted to know this.

"Your mum's so anal that before she slit her wrists, she sterilised the knife."

"Your mum's so fat she had to slit her wrists with a chainsaw."

In the end, everyone at school just cut to the chase and told each other that their mum had died. *"Shut your mouth, you dicksplash, your mum's dead."*

"Fucking give me back my cricket bat, you wanker, your mum's dead."

Not that you gave a shit what people wrote on your walls and your school exercise books and stuff. That's what Facebook walls and exercise books were basically for – like plaster casts and toilet cubicles. One time, even your dad wrote something. Once – he once wrote your name. On the cover of your first-ever exercise book, which was for drawing in cos it was before you'd learnt to write – except basic words like Cat and Dog and Mum and Dad. He'd crossed out your name and written "Dylan" in marker pen. Then later, your mum crossed out "Dylan" and wrote "Dhilan" in darker pen.

"Nice trainers, shitface – shame your mum's dead."

Google told you about some other bone-strengthening technique that involved injecting her hip with cement.

"Good morning, dude, your mum's dead."

Google told you about special private clinics that did special hip cement. Even told you the name, phone number and fee for each clinic – cos, after all, ads are basically answers.

Back in them days, though, Google mainly decided what stories and info to hit you with depending on how often your keyword appeared in each webpage, and the website's popularity.

i.e. before ads and search results became fully custom-tailorised according to your search history and personal data. Your tastes, your fears, your twistedness.

i.e. before Google started trying to guess the shit you were looking for before you'd even finished typing your search query.

i.e. before Google started hitting you with ads for morning-sickness tablets, boob-job clinics, books about Oedipus.

i.e. before search engines became psychic and started pumping out prophecies. Data-crunching your future based on what you done in the past. Predicting where the sickness would spread to next. What would happen next.

How you'd feel.

What you'd do.

19

"SHOULD'VE WANKED. YOU'D be more relaxed."

I look at Ramona like I ain't actually for sure if she's joking.

"I could even loan you my insoles. Though let's be clear: that'd be the limit of my participation."

Minor spillage of my McDonald's milkshake while I'm like, WTF? Scanning around to check ain't no other diners are eaveslistening.

"Or maybe you could've just scored some weed or beta blockers? Or even morphine."

"What?"

"There's no shame in it, Dillon. I mean, I'd be freaking out too if I were you."

"I'm fine. Ain't freaking out."

Five minutes later, I start freaking the fuck out. Start wishing we'd picked somewhere with table covers just so I could hide the fuck underneath one. Ramona reckons swanky restaurants are some vulgarity crime against humanity, but even *she'd* ripped the fact that we was having a meet in a McDonald's. "Couldn't you at least ask for an upgrade to Pizza Express?"

Ain't necessary to describe a McDonald's. Plastic furniture and A&E lighting. Don't never see a dimly lit McDonald's.

She reaches across the table and taps my clenched fist. Last night's red, porcelain fingernails now more like patent leather. I count to five then turn round in my seat to check out the entrance.

"No, nobody's there," she says, "That's not what I meant."

Even though we in a Maccy D's, we in a Maccy D's in London's Wall Street district – right by an entrance to Liverpool Street Station, i.e. no truants, no twisteds, no trainers, no teenage parents with ketchup-blotted toddlers. Nearest we get to violent gang factions is when a posse of old men hobble in, rocking blazers and berets and bravery medals. Guess he's an old man too now, though not as aged-out as this crew. Plus he probly never won no medal for diddly nothing and he deffo didn't fight in no battle. *Why is it that wrinkles don't camouflage scars?* Not for custody anyway. Still, I can live with calling him the Old Man. Can be comfortable with that. All the other options are so over-emo, they'd make me vomit in the back of my throat. (*Pops*, for instance.) (Or *Papa*.) (Don't even mention Dad or Daddy.) (And obviously you can forget the fucking F-word.)

Take another hit of my milkshake.

One time I tried to cover her scars with the opposite-of-stretch-marks.

When my Old Man finally shows, ain't no apologies for his thirty minutes lateness. No apologies for not calling or texting ahead. No apologies for making us meet in the corporate capital of cow-genocide when we meant to be Hindu. No apologies for anything at all. Just stands there in the entrance/exit like he expects some standing ovation for showing up. Shoots me a nod just one notch up from nothing – like he's trying his Keanu Reeves-best to de-emotion this shit. Then he heads to the counter to order his meal. Ramona's like, "What the fuck? Who the hell gets their food before saying hello?" But I'm too busy judging to care. Some new or maybe old moustache. The kind he should keep tidy with scissors, not a beard trimmer. New or maybe old glasses. Who the hell still has gold rims? And still a full head of hair. Phew, thank you, high five, fist bump, actual tequila shots. Ain't no need to note that he's gone greyer over the past ten or so years. But thing is, I always thought of him as being old. So even though the man's clearly aged out, he's basically become closer to how I always thought of him anyway. Realise I'd been hoping he'd have a matching-grey beard. First I've known of me wanting him to have a beard. Still, he's donning some telltale newspaper – we talking the kind you actually gotta pay for. Rolled up under his arm like as if it's making some holy cross with the sleeve of his battered raincoat. Yup: to round off the whole Divorced Dad look, he's rocking a regulation lonely-old-man's beige raincoat. Some poncey yellow scarf that snubs his throat – like he's wearing half a McDonald's arch.

"Seriously, what the fuck?" Ramona goes again. "Is it shyness or is he just clinically chickenshit?"

Ain't no reason why me and him lost contact – way back in them plastic-action-figure days. Those Saturday afternoons just came round less and less regular. Done and done, no big deal – all my non-Disneyfied friends went through the exact same thing. They call it the "post-divorce divorce".

So don't be a pussy about it.

Don't start listening to Coldplay.

"Dillon, doesn't he realise how lucky he is to even be getting face time with you?"

Ramona didn't even need to ask why me and him weren't in touch. Way she saw it, custody arrangements when parents split are the same as antitrust agreements when businesses merge: you promise the regulators you won't fuck up the market, but a few years later everyone just forgets all that shit.

No big deal at all.

So while I watch him wait in line, I check myself again to make sure I ain't gonna be some sappy, sentimental spunkwash about this. Make sure I haven't started listening to Green Day. That I don't even wanna know what his favourite fucking colour is. And for definite none of that *backslap/that's my boy/thumbs up/attaboy* crap. Or anyshit that even starts to sound like *My advice to you, son . . . Whatever you need, son . . . Let me buy you a beer, son . . . Let me teach you how to ride a bike/tie a necktie/shave without slicing your pus-filled zits/wank while shaving without spraining or slitting your wrists . . .* You remember that useless cuntfart at school who needed a probation officer and a course of CBT just cos he lacked a source of paternal authority? That waster wasn't me. Or that gibbering dicktard who probly still lacks direction and still can't make decisions? Not me either. Cos just as Mum once said after getting paid a backhanded compliment by some uptight sack of sanctimony-in-a-sari: *"A father's just an optional piece of furniture."*

My Optional Piece of Furniture is still transacting at the McDonald's counter. See him there in the actual fact flesh – still feels like seeing him on a screen. Proper HD this time, though. (How is it that I clock more of this guy's facial features than I ever done for Mum?) Man seems to be chatting to himself. Over and over again – like he's repeat-playing some special hamburger mantra. Fuck's sake, surely he's rehearsed this lunch enough times before? Not as often as I have, maybe, but once or twice at least; at least once. In the eight years and two months since we last met for lunch. The small talk, the smaller talk; the football scores. Me, I plan to just begin with and end with just asking the question. Then thank him for the answer. Then get up and go. Cos surely he'll have an answer? It ain't some deep and meaningful drama-queen question. Ain't even remotely soap-opera or emotional. Ain't about me waiting beside the house phone for a birthday card or beside the letter box for a birthday fucking phone call. It's just about his career – his blacked-out news stories. So, once again, just ask him the question, thank him for the answer, then get up and go. Okay, give him your fucking mobile number if you really gotta be all Drake about it, whatever feels right. But then thank him and go.

Cos custody arrangements are the same as antitrust agreements. No big deal at all.

When my Old Man finally rocks up to our table, he announces, proper loudspeaker-style, "I realise it's depressing to be meeting in McDonald's, but I find all those coffee chains round here too plasticky and commercial."

Stares at Ramona instead of sitting. And then back at me – though not to *thumbs up/high five/attaboy/backslap* me. More like that bear from Goldilocks, the one who says, *Who the fuck been sitting in my chair?*

"Oh, this is my friend Ramona," I go. "We just happened to bump into each other just here. Not here in McDonald's – I mean in the train station."

When she's done looking disappointed in me for not braving up about the fact that I'd needed her help to brave up, Ramona stands up and tries rebooting the situation. Shakes the Old Man's hairy hand. Says she's pleased to finally meet him. Calling him shit like "Mr Deckardas". Hopes she ain't intruding. First time she's ever met one of my relatives and it's some relative I don't hardly even know myself.

"Nonsense," he goes. "It isn't as if we've booked a table for two here."

Ramona stays standing as my Old Man sits down. I thank him for agreeing to meet me and for making the time. Then he starts thanking *me* for meeting with *him* – for making the time to meet with him. Each of his sentences just following each other like the carriages of one of them not-in-service Tube trains: "I know it must have seemed strange for us to be talking again on the phone out of the blue like that, Dylan. So the first thing I want to say is I'm sorry if I unsettled you by calling you—"

"But wait," I go, "You didn't. I mean, *I* was the one who—"

"—So I want to quickly set one thing straight, son: there's nothing the matter, nothing wrong – I'm not dying or sick or anything like this. I just thought it was high time that we started meeting each other again."

Hadn't even occurred to me he might be dying or sick – that he'd be anything other than fine and dandy. After that, my Old Man goes total mute button. Like those people who've offered their blessings and get-well wishes and then can't wait to bail.

I ask him if I can ask him a question.

(Cos, hey, even soldiers request permission to speak.) (Cos politeness, etc.) (Cos Mummy taught me good manners.)

"Are you sure that *you* foned *me* and not the other way round?"

"What do you mean, son? Of course I phoned you." Behind his gold-rimmed glasses, some kinda twitch action starts blinking back to life. I full-on proper forgot about his twitch.

"But—"

"Actually, excuse me a moment, Dylan, I meant to ask for some barbecue sauce." My Old Man-shaped Optional Piece of Furniture turns to look for a waiter or waitress. A woman at the counter pretends like not to notice him, so he pretends not to notice her back.

I tell him I don't think they do table service at McDonald's.

Next, he tries calling over this guy who's mopping up a puddle of freshly spilt milkshake. Each move of the mop exaggerated-style, like he's stabbing the puddle with a spear or someshit. All the different milkshake flavours the colour of a different type of bodily fluid. The mop man cuts my Old Man a look then holds up his mop as if warning us to stay the fuck away.

I weigh up whether to go get the barbecue sauce for him, but then muster all my manliness to shut that shit down.

He aborts the whole barbecue sauce thing.

"So, you were in the middle of telling me something, son." His twitch doing some kinda guitar solo.

"I was asking if you're sure that *you* foned *me*?"

"Of course it was me – who else would it have been?"

"No, I mean are you the one who contacted me or was it me who contacted you?"

"I'm sorry, Dylan, I'm not sure I follow." Checking about now like he reckons he's on TV – like he thinks maybe someone's playing one of them plebby prank-show pranks on him. "Dylan, of course I'm the one who phoned you. I phoned you, you picked up the phone, we agreed to meet and now we're here." He cuts a look at Ramona.

I try asking him again, even though I already know for definite that *I* was the one who called *him* and suggested this meet and that *he* was just the one who suggested we do the meet in Maccy D's. "So, far as you're concerned, it wasn't *me* who contacted *you*?"

"Look, what is it exactly that you're trying to say, son? That you were *going* to contact me?"

"That's what I'm trying to ask you. Who tracked who down? Who came looking for who?" Try focusing on his right eye – the one that don't twitch. Then I realise there ain't no more twitch – like as if the calibration's all off so that the twitch actually cuts *out* when he gets vexed or pressed.

Ramona asks if I'm sure I don't wanna eat nothing. "I mean something proper, Dillon. Solids." Holding my hand under the table now.

Ain't about my lack of nourishment. Anycase, lunch ain't even an issue for me – normally I can always eat something for lunch. The involuntary morning vomiting malarkey means normally by then I'm starving – though normally I take lunch on the late. Like, 3pm at the earliest – soon as the sickness in my throat clears and I can tap the hunger in my tummy. How to explain all this shit to Ramona without sounding like some wuss-ass feeble fuck-up with a sick note for every occasion? Or without telling her the truth about the woman I started puking in sync with.

"So I just wanna get this straight," I go to him – trying once again to fix this whole father–son screen-freeze problem. "You're saying for definite that you—"

"Okay, what's going on here, Dylan? If you didn't want to meet me, you could have just told me on the phone – you didn't have to agree to it just so you could come here with your girlfriend and make fun of me."

He grabs his newspapers like he's about to bounce – I gotta shoot out my hand and make actual body contact to stop him. His arm somehow bonier *and* podgier than I remember. "I ain't trying to make fun of you, Dad – I swear on my mum's life."

Starts spluttering and coughing up my name, but I'm too busy dealing with how piss-easy it just was to say the word "Dad". I try that shit once again. "Of course I wanted to meet you, Dad." Is it okay if it's easy to say the word Dad? "Just ignore everything I just said, Dad." And now that I said the word Dad, I can't exactly go back and not say it. "I'm just being a dumbass, Dad."

"Look, about your mother, Dylan – I mean, how are you . . . doing? How are things now? These days, I mean."

"Things are fine, but, Dad, like I said on the fone, I don't wanna talk about her. It wouldn't be right."

"You know, she—"

I tell him again that things are fine. Take some major slurp of my McDonald's milkshake to show them both that I mean it.

"But you know, she didn't even call me to tell me," Dad goes. "Perhaps I could have been doing something to help. Instead of always hearing from other people – from our mutual friends. Not only telling me she isn't well, but also that I'm not doing anything to help."

"You didn't tell me your mum isn't well," goes Ramona.

I tell her that it's nothing – ain't no biggie. I tell her my mum's much better now.

"Well – next time tell her to take some echinacea, Dillon."

"You also, Dylan," Dad presses on.

"What?"

"I mean it's been the same thing with you: you've never called to tell me how you've been keeping. For instance, how well you've been doing in your studies. Your GCSEs and your A levels. Getting into LSE. Once again, I have to hear that news from my friends. Not only that you're doing so well but also that you're doing so without my help."

Him hearing about my kick-ass exam results from other people used to be one of my recurring daydreams. Now that I know that shit actually came true, I have to check myself so that I don't high-five myself or someshit.

"Still, no point dredging up what's already done – I'm very glad you've done so well, son. It's good you've gone to a good university."

Ramona leans forward like she's gonna set him straight – tell him how working your guts off to get to a good uni now marks you down as too educated and elitist by people who are sick of experts and that. "Mr Deckardas, I think Dillon has another question he wanted to ask you today."

After that screen-freeze over who foned whom, last thing I wanna do now is ask him head-on about his blacked-out news stories. Man'll think I only wanted to hook up with him so I could jump him with cross-examinations and challenges. I know from dealing with my side-effected mum that the best way to tranquilate these situations is to make your questions general and non-confrontational. So I ask Dad if he'd ever done anything different.

"Do I wish I'd done things differently?"

"No, I mean did you ever try out a different career, for instance?"

"Such as what, son?"

"I dunno – anything other than working in life insurance. For instance, were you ever, say, I dunno, a journalist?" Fuck it – obliqueness is overrated anyway.

"But I *am* a journalist, Dylan. Always have been."

Now both of them hit me with that look. "Nah, Dad, don't play around with me now – I always remember you going to work for some insurance company. And Mum and Masi have always said you worked for an insurance company. That's how I first learned what insurance even *was* – about forecasting and predicting and that. How is it all my family could keep telling me that if you're actually a journalist?"

"All your family?" His raised eyebrows look more natural when he smiles. "You mean all your mother's family. They all liked to say that I worked for an insurance company because they thought that sounded better paid and therefore more prestigious than journalism."

I tell Dad that if he's seriously really a journalist, then how come I never ever come across any stories written by him? I know this sounds like exactly the sort of confrontational vibe I'm trying to avoid, but just wait for the butt-kissing pay-off. "I mean whenever I google you, Dad."

Man looks more spooked than suckered, though. No shitting – even his shirt collar shrivels. "Go on, Dylan. Continue."

"Nothing, that's it – there's nothing on Google."

He lets the convo just marinate on ice – like as if I'm somehow meant to elaborate on the word "nothing".

"But anyway, even back when you were living at home, I'm positive you even told me yourself you worked for an insurance company."

"I did. I do. But you were seven, Dylan, so I didn't go into the nuances. I'm a journalist for a news service that sits on an insurance company's website."

I tell him that, actually, I was six.

"It's a way of jazzing up their home page – making them look more dynamic. The reason you've never found anything I've written when you've googled my name is because we don't have bylines on our news service. That's all. There's no mystery, Dylan."

Twitch comes on again.

I now got no choice but to hit him with more specifics: "Dad, I have one more question. Did you ever work for a proper newspaper? Say, for just a year or so? Say, in 2001?"

Twitch off.

Starts having some kinda stare-out with his half-eaten Big Mac – like as if it's only just hit him that Hindus ain't meant to eat beef. Chucks it onto his tray, wipes his mouth, his moustache. Then just sits there for twenty or so secs before standing up. "If you want to think less of me just because I write for a website instead of a 'proper' antiquated paper, that's up to you. But I'm a journalist, Dylan. And whether a journalist works for a newspaper, a TV channel, a news website or some other kind of website, the one thing we all have is deadlines. And I'm now very late to meet mine. You may have already noticed I've been running late all day today. So thanks again for agreeing to meet me, son. It's good to know you're getting on well – doing well without my help. And it's been very nice to meet your friend." Before either Ramona or me can even process this sudden-like

TV-talent-show strop, he's grabbed his raincoat and newspapers and bounced.

Ramona stares at the remains of my Old Man's Big Mac. Her hands around my clenched fist like we're on some kinda rock, paper, scissors thing. "Hey, on the bright side, at least I finally understand why you never want to introduce your family to me." Flexing a smile to make sure I mimic it. Through the window, the light inside Liverpool Street Station is like the light in a shopping mall – wouldn't even know for shit if it was daylight or night outside. "And at least his mad rush deadline explains why he chose fast food instead of taking you for a proper pizza or something."

I tell her I thought pizza *was* fast food. All them Saturdays straight after they split when he took me to Pizza Hut so that he could get me back home before on the dot. Cutting off the crust just to hurry me up. All them times we went for even faster food and them times he didn't wanna risk no untried and untested *un*chain restaurants cos he was scared shitless of taking me home with an upset tummy.

By the time Ramona's finished making everything okay again, I've come up with two more reasons for why maybe he wanted to meet in Maccy D's: Firstly, for the same reason people eat in McDonald's when they travelling in countries where they wanna take the safe option – places where you drink Coca-Cola cos you don't trust the water.

Secondly, maybe he wanted to meet in McDonald's cos that's where we'd left off.

20

"SEE, DIDN'T I tell you?" Botched-Botox man standing in front of me like he's some human pop-up ad. Nodding at the essay on my screen. Still donning his dickhead biker jacket, but this time with some piss-take preppy necktie. "I told you to just focus on your degree."

I'm studying in the office instead of data-entering. Popping Pro-Plus tablets instead of munching a Pret a Mortgage sandwich. Takes me a second to remember this guy's now the Acting Head of IT in this place. I play along – apologise for doing degree stuff in the client's office and on the client's time. Tell him I'm falling behind at uni.

"I told you that you would." He starts walking away but then doubles back to re-inspect my screen. Scans the other desks of data-enterers, digitisers and Website Functionality Enablers. "We'll continue in my office, Dillon. Just give me a minute to go get a sandwich. And then why don't we continue in my office."

And once again with the walking-away-and-then-turning-back routine. As if he doesn't realise that same shit is pulled by every limpdick line manager on the planet. Always forgetting their wallet/umbrella/scarf so they can catch what their undergimps get up to when they gone. Except this time when he turns back, it ain't to scope out my screen. "Can I get you anything, Dillon? A soup or a sandwich? Some chocolate chip cookies?"

Ramona had wanted to link up for lunch today, but thing is, sometimes I bail on autopilot even when I'm properly down for seeing her. Even when I'm done with all my involuntary morning vomiting malarkey. Even when I done whatever Mummy needs doing. Even when I been daydreaming about Ramona during my sleep dreams. *Young Carer's Playbook #472: Of the three forms of social exclusion – self-exclusion, forced exclusion and officially sanctioned exclusion – the first one typically leaves the largest deficit in a young carer's personal development.*

Fine, Ramona said. She'd grab lunch with some other J. Doe instead. One of those brand-new oldest best friends.

The botched-Botox man ditches the bread, just eats the sandwich filling with some plastic fork. Apologises for eating while chatting – packed schedule, etc. "Four days I've been doing this job and dealing with these people, Dillon, and already I'm sick of the digital archive." Stool he's got me sitting on is on some proper wobble. Maybe cos he's just the Acting Head of IT, they given him an acting office. A name on his door and on his brand new business cards, but I figure that's just some acting name. "As if they don't even realise that *everything's* a digital archive now. Doesn't matter whether it's a newspaper or a person or a grocery store – supermarkets are archives of product info and whining customer reviews." Nods to himself like he's nodding on my behalf. "*Searchable* archives. That's the key. Everyone's now a searchable archive of their own search histories. The logic of the database, Dillon – searching is the most performed activity in the digital world. So easy to do it that there's no excuse not to."

Figure ain't no point in me even trying to swipe away all these lectures of his. The man's digital media sermons been hooking me in just like actual digital media does – like as if he's on some mystical-knowledge-type shit. Like how everyone keeps going on social media to share articles about the effects of social media. Fuck it – people been logging onto the internet to read about the internet from jump.

I tell him that the archives are just some side effect of custom-tailored personalisation/advertising/surveillance. Or is it other way round?

He looks at me like why's he even wasting his time with this.

"Tell me, Dylan, you wear braces?" He's now on sandwich number two. Raw steak that actually bleeds into the bread. Swallowing half of it whole before once again ditching the bread.

"On my teeth?"

"Over your shoulders – to hold up your trousers. Folks back home call them suspenders. Imagine the kind of transatlantic confusion that causes."

I tell him I don't wear braces or suspenders.

"Because the trouble with the so-called 'belt-and-braces' approach is people then neglect to fasten the belt as tightly as they otherwise would." He munches another forkful of sandwich filling. The steak now so raw it's like a lump of liquid, like it's travelling back in time right in front of me – all the way from well done, to rare, to flesh tissue, to inseminated egg of a cow. "Or to take an example closer to your home, it's like neglecting to wash your hands before making her breakfast just because you'd worn latex gloves. You see, in my case, the belt was me taking this fucking ridiculous job to overhaul the management of the digital archive project. The pair of braces was that terribly tragic accident in the external storage facility that closed off access to the physical stock of back issues. You'd think those two measures would have been sufficient. But, apparently not . . ."

Accident had been in the news all week – not the accident itself, the row about the road closures above it. Oh, and also the victim – the woman who got crushed by papers when the tunnel collapsed. I been checking for bulletins, updates, refreshing every page. *This story has been amended since its original publication to reflect the fact that the victim isn't critical.*

Correction: Actually, readers, it turns out that she's dead. This story has been amended accordingly since its earlier amendment.

Clarification: Not dead, just dying.

Allow all that crapfuckery – if she dies, she'll just stop producing new data is all.

"By the way, I understand that right before your little expedition to the external storage facility last week, you walked into a hardware store and purchased a flashlight. I need to know why."

"Case it got dark."

"The place was fully lit. Backup generators, power couplings. Anything goes wrong, the dehumidifiers cut out but the lighting always stays on. Plus your cellphone has an inbuilt flashlight. All three of them."

Figure if I just stay hush, probly he'll answer his own question. Or at minimum vomit out more intel. Dude's proper addicted to mansplaining. Real question is why.

"Well, I apologise for being remiss. I could have just given you a flashlight, Dylan. I appreciate that the micro-targeted ad for it kept following you around everywhere, popping up in every story you read, but, still, twenty-five bucks for a single-function flashlight is pretty steep for a student. Plus, I feel like I really ought to be giving you something – some kind of tool. How about I give you a single-function digital camera to make up for my oversight? Or a single-function watch or alarm clock? Maybe a single-function voice recorder?"

"A dictaphone?"

"Well, I usually just dial with my fingers."

He longs out the silence while waiting for my non-response.

"Okay, look, Dylan, I know you've been desperately distraughtly distressed about the fate of that security woman down there. You need to forget about her. Move on. You've got enough bearing down on your conscience as it is." Next, he starts slapping out some drum roll on his desk. "Cried for her mummy, she did. While the paramedics were trying to free her. Pissed her panties too, apparently. Though that may have just been bladder compression rather than fear."

Check my face as he says this. I'm like the ghost of a goth with a sun allergy. How the fuck did I have the balls to hook up with my dad yesterday when I been warned by this maybe-actual-badass to stop poking the fuck around? Meeting him in broad train station daylight, even. Problem is, being told not to search for something is like being told not to think of something. Even more so now that you can reach into your pocket and look up anyshit you can think of. And because you can track down answers so easy, ain't no excuse not to. And so you basically *have* to. Meantime, the time between wondering someshit and knowing the answer is shrinking all the time. Even if you try and block it or blank it or just long it out.

Botox man pulls out his string of beads, starts meditating or mindfulating or whatever.

"The fuck is with those beads of yours?"

"Calculator."

"You what?"

"It's a single-function calculator, Dillon. Very early model, of course – pre-Casio. Pre-abacus, even. Anyhow, as I was saying a few moments ago, my failsafe belt-and-braces approach seems to have come undone. In its infinite cost-cutting wisdom, this company has now decided to reverse the decision to get rid of all you freelance data temps. They claim it's too expensive to bring the digital archive project in-house. In other words, too expensive to hire enough staff. In other words, too expensive to do things properly. To dot all the i's and cross all the t's and check all the fucking facts. Idiot blubbering bean-counters. I should've had myself drafted in as Acting CEO."

Man lets rip a fart like he's signal-boosting my sigh of relief. My relief ain't got shit to do with what he just said, though – it's cos he clearly ain't wised up to the fact I linked up with my dad.

"Of course, the company's U-turn means you'll now get to stay on this project. Should you wish to. Though it also means that my job now entails making sure you *don't* wish to. You see, I can't just have you thrown off for performance-related reasons because the

Managing Editor now has a sob soft spot thanks to all your young carer problems. And I can't plant porn in your browsing history because, let's face it, what could be more disgusting than the sob-story post-surgical porn you've already downloaded with apparent impunity. So you're going to have to help me out here, Dylan. Because I wasn't trained to deal with corporate compassion." Anyone striding past his office will probly think we're on that trendy reverse-mentoring crap, where the young digital native has to school up the C-suite dinosaur. "And to confuse me even more, I'm no longer even sure that even *I* want you thrown off."

When I ask him why not, he shrugs and comes out with some bullcrap about me not having much of a client roster – says I could use this place for references. "But in return for keeping you here, I want you to agree to something: I want you to continue doing exactly what you were doing when I walked up on you earlier – use the office facilities to help you with your studies. You're smart enough to get a first if you put your whole mind to it. If nothing else, a first-class degree should land you a better position in the dole queue. You'll need all the help you can get, seeing as how your parents' generation have gang-banged the economy." And again with his nodding on my behalf bullshit. "In any case, kid, you really need to stop feeling so guilty about studying. You've been acting like it's a felony since primary school and, well, frankly, it's getting irritating."

He's now having some serious struggles trying to open a can of Diet Coke. Keeps fat-fingering the task. "By the way, Dylan, how come you don't ask me why I've gone to all these elaborate aggravations and shenanigans? Even when I first took this job here, you just acted as if all this is to be expected."

Ring-pull now busted, he pulls a pocket knife from his double-breasted biker jacket and just cuts into the Coke can. Drinks straight from the stab wound. Laying the knife on his desk like as if he's trying to show me it's actually a surgical scalpel. Instead of shrivelling my testes as no doubt intentioned, the sight of the blade just morphs my balls into some same grade of stainless steel. I tell him that if he was gonna clue me in about what the fuck this is all about, he'd have already told me by now.

"Come on, Dylan, just look at my fucking face. Because contrary to Hollywood and literary stereotypes, deformities and scarring don't actually indicate villainy." He chucks his sandwich wrappers and the uneaten bread in the bin. Followed by the stabbed-up Coke can. Followed by the scalpel. "And in any case, you don't even really know what you're doing, do you? Which makes me wonder why the hell you're persisting in doing it. I mean, okay, sure, kid, I don't need a flashlight or magnifying glass icon to see that you're trying to make things right. But you got no idea what it is you're trying to rectify. You already know that there's no point trying to make sense of what's happening here. And you know that exercising your intelligence without being in full possession of all the information is worse than ignorance. You know this. Yes. It's known that you know this. After all, you've read all those stories about Oedipus."

Thing about Oedipus is he weren't being foolish. Dude was actually acting proper rational, logical, flexing his brain cells. Got the hell outta Dodge to dodge the oracle's prophecy of marital relations with his mum. Assumed he was innocent even when others started getting sus. Accusing all the haters of treason. Problem was he just didn't have all the info.

That's all for today about Oedipus.

"What are you trying to tell me?" I go. "Why keep longing out all these lectures? Why can't you just fart out whatever the fuck it is you wanna say?"

"I *am* telling you everything, Dylan. I'm telling you that *you're* telling us everything. I'm telling you everything *because* you're telling us everything. You people are so blasé about just giving it away. You give it away so easily because it's invisible. If you could actually see all your digital data printed out on paper, it would be a very different story. Facebook alone probably has thousands of pages on you. Google maybe twice as much. You keep talking about my flatulence. Well, let me tell you that across the entire population of America, there are more Facebook likes per minute than then there are human farts. Every millisecond, Dylan. Every pixel of every moment. They should call it big*mouth* data. No wonder you people binge on eight-season boxsets, six-volume autobiographies and overwritten novels." He stops talking just long enough to decide not to stop. "And of course if you're reading those overwritten novels on a handheld digital device, then the story is also reading you. Every page you skip, every paragraph you linger over. All of it adding it to your very own digital archive to help the algorithms determine what you read next. But, of course, you don't read novels, do you, Dylan? Should give them a try sometime – I promise they don't all read as if they were written by writers." Next thing, he starts busting out some personalised book recommendations but then checks himself and clicks back to sermonising. "Or maybe you people act blasé because you're lulled into a false sense of fluency by the term 'digital native'. Of all the idiotic buzzwords. Absolves adults of the responsibility to tell you the things that I'm trying to tell you. Makes grown-ups dependent on you youngsters. You show them how to use their smartphones so that Mummy and Daddy can make their own way out there in the world – their faith in all this stuff based solely on your faith. Meanwhile, *you* outsource your faith in your gadgets to the gadgets themselves. It's as if technology believes in itself on everyone's behalf."

"For fuck's sake," I give it. "All this fronting and badassery and basically you just some jumped-up Media Studies teacher?"

"Come on, Dylan, you've already figured out that this isn't about the media or online privacy – or even digital data. It's about what your data does to you when it's crunched up and processed and fed back to you."

He stops to let his breath sink in.

"You chatting about Oedipus again, ain't it? Predictions and recommendations and prophecies? Like how all our own digital archives are side effects of surveillance, predictions are side effects of the archives."

Starts scratching his face now – his Botox, his stubble. Same old salty dandruff (or ash or pixels or whatever). I still get dandruff in my knuckles from being so extra when washing my hands. Now an ad for hand sanitiser – antiviral as well as antibacterial. A story about people with OCD.

"You saying they was right, then?" I ask him. "I mean Google and that. But if they was right, then that means that I was right too – to do what I done."

"Wherever you're going with this, Dylan, I wouldn't go *that* far."

"Look, even if they *were* right, the predictions and recommendations and stories could've changed as a result of the teeniest little thing. Like if, say, I hovered my cursor over some story about Oedipus for just a couple seconds less, then the algorithms might have decided something different about my personality – about who I am. And then the predictions and recommendations would've been different. Wouldn't have dragged me out so far."

That's all for today about Oedipus.

The botched-Botox man taps another drum roll on his desktop. "Now you're talking, kiddo. Except of course, those stories you were hovering over in the first place were most likely recommended for you by the algorithms. They fed you stories about Oedipal relations because they figured out those were the stories you'd be most likely to click on and stay on according to your data-crunched vulnerabilities and triggers and weaknesses. Laser-guided precision targeting. Pull to refresh. Cleverly designed push notifications to make cellphones more addictive than slot machines. In junk news industry parlance, it was a perfect triple-whammy, playing to your fears, your perversions and all those convenient prejudices against over-baring mothers. So you see, there's no scenario in which you aren't being nudged towards Oedipus by algorithmic prophecies."

He tells me it's the exact same shit as people who emit bipolar signals getting nudged towards online casinos. Or people with a mild intolerance getting nudged towards neo-Nazis. Says the only thing that could've saved me from Oedipal predictions would've been if the likes of Google and Facebook had completely different business models that didn't involve baiting people's eyeballs with the cleverest hooks ever constructed in order to generate ad revenues. If they didn't stick you in some custom-tailorised bubble of self-reinforcing thoughts. Still can't puzzle out exactly what he's trying to tell me with all this red-pilling of his – if he's on some particular specificness about things that gone down between me and Mum. But I'm feeling like maybe now I might actually understand this guy if he ever does decide to just tell me whatever the fuck he's telling me.

Stand up from the stool like we all done here, like as if my cursor ain't still fumbling about in the search box.

The Botox man scans a look at his single-function wristwatch. Tells me he knows I ducked Ramona's offer to link up for lunch today – even claims he knows why. "And I know that my knowing this won't surprise you, Dylan. But I strongly suggest you reconsider. Don't shit the bed on that front too. Plus you could clearly use a square meal. Some proper slap-up red meat. Stop trying to steel yourself against the day by siphoning your mummy's iron supplements."

"So now you dosing out dietary advice?"

"Fashion advice. Couple more pounds and your trousers might actually fit you. You ever considered wearing a belt? Or braces? Or, better still, both? I mean, just to be safe."

21

RAMONA'S GOT COMPANY. The girl's got her back to the entrance so I can't clock her face. But she's rocking an afro like a crown of crushed-up rubies. Some signage tagged across her chair – hashtag BFF. Like as if to tell me that this is Ramona's brand-new oldest best friend. *Why the hell is there signage?*

I walk towards their table.

If she's a crap friend, this'll all be safe. But if she's a good friend, we're riding straight to Awkward City: legislative capital of the Confederation of Autonomous Awkward States. Cos here's the thing about Ramona's BFs: you can change the topic of convo all you like. Can offer to go buy another round. Can leg it to the bar or the bathroom or that counter with the milk and the bogey-blocked sugar pourer. But you can never outrun the words "he's my *sort-of* boyfriend".

Best-case scenario: when that girl called Jen told Ramona maybe I was moonlighting for MI5 or someshit.

Or Trish, who'd told her I'm probly just a highly committed commitmentphobe.

Then there was Beatrice, who told her I obviously had a defective dick.

And Wai-Liu, who told her maybe I was shamed of some other defect – like midnight bowel movements or post-coital halitosis (apparently that's actually a thing).

And then of course there was Gita and Myra and Deidre and all them others who'd told her must be I was cheating on her – as in actual cheating, not just thinking about possible rebound options for when Ramona wises up and dumps me.

Allow it – just be chill.

Roll up to their table.

Apologise for crashing their lunch.

"It's long after lunch, Dillon." Ramona doesn't ask how come I managed to find her here – in all the pop-up cafés in all of London. And so I don't ask myself either. "This is Naliah. My new friend."

Before filling out all the mandatory nice-to-meet-you fields, I tell Ramona I swear down she told me earlier she was meeting an *old* friend.

"Well, a week's a long time." Smiling as she says this, though.

Tables are all wearing, like, wedding gowns or someshit so Naliah's face has gotta front for her footwear. Sunglasses fronting for her eyes. No make-up, no lip gloss, no nothing, just those ruby-red highlights in her afro burning all the way down to the roots. Why is it that women feel they gotta keep highlighting or dyeing or straightening or just generally self-mutilupgrading? *Hug her tighter and tell her again that she don't need no hair to be prettyful, don't need no breasts to be prettyful, don't even need to lose the nasal feeding tube to have a prettyful smile.* When Naliah takes off her shades, her contact lenses are green. Ain't *so* green that they order you to stare at her, though, they just tell you that they there. The TV's still on standby. The car alarm activated, i.e. zero distraction as she answers all my stock-standard questions: chemical engineering, Imperial College, tea rather than coffee, Samsung, Camden, purple, her parents are from Angola though they split when she was nine. And all the time that I'm nodding and asking and nodding, I'm basically just trying to sus out if she's a crap friend or a good friend. Can I really, like, love Ramona for real if I want her to have crap friends who'll just shoulder-shrug all my sneaky shiftiness? But could I really love her for real if I wanted her to have good friends who'd tell her to chuck me? Naliah's now asking me her own set of user profile questions so I do my best to bore her. Basic strategic manoeuvre straight outta my *Young Carer's Playbook*. It's all about boundaries. Being boring is less rudeful. Less shitty than bullshitting. Less convoluted and extra than pretending you got a cold when her white blood count is low. So I hit her with the precise distances between Piccadilly Line Tube stops. I hit her with linear regression econometrics. Hit her with how variable datasets affect financial forecasting. She reaches across to check her rejuicing phone – shoes squawking like they on some error alert. So not just flats, but trainers. Probly them dickless hipster plimsolls.

"Sorry for squeaking," says Naliah. "I'm wearing trainers – not by choice, just for work. My job requires the wearing of flat shoes." And then once again with the squawk of the score for a horror film. Scalpel on a hospital whiteboard. Now giving aggro to the table cover as she sits straight again and crosses her legs.

"Barista, right?" goes Ramona. "I barista'ed last year – totally fucked with my feet. So now I'm just going to pay for uni by selling one of my kidneys."

A real, actual barista then pops up right in front of us to clear away the table stains. Naliah can't tell if Ramona was joking about selling a kidney. Solid indicator of low-level friendship and so my muscles kick back in their sockets or tendons or sofas or whatever.

"No, I'm not a barista," says Naliah when the actual barista has gone. And then she locks on me. "I'm a part-time professional foot model. Officially voted the sexiest feet in Europe."

My eyes on Ramona to see if this shit is her idea of a practical joke. Ramona just looking like the joke's on her. Next, Naliah starts busting out some blatantly well-trodden spiel about foot modelling – saying how regular fashion models don't get hired for close-ups of feet cos of all that strutting their stuff up and down catwalks: "It isn't just the blisters that count them out. A lot of catwalk models like filing down their toenails, which pretty much rules out modelling sandals or stockings or barefoot shots for verruca treatments. Plus they're all so lanky, which means larger and skankier feet." Starts telling us how people are biologically programmed to prefer seeing women's shoes modelled on small feet – like as if I don't already know this shit. (FYI, it's cos oestrogen limits the growth of foot bones.) (And also cos pregnant women have bloated feet.) (And cos sick women have swollen, fluid-filled balloon feet.) (And cos our infant minds develop while we crawl at our mum's and dad's feet – and our mummy's feet lead to the milk.)

"But really it's about more than just slenderness," Naliah presses on. "For instance, I also won my Sexiest Feet in Europe Award because of softness, sheen and scent. Plus I've been blessed with a perfect toe cascade and a really deep nail bed, which means I've got shorter nails that look longer." She carries on listing her foot modelling credentials like she's trying to give me a hard-on filled with helium. Fucking laughing gas, more like. "Exfoliating helps with texture but also improves the taste of my toes by counteracting any clammy tanginess . . . I usually just rub against cold metal table legs to tone and tighten my ankles . . . It's good practice for when I model stainless-steel ankle-cuffs because the steel is usually coated in coolant to stop them conducting the heat of the spotlights . . ."

Reroute my stare three tables to our left. Some guy's holding up a Polaroid foto of the blueberry pie on his plate. Starts telling random strangers why he reckons the taste is "underwhelming". Another diner joins in by listing various blueberry-bush pesticides that studies have found to be dangerous.

Naliah drops a throat-clearance cough and so I swipe back to our table, "Thankfully, though, leather ankle-cuffs don't conduct spotlight heat . . . And of course steel stiletto heels are generally insulated by plastic . . . Did you know women are more likely to wear high heels when they're ovulating? It's true – even female baboons walk on tiptoes when they're on heat . . ."

My mama falling over and crying despite me begging her to wear her post-op plimsolls instead. Can't use crutches if they cut out half your latissimus dorsi.

"It's because high heels push forward our centre of gravity," Naliah explains, "so they alter our hips, chests and pelvic muscles." Next, she starts going on about her bunion immunity, which apparently means she can model the soles of fishnets without any bumps disturbing the lattice. "All things being equal, though, I prefer modelling shoes rather than stockings – especially those slingbacks with the straps that pull tight on your toe cleavage like the rein of the rear of a thong."

This is when I finally step up and ask both of them what the fuckness is going on here. Even stand up for dramatic effect – though I think maybe I mainly do this just to prove to Ramona that I ain't got a hard-on – not even semi. Another handy manoeuvre straight from my *Young Carer's Playbook*.

Ramona scrunches her nose and then facepalms as if to hold it scrunched. Whispers through her fingers, "I think that maybe . . ."

"*I'll* tell you what's going on," goes Naliah. "I appreciate Ramona and I have only been friends for a couple of weeks, but all the same, I like to look out for my friends."

"Oh, really, is *that* what you think you're doing?" goes Ramona.

"Why'd you go and blurt to your new friend that I'm into feet?" I ask her. "Exactly how is that something to front about?"

"Well, I didn't know she was going to stage an intervention."

"So tell us, Dillon, did you like the sound of my award-winning feet?"

"So what if he likes your feet?" goes Ramona. "It'd be unhealthy if he wasn't attracted to you."

"But I'm not attracted to her."

"No bunions, Dillon. No fungal infection."

"It's okay to acknowledge that she's gorgeous – I'm not asking you if you want to fuck her."

"A lingering Red Leicester aroma but with no sharp aftertaste."

"And besides, Dillon, you know how I feel about liars." After Ramona drops this line about liars, I need a friggin Dyson to gather my shit back together. But then Ramona backs up a bit – tells

Naliah that, actually, for all my various headfucks and defectments, at least I've always been *honest.*

"Wait, what? So it's okay for him to treat you like this just so long as he's honest about it?" And then to me: "Can't you see what you've done here?"

"Look, I don't know who you're meant to be or why you're being so extra about all this. But ain't anyone ever told you it's rude to make fun of someone's personal hang-ups?"

"Oh FFS, Dillon, this isn't just about your twisted sexual preferences. It's about the way you don't even *see* Ramona, you only see her feet. You stay safely at the fringes, leaving her dangling around like a rag doll. And believe me, I know what I'm talking about – I watched my mum waste her forties being some slippery shithead's mistress."

Now Ramona steps back in. "Dillon, I think that Naliah's just trying – I mean Naliah and me – we're just trying to figure out what this is."

"Well, at least now you're being straight with me."

"Oh *please*," goes Naliah. "A woman is seriously suffering here and you're making out as if *you're* the victim."

I start splintering one of the wooden coffee stirrers.

This is when I realise that all the chairs in this place have got #BFF tagged across the back. Ditto the menus. Guess it's the name of the café.

"You can't just keep blowing hot and cold on her, Dillon – she isn't a row of painted toenails. If you want to be free, then go ahead, leave and be free, but don't just keep loitering in the doorway. Do you have any idea how much that's been torturing her?"

I wanna tell Naliah this shit tortures me too, but I can't without telling the truth about my mother. And then watch Ramona's face as she clocks all those thousands of little lies I've told her. I know full fucking for real it seems like I'm just stringing Ramona along. But truth is I'm also stringing my own ass along.

Lay my hand on Ramona's and tell her I'm sorry she felt she needed to sign up Naliah for all this – that she should've just talked to me about it.

The scrunch in Ramona's nose climbs up her forehead. "Sure. And then watch you run a mile. Well, I'm sorry, Dillon, but I needed to talk to someone who'd actually stay in the room and listen. And it isn't like I can talk to any of my other friends about us because I know full well what they'd tell me to do. I can't even talk to the student counselling service because I know they'd tell me to do the same thing."

Of course, Ramona knows diddly-fuck about my own covert-op counselling sessions – not the mother–son marriage guidance therapy, not the pre-bereavement bereavement sessions, not the general purpose emotions-are-as-valid-as-facts sessions. But the even bigger false advertising is she doesn't even know that I *need* counselling. I try and look away from Ramona's eyes but without looking like I'm looking away. Without looking like I'm gonna cry or someshit, but also without looking at the floor. I look at her smile-proof mouth – as if clamping roll-ups in place has worn her lips down thinner than blue-grade Rizla. Ramona stopped smoking just before our A levels. Never dramafied it or discussed it. Just quit. And I knew right then that she wouldn't have no trouble just quitting me on the spot.

"So what is this, Dillon?" Ramona asks. "To you. What is it to you?"

Even *I'm* sitting here waiting for my response when, for some reason, Naliah saves my ass from having to answer. "Look, maybe the real question here isn't why do you treat Ramona like a sack of shit. Maybe it's why do you put her on a pedestal, Dillon?"

I nod – I know where Naliah's coming from. Thing about being a masculinity asshole is you ain't gotta be some blatant dickhead. Ain't even gotta be one of them silent sense-of-entitlement guys who blames women on the quiet for all of his personal fuck-ups and failures. Truth is, many masculinity assholes reckon they adore women – that they worship the ground beneath their feet. I weigh up whether to tell this to Naliah – show her that I been thinking about this. Problem is, I'll probly just sound like I'm virtue signalling on social media or someshit. That happens to Dhilan a lot. Even though accusing someone of virtue signalling implies that you yourself are somehow above virtue signalling – which is basically virtue signalling, right?

Turns out Naliah's got her own angsts. "I hope you appreciate what it takes for me to speak the truth, Dillon. The things that a person risks. For instance, I've just risked my friendship with Ramona. I've probably risked being labelled an angry ethnic woman or something just to keep me in my place. And I'm risking a lot more besides. But when I heard how much Ramona's been suffering here, I really wanted to help her." And then to Ramona: "Sorry for talking about you in the third person."

Ramona shrugs her fingers.

"Okay," I step up. "So you wanna know why I put her on a pedestal? Or is it you wanna know why I put her feet on a pedestal?"

"We've finished talking about feet," goes Ramona.

"Maybe you simply have low self-esteem issues?" Naliah doesn't let me answer then takes my silence as a denial and an access-all-areas invite to guess again. "You have mother issues? No – a little too clichéd for you? Well then, how about your father?"

I wanna tell her that I don't know my father. That I ain't nothing like my father. That my father ain't some misogynist womaniser, he's a lonely, woman-losing loser. But before I can speak, Ramona cuts in. "Naliah, listen, I get what you're trying to do for me here. And I get why you have to be extra just to shake us out of our zone. And I appreciate it – you've been really good to me these past few days. But it isn't really your place to talk about me like this and it certainly isn't your place to talk about Dillon's hang-ups or Dillon's parents."

"But come on, Ramona, you don't know even know his parents. You said so yourself that you only just met his dad yesterday. Your so-called boyfriend has somehow managed to convince you that meeting his family doesn't equal natural progression."

I stand up and put on my jacket.

"What's the matter?" goes Naliah. "Can't face facing up to any more of this?"

"Stop fronting like you're trying to straighten me out when you're clearly scoping after something else. So how about you just tell me straight why you're so interested in my father?"

"Who said I was interested in your father? I'm just trying to help Ramona. Although she did happen to mention that the reason she couldn't meet me for lunch yesterday was because she went with you to meet him. In McDonald's. Apparently you didn't even know what he did for a living. Is that true, Dillon?" Then she looks at Ramona. "So now that we're on the subject, tell me, what's the deal with his dad?"

22

TOXICITY DEPENDS BOTH on dosage and the individual exposed to it. For instance, even water can be toxic if you drink too much. Mum's medicines ain't toxic enough if they don't make her sick. Scroll back to that time I somehow convinced myself that one quick fix to cut down my own toxicness was to find the one person in the worldwide world for whom my toxicity level was as low as possible. Check my relief back in my first year at uni when I realised that person was probly Ramona. And the whole epiphanation was all down to some random fool named Johnny.

Johnny fronted like he was in some unspecified contest with every guy on campus. Like as if somewhere along online, his mission to be some biggest swinging dick had gone full bareback and become a competition to be the biggest asshole. Kind of masculinity asshole I'd point to whenever some quick-fix counsellor or therapist suggested I try and "cultivate more male friendships". (Though don't be getting fooled by all them gentle-souled hipsters either.) (Trust me, they got their own schemes and ploys.) (Only reason they grow big beards is cos apparently the symmetry makes a guy's general genital areas look less repulsing.)

Johnny came up to me and introduced himself after seeing Ramona storm off in Starbucks one time. Didn't know jackshit about me or nothing, didn't even know if I was at LSE, King's or

UCL. Just a backslap outta nowhere and some big declaration that he was more toxic than me. Like as if the fool was on some kinda bragging trip. Wouldn't ease up, even – was like he really, really *needed* to hear what an asshole I'd just been to Ramona. As if he wanted to compare notes or someshit. I remember thinking maybe he pulled this same routine with other random anonymous strangers. I tried clicking away from our convo but he kept backslapping me, pulling at my arm and that. And so, fuck knows why, but I ended up telling him that the reason Ramona had stormed off was cos I'd been trying to pressure her into sleeping with me. Even though, truth is, I'd actually been doing the exact opposite. Truth is, I'd actually been telling Ramona that I weren't ready to take things to that level yet. She hadn't brought it up or nothing – I just wanted to get pre-emptive cos I was angstipating about that whole student sexpectation thing. But then things got proper messed up cos it turned out Ramona wasn't ready for it either but she thought I was trying to pressure her by not pressuring her.

Anycase, soon as I falsely fessed up to this random Johnny guy that she'd bounced cos I'd been pressuring her, he started telling me how he "handled" his own girlfriend. And let's just say he didn't use the term "girlfriend" – not even the "GF" bastardbreviation. Told me his "problem" was that his girlfriend had two completely clashing goals. On one hand, she wanted to hang onto her virtue and innocence until she found potential husband material. On other hand, she wanted to have the grown-up undergrad street cred that came with having a sleep-in-the-same-bed boyfriend. Johnny's fix for his girlfriend's dilemma? Said he'd convinced her to "preserve her virtuousness and good wholesome goodliness by *only* taking it up the butt".

The fuck do you even say to something like that?

Told him I was late for lectures.

He grabbed my arm again, started longing out his bullshit. "I also told her she could remain as pure as a snowflake by *only* sucking my cock." Next, he reached into his rucksack and pulled out a flyer for a "men's rights advocates" forum, a story about "female social justice warriors", a print-out of a blog post about women being locked into their "sexual market value". An article about single mothers on welfare.

This is when I finally fronted with some toxic masculine assertiveness and told him to fuck off. Not that I was in any position to judge his little anal-only racket or whatever – but maybe that was the whole point. That random Johnny bloke made me think I could maybe take some kinda easy-fix shortcut to being less of an asshole, less toxic – even nontoxic. Neutrality through a parity of hang-ups. Find the one person for whom your toxicity level was as low as possible.

Next time the whole sex convo came up with Ramona was after I'd moved into student halls. *Outcome:* I promised not to pop her cherry and she allowed me to lick her feet way beyond normal foreplay. That's been the basic deal between us ever since. Everyone's a winner – and butt-fucking don't even need to come into it because buttocks remind me of breasts.

Two nights later, Ramona was in my bed, washing my cum off her hands with a bottle of diluted bleach solution that she'd brought to my student halls especially. As for my saliva on her feet, she made do with one of them bumper packs of antibac wipes my mum had planted in my suitcase. Protein smell of cum and cleaning products filling the vacuum of post-non-coital awkwardness.

"Dillon," she threw me an antibac wipe. "I just wanted to say thank you."

By then I was sitting at my desk, firing up my laptop or fone or whatever while savouring the vinegar taste of her toe cleavage. "Thanks for what?"

"For respecting me. Thank you for respecting my chastity or whatever. Pretty sure most guys wouldn't be so patient."

I told her she was welcome. Told her it was a pleasure.

Ramona had wanted to crash in my student halls that night so that in the morning she could slip back into her dress and do a proper walk of shame back to her own halls. She'd checked when her friends were meeting at the front desk for brunch so that she could make some perfectly timed entrance. "Please, Dillon?" she'd asked. "It'll be so much better for me if they think I'm a slut rather than them thinking I'm frigid."

"Fine," I'd said. "But just so you know, if you dare try to have proper sex with me, then I'll tell everyone that we didn't."

When she was done with her bleach solution, Ramona put on a pair of pyjamas like as if to make me feel more comfortable. Not trackie bottoms and a T-shirt, we're talking an actual pair of pyjamas. Night socks to seal in her scent. (And in case you're wondering, it's completely wrong to assume a woman will have sweaty-tasting feet at the end of a long day.) (Turns out sometimes they still taste of feet – like the sweetness that stays between the toes of freshly washed feet.) (Other times, they taste of whatever lotions and creams she uses to keep the skin beneath her ankles smooth.) When she was done buttoning up more buttons than her pyjama top actually had, Ramona started throwing down some random convo.

"Dillon – since when the hell did you play cricket?"

I kept this random cricket bat strategically placed on top of my drawers to help create the general impression I could afford to fuck around playing poncey sports. Could see it from my pillow whenever I woke.

"You know, it's wrong to hide something like that from your girlfriend – that you're secretly into sports."

Couldn't figure out if she was trying to get all up in my business or if she was just feeling awkward or anxious, i.e. I didn't know whether to help her. If it's just anxiousness you can still safely tuck her up in bed. Tell her to be calm – help her with her meds, sedate her with a story. But if it's awkwardness, it's best to just go chill with your laptop or your fone.

I told Ramona that the cricket bat was just there for random acts of violence.

Next, she started flicking through the mags by my bedside. My teenage stash basically just student-discount copies of *The*

Economist. Nothing even remotely dodgy. Not even softcore or arty. Not even them lads' mags for guys too pussy to buy proper porn. Maybe a couple of women's shoe catalogues and my hardcore brochures for underfloor heating solutions. Ramona's groan of relief as she realised that I really wouldn't be trying to get my jimmy into her jenny.

Weird thing is, even though I was on some fone or tablet or laptop, Ramona didn't try to eavesread my screen. Didn't even move from my bed. I was reading a random blog post from a random month four or five years back – back when the blog I wrote from my mum's perspective first started contradicting whatever reassuringness she was saying to my face. Just reading it like some children's bedtime story that I wrote for myself. Weighing up whether to click open the ads and recommended articles, or whether to first wait for Ramona to fall asleep like how all those online-porn addict husbands do.

"So, Dillon, how come *you* didn't thank *me*?"

"Sorry?"

"Well, I seem to recall thanking you for respecting my chastity just now, but you didn't thank me for letting you lick my feet."

I powered off the fone or laptop and spun the fuck around. Ramona's mind on my pillow but my eyes to her feet. Like as if her body on my bed was just some idiot e-cig. Sugar-free chocolate. Decaf coffee. Non-alcoholic beer. Been trying to get some support by clicking on them foot-fetish web forums. Worst case, you just end up feeling validated. Best case, you sign in under some different name and upload different personal details – and then it doesn't validate or non-validate diddly nothing, it just makes you feel like your freakism is someone else's. Hated myself for clicking on all them other forums. Hated how the web always made me hate myself a little less.

"I mean, it's probably important or something, right?" Ramona pressed on. "Essential for our ch'i or something that we thank each other for respecting our respective boundaries."

So how the hell were you meant to wean yourself, then? Kick the feet, set yourself free? Apparently there was some kinda methadone programme for shrimping. You were supposed to gradually move from toes to earlobes. From ankles to armpits. From toe-clippings to clits. But, thing is, I couldn't figure out if you needed clean-cut transitions between each stage or if they could overlap a little.

"Okay then, Ramona," I told her. "Thank you for letting me lick your feet."

"You're very welcome," she said. "Maybe next time I'll even clean them especially before I come to your room. Wipe them with my love juices."

And after that, we couldn't stop laughing the whole night. And hugging – lots of non-toxic, non-penetrational hugging.

And that basically was our first time.

23

FINDING OUT WHERE he lives was a piece of piss. Buzzing his flat number, even easier. Like as if I already knew he wouldn't be in.

Technical term for this shit is "doorstepping". Probly saw it in some film about a journalist. Clark Kent for the *Daily Planet* in *Superman*. Peter Parker for the *Daily Bugle* in *Spider-Man*. Vicki Vale for the *Gotham Globe* in *Batman*. All of them scooped to the post by Lois Lane. When someone gets busted and won't talk to the press, go to their front door. When someone's crying and screaming cos their kid got stabbed and raped, go to their front door. Knock. Talk through the letter box. *Your side of the story, sir.* But you can't exactly doorstep your dad if he lives in some block of flats with a twenty-four-hour security desk. All you can do is doorstep the intercom.

Block looks more like some nursing home or private hospital. Awkward among the terraced houses. I wait for him in a phone booth across the street. Could be any old Zone Four suburb – same road signs, same coffee chains by the Tube station – but feels like I come to some different country. Like if I walk into one of the corner shops there'll be completely different brands of biscuits, tissues, painkillers. Allow that strangeness – even Mum once said it'd be good for me to reconnect with him. Exact word she'd used was "maybe". That one time she said it, she'd said "maybe it might be good for you".

Phone booth actually contains a payphone. Also a wife-beater brand of beer can, regulation cum-stained newspaper, entrails of old-school audio cassette tape. One side wallpapered with badly printed sex workers' pap. Photos too X-rated to describe, except for those that look like careers advisory leaflets. We're talking headmistresses instead of schoolgirls, doctors instead of nurses, policewomen and female soldiers. Rip em all down and find an ad for ChildLine behind them. Look once again at the payphone, pull out my mobile; consider texting Mama to ask for her permission. But, fuck it, she's already told me maybe this might be good for me.

This time I've wrote down a list of questions to ask him. In his living room or the hallway or the doorstep or the street.

Your side of the story, sir.

I'll even tidy my room and finish my greens, Daddy, if you just promise to just tell me the story.

Oh, and guess who else gave me permission to do this? Proper green-lit blessings. Like as if I been going round with some cap collecting consent. The botched-Botox man. No lie – dude told me to go ahead and meet my dad.

Pull out my fone and reread my questions. Kinda dickless to be hiding like this in some phone booth so let's just say I'm in here cos of the rain or the wind or, whatever, the darkness. Anycase, Botox man already knows I'm doing this so ain't no need to be on some subterfuge bullshit. Like I say, the man even gave me permission.

Right after today's lunch with Ramona and her brand-new best friend, I made a beeline back to the Botox man's office. Didn't bother knocking or nothing – just walked straight in and told him he'd sworn down that he'd leave Ramona outta this.

"That I did. And it appears I've even kept my word. After that morning when we visited you in her student halls, no one has ruffled a hair on Ramona's head. Or anywhere else. So, you see, I've even kept my word."

Told him to quit beating around the bullshit – that I knew he'd been in on the whole lunch-hour head-fuck. "You was the one who pushed me to go meet Ramona for lunch. And then her random new friend starts interrogationating me about my dad. Here's a pro tip, old man: next time you try and plant a spy as Ramona's mate, you might wanna make it a bit more covert-ops."

"You're suggesting your girlfriend's new girlfriend is some sort of femme fatale? Seriously, Dylan?" He sat on his desktop like as if he was trying to cover up some secret document/porn mag/X-Ray/CT scan. "A spy? As in a mole? A data-miner? An undercover honeypot, no less. Of course, of course – of course she's a spy."

"So you admitting it, then?"

"No, I'm ridiculing you, you fuckhead. Why would I need to spy on you when I already know everything about you?"

He made me explain all the fuckery that had gone down at the café – from Naliah's OTT foot-model routine to her Congressional Inquiry into my daddy issues. Tried telling me the whole thing was probly just some coincidence. Kinda shit that happens all the time. "For instance, only this morning, Dylan, I was thinking about buying a milkshake blender – doubtless triggered by a recipe or some other kind of story I read. Then a few hours later, up popped an ad for a milkshake blender with free next-day delivery. All I did was think about it and now tomorrow it'll be on my kitchen counter. So, you see, these kinds of coincidences happen all the time." Cutting me a look to make sure I'd clocked his ironicalness. "And then just think of all the coincidences that have to happen in movies and plays and novels. For instance, just to take a completely arbitrary example, think of all the coincidences in the story of Oedipus. That he should randomly encounter his real father at a crossroads. Of all the men to run into. Or that he should end up marrying his real mum. Of all the women to ruin."

Weren't no point telling him the coincidences only happened cos Oedipus was rolling in response to the oracle's predictions. We both already knew this.

That's all for today about Oedipus.

"So as for this Naliah-the-Foot-Model, if I were you, kiddo, I'd take her and her feet at face value. Most likely she was genuinely looking out for Ramona. Perhaps she's even trying to steal Ramona away from you. Or perhaps she's genuinely a foot model who just happened to find her way to the feet of a foot fetishist. Isn't exactly difficult to find out what turns a man on – what images his fingers click on or his eyes linger on. Half of you fools now wear fitness bracelets that betray the people and playthings that quicken your heart rate. As we've surely already established during our chats, Dylan, with enough digital data and the right algorithms, you can tell if someone's going to turn into a foot fetishist before they even know it themselves. Same if they're going to be gay, ungay or a bit of both. Same if they're going to fall sick. Same if they're going to go seek out their estranged father like the star of their own pointless soap opera." Upping his chin at the stool like he knew I needed to sit. All my pumped-up front now hiding behind my back.

Okay, so the man knew I met my dad. Guess either that girl Naliah had told him or he'd been watching me in the station himself. Standing on the concourse – face hidden behind some old-school newspaper like some parody of a spoof of a spy.

"Still, at least give me some credit for not obstructing your cosy little lunch date with Daddy. After all, clearly it would be better for us if you didn't meet that man. Be better for him, too. In fact, everyone would probably be a lot better off if you never met him again. And yet . . ." shooting me his most fakest, most badly Botoxed smile ". . . and yet apparently boys need a father – isn't that what all your aunties and uncles told your mother?"

"Okay, how the hell you know they told her that? Ain't like they said it in emails or texts or WhatsApps."

"Actually that one was just a lucky guess." And once again with his string of meditation beads – or abacus or single-function calculator or whatever. "Way I see it, you're a teenager, Dylan. You're at the age when you'd want to seek out your father regardless of any of this other bad business. It's imprinting. It's thousands of years of data bound up in men's collective DNA. In primordial societies, boys would reach a given age and start to go out hunting with their fathers. Spend every minute of every day together. The switch from being mummy's boy to daddy's daily hunting partner was a big fucking deal – even came with all kinds of traumatic initiation rituals designed to give meaning to the pains of growing up. To suffering and loss and heartbreak and tax return admin. That way, the young men wouldn't slip back into being perpetual adolescent mummy's boys who try at all costs to cushion themselves against discomfort and rejection and contrary opinions. Or who try to seek out other kinds of validation." He started scrolling through a bunch of For Examples – chatting about sports cars and strip bars and that. Gangs, terrorism, football hooligans, locker rooms, boardrooms, groping, arrogance, over-explaining. Said one reason that men keep getting twisted online is cos guys need more validation generally.

I asked him to tell me again the bit about over-explaining.

"And then along comes a digital economy that's practically designed to turbocharge these tendencies – to tell them what they want to hear, bolster their fragile egos, wrap them up in their own tailor-made cotton-wool kindergartens. So you see, Dylan, in light of all this, how could I possibly in good conscience stop you from seeing your father?" And then scrolling down to some next slide: "However, I would say this, kid: you've done okay without having a daddy in your life – all your teachers and tutors and heroes are in agreement with this. All the symbols and metaphors that have more than performed the paternal function. So try not to undermine things now by pining after some fuckhead father figure like some self-pitying, therapy-addict patsy."

"Okay, what the hell does that even mean? You want me to meet my dad in *theory* – for some random anthropology reason – but not in *practice*?"

"I mean scratch your itch but not your scab. I mean stop clicking on every single link. I mean meet the man if you must do, Dylan, but don't talk about things. About what's going on here.

Me, the digital archive – don't even mention that you work here. Don't give me cause to regret this."

"I ain't got a fucking clue what's going on here anyway and you know it."

"Well then, that'll make it easier for you not to talk about it."

"Look, why do you keep longing this shit out? Why can't you just cut to the season finale smackdown and just tell me why they blacked out my dad's stories?"

"Sure," he said, "why didn't you just ask me that in the first place? Your father's stories were redacted because we didn't want anyone to read them."

Even before the taxi pulls up, I already know my dad's the passenger. Knew it soon as I clocked the headlights appearing at the top of the road. Push open the door of the phone booth with elbow instead of hands to avoid snot/phlegm/jism, but then the payphone starts ringing – the jump of it making me shut the door instead of stepping outside.

Payphone stops ringing.

Again, I elbow open the door and, again, the phone rings. Shut the door and phone shuts up. Dad don't notice any of this shit – first he fumbled for his change, now he's fumbling with his keys. Now he's indoors, fumbling with his umbrella, talking to the woman who mans the twenty-four-hour security desk. Once again, I elbow open the phone booth. No gold stars for guessing what happens next. From inside the booth, I try scoping out the street to spot whoever it is who's fucking with me. Nearby parked cars, the windows of nearby houses. But it's dark and drizzling and dying and so on, so I can't make out diddly fuck. Then what I do next is, I start opening and closing the door on the quick – so quick that whoever's messing with me won't have time to keep hitting redial. Have to use my actual hands to do this instead of my elbow, but that's fine, whatever – I'll be sure to shake my daddy's hand when I'm done. Don't matter how fast I push the door open and pull it closed, though – ringing just carries on starting and stopping in sync with the hinge. This fuckery goes on for a couple more minutes before it even occurs to my dumb ass that maybe I should pick up the phone. But I don't. Because my dad's now standing outside his block of flats, watching my random display of dicklessness.

"So you came to see me then, Dylan."

Finally, I step out the phone booth. Ain't walking towards me, though, just standing and watching. Him lifting his umbrella a little, me losing my hood.

"Why were you fooling around with that payphone?"

I tell him the phone was fooling about with me. He looks up and down the road, says it's probly just kids, switches from holding his laptop case by the handle to sliding his arm through the strap. I do the same with my rucksack.

"So I take it they've spoken to you," he says instead of asks. "Well, let's hear it, then. Let's go for an evening stroll and talk about it. Let's see how many blocks we can make."

I tell him ain't nobody's spoken to me.

"No point playing dumb, Dylan. How else would you know where I live?" Damp streetlamps making his moustache look dunked in tar or someshit. "You should have phoned and told me you were coming to see me. We could have planned something. I could have kept myself free. To talk about it properly – to discuss what you've been told. I'm supposed to be going out for dinner in an hour, but we can walk for thirty minutes. We can get all the whining about being fatherless out of the way. All the struggling to survive your single-parent upbringing – that self-indulgent nonsense they picked up from the news. It's fine, Dylan – as a matter of fact, I'm glad that you came. Actually, why don't we just go inside and talk in my flat."

Before I left his office, the Botox man hit me up with one more sermon of advice. Said that all his talk about our "ancient tribal forebears" had reminded him of something I might find helpful.

"When you meet with your father, be mindful not to rely on reason or logic."

"Mate, I know I ain't got much experience, but I'm pretty sure that same shit could apply to all sons and dads."

"Just accept what I'm offering you here, Dylan. A few hundred years ago, I'd be giving you a fucking sword or a magic wand or something. I still feel remiss for not providing you with a single-function flashlight the other week. So let me at least give you data. Info. Information about information – I believe the technical term for that is metadata. When you meet with your father, your feelings of kinship and clanship will dramatically impair your ability to use reason or logic. This won't be because of heightened emotion or sentimentality, but because logic is basically a tribal tool, not a tool for establishing the truth of things. That just wasn't originally its primary purpose, kid. The human mind's ability to mentally reason was developed for a bygone age when the key to survival was to foster basic social collaboration – to convince people to go hunting together in packs. To keep each other on the same side. It was about the formation of clans rather than correct answers to empirical questions. And since then, the human mind simply hasn't had enough time to readapt. That's why people seem hardwired with all those crapfuck cognitive biases that we now consider to be mental design flaws. Defects that distort their decisions and make it harder for people to figure out what's true. That make them seek to corroborate what they already believe, to ignore or reject contrary facts. It's why a digital economy that places such a high value on clicks and shares rather than on the truth of the information being clicked on has proved such a clusterfuck. But it's also why family and kinship units are so vulnerable to fictions and untruths. It's why families seem stronger in less developed, less science-centric societies. It's why truth always seems to be the first casualty of divorce – the dissolution revealing all the fictions that glued the marriage together. It's why family units tend to shut out the wider world of threatening facts. And it's why your burgeoning father–son relationship will be particularly fraught. And I just think you should be armed with this data."

So like some try-hard who always sits in the front row of the classroom, I told him that maybe this was also why Oedipus got his ass in such a shitstorm – dude kept relying too heavily on these twisted tools of practical reasoning and logical deduction.

"Exacerbated by his reliance on incomplete information, Dylan. That's why the shitstorm hit the cyclonic fan."

That's all for today about Oedipus.

Fuck knows what triggered Mum to tell me "maybe it might" be good for me to link up with my dad. Coulda been some story she read on Facebook. Coulda been that time this dicktard in Physics lesson wired up my orthodontic braces to a nine-volt battery. Coulda been that first time I puked in sync with her – even though she didn't even know I was upstairs puking. Probly just thought I was just wanking or something. I laid down some decoy action, you see. You wouldn't believe how well online porn videos can camouflage the sound of retching. It's like it's the exact same sonic frequency or something.

Might just be cos of the weight of the rain, but Dad's coat looks longer. Ain't never met a man in a long coat before. All my schoolteachers wore anoraks.

Security guard assumes he still can't find his keys so she tries to buzz us in. But Dad stays standing at his own doorstep.

"We don't have to do this, Dylan."

"Then what will we do?" I ask him.

Then we enter.

24

FIFTH TIME YOUR mum told you she had the C-bomb, it sounded as if she was telling you something else. That she was scared. Over-the-counter sleeping pills and a lavender-scented candle. That it sucked. That the treatment was just another symptom and so on. There was a light above her dressing table that hadn't worked in years – though sometimes you could still hear it sizzle. That she was sorry. Confession, plea and apology all rolled into one. That you needed to learn how to drive.

You wiped away the bloody discharge. Told her it weren't her fault. That it happened because of your shaky hands.

Maybe she was always saying something else when she said it? *Announcing* something else – some official secret statement. A Declaration of Co-dependence.

When the discharge wouldn't stop discharging, you weighed up foning NHS Direct. Or the after-hours GP. Ambulance, even? Be six more years before you were old enough to drive. (Later you'd learn never to mention the future like that.) (The future brought up sad memories.) (Better still, don't even think about it.) (Nobody actually *needs* to go to university.) Who the hell puts 999 on speed-dial?

Decided to give it one more shot. Resterilise your hands. Brand-new gauze pads. Fresh pair of latex gloves. Started cleaning from the centre of the wound and then worked your way out to the suburbs. Standard procedure, standard.

"Dhilan, baby, what's wrong?" Her brave face just a data visualisation of pain levels. "Why the bloody hell are *you* crying?"

"Because I hurt you, Mama."

And that was the fifth time she told you it. Confession, plea and apology all rolled into one.

You told her it weren't her fault. Immunity issues and so on – weren't even her fault it'd got infected.

Truth is, you were glad for the change. To be changing a dressing on her leg for a change.

At first they thought the leg pain was septic arthritis cos of her compromised immune system. Or bone weakness from previous rounds of treatment. Or postural realignment problems. You couldn't decide if it was better or worse to not even know. Back when it was just minor level, just a scent-free biopsy lesion. Better to not even know the why of the wound.

After cleaning, don't rub dry – just gently, pat it, gently.

Avoid the sutures. (*Duh! Obviously, etc.*)

Check if drainage or discharge has become darker or thicker.

Couldn't never predict which part of the process would hurt her, though. You'd think it'd just be the antiseptic or the surgical tape. Or maybe you were just crap at doing this – same way some kids were just shit at Maths? Wasn't even any body hair anyway.

I'm sorry I hurt you, Mummy.

I'm so, so sleepy, I'm sorry.

Never got angryfied with you for hurting her, though. Or for any other carefulness fuck-ups. Not yet, at least, not then. For bruising her veins. For looking away. For changing the subject. For suggesting a sedative. For contaminating her pillbox with those candy love hearts. For offering all those reassurances that you didn't really believe yourself. For getting all mashed up inside every time you tried to be her rock. One of the district nurses had told you to call her if you ever had any problems and that. Didn't never fone her, though, because you always had problems. And because you'd have to tidy the house – clear away all the tissues and laundry and stuff. And because having an actual nurse in the house would make it seem like now your mummy was really, seriously, really sick. And because you *wanted* to do this. Didn't matter that government policies and cutbacks that were designed to attack sick people basically forced kids into doing district nursing work. If she'd got stung by a bee or burnt her finger on a milk pan, you'd want to make her better, standard. Size of the wound shouldn't make no difference. Love and compassion and so on, not duty or obligation or some audit-style give-and-take vibe (though you thought of all the splinters she'd removed from your fingers). (Her magnesium sulphate magic trick.) (Weren't as if she'd got traumatised by changing your nappies.) And so, soon as you got stuck with the whole "young carer" label, you tried to show your mum that being a young carer weren't a bad thing. Even put it on your CV even though primary school kids didn't even need CVs. Even lobbied your school to hold a first-aid course so you could boss it and get a certificate. Even advance-schooled your technique by scoping out videos on YouTube. Anyway, who the hell else was gonna help her unzip her evening dresses and take off her necklace? Deffo wouldn't want some district nurse doing it for you. You just needed . . . You didn't know what you needed.

"Dhilan," she whimpered when you were done with the new dressing. "Sweetheart? You remember when you first started going to school and I'd come and pick you up at lunchtimes?"

You just needed steadier hands.

Or stronger hands.

Sometimes you told yourself that it wasn't *her*, it was just her body you couldn't be near. Then you told yourself it wasn't her body – that you weren't some masculinity asshole who couldn't stomach her body – it was just *her*.

"I'd bring you home to give you proper Indian food – instead of the school dinners with the beef and the overboiled vegetables. Saved you from all those moody dinner ladies. You remember?"

She took your non-response as a sign you were struggling to access the memory.

"It was just for your first year at primary school. I'd bring you home for Indian food."

You remembered the safe-disposal protocol for binning old dressings.

"What I didn't realise was that all your friends gobbled up quickly and then went out to play. I thought they just went to the dining hall and had to sit there for a whole hour being shouted at by the dinner ladies. Dhilan, I didn't realise the school lunchtime was also a playtime."

Fuck the protocol. You chucked the old dressings in a torn Tesco carrier bag. None of that double-bagging bollocks – not for your own mummy.

"And then when I found out, I got upset with myself for dragging you back home every lunchtime. Because I didn't want to be that sort of mother, Dhilan. I *want* you to have friends. Even girlfriends – lots of girlfriends. You could be in the playground or in Gunnersbury Park. I never wanted to be that sort of mother. I don't *want* for it to be like this."

And then the crying came. Proper hurricane hitting a burst water main. On top of the Niagara Falls.

Young Carer's Playbook #272: Could switch your brain off for all the practical tasks – even the sterilised scissor tasks – but when it came to being a shoulder to cry on, you gotta keep your head.

To begin with, she'd just cry on the downstairs landline. Carry on crying as you got ready for bed. Take five to kiss you goodnight and then, when she thought you were sleeping, she'd phone the other person back and start up again with her crying. Saying all kinda things in between her sobs – and sometimes the things she said were actual words. You figured maybe she was talking to one of her work colleagues or some loosely defined aunty. Something about being sorry for whatever she'd done to deserve all this. But after three or four months of that same bedtime routine, you started getting proper curious. *Who the hell is she always howling to and why the hell don't they just come to the house?* Didn't exactly need to be James Bond to creep into her bedroom one night and listen in on the upstairs landline. Waited for her next round of coughing and then just, careful like, lifted the receiver. The person on the other end was silent while your mummy finished coughing – like they were holding the phone away from their ear. Stayed silent while she cried. Stayed silent while she told them how sorry she was. Carried on staying silent until it finally hit you: *maybe there weren't no one on the other end of the line?*

Took your chickenshit ass another month to bring it up. To tell her it was okay for her to cry in front of you. That you *wanted* her to.

Talk about opening the floodgates.

Her panic and fearfulness.

Her loneliness.

"Dhilan, you must believe me. I don't want for it to be like this. I never *wanted* it to be like this."

You wiped away her eye saliva.

Hush now, Mummy, don't you cry, etc.

Make her calm. Make her watch some television.

Curfew her mobile fone use.

Suggest some random budget wellness break for when she'd beaten it.

Standard procedure, standard.

Your mummy was right the first time, though. Truth was, you just wanted to hit the playground in Gunnersbury Park. You were up for all the practical tasks and the drainages and the discharge, but when it came to all this crying shit, you just wanted to go Gunnersbury Park.

25

STRETCH MARKS ON the armchair he's slumped in.

"So, what do you want – money?"

"What?"

"Do you need some money, Dylan? Will that do?"

Now that he's lost the raincoat, his shoulders look broader. His neck proper solidness without the poncey yellow scarf. I tell Dad I don't need no money, thanks – thanks all the same, though. Thanks.

"My chequebook's just in the kitchen. I keep it hidden inside an old milk carton."

I tell him again I don't need his money. Just like we didn't need it when I was at school. He rolls with this like it's some fist-bump instead of a punch.

"I could do an online bank transfer right now."

"Why do you keep making out as if I want money?"

"Well, you've come to see me."

Switch to scoping out his flat. The scent of pizza and printer ink. Telling him there's so much light and space, like I'm some bubblefart Foxton's estate agent. Cos what the hell else am I meant to say? That I like his pet ants? Way each of them seems to divide into two as they exit the light switch. Or that his walls are more maroon than shit-brown? That who needs wardrobes anyway? Or do I tell him I reckon it's really right-on and enviro-friendly the way he reuses envelopes and newspapers as coasters and placemats and table covers and even as actual tables? That the skid-marked bath towel makes a surprisingly versatile substitute for a Persian rug?

"Well at least sit down then, Dylan."

The fuck has it taken me twelve whole years since the divorce to figure out the man didn't just lose a home, he lost an actual house?

"Son, please sit."

A three-bedroom semi, now with accessible downstairs bathroom and planning permission in place for some crazy optimism loft conversion.

Dad's moustache starts moving up and down. Asking me if I'd like some almonds or someshit. When I don't respond, the moustache tries again: "Cashews?"

"I just wanted to talk."

"I think I have some pistachios somewhere . . ."

I tell him I been allergic to nuts since I was born – that apparently he'd had to take me to A&E once. Then, when I finally step up and tell him I've come here to ask about his journalism, he thinks I'm trying to tap him for work experience. "I see – so a back scratch instead of cash?" The moustache now doing actual Pilates – not just stretching to smile at me, but taking it to some next level, like he's smiling at the fact that he's smiling at me. I shut that shit down with a quickness, tell him that if I needed an internship I'd score my own placement.

He fiddles with one of the improv coasters on his improv coffee table. The table's just another stack of newspapers. The coaster basically this plastic Save-File icon. "Your mother used to be impressed with my profession. But never genuinely interested in it. Then I'd try so hard to interest her that in the end she stopped being impressed."

I tell him I didn't come here to talk about Mama.

"You know, your mother never—"

Tell him again: I didn't come here to talk about Mama.

"Yes. Yes, apparently you came here to talk about my journalism."

Before I can bring up his blacked-out stories, Dad just starts throwing stuff out there, proper rapid-fire – like as if he's trying to demo that my asthma ain't hereditary. Telling me all about the news service he runs as part of that insurance company's website. How much web traffic it brings to their home page cos news spreads faster than policy premium smallprint. How he basically rewrites stories from news agencies, plus a handful of longer, in-depth stories of his own. "So just a low-key operation, Dylan. Actually, as far as the branding goes, it doesn't have the most original name for an online news service. We just call it *Latest Headlines*." He scratches the armrest like as if it's got a rash. "Though sometimes I wonder whether we shouldn't just call it *Latest Deadlines* . . ."

I shoot him some semi-smiley emoji – tell him how all the journalists I see in films are always on some mad dash deadline. Should probly have sirens attached to their keyboards or something.

"It's got nothing to do with being on the clock," goes Dad. "It's because we accentuate the death tolls, of course – otherwise what would be the point in having a news service on a life insurance website?" Nodding with his moustache instead of hs neck. "Now I know what you must be wondering, son: but what if nobody dies in the story that I'm writing? Well, even if there's no actual death toll, you can always speculate that people could have died or they might die – or maybe that they're in the process of dying." Then he throws down a For Example: "Your university must be having a student newspaper, Dylan. Well, any story they publish about any aspect of campus could easily be massaged a little in order to add one or two paragraphs about the number of students who commit suicide each year because of exam pressure – even if it's just a story about something boring and non-lethal like library funding. You just stick in a sentence that says libraries also provide sanctuary for students who otherwise would get anxious studying alone in their bedrooms – followed by all the suicide statistics. And then, like that, the boring library-funding story becomes a death-risk story. In my job I've found that there's always a death-toll angle or a death-related tangent – doesn't matter what the story is."

I'm all like "erm" and "um" and shit – fat-fingering my response again. Finally, it comes out like this: "So you basically saying you *are* an insurance salesman after all?"

Neither Dad nor his moustache gives a ruffle. "I'm sorry, son, but I think you must be having a very naive impression of the dishonest mainstream news media. Even when I worked for the newspaper, the editors there would get squeamish if there wasn't enough death in a story. Because all news stories are about selling something, Dylan, only usually it's about selling the news. If a local council opens a new school, the local media outlets can't just report on the school, they have to find the one person on the planet who happens to be unhappy about the school so that they can report on a row. The conflict and the division. And if there isn't a row, they'll find a row about the lack of a row. Well, tell me, son, how is that different from me highlighting the potential death tolls from a new school because of the increased road traffic? My stories have to sell life insurance; their stories have to sell the news – the point is neither of us is really telling the reader all that much about the actual school." He hits his pause button for a few secs, but his moustache carries on going without him, like as if it's revving up for the next bit. "And it's the same damn thing when the news media tries to be balanced and neutral. They think that being balanced makes them objective. Tell me, how the hell is it objective to balance out a story by airing the views of hate preachers and far right neo-Nazis? Or by giving space to climate-change deniers spouting falsehoods sponsored by oil companies?"

Dad starts telling me how being balanced and telling the truth are full-on different things. Says balanced stories are contradictory – that you just end up telling two contradictory facts. Says balance should just be some last resort for when you can't actually find out the actual truth. Carries on chatting about the "dishonest mainstream news media" while chucking actual newspapers onto his improv coffee table – so basically it's like he's just building a bigger coffee table. "And of course these days they have to sell the stories even harder." Thud. "Everything's now on the same screen so people assume every piece of content is equally important, equally credible." Thud. "It's like having to sell broccoli to kids inside one big giant sweet shop." As he starts shit-fitting about all these tooth-decayed kids, Dad starts jabbing a paper in my direction. Won't even let me cut in with my own side of the story. Starts going on about clickbait and that – like as if he knows that's exactly the topic I wanna click on. "And, sure, people may *say* that they want calm and factual, good-quality journalism. But believe me, the web-traffic data suggests there's a big difference between what people say they want and what they actually click on, son."

I try jumping in – show my daddy that I know someshit. Tell him the reason that crap content and proper stories all look the same is cos fone screens are small so you gotta simplify the design of everything.

Dad actually laughs at me. Says the tech giants have made fortunes by blurring the lines between advertising and journalism and promotions so that it all just becomes "content". Says that, compared to all them blurred lines, him using news stories to openly sell life insurance is pretty harmless.

I grab my rucksack like as if I'm gonna bail. Like as if I don't wanna know where he's going with all this. Tell him again that his flat has so much light and space.

"Wait, Dylan, listen to me," he says. "Why can't you people be patient enough to listen when a man needs to properly explain something? I'm trying to tell you that not every media outlet or journalist acts admirably when they're compelled to compete life and limb for people's increasingly dwindling attention. Much less when they're forced to compete for their own son's affection."

After that we both just sit there in silence like one of them mis-married couples who shoulda got divorced while they still had functioning sex organs or something. Cos what the hell are you meant to say to something like that? Only thing I know for cert is that there ain't no bailing now – for me or for my dad. He fones his friend or colleague or story contact or whoever to tell them that he's sorry, but he's gotta work late in the office. "I'm sorry. What can I say? I'm always working late. You all go ahead, though – the reservation is under my name, Nick Deckardas."

Soon as Dad hangs up, he clocks my fuckstruck face. "What, Dylan? So I lied about working late in the office. It's hardly a crime, son."

I ask him why he said his name is "Nick".

"Because I changed it when I started this job. My colleagues couldn't pronounce Ramnik. I tried using the name Ram for a while, but they thought I was talking about RAM data storage."

I tell him it stands for random-access memory. I tell him I prefer the name Ram to Nick. I don't tell him that Ram is also my secret pet name for Ramona even though Ramona doesn't do pet names.

"Of course you prefer Ram to Nick," he goes. "Ram is an Indian name. And your mother's family never thought I was Indian enough."

I tell him I didn't mean Ram in the Indian sense. I meant it as in the male animal thing.

Dad just grunts and heads to the bathroom or toilet or men's room or whatever – and let's just say it ain't exactly soundproof. That time Mummy told me about his bowel issues. Felt like she was actually dissing me – or at least dissing half my DNA.

"There's some beer in the fridge, son."

I take the hint and take my ass and my rucksack to the paper and cardboard recycling plant he calls the kitchen.

"Do you want it in a glass, Dad, or is the bottle fine?"

"Let's not have a conversation while I'm in the bathroom, son."

If I was going for the full Kleenex-and-violin effect, I'd tell him I've chatted to Mum in the bathroom on the regular. Her holding the flush handle, me holding her hand.

"The glasses are in the cupboards along the top," he calls out. "Not the cabinets along the bottom – the cupboards along the top."

So of course I start opening the cabinets along the bottom – just for the fuck of it, like I need to rack up some acts of teenage disobedience. Check out all his top-secret frying pans and saucepans while my dad is on the shit-pot. Also, crockery, Tupperware, obligatory unopened rice cooker. But, wait – what the fuck? – also his socks, boxers, pyjamas, woolly jumpers. In another kitchen cabinet, his vests and T-shirts. In another, his shoes, flip-flops, bedroom slippers. In another, books, more newspapers, more books. One big fuck-off book in particular – some black, leather-bound beast of a book lying right at the back like some well-fed rodent. On the cover, the word "Cuttings". Inside it, scrapbook pages rammed with newspaper clippings that have literally been cut-and-pasted. Yup, I shit you not: each clipping is a story written by my dad during the year he worked at the paper. Only this time, ain't none of them are blacked out with marker pen. Soon as Dad flushes the toilet, there's some tremor action in the tower-block of dishes in his kitchen sink. Like as if his crockery is warning me not to.

Dad don't ask why the hell we're drinking beer outta teacups. He just says, "Cheers." And then: "Son, I'm sorry it's taken us so long to have a beer together." And this happy moment right here is where tonight's episode should end. Dad's gesture of fatherly fatherliness and whatever. His stories weighing down in my rucksack like some cliffhanger in a doggy bag. Shouldn't even take time to down my beer, what with it being in a teacup and all. But turns out that Dad's got other plans. He pours another cupful then hits me up once again with the question: "Do you want money, Dylan?"

"Dad, didn't we just do all this already?"

"Yes. And you said you wanted to talk about journalism. Well, now we've talked about it." He nods towards the old milk carton.

"You don't need to keep telling me where you hide your chequebook. If I needed some bucks, I'd earn them myself – I got my own business."

"What business? You're a student."

So then, mainly to just change the channel, I give Dad the download on my start-up. *The Dumbfuck's Guide to Data Entry.* A day in the life of a data temp. (Also: how tons of students have now got their own business on their CV.) (How your actual degree is just the footnote.) (How I set the thing up so that I could chip in when Mum's sickness made her too sick to work two different jobs.)

"So does this business of yours have a name?"

"I just call it Company A."

"Eh?"

"That's just what they call companies in our Business Studies module. As in, Company A merges with Company B and together they appease the regulator by spinning-off Company C."

Dad asks how come I didn't mention my start-up when we linked up yesterday. I tell him he didn't ask – didn't even ask what subject my degree is in. Then he starts sipping his teacup of beer like it's actually tea – sweet, milky tea. And, fuck knows why, but the sight of him doing this makes me tell him that I got a confession. And, next thing, I'm vomiting it all out to him like some sickly child who chunders just to get hugs and cuddles. Tell him about the digital archive I been helping to compile for my start-up's latest client. Tell him I know he worked for the same newspaper for a year – back when I was a baby or a foetus or, whatever, a semen. And I tell him about how his stories ain't allowed to be entered into the online archive. But I don't tell him about my run-in with the managing editor who tried to suss out if I was related to him. And I deffo don't shoot my mouth about the two Botox men.

When Dad lowers the cup from his face, I have one of them freaky facial-recognition moments. The man's wearing the exact same look that our GP did when she knew straight away for sure what was wrong with Mum without having to hedge shit or refer her to a specialist. Her stethoscope underlining an actual smile on her face – not cos it was good news, but cos at least this time she knew exactly what to tell us.

"Dylan, you make it sound as if there's some big mystery going on with my stories. The reality of the matter was more straightforward. Cost-cutting. Profit-maximising. More content to churn out and less time for each story. The more they cut the headcount and increased the workload, the more the rest of us had to obey the basic laws of physics and cut corners."

I tell him I no longer follow him.

"Well, obviously I made things up, son. Not the actual stories, you understand, just the quotes. Of course, not the quotes from government or corporate officials, just the eyewitness quotes from random members of the public, who I also made up – Joe Bloggs from Buckinghamshire or whoever happened to be visiting the brand-new shopping mall or stuck in the traffic jam or walking past the fire or what have you." He hits me with another For Instance: "*Peter Smith, an accountant from London, was cycling past the arson-damaged school on his way to work: 'Flames were coming out of the windows like wings,' he said.* That sort of thing, Dylan. I mean, you have to appreciate what happens when stories become sausage meat for these giant digital content machines. I mean, it's not as if—"

"Wait, Dad – just press pause for one sec. Just tell me straight up, yes or no, are you actually saying you wrote fake news stories? You actually made shit up?"

"Not the stories, Dylan, just the eyewitness quotes. Just the ones from Joe Bloggs from Buckinghamshire or whoever from wherever. It wasn't fake news – fake news is when you deliberately present falsehood as fact. This was just about cutting corners to keep up with the workload. It wasn't fake stories, it was just fake quotes. And fake names." My eyes hit the deck. "Everybody did it in some form, Dylan. Either they just rewrote press releases or they didn't properly verify things or they just made things up. Same difference. But I got caught, and because I was the newbie in the newsroom I was made an example of. Although nobody except the editor and managing editor even knew just how many quotes I'd actually faked – everyone thought I got fired for doing it just the once. A one-off occurrence by a one-off rogue reporter. That's how the paper managed to own up while at the same time hushing the whole thing up. And I suppose that's also why they blacked-out all my stories."

I try not to topple Dad's leaning tower of rotting Domino's pizza boxes as I once again lift up my rucksack.

"It wasn't a big deal, Dylan. It wasn't fake news stories, it was just fake names. Fake quotes. It was merely misinformation not disinformation. The motive wasn't malicious."

After they first got divorced, I used to reckon it must be pretty cool that Dad could order a pizza whenever he wanted – that he could tip the delivery man whatever he wanted.

"In any case, most fake news stories don't even contain things like quotes or names, just as they don't contain numbers or statistics. Makes it harder for people to verify the facts. So, you see, if I'd been involved in writing fake stories, I wouldn't have included any quotes at all."

His tower of pizza boxes is low-rise compared with the floor-to-light-switch stack of newspapers. We're talking call the structural engineers.

"Come on, Dylan, this whole stinking century started with a bullshit news story. You ever heard of the Y2K bomb? Not many journalists checking the facts on that one. It was just too good a story."

Instead of just owning the fact that he's clearly full of fake news and bullshit, Dad keeps switching back to dissing the "dishonest mainstream news media". I mean, how fucking childish is that?

Stare again at all his newspaper stacks and it's like some video glitch in my head – all them mental video clips I'd put down to Mum's side effects start making a little more sense. That time she got upset that I'd started watching Channel 4 News. That time she'd caught me spending my birthday bucks on *The Economist*. Her full-on meltdown when she found out I'd been saving my copies of *The Economist* – stashing them under my bed like a stockpile of painkilling porn.

"But I thought you'd been putting all these out with the recycling, Dhilan . . .?

" . . . I'm not saying don't use them for your coursework, darling, but these days you can get everything on the internet . . .

" . . . All these piles of them here – they're a health hazard . . .

" . . . Stop being such a smart alec, Dhilan – a fire hazard is a health hazard."

And then starting up with her howling and weeping and howling and screaming and howling and banging her head against my bedroom wall.

The sight of Dad's stacks makes me wanna tell him the exact same thing: that these days he can read any story he needs online – on all them digital archives.

The sight of Dad's stacks makes me wanna pull out my own fone right here and now and dial my mum. Tell her that maybe my own stacks were just genetic – like birds got genes for building nests and spiders got genes for building webs. Ain't no more significant than my hairy knuckles. That I ain't nothing like my dad.

26

SO WHY THE fuck would anyone do this? I mean even anyone in their *wrong* mind. It's like the scene in the horror film where the characters think, *Oh look, there's a creepy, derelict house in the middle of the forest – I know, let's go inside.*

I've got my office security pass. Ramona's got her student card pinned to what I think might be her bra strap. Cos a student ID card ain't just some ticket to cheaper cinema tickets: if you use that shit correct, it's a VIP, access-all-areas-cos-I'm-only-on-work-experience pass.

What's that you said? The switches in this creepy, derelict house are busted? No sweat – the windows will let in the light from the full moon outside.

The late-night security guard spends more time checking out *my* pass. Holds it up to a light that catches her blingy shoulder epaulettes. Kind of light that says, *Go to bed now; go to sleep*. Bag-checks my coffee cup as well as my rucksack.

Guys, check out this red splodge of modern art they've painted directly onto the floorboards. Neat. And that spillage of strawberry syrup. Awesome. Come on, let's go upstairs – it'll be fun.

Security guard writes down both our names. Claims it's some fire-regulation shit in case the office burns down while we're inside it. Says goodnight as she lets us through.

Inside, most of the night staff are now stuck on power-saving mode. Just feeding the website with stories from America. They do that up in the newsroom, though – the IT department should be dead.

In the stairwell, a wall-mounted security camera swivels. Ain't ever noticed they swivelled before. That settles it, then: we're dropping the lift plan and taking the stairs.

"So this is what a white-collar working environment looks like," goes Ramona. "I should take a photo for posterity. Put on my CV that I once set foot in one."

She holds open the door to the IT department and starts scoping around for a light switch. I tell her the lighting is motion-detector; she starts busting out kung-fu moves.

"Fuck's sake."

"You wouldn't complain if I was twerking."

Turns out the lighting is on some kinda double-lock type shit: we have to play Hunt the Light Switch in order to activate the motion sensors. Shoulda just brought my brand-new single-function flashlight. Ever been to a wedding when something goes wrong with the lighting or the mic or whatever and so someone yells, "Technical hitch!" and then everyone else starts LOLing? Why the fuck is that funny?

While we try and fix our lighting issues, I realise I been rolling out the wrong horror movie cliché for what we doing here tonight. This ain't like entering some creepy derelict house. When people in them films voluntarily walk into the creepy house/ attic/basement, they're flexing shit like choice and judgement – stupid dumbfuckulous idiot judgement, but still choice and judgement. Whereas me, I ain't choosing to do this. Wouldn't be such a fool. What's going down in this office tonight is closer to the more modern-day horror movie cliché – the one where the person's hand is forced by a technical hitch. Lost in a forest full of werewolves? Damn, no network coverage. Stuck in a haunted mansion? Fuck, no signal. No battery. No data allowance. All those handheld hotlines to the cops or your mummy or Google turned into uselessness slabs of plastic. But whereas in the horror films people are forced into doing things cos their tech has been disabled, I'm being forced into this thing here tonight cos the technology *enables* it. Compels it. It's like that unwritten law for every illegal file-sharer: if you're able to do it so easy, then surely you must be allowed to?

You'd be dumb not to.

You *have* to.

All the same, I deploy the whole belt-and-braces approach.

Just in case.

Belt: Ramona stands by the doors to the department so she can warn me if someone heads this way.
Braces: I clip a mirror to my laptop screen in case someone approaches from the other direction.

Belt: Plug in my laptop at some desk I ain't never been known to use before – i.e. one of the ones by the coffee-dispensing conversation machines.
Braces: I log in as someone else – this other freelance data-enterer who always annoys the shit outta everyone by reading out loud as he types up the corrections to craply scanned stories. Doesn't do this cos he's some thickshit who can't read without moving his lips, though – he does it cos he reckons the scanning errors are *just fucking hilarious.* Helpfully, the dipshit also mumbles what he's typing when he enters his username and password.

Belt: I disable the automatic email notifications that get sent to the Project Manager whenever a new story is created.
Braces: Just in case this don't work, I already created a batch of brand-new stories earlier on – during normal office hours.

Belt: These stories that I created from scratch ain't just blank – otherwise someone else on the team might've noticed they were blank and hit delete.
Braces: Instead of just filling these stories with gobbledegook, I filled them with text from a bunch of random other stories that are already on the online archive – i.e. it looks like they just been duplicated by mistake.
Staple-gunning the trousers to the waist: I gave these duplicate stories the exact same filenames as the originals. Technically that shit shouldn't be possible, but the system lets you do it if you just replace all the full stops in the original filenames with italic full stops in the duplicates. Apparently there's a night editor on this paper who's famous for being able to spot an italic full stop at fifty paces. That's how I got me the idea.

As a result of all this prep, what I do next is as piss-easy as it is inevitable. Remove my dad's cuttings book from my rucksack, open it up at the first page.

Because you're able to.

You'd be dumb not to.

You have to.

The book is proper heavy. Leather-bound. A latch, but no lock. I open it up at the first page.

Leather on the cover is old and frayded.

I open the book.

Ain't no markings on the cover – no gold-leaf initials or branding or nothing. I open it up at the first page and start typing his stories directly into the digital archive.

But as a favour to both him and my client, I make sure to leave out all the stuff Dad told me he'd faked – i.e. all his made-up names of eyewitnesses and all their bullshit made-up quotes.

Another belt: Don't include my dad's byline. This means his stories look like the ones you see in *The Economist* – where they don't tell you the name of whoever it was who wrote the story so you just assume they was all written by some big-dog uber-being called *The Economist.*

Another pair of braces: Don't fix up any of Dad's stories with character-recognition software or metadata – i.e. they don't contain any keywords – i.e. they won't come up in any search results – i.e. they probly won't even be read by anyone ever again in the history of ever.

But now that they been digitised, at least they'll still exist.

And another belt: Because Ramona's standing over by the door, she doesn't know what I'm actually doing. Reckons I'm just downloading and printing out stuff for free to help me with my dissertation.

And another pair of braces: Even though Ramona ain't clued in on what's really going down here, I made her swear to keep tonight's doings on the hush. Told her don't even mention it to her friend Naliah the foot model – i.e. ain't no way word will get back to the Botox men.

Even without including Dad's fake content, typing up and digitising a whole year's worth of press cuttings ain't exactly a cakewalk – even for some turbo-typist like yours truly. Even though I'm using one of them detachable ergonomic keyboards. Even though I pre-rubbed my fingers with Nurofen ibuprofen gel to stop them cramping with the speed. Even though I already read, reread and practically memorised all his stories at least fuckty-two times before we came here.

The stories themselves fall into three general categories: boring, less boring and weird-but-boring.

The boring stories are mostly about commuter misery and struggle and suffering.

The less boring stories are mostly about transport accidents that disrupted people's commutes, strike threats that might disrupt people's commutes, plus various civil disturbances, campaigns, marches and demos that disrupted traffic, public transport and other forms of commutes.

The weird-but-boring stories are about one of them campaigns in particular. I ain't wanting to make a big deal outta them just cos they weird. After all, some stories always gonna be weirder than others – that's just the way shit goes. And, anycase, only about seven or eight of Dad's stories actually fall into the category I'm calling weird. All of them are about this crackpot who was campaigning to force the government to change every single internet domain name. My dad had reported on the whole campaign – from the initial petition to some final fancy-dress protest. Could probly paste some of the newspaper clippings right here to give you a picture. Or I could include some web links. But who the hell's got that kinda time? According to my dad's stories, the crackpot's problem was basically this: turns out that in ancient Hebrew there ain't no numerical signs – instead, numbers are repped by letters. And apparently the letter "w" – as in "www" – represents the number six. Given that, back then, everyone and every organisation was falling the fuck over each other to stick the letters www in front of their names, this crackpot was freaking out cos he thought that the biblical warning made famous by various assorted Hollywood horror films was finally kicking off – the one about everyone bearing the three-digit number of the beast. So obviously when I read these stories, I was like, duh, maybe this might possibly be of some significance? Maybe I should start getting scared or cold or anxious – or at least grow a few goose-pimples outta respect. But, way I saw it, the guy was just another of them whining cranks who reckons the whole internet is some big, bad force of evilness. For starters, his campaign only got about as far as second base – Dad's stories about it stop after the guy gets arrested for climbing up some random town hall wearing a pair of red tights, plastic horns and carrying a pitchfork. Secondly, according to Dad's stories, various linguists and theologists were having bust-ups over whether www actually meant the number of the beast anyway – some of them reckoned www simply meant six *multiplied* by three. If you punch that into the calculator on your fone, you'll find it works out as eighteen. Thirdly, turns out that the protestor was locked in some longed-out battle with a cyber-squatter who was sitting on the www domain name that the protestor wanted for his own internet start-up – a company that just happened to be in the business of selling, yep, internet domain names. Dad's cuttings book also contains another bunch of weird stories about red herrings. For real, though, he literally wrote stories about these red-tinted herrings that they found in the Thames.

So I'm uploading the last of Dad's stories onto the digital archive and truthfulness I can't wait to be done with them. Not just cos of their boringness or pointlessness. Not just cos I wanna get a move on for security reasons. And not cos Ramona is now getting antsy and starting to rush me something serious. It's cos *I'm* getting antsy. Don't even send a goodnight text to my mum. After I'm done with Dad's stories, I re-rub my hands with Nurofen gel, then actually do what I'd told Ramona I came here to do: I download and print out about 200 pages of dissertation research using the client's printers and paper and staplers and basically anything that could be defined as Misuse of Corporate Property. Make sure to sign in as myself for all this in order to leave a decoy digital footprint. After all, who's gonna suspect me of doing something I shouldn't be doing if I get caught doing something else I shouldn't be doing? Something pretty bad but not technically criminal. Something that'll inject this whole 1am mission with a dose of alternative truthfulness. *Young Carer's Playbook #456: When engaging in necessary subterfuge, always make sure your bullshit can blend with the truth to form an alternate truth in case you get busted.* And in the same pulsating vein, it's now time for my belt-and-braces coup de slam-dunk. You see, when I said Ramona had pinned her student ID pass to what I think is her left bra strap, what I forgot to mention was there weren't hardly anything else on her torso for her to pin it to. When I'd run this part of the plan by her, she took some serious arm-twisting. Asked me if there was something properly wrong with me. And then, all sudden-like, she said she was up for it. Even suggested she'd wear fishnets – but we figured they might not let us in if they thought she was a hooker.

Removing the belt: First we make out in the stairwell and then in a meeting room named after the newspaper's founder.
Removing the braces: We don't bother with the bathroom cos ain't no security cameras in there.
Removing the bra straps: And maybe cos we on camera, I steer clear of both her footwear and the feet inside them.
Removing her high-hip, lace-trim briefs: And cos I steer clear of her feet, we're basically miming actual, standard-issue, non-dysfunctional sex. I think the technical term for it is dry-humping. Next thing, shit gets real. As in proper. I mean, it ain't like I can just use my fingers cos my hands are still covered in Nurofen gel.

It happens in the kitchenette rather than the stairwell. Ramona reflected in the rows of microwave ovens. Saying the words "Don't stop, Dillon" like she's asking a question.

As we exit the office, we can tell we been busted from the look on the faces of the ground-floor security desk. None of them saying nothing – I guess cos it would involve talking about sex.

While we're in kitchenette doing whatever it is we're doing, I keep replaying those three words in my head: *"Don't stop, Dillon."* And eventually I end up hearing a full stop between the words "don't" and "stop". And so of course, what I do is I stop. Both of us still pumping some horror film adrenalin rush as I buckle up my rucksack and stuff.

No one's calling the cops on us, though. The late-night security desk will just hand a report to the day desk like a scribbled-down note of some hazy 3am dream. Maybe throw in some security camera footage so they ain't gotta actually write the word "sex".

Next, I try and think of things I could maybe do for her – make her feel more comfortable. But it's hard to make someone feel comfortable in some scuzzy kitchenette. Dirty coffee mugs and the stink of expired milk cartons. Skirting boards lined with plastic boxes of rat poison.

We say goodnight to the security desk and carry on walking out the exit. Tomorrow they'll literally report my ass to HR. Then they'll probly bust me for misconduct and kick my butt off the online archive project. But fuck it. My work here is done.

I step towards one of the vending machines and ask Ramona if she'd like anything. Even open the fridge – some big fuck-off chocolate cake with icing that says "Good Luck in Your New Job".

"Dillon, did we just? For a minute or so just now. *Did we just have actual sex*?"

I tell her there are lots of different definitions of sex.

"Okay, well you have fun talking about all those definitions because I'm going to talk about what actually happened."

"I think that, as a couple, we definitely just took a major step towards being less sexually defunctional."

"Oh wow, if only you'd sold it to me that way two years ago, I'd have dropped my knickers in a heartbeat."

We leave the kitchenette and head towards the lifts.

"I can't believe that we finally did it," she says. "Shit. And I can't believe I was dressed like this. Wearing this stupid dress."

"What would you want to be wearing? I mean, for our first time."

"Well, I didn't exactly have a specific outfit picked out, Dillon." She presses the lift button. "Though I guess some people do – some people even buy special lingerie for it. But that doesn't make me feel better."

"I've got a pair of lucky boxer shorts," I tell her. "And I guess, if I'd known, yeh, I'd have probly worn them tonight or something."

"Oh for fuck's sake, Dillon. You're not getting this at all, are you? I don't care what dress or underwear or footwear I wear, just so long as I wasn't dressed like *this*. I mean, I thought we'd just be play-acting and so I dressed the part. For laughs, Dillon. Like how dressing for Halloween parties suddenly became all about dressing slutty. But how do you think it makes me feel to know that the first time we finally did it, I had to dress up like some fucking slut?"

27

NALIAH WANTS TO link up. Keeps trying to get word to me, telling me it's code-red critical. Carpet-bombs my timelines and time-bombs all my messaging apps. Every comms channel possible except the obvious option of contacting me via Ramona.

When and where's good for me?

I'm Ramona's friend, remember we met

Hits me up with half-finished DMs, one-line emails, quarter-sentence texts. Even handwrites half a Post-it note and leaves it for me at my student halls.

Hopes she didn't offend me

How am I?

Each message like some afterthought to her next message or a pre-thought to her previous one.

Sorry we got off on the wrong foot

Rapid-fire think-clicks and random emojis. Like as if she knows there ain't no point trying to straighten out my thoughts.
She'd like to set a meet

i.e. she's doing that thing where you hit the Send button instead of the full stop. That's how the apps are structured and therefore how they structure us. Paying proper close attention to this kinda stuff cos if my start-up's gonna expand on its own two feet I gotta diversify away from corporate clients, start tapping consumer markets.

Is this the right address/profile/handle/fone number for me?

So how the hell does Naliah access me even though I blocked her, blanked her, rejected all her Friend requests? Simple as pissing in a barrel of fish: she comes through as Nayeesha, Nadina and Nadia. Maybe even Naliah ain't even her real name – best-case scenario it's a true fake username. All her assorted online personas easy enough to ignore, though. Shit only got real when she started tracking down all of me – @Dylan, @Dhilan and so on. Can't risk her telling Ramona about all of me so now ain't no choice but to respond.

@DHILAN: WHAT DO you want?

@DYLAN: THE FUCK do you want?

@DILLON: WHAT?

We agree to talk face-to-face. Coffee's just another word for outside your fone. She suggests Starbucks in Holborn, I switch it to McDonald's. If we gotta suck down corporate American crap then might as well be honest about it and go hit McDonald's.

But first, the big hairy butt-kicking.

One random benefit of hot-desking: ain't no need to clear out your desk when you get booted out. Before my client finally fired me, I got a tag-team bollocking from the Online Archive Project Manager and the Head of HR. Then the Managing Editor hauled my ass in to tell me what a "crushingly disgusting" disappointment I been. My post-surgical porn, she'd been fine with. Me blogging as a pre-surgical online alter ego for my mum, she'd made allowances about. But me having real-life actual sex was "filthy, lewd and unforgivable". The security footage of Ramona and me playing on their desktop monitor – like some random teenager's standard daydream.

Didn't bother telling them that, actually, it was the most respectful sex I ever had with her cos I didn't waste her time worshipping her feet.

Didn't bother telling them that if their security cameras had an audio feed, they'd have basically heard her back up their own interpretations.

Didn't bother telling them anything at all.

But after my contract was formally terminated into shreds and I'd handed over both my office and offsite security passes, I asked them why the Acting Head of IT hadn't tagged himself in for their joint-action smackdown?

They told me he was on some urgent emergency crisis meeting.

As I head to my link-up with Naliah, it daybreaks on me that, actually, *I'm* the one with a shit-ton of questions for *her*. And now I been forced into a meet, ain't got no choice but to ask them.

"What time do you call this, Dillon?" Those words soon as I step inside – hitting even before the smell of French fries and sugary bread-buns. One thing about McDonald's: I can't never smell the actual meat.

"Sorry. I got held up getting fired."

The botched-Botox man kicks out a plastic chair for me. It's bolted to the floor but he kicks it out anyway. Back of his neck sweating like a stump of shawarma.

Like a dumbass I tell him I was meant to be meeting someone else here. He turns in his seat to scope out the other tables. Only person sitting solo is a woman who looks like she been sponsored by Louis Vuitton. He ups his chin in her direction.

"Yeh, like as if you don't already know what Naliah looks like."

Now a text from Naliah telling me she's running late – *so sorry,* etc. Now an ad for Louis Vuitton. A story about fake products. An article about fake stories. Botox man jacks my fone out my hand like he gonna ghostwrite my reply. Instead he powers off and surgically removes the battery – we're talking screwdrivers and forceps and scalpels. Doesn't need to explain that all fones are tracking devices. I hand over my Dhilan and Dylan handsets.

"I hate the plastic prosthetics too, Dillon." Screwdriver slips and scratches one of my touchscreens. "So, this girl you're meant to be meeting here – you're still sticking to the outside possibility she's being less than truthful with you?"

I tell him the outside possibility is the one where she *is* telling me the truth.

He grunts and carries on gutting my fones. Even knocks out the camera lens and the tiny inbuilt flashlight. "There we go. Lights, camera, deactivation. Now we can talk. Like we used to talk." Veins across his temples like some spam alert for his smile.

And once again with all my angstipating about whether or not I should be angstipating – that old familiar time-wasting timesaver. Checklists, flow charts, *if this then that.* Critical or just life-threatening? Urgent or emergency? *How may I direct your call?*

Basically, am I busted?

Does he know I uploaded Dad's stories onto the digital archive? No matter how carefully I encryptionated my footprints. No matter that my decoy felony was so convincible it got me fired for sexual misconduct. No matter that I fixed up Dad's stories without any keywords, metadata or character-recognition software so they won't never show up in any search – i.e. ain't no one, not even Google, should ever even know they there. Outside the window, a pigeon pecks at the corpse of a Big Mac. Beak dripping with that dirtypink Big Mac sauce.

The Botox man pockets my handsets and slides me something across the table. From the shape of his hand, I figure the object beneath it is either my fone batteries or those tubs of Maccy D's ketchup. Turns out it's a triple-pack of jimmy-hats – ribbed for extra pleasure. "It was noted from the security footage that you didn't appear to use one." He raises his cup of coffee. "Here's to you getting yourself thrown off the archive project in more salacious style than even *I* could have orchestrated." When he burps bourbon, I realise he's drunk.

After he's done with all the back-slapping and big-ups and congrats, he asks me what I intend to do now.

"Now that I've had proper penetrative intercourse?"

"Now that your little adventure at the newspaper is over. What will you do, Dillon? Pitch for a new temping gig? Or just be a student – a *single-function* student? Or maybe you'll just spend more time by your mother's hospital bedside or graveside or memorial website or a post-mastectomy porn site?" Clicks his fingers. "Why not just ask Google what you should do next?"

"Okay, first, why the hell would I wanna do that? Secondly, you just confiscated all my fones."

"*What shall I do next?*" – he drops this question like it's an answer. "As you know from your student start-up forums, the holy grail of search engineering is to be able to answer the question *What shall I do next?* Not merely what should I purchase or click or watch or read or think or visit or study or eat or date or fuck next – *what shall I do next?* The destination that's driving the engine. Though for many data-gatherers, the best thing about predicting people's behaviour is that it becomes easier to manipulate them."

I ask him if this is gonna be another one of them chats where he gives me some fucking Media Studies lecture instead of just saying what he's trying to say.

"Your own personalised, data-crunched destiny, Dillon. Delivered straight to your cellphone."

"Dude, how much commission they paying you to keep dropping all these taglines?"

"Fine – if you'd rather not ask Google what to do next, then by all means ask someone else. In fact, why not ask your father?"

I figure he's just phishing so I say nothing. On his tray, there's enough fast food to feed a whole family. You know – of three. Bit by bit, he's been sticking half of it in front of me. Not like he did with the jimmy-hats, though. More stealth-style, like he hopes I ain't noticed.

"The hell would I ask my father for? Man hardly even knows me."

"You'd be surprised how helpful ignorance can be in some situations, Dillon. The more information a person has about a given topic, the less likely they are to take into account information that challenges what they already believe. They'll just select the information that suits them. Even more so if all the information looks equally credible because it all sits on the same platform. Advertisers have known this for decades: the more options a consumer is presented with, the more open they are to persuasion and manipulation. Whereas the less information they have, the more they'll exercise their critical thinking muscles. Also, there's more of a mystery, kiddo. Mystery begets curiosity. And curiosity happens to be the one thing that makes people more open to information that doesn't reinforce their own opinions. This is because curiosity involves a very different kind of motivation. So, you see, your father's ignorance might make you more open to reaching better conclusions – provided you don't rely too heavily on logic and reasoning, of course."

Even with his white stubble, I still can't mentally Photoshop what the Botox man would look like if he went full beard. Stubble is normally the template of a beard, but ain't so with this guy. He's one of them men with a face that just won't be bearded.

"Plus, let's not forget that boys rebel against their fathers a lot more wholeheartedly than any kid ever rebelled against technology."

Botox man carries on longing out his point the way he does while I try to picture him fully bearded. Ain't gonna lie, I reckon

I'd like him to be rocking a beard – like Gandalf or Dumbledore or Obi-Wan Kenobi. That's the kind of dipshit gimp I can be.

Seems like he's basically saying that our smartfones ain't simply replaced other sources of info and authority, they've replaced the positive impact of parents' dumbassery. "Which is to say, if your father should ever tell you that he doesn't know the answer to a question, Dillon, then know that his ignorance is probably good for you. The four words *'I don't know, son'* are words that you should cherish."

"Fuck's sake. All this brainful red-pilling and you just trying to throw me off the trail again."

"I'm just saying that the mystery will be much better for you than answers."

"Why do you keep doing this? Always warning me off the garden path, but being so obvious and extra about it that you're basically also encouraging me?"

"It isn't complicated, Dillon. I want you to search but I don't want you to search. You of all people should be used to that kind of conflict. Plus, of course, I'm just trying to cover my own ass."

I remember something I read one time: for all them brainful debates about whether or not Oedipus is trapped by some kinda predestinated fate fuckery, the one freedom he clearly flexes is the freedom to search for the truth.

That's all for today about Oedipus.

"You deliberately got fired, didn't you, Dillon?"

"The fuck would I do that for? The newspaper's my most high-margin client."

"Because you no longer need to be there. Because somehow you've managed to obtain your father's scrapbook of his old news stories – the one he claimed he never kept. Now, either your dad doesn't know that you took his cuttings book or he gave it to you out of some sort of inverted parental pride. Either way, you have his stories now. I'm assuming you've stashed it away in your student halls?"

He pushes a bag of French fries towards me. I slide him a tub of barbecue sauce.

"My dad don't know that I took it."

Turns out the Botox man thinks I just been reading the scrapbook. Like as if I just took it to semi-skim Dad's stories. Has diddly-zero clue that I've uploaded the stories stealth-style onto the digital archive. Even though it makes fuck all sense that I could be one step ahead of him like this.

"Dillon, I'm inviting you to stop dicking around. Haven't I been a friend to you? I've helped you out on several occasions. In fact, we're now way past little helpful gestures – now I'm fully trying to protect you." He pulls out his fone to show me he's removed his own battery as well.

"Okay, so you gone rogue. Good for you. Least that explains why you ditched the other guy, then – the guy who looked like a younger version of you. Where's he at these days anyway?"

He drops a snort that blends mashup-style with the sound of him unzipping his pockets. Turns out one of my fone batteries is the same type as the Botox man's. He makes some big-budget HBO drama of switching them. "Think of this swap as something akin to a blood oath, Dillon. And as for that other man – the man who looks like I used to look – well, whenever I'm in the newspaper's office being the Acting Head of IT, he sits in my actual office being the acting me. Though this afternoon he's running one of those mission-critical errands. Not too far from here, in fact."

He slides me a semi-skimmed milkshake.

I fumble about trying to find a straw.

"Just scrape out the froth with your tongue, kid. It'll be good practice for you." When he winks, it's like all the botched Botox disappears for a sec. Then he gets up with a quickness that makes me flinch.

I watch the Botox man exit while Naliah keeps me in check, telling me how sorry she is for showing up late. Carry on watching him through the window while she talks about Tube delays. Just standing in the middle of the pavement winking at us. Making actual wanking gestures in the general direction of Naliah's foot-model feet. Pumps instead of plimsolls today – heels, not flats, though you can't really tell cos they're wedges. When the Botox man is done making wanking gestures, he pulls out his fone and either reads or sends a message. Drops his handset onto the pavement and starts stomping it to shitness. Then he turns left towards High Holborn instead of right towards the client's office.

"You ate all this food yourself?" Naliah asks. "Now I feel like my lateness has been bad for your health."

I tell her that I'm sorry but I have to leave – I gotta go student halls. Now. I tell her I gotta go there now. I don't even bother to bin the remains of the lunch.

By foot, my dorms are five minutes away. Ten minutes tops by bus. I run a different route so as not to run into either of the Botox men – finding me some shortcut I didn't never even know existed. Film-set back-alleys and restaurant dumpsters. Junkies, rapists and serial killers, probly – I don't exactly stop to ask them. But when I get to my floor I can tell straight away that the lock on my door has already been jimmied. The smell as I open the door coming from dog shit that's been smeared into my carpet. Mess of papers, essays, bank statements. My copies of *The Economist*. First, I check for my laptop. All present and accounted for. My external hard drives, they all there too. My mother's letters still in the fireproof box, tucked in beneath the slowly siphoned fotos, home videos, unwashed headscarves and stolen wigs. *How the hell do you misplace a prosthetic breast?* My chequebooks, my debit cards, my cash – everything worth jacking is still where it should be. So now I ain't got no choice but to check for Dad's cuttings book.

28

SOON AS NALIAH steps into my room, she pukes. Vomit on my carpet, vomit on my laptop. Weird to watch someone so healthyful puke. Puddle of puke by her foot-model feet. Splash-back dripping down from the lips of her ankles. The lips sheltering the space beneath her ankles. Next, vomiting out her apologies.

Young Carer's Playbook #514: Never ask a puking woman if she's okay.

Young Carer's Playbook #515: Never tell a puking woman that it's okay.

I ask Naliah how the hell she got here so quick.

"You didn't hear me shouting out your name? I was running right behind you. Why do you think I'm so out of breath?"

I tell her I thought she was just breathless cos she'd vomited. But this ain't even true – I didn't think that at all. If anything, for a moment, I was hoping it was the other way round: that she was vomiting *because* she was breathless. Or cos she had a tummy bug. Or food poisoning. Or morning sickness. Anything except the stink of dog shit in my room. Or I think that's what I thought. Anycase, the smell of it – it makes it difficult to think. Her vomit adding to it. I mean to the memories of it.

Later, what Naliah'll want to know is this: why ain't I told Ramona about my mother?

She'll say that when she brought up the subject, Ramona was like as if my mum just had a bout of food poisoning. Followed by a bad chest infection. Followed by a broken hip. Even a medium-term timeframe can make all that shit seem unrelated.

"But don't worry," Naliah will add, "I did you the courtesy of not correcting her. At least for now."

Then I'll ask her: "And what the fuck do *you* know about my mother?"

"Come on, Dillon, I've read your social media posts," she'll go. "I mean your @Dhilan and @Dylan posts. You tweet about looking after her in hospital and then you tweet about the passing of her death anniversary. And then you tweet about her as if she's just fine and dandy."

Then she'll ask me why I didn't just pick completely different names? Why three different spellings of Dillon?

But all this'll be said later on. After we're done with the vomit incident.

Naliah starts dropping paper napkins on her puddle of puke. "I know students are supposed to live in pigsties, but how the hell are you living like this?"

"The fuck? This ain't *my* mess."

"The place is a little too poky for you to blame it on a roommate."

Then she looks at me like I'm captain fucking dumbfuck for not getting she was joking. Then she apologises for joking – says she was just trying to cover up her shame over vomiting. Then she apologises again for vomiting.

Later, what Naliah'll want to know is this: do I really love Ramona for real or am I just dicking her around?

And I'll tell her: "Depends how you define dicking around."

Also depends how you define hot and cold.

On and off.

Ask a set of strobe lights and they'll tell you that on and off is actually on.

"Because if you aren't really into her," Naliah'll say, "then why can't you just let her move on?"

Cos I'm addicted to the smell of her thoughts.

Cos without Ramona, I'll feel like I'm trapped in someone else's body.

Cos I wanna fess up – swear down I wanna tell Ramona the truth. Just don't wanna tell her about my lies.

Cos I didn't actually mean for her to live in an alternate version of reality that I bullshitted to existence.

"Say something, Dillon – I mean, what are you? Fourteen?" she'll ask. "You know why Ramona's so keen for you reconnect with your dad? She thinks it'll help you finally man up for her. Damn it, Dylan, stop being such a sadist."

I'll consider telling Naliah that I ain't sadistic, I'm exploitative. But that shit ain't the truth.

"And what the hell is with that whole platonic online harem of yours? Are those girls even real or are they your ivaginary friends?"

I could tell her I'm just keeping my rebound options open for when Ramona wises up and dumps me. Or I could tell her that to eight-time Ramona is to nine-time my mother and so I'm aiming for double figures. Or I could tell her the truth – tell her how young I was when I first went online to find me some solid bereavement rehearsal buddies.

She'll suggest that I start this whole process of manning the fuck up by coming clean about my mother. "In fact, that's the other thing I wanted to ask you. Why on earth haven't you told Ramona about your mother?"

But all this'll be said later on. After we're done with the vomit incident.

I hand Naliah a bottle of mineral water and tell her to stop worrying herself sick about vomiting. Even if she's just puking cos she can't hack some dirty-ass stench. Try and make her feel better about it by pointing out that, actually, puking is probly a healthier response to the shit that someone's smeared into my carpet – that maybe she just has a 2.0 nose. "You see, technically, Naliah, the scent of the shit actually consists of shit. Tiny particles of shit drifting into your nostrils and your mouth."

Then she vomits again.

After that, I'm back on my hands and knees. Cleaning up vomit and shit. The Dettol and the bleach solution. The sponge, the bucket, the paper towels. All the tools and apparatus magically appearing in my bathroom as if the burglar deliberately left me a token of my misspent youth.

"Let me help you," Naliah says.

I tell her I'm okay.

"Well, at least let me mop my own vomit."

"I'm okay. I got it under control."

Pro tip: take the edge off the stench by lighting a match. Take the edge off the visual by leaving the lamps switched off. Just the light from the corridor outside my still-open door. The green backlit fire-exit sign. Glow from the traffic lights behind my always-drawn curtains.

"Shouldn't you call the police, Dylan? Or your student hall security? Shouldn't they see this?"

I'm okay.

"Dhilan?"

"I'm okay."

Naliah now crouching down to help out. I keep shooing her away. *Fuck off, Naliah, I've got this.* And now I even got latex gloves on. From where the fuck did I get latex gloves?

"You just mix it in like this, you see, Naliah? Then you squish it. Easy."

"What?"

"You see that, don't you?"

"Dillon, perhaps we should open a window? Maybe you shouldn't be inhaling so much bleach and Dettol?"

"It's okay. I've got it. The right kinda sponge can soak the right kinda shit right up."

Again Naliah trying to help. Again me shooing her away. The stink of it. I try shooing away the stink of it.

"Why won't you let me help you, Dillon? After all, it's my vomit."

"It's mine."

"What?"

"It's my job. My room, my job. And this is what I do."

It's true – this *is*. This is what I fucking do. While the others are sitting in art-house cinemas or keeping it real by watching YouTube.

Naliah ain't no longer waiting for my permission. Just walks over to the window to force it open. Can't even open the curtains, though.

Or while they listening to some latest hip-hop tunes to convince themselves they got the faintest, foggiest, fucking clue.

Then she goes to my en-suite bathroom to look for another bucket. Er, why the hell would I have two buckets, Naliah? Why the fuck do I even have one?

And while they taking tennis and dancing lessons. Dissing some sunset on TripAdvisor.

This is what I do.

Young Carer's Playbook #516: Carry the bucket to the bathroom and empty it into the toilet. Minimise splashback in the eyes by kneeling and, gently, tipping gently.

"Dylan, please, let me help."

"No sweat, Naliah – this is what I do."

"Oh no – look at your shirt, Dylan. Quick – which of these towels can we use?"

"No. No bath towels. Ain't no good using bath towels. Always sponges and paper towels. Loo roll if you have to, but it tends to shred."

"I'm so sorry about all this. It'll teach me to have such a big, decadent breakfast – tell you the truth, I think most of it was profiteroles." Grab her arm to stop her wiping her puked-up profiteroles off my shirt. The warmth of a vomit-tinged handgrip. The stickiness of dirtied bleach. So, next, I'm wiping my dirty scumbag paw prints off her arm. "What's that noise?" she asks, clearly shit-scared of the answer. "Dylan, what the hell's that noise?"

The cocktail of vomit, shit and bleach solution flushed down – I swear, it definitely did flush down. Of course the usual remnant spatterings around bowl and rim, but the body of it flushed down. The plumbing now making a sound like it's weeping. Snivelling and retching and snivelling. And weeping. And snivelling. And weeping – turns out even my toilet weeps while it pukes.

"Dylan, what's going on?"

Naliah now stops offering assistance. Each time the toilet backs up, she backs up a few paces herself. Freaking out not just cos of the smell, the mess, the smell, but also cos the cocktail now consists of full-on different colours. Her puke was beige, the bleach was blue, the shit was, well – you know. But the puke the toilet starts throwing up is some next shade of pink. Maroon. A kind of reddish purple.

Or while they're complaining about some book they just read. Quibbling about the rap lyrics. Whining about the obstructed view.

Naliah now backing away into the bedroom and towards the window.

This is what I do.

No – now backing away from the window and towards my open doorway. Trying to make it out into the corridor. Next, it's as if the doorway starts retching and heaving and retching – Naliah hurled back into the bathroom like she's gonna smack me. Instead, she leans over the basin and begins another bout of vomiting. And finally – once a-fucking-gain – I find myself kneeling and vomiting in sync.

Afterwards Dhilan and Naliah don't talk about it.

Trust me, you never do.

Even more hush-hush than all that post-non-penetrative awkwardness.

Despite all the supplies in his en-suite student bathroom, Dhilan's all out of air freshener. Ends up unloading a whole spray can of Lynx. Two cans. Even sprays his bedsheets as if he's trying to get inside her night socks. Chucks the emptied spray cans in his bathroom bin. Along with the empty bleach bottle and another bottle of spent Dettol.

Naliah asks him if he knows what the burglars even stole. He lies and tells her a laptop. Then she follows him to the window. Chaos of essays and invoices beneath the window. He starts sorting through the mess, separating the essays from the invoices from the bank statements. Notices the way the bleach solution has started to fade the carpet. Just like he knew it would.

Naliah asks if I'll at least let her pay for the carpet cleaning – by which I'm guessing she means professional carpet cleaning.

I tell her that you can't clean a bleach stain. Not even with a pack of never-used ladies' hair dye.

"Well then, let me pay whatever you get fined for the damage."

I tell her I don't need any money.

"It's not a problem, Dillon – I make a decent enough amount."

"From foot modelling?"

"Yes, of course – what else from?"

"You don't need to bullshit me no more, Naliah. We've puked together. We're *connected*."

"I'm not bullshitting – I can afford to pay for the cleaning. Okay, I'm not saying the money's great – just like any other body-part model, we foot models don't get royalties and repeat fees every time an ad is shown. But, on the upside, because we're pretty much unrecognisable there are no conflicts of interest or divided loyalty issues when it comes to working for competing brands."

"Here's a handy tip for lying: don't overdo the prep. It shows. Trust me, I know this stuff."

"You want me to take off my shoes and prove it to you? Only, do you think we could first clean up the rest of the mess?"

I tell her I got a better idea – how about she tells me why she wanted to meet me today.

"Because there are a couple of things I can't ask you in front of Ramona. Well, technically three things."

Later, the third and final thing Naliah'll want to know is this: why the Dillon and Dylan and Dhilan?

"They're just online identities," I'll tell her. "Ain't no big deal."

"Okay," she'll go.

"Why is it okay?"

"Because they're just online identities."

"But you already know that they're more than that."

"And you already know that I know."

"All you know is they roughly correspond to different states of my mother's well-being."

Naliah will shrug and start getting ready to bounce.

"My dad wanted it spelt D-Y-L-A-N," I'll blurt before she goes. "But my mum wanted it spelt D-H-I-L-A-N. They used to have big bust-ups about it. Apparently there were five drafts of my birth certificate – turns out they become void if you cross shit out."

"Or if you delete them with big black marker pen."

And you'll go: "What the fuck did you just say?"

She'll point to a patch of unbleached carpet: "There's a copy of your birth certificate lying among all your bank statements and stuff. Couldn't help noticing that you've blacked out your name with marker pen and spelt it D-I-L-L-O-N."

"Ah yes," you'll go. "That's the way I been spelling it ever since I was ten or eleven." Then you'll let out what'll probly sound like a laugh. "I told Ramona all the teachers before secondary school had been spelling it wrong. That's why she's never bothered following anyone called Dhilan on social media."

Naliah's sharp. She'll know it weren't no laugh. She'll press her fingers against her forehead and then drag them down to protect her nostrils from the odour of bleach and disinfectant. And the truth. "Fuck," she'll say. "Fuck, fuck, I get it now, Dillon. All the lying and lying and lying you must have done over the years to keep that up – she'll forgive you for the big lie but never for all the little ones. No wonder you can't ever tell her about your mum."

29

SIXTH TIME YOUR mum told you she had the C-bomb you ran away. Fled the scene of the crying. Not to go AWOL or nothing. Not to blow off steam, or vape, or vandalise a payphone or whatever the fuck it was that moody teenagers were meant to do. You hopped a bus to some nearest Waitrose. Some slap-up gourmet superfood – plus profiteroles in place of her traditional after-news-of-new-tumour cherry and raspberry mousse. That was your way of rebellionating – of sticking it to the system: stealth-stocking your mummy's fridge with healthy food. Coulda gone Tesco but you wanted a proper three-arm candelabra. Goblets and napkin rings. Also flowers, bath salts, lavender oil, scented candles, bag of floating rose petals. Google had told you it was up to her partner to properly pamper her. Reassure her that she weren't no less of a woman.

First time she mentioned the side effects, she warned you she'd have her good days and her bad days. Didn't never say nothing about the good minutes and bad minutes. The woman minutes and man minutes. Hated yourself for even thinking about her womaninity, but *she* was the one who called those pills her "man tablets". Technical term for it was anti-oestrogens.

Your mummy limped down the stairs and was like, what's all the commotion? Took her a whole minute to clock the dining table. Then hiding her eyes behind her camerafone. Sometimes you told yourself to just call these things practice runs in case you ever got married or something. Couldn't just stick with kitchen table stir-frys and blended breakfasts in bed. Increasing resistance so increase the dosage. Just enough to make her smile, but not too much, not to set off all her weirdness facial stuff. Like as if she was peeping into some future in which both of you somehow stayed together.

Then she started cold-staring the chocolate profiteroles.

Oh gimpdick – what the fuckery was you thinking, serving dessert same time as the food?

You were thinking: chocolate was the thing she missed the most whenever the chemo shot her taste buds to shitness. All them times you'd got her to eat some breakfast by lacing her Coco-Pops with Nesquik chocolate milkshake powder. How the milkshake stopped her from sealing her lips shut. If every decision or dilemma could be boiled down to a trade-off between making her happier or healthier, then chocolate was the appetite booster that did both. Other times just basic blender action. You like a boy-shaped fruit fly, liquidising her food before she chewed it. (Later, making sure there weren't no air bubbles in the liquid.) (Pulling back the plunger on the nasal feeding tube to check for gastric juice.) (Trying not to push down the plunger too quickly or too slowly.) (Your hands always shaking to shitness.)

Cos fuck all them side effects. Those anti-sickness tablets that listed *nausea* as a side effect. You knew better than to even read the side effects in the Origami Olympics *Before-You-Take-This-Medicine* leaflets. Anycase, Google clued you in on all the need-to-knows. Told you the reason for the anti-oestrogens was cos most breast cancers needed oestrogen like babies need milk. Cut off the oestrogen and you cut down the tumour's food supply. Younger women make oestrogen in their ovaries, whereas older women make oestrogen by file-converting the male hormones in their muscles, fat cells, liver and whatever breast tissue the C-bomb hasn't bombed yet. The conversion involves a chemical called aromatase. But they couldn't just give your mummy meds to block her aromatase cos she was still producing oestrogen in her ovaries. Cos she hadn't hit her menopause yet. Cos she was way too young to be fucking dying.

"Dhilan, the profiteroles . . ."

Couldn't tell if the vibes on her voice were sandstorm or sherbet or old-school TV static.

". . . they look so yummy. Chocolate is the thing I miss most whenever my taste buds go."

"Well, just as well I foned you from Waitrose, Mum." And you realised that, actualtruth, it was *your* voice, not hers, that had all the hostile vibes on it.

Back in Waitrose, you'd spotted some woman in navy-blue pump-style shoes with plunging white-trim top-lines. *She* wouldn't go ballistic over some minor-level feeding-regime fail. The brunette in beige suede ankle boots – she'd just laugh if your DIY shelving unit collapsed. If you used too many pans to boil the pasta.

"But you didn't need to phone me from Waitrose, Dhilan – you could have just surprised me. This whole dinner is so beautiful."

The redhead in peep-toe slingbacks: she'd just shrug at your sick-note postal oversight. Or if you fucked up that hospital minicab booking.

"Well, I did *want* to surprise you, Mum." *She weren't even angryfied with you so why the fuck were you escalating?* "That's why I went to Waitrose instead of Tesco."

The blonde-haired goth: she wouldn't keep waving the minicab card while shouting the words "One little thing" – meaning she'd only asked you to do that one little thing. You like some dickless limpdick telling your mum that, in your defence, she'd only asked you to do that one thing once. Wishing you could drive her to chemo yourself. But to do so you'd somehow need to turn seventeen and then pass your driving test in the next fourteen minutes.

"But then why didn't you just surprise me with the profiteroles, darling? Why to be so scared of these things? Why waste a phone call from Waitrose to ask me if I wanted profiteroles or cheesecake?"

Tearing up the minicab card before tearing off her wig and her work clothes. Smacking her still-bald-from-the-last-C-bomb head. Straightening the crotch of her tights as she slipped on her peach summer dress.

"I foned you from Waitrose because of what happened last time – with the ice cream."

"But I never complained about the ice cream, Dhilan, I just didn't eat it. It was strawberry flavour, sweetheart – I was in a bad way that day and, I don't know, I just didn't like the smell of it."

"Well then, that means that I was right to be scared about whether to buy profiteroles or cheesecake – because the only cheesecake Waitrose had left was *strawberry* cheesecake."

"Please, Dhilan, why are we arguing about this? Anyway, if they only had strawberry cheesecake then in that case why couldn't you just make the decision to buy profiteroles instead of cheesecake without phoning me?"

Then driving off to the Department of Nuclear Medicine by herself even though she was too thermo-nuclear angryfied to even walk straight. Even though they'd nuke away any strength she had left to drive back again. Even though she was still with pin-and-plated hip and partially removed pecs. And before you could tell her it'd be dangerful for her to drive back afterwards, she guessed it and told you it'd be even more dangerous to leave her tumour untreated. And before you could tell her to take the bus or the Tube, she guessed it and told you that public transport was even less reliable than you. Tyres weeping, eyes screeching – didn't even look at you standing like some dickless pussy in the disabled-access driveway. Telling yourself that it weren't her, it was just the anti-oestrogens. Or some pre-treatment side effect of the treatment. Reminding yourself that when someone ain't well, people always say, *"They aren't themselves."*

"Look, Mum, we been through this a thousand times in couples therapy: ain't no point in me making decisions about profiteroles or cheesecake or pasta sauce or soap when the consequences of me making a decision you don't agree with are so stressful."

You followed her, of course. End of the day, you'd bunked off school to go with her. Just like you done for her scan – though she still never let you bunk off for her routine check-ups and stuff. Told yourself that's why you were following her – just to square the fact that you'd skipped school. Not cos you were worried or nothing. Not cos you literally worried yourself sick if you didn't go to her appointments with her. She never knew it, but you hopped on the Tube, legged it to the hospital, shortcut up the external stairwell, past the wig-recycling bin, watched her having her chemo through the hospital window. Just stood there and watched her face. From angry through worried to absolutely nothing – the most nothingstruck expression you'd ever seen. Her lights going out soon as the cooling packs were placed on her scalp.

Hated yourself for being so sensitive, so over-absorb-imental. Technical term for that shit is "too porous to her emotions". Except it weren't just absorption – it was also the shock. Every time she got angryfied it still jumped you outta nowhere. Used to be a time she couldn't tell you off without laughing – laughing at whatever you'd done.

Your mummy sat down at the dining table like as if you were back in some mother–son marriage counselling room. You didn't even bother to light the candles or scatter the rose petals. Just eating her food in silence. Sniffling through her eyes. Downing the wine glass of beetroot super juice. Standing up and smacking the pyramid of profiteroles – we're talking full-on karate fork. Then picking up the profiteroles from the table and laughing at you like the two of you was having some kinda food fight. "So I complained once about the strawberry ice cream. So what, Dhilan? So what? Would you rather I lied to you and told you that I liked it? That I loved it and wanted to lick it off your face?"

"Please, Mum, let's just forget it. It's only profiteroles. I got the right dessert, even if I didn't get it the right way." You hated the way your voice went shrill whenever you tried fronting with her. Like you were shooting for high pitch cos your dumb ass couldn't hit high volume. "Anyway, Mama, we haven't talked about your cancer yet."

"What's there to say about my cancer?"

"Well, how about what the gameplan is?"

"You mean the 'prognosis', Dhilan – it isn't a bloody idiot game. And, no, this isn't only about the profiteroles. It's about why is it so bloody difficult for you to make any decisions."

Truth is, you couldn't even decide if you really did have some chronic inability to make decisions. Obviously couldn't make decisions involving the future. *Did having dinner count as having a future?*

"But why do you always need me to decide everything, Mum?"

"What everything?"

"Your wallpaper, your wigs, your underwear, the curtain rod – what do I care what kind of pasta shape the ends of the curtain rod look like?"

"But why wouldn't I ask you what kind of pasta you wanted, Dhilan? I cook it for you, not for myself, not for anyone else. Why the hell can't you just make decisions and be a man?"

You wiped some profiterole cream from your face and laid down your fork. Loud and deliberate-like. And manly. Scraping your chair as you stood up. Chucking your napkin ring on the table like some wedding ring. Like a post-vomit dollop of flickable phlegm. Like a fifty-quid note on some stretch-marked bed. "Why the fuck can't you just chill the fuck out for once, Mum? For fuck's sake, it's only profiteroles – ain't like anyone's dying."

30

MORNING. THE CURTAINS. I sit up. The curtains. Know I had that dream but I don't remember it. I don't remember which appendage.

The curtains.

My student room.

The stink of disinfectant still on my bed sheets.

At first I reckoned that making my bed counted. Another tick in the list of the things I helped her with. This was back before my bed became *her* bed. *Our* bed. Whatever. Back when I used to keep score.

"You want a gold star for making your own bed, Dhilan? What do I get for making you?"

"Stress and school runs and errands and headaches."

"I'm only stressed because at this rate I'll run out of gold stars."

The curtains, the smell of Lynx deodorant.

The bleach stains on my carpet where Naliah had vomited.

Now the sink and the taste of my mouthwash.

Empty bottles of Dettol inside my bathroom bin.

I look at my face in the mirror and see my father's.

Ain't talking about me having my father's eyes or his hairy ears or some other lonely loser resemblance. I mean I see my actual dad.

Standing right behind me. Fronting like he's been in a punch-up. Doesn't even give me time to freak out. "Dylan, we need to talk."

"Where the fuck did you come from?"

"I was knocking. Your room door just swung open – did you know that your lock's broken?"

I tell him I had break-in.

He asks me if I'm sorted for contents insurance.

There are three different brands of toothpaste in the corners of my mouth.

Dad's got zero bants today. Waits in my room till I'm done brushing. Asking on repeat play how long I'll take. *How long is a piece of dental floss?* Now pretending I'm taking a dump so that I can shut my bathroom door. Truth is I just ain't ready to have a father watch me shaving.

"I don't have much time," he goes when I re-enter my room. "So can I please just have it back?"

I look back towards my bathroom. But it's too late for that other play – the one where you pull the flush and just pretend not to hear your parent.

"Look, I know you took it," he goes. "I've had no one else round to my flat. It isn't exactly a place for entertaining."

I tell him I liked his place – there was so much light and space.

"Do you know how difficult it's been for me to come here and confront you? I was agonising for days over whether this was the right thing to do."

I tell him it's only been one day. Two at most. Fuck – maybe three. This is the problem with mainlining Red Bull.

"So first let's be clear, son, I'm not angry with you or accusing you of doing anything wrong. But that cuttings book that you took from my kitchen the other night – I need to have it back."

The light from behind my always-drawn curtains is a mash-up of morning sun and backlit billboard. Enough light to zoom in on what I'd thought were Dad's bloodstains but are probly just ketchup stains. Guessing this is cos of the milkshake stains.

Whiff of Egg McMuffin. The all-over glow of breakfast at McDonald's.

"I just wanted to read your work. Just semi-skim your stories. I'm sorry, Dad – I know I shoulda asked."

He starts scanning my freshly Lynxed and bleached dorm room. The tidiness is proper shameful. Like I got way too much time on my hands. Like there's too much room in my headspace. Like I had parents who pegged some poncey pocket money package to the completion of household chores. The room ain't much more than an en-suite box room – the floor just a path between fitted-in furniture. But Dad's now moving about as if ain't no furniture in here at all.

"No harm, Dylan. Nothing to worry. Where is it?"

The desk. The files. The chest of drawers.

"Is it in one of these?" He points.

The shelves. The bed. The clothes that sit on my chair.

"Or up there?" he says to the shelves.

The box files by my radiator. The box files by my bedside.

"Here?" He pulls open my top drawer. My socks, my self-bought boxer shorts – well, at least I don't store my garms in kitchen cabinets like how he does. Now again my desk, again my bed, my socks, the other socks. Blanking all my pre-bereavement bereavement props like as if he knows to don't even go there.

"Dad, you *do* know that it's rude to just rummage through someone else's stuff, right?"

"Well, I don't *want* to." He starts checking the cabinet in the bathroom. "Why don't you just give it to me, then, instead of just standing there?"

Now *he* sees *me* in my bathroom mirror.

"Well, where is it, son? Your mother's house?"

"What the hell? Why'd I take it there for?"

Next that big blue Ikea bag I use for dirty laundry.

"Okay, look, Dad, your book was stolen when I had that break-in."

"Oh, come on. What kind of burglar steals a scrapbook?"

I try and smooth the flames by acting stupid. Ask him if he needs his cuttings book for a job interview.

Dad's moustache relaxes. "Dylan, listen, I'm very flattered that you took it because you wanted to read my work. But nevertheless it belongs to me. It's my property."

"This is about your fake news stories, right? Your made-up eyewitness quotes."

"It's not important why I want it, son, what's important is that I want it. And that I don't believe for one second that it was stolen from you. Come on, Dylan, I don't have time for this nonsense. I mean, have you told the police?"

"About the cuttings book?"

"About the break-in."

I try fronting non-responsive but I guess something in my eyes shakes its head.

"No. Didn't think so. The lock on your door looks more like it's been broken by a drunken student – probably trying to enter the wrong room."

"You saying I'm lying about being burgled?"

"You've already proved yourself capable of stealing – when you took it from my kitchen."

"I only borrowed it."

"Well then kindly give it back. That's what people do when they borrow things."

Dad sits at the foot of my bed. Unbuttons his navy-blue suit jacket. I keep staring at his dandruff – like as if his shoulders are lumps of sky on some clear night. Fingers on his forehead, he nods at my kettle.

I ask him how he takes his coffee.

"But you don't have a coffee machine, Dylan."

When Dad tells me how many sugars he takes, I do my best not to memorise it. Just chuck in the asked-for two lumps and then, quick time, I start thinking of other random numbers to confuse myself.

Hi sniffs the jar of freeze-dried instant. "Why does your room reek of deodorant?" Doesn't clock that I'm using baby formula instead of coffee whitener. "And why does your deodorant smell like disinfectant?"

Ramona had thought I'd sprayed my bed sheets for her benefit. To encryptionise the scent of some other girl's perfume. Took me half an hour to convince her. And then, when she finally began to believe me, I started to feel some proper guilt – even though, for once, when it had come to my efforts to disguise the smell of another woman's vomit, I'd actually been telling her the truth. She kept asking me to explain once again what the hell Naliah had been doing in my room in the first place. So I kept telling her everything all over again. Everything that happened after Naliah had shown up – the dog shit, the vomit, the bleach stain on my carpet. Left out Naliah's questions about "Dhilan" and my mother, of course, but otherwise I pretty much just told her the truth. Could really get used to just telling Ramona the truth.

"Okay," Dad goes. "Coffee break's over. Where the hell's my scrapbook?"

I tell him again it was stolen when my room was burgled. He tells me again he don't believe me. We roll back and forth like this for another ten minutes. Just like our meet the other day in McDonald's when we kept screen-freezing over who'd been the one who got back in touch with whom. And just like he done back then, Dad all sudden-like starts accusing me of piss-taking. Pointing at me with his coffee mug. "You're just trying to play games with me, aren't you? Don't think I don't realise it. That I don't notice. Like the way you always leave the father field blank."

"What?"

"In your online profiles. Father's name: *blank*. Father's occupation: *blank*. Or the way you put on Facebook once that you don't have a father – that your father's estranged. As if you want the whole world to know you have no relationship with me."

"Why the hell you been scoping out my Facebook page?"

"Because apparently that's what parents do." Then he throws down the mug of coffee and stands over the brand-new stain. "Stop bloody messing me about, Dylan, this is serious. I need my cuttings book."

"Okay, just tranquilate, yeh. I think I know who took it."

"Who? Who did you give it to?"

"I didn't give it . . . Look, there are these two guys who've been hassling me. At uni, I mean. Two old dudes. I reckon they the ones who broke into my room."

"I'm sorry, son, but I don't accept that."

"But I swear down it's true."

"And I swear that it isn't."

"Dad, why are you being like this again?"

"Are you being slow on purpose, Dylan? I'm certain these men you talk of didn't break into your room because *I* was the one who broke into your room. And I couldn't fucking find it then either."

What Dillon does next ain't easy to comprehend, even to himself. Dude tries to comfort his father. Even though the man had bust into his room, staged some burglary, fucked up his shit, smeared *actual* shit into his carpet. Ain't cos Dillon's trying to be big about it. If anything, he's being little – doesn't want to fight with his daddy. Doesn't want a drama-queen father–son bust-up. In fact, Dillon doesn't even mention the dog shit. He just points to the bleach stains at his father's feet. "Look what the bleach did when I tried to clean it."

"What the hell has your carpet got to do with this, Dylan? I've got milkshake and ketchup all over my suit. I'm trying to protect you from something you won't understand and you're more worried about some stain on some dormitory carpet. And anyway, why would you even need to clean your carpet?"

Then his father starts pacing again – pumping out aggro with his legs to offset the way his mouth is now begging Dillon's forgiveness. "I'm sorry, son. I'm sorry I broke your door lock. I didn't want you to get accidentally involved in something you shouldn't get involved in. So I thought I'd just take the scrapbook back and then you'd tell me that it had been stolen and I'd tell you not to worry about it – that it wasn't important. And that would be that. But then I couldn't find my scrapbook, Dylan. I couldn't find my scrapbook."

"It's okay, Dad," Dillon says. "It's not important."

After that, Dad hits the bathroom to clean up his face.

"What now?" I ask his image in my mirror. "Are you at least gonna clue me in about what this is all about?"

It's like we're playing some kinda poker-face game in my bathroom mirror – just me, him and my male grooming products. I curse the never-opened box of condoms. The stray strands of used dental floss. Dad staring at the floss like as if somehow he knows the red stains ain't from bleeding gums – they're from the flakes of Ramona's toenail varnish that got stuck between my teeth.

Then, from fuck knows where, a question lands slap on the basin like some Tarot card: "Dad, this is about them stories you wrote about www, ain't it?"

Can't tell if his AK-47 look is shot at me or at his own reflection. "Double what?"

"The letters www – you wrote a bunch of stories about some guy who was lobbying the government to scrap www in internet domain names. Something about the Hebrew numbers that correspond with the letters." Don't ask me why I can't just say the actual number six. Ain't like I'm superstitious or nothing. After all, Mum had started breaking mirrors *after* her bad luck, not before it. Dressing-table mirror on the regular.

"Oh," he goes – still talking to my reflection. "You read those stories." Dries his face with a flannel that belongs to Ramona. She'd even tagged it with marker pen – just the first three letters: RAM. "I made up most of the quotes and content in those stories too." He relocates our convo back to my room as if the carpet is safer ground than the bathroom. Fronting like it ain't no biggie, like as if all this is just some nothing, as if the shitstains between us don't exist. "Dylan, why can't you bring yourself to say the actual numbers? Why do you use the letters www? Are you spooked, son?"

"I ain't got a problem with saying the numbers. But internet domain names start with letters, not numbers, so obviously I'm gonna say the letters. If I said the numbers, then we'd be talking in Hebrew and we can barely even manage Hindi."

"Ah – of course. Your mother's family – they think I'm too anglicised just because I forgot how to speak my mother tongue."

"That ain't what I meant, Dad. I didn't even know you forgot how to speak your mother tongue."

"It isn't a question of forgetting the words, Dylan, it's a question of forgetting how to reach the volume they think words should be spoken at." Buttoning up his suit jacket. "Anyway, Dylan, do *you* know your mother tongue?"

Wanna tell him I know my mother's *ulcerated* tongue. And we ain't talking them tiny sores you take out by unloading a few rounds of Bonjela, I'm talking ulcers like bullet holes. Big, black immunocompromised cigar scabs that even my kisses can't cure.

"Son, those www stories were fake. Not only did I fabricate the eyewitness quotes they contained, but 99 per cent of all the experts I spoke to told me that, numerically, www doesn't even mean three sixes in Hebrew. It just means 18. I just found one crackpot who thought differently to all the experts and, by giving him an equal platform, I made it look like there was confusion around the subject – that the facts of the matter still needed to be debated. Made for a much better story. It's the same basic trick the tobacco industry used and what climate-change deniers do today – just keep generating doubt. Because, when faced with doubt, son, people often just believe whatever sticks in their mind – and lies usually stick better because they're simpler."

"Wait, what? Dad, why are telling me this?"

"To show you that there's no big mystery, Dylan. So when you remember where you've hidden my scrapbook, please do me a courtesy and kindly return it."

31

MY STUDENT HALLS again. My bed. My desk. Again my door opens. This time, Uncle Deepak rolls in. "You know your lock is broken, Dhilan?"

Great. First my factual father and now the nearest thing I ever had to an actual dad. I peek out my door and scope up and down the corridor – like as if I'm expecting Mum to be visiting next.

"I came by myself," goes Uncle Deepak. "I told you I'd come. I told you I'd come and find you in your student halls." He's packing a pink umbrella and a brown paper bag. He can't weigh up whether he should drop the bag on my bed or my desk so just holds it. "Didn't I tell you I'd come? On the voicemails I left you. I said I'd come here and so I'm here."

Uncle Deepak always gives off the vibe of a man who should don a hat with his coat. Stride the fuck around in an old-school fedora. Probly be a bit difficult though – what with his turban. Wears it on the daily even though my family ain't even Sikh. He converted all his files to Sikhism when he was in his mid-thirties. Picks and chooses, though. For instance, he ain't got a beard. I reckon he'd look better if instead he'd selected a Sikh man's beard and a non-Sikh fedora.

"We said we'd give you one or two days before one of us came," he goes. "But then after we got the visit, I decided better I waited a little longer. So now I've come here today."

"What visit?"

"I told you I'd come and visit, Dhilan. Why they don't give you a bigger room?"

When I'd first moved into student halls, Uncle Deepak had offered to drive down from Birmingham to drop me off with all my stuff. That would've meant he'd have driven for three hours from Birmingham to Mum's house in Acton just to give me a forty-minute lift to my student halls in Holborn. That's just the kind of thing he does. *"But what you will do?"* he'd said when I told him not to worry. *"You can't carry all your books and computer on the Tube."*

If I'd gone to Cambridge, then probly I'd have accepted his offer to help with the driving and dropping and consoling and crate-lifting and consoling and tear-wiping and mopping and consoling. Anycase, he and Aunty Number Nine have now moved from Birmingham to Acton to take care of things. He's Mum and Masi's first cousin. Sometimes I feel proper fraudulent tagging myself a "young carer" cos of everything he and my aunts have done. Are you still technically a marathon runner if you drop out before the final couple of miles? If your pre-bereavement bereavement peaks too early?

"What visit?" I ask again.

"I told you, if you don't come back to Acton, I'd come and visit you here. And now I'm here."

"Oh, okay, sorry. For a minute I thought you meant that someone had visited *you*."

"Yes," Uncle goes. "Of course. We got that visit from your boss."

"What visit?" Watch me working double shifts here to not drop an F-bomb. "What boss?"

"Your boss from your typing business."

"But *I'm* the boss of my typing business. It's *my* business – my start-up. And, anyway, it ain't a typing business, it's a data-entry business."

"I don't know the ins and outs of such things. He told us he was the one who hired you."

"One of my clients?"

"Can I ask you something, Dhilan? And answer me please truthfully. You are working for the government or something like this?"

"Who the what?"

"Like on the TV. For MI5 or whatnot?"

"What?"

"Because of the way you're living. All the sneaking around and around, all the money you're making. And also when your boss came to see us he knew everything about us. *Everything.* When and why I converted to Sikhism. What's in my bank accounts. *Everything.*"

Ain't no need to ask Uncle Deepak what this boss man looked like. Nonethefuck, he starts describing an old man wearing a shirt and tie with a leather jacket – "Like the leather jacket Marlon Brando wore. What do you call them? With the two zips? Double-breasted."

"Well, what did he tell you – this boss man of mine in a biker jacket?"

"He told to us that we should stop harassing and WhatsApping you in the office. That we should give to you the space. That you were his best employee and he needed for you to be free from the stress so you could do your job and your degree."

"He didn't threaten you, did he?"

"What threaten? He helped me to fix the carburettor. And so now I've come here to tell you that we're giving you the space." Uncle stays standing a full five metres away like he's trying to do a demo. "Do you need anything, Dhilan? I know you have your typing business, but do you need any money or anything?"

"No, I don't. Thank you. I have my typing business."

He clocks the bleach stains on my carpet. Feel like fessing up that, yes, they're from bodily fluids – but not the fun kind.

"Also I came to give you this." He drops the brown paper bag like a dead animal on my desk.

First time Mum went in for surgical drama, she filled up empty ice-cream tubs with her freshly made sai bhaji. Frozen bricks of spinach to keep me strong and so on. Two tubs for while she was in hospital and an extra ten in case she never left.

"What, so that's it? We're done?"

"Yes, this is all I've come here to say."

"Why? Why is that all you have to say? What did that man – my boss – what did he tell you to make that all you have to say?"

Uncle dodges the bleach stain as he steps towards me. His forefinger flexed. "Truthfully, I don't even care what your boss said to us. What I have to say is this: you don't need to discuss with him or anybody else about our family matters. I don't care if you're working for the MI5, the CIA or Inland Revenue."

Fact that I ain't even discussed my complicated family-related shit with the Botox man ain't even the point now. "Who do you want me to discuss it with?" I ask him. "With the mother–son marriage guidance counsellor or with the pre-bereavement bereavement counsellor?" Takes some proper effort to keep my voice levels in check – technically you ain't allowed to shout down your uncles or aunties.

"But why you did all this counselling-bouncelling nonsense? You should have discussed these things with us – this is what the family's for."

I tell him they only wanna think what they already think so what's the point in talking to them? Again working hard not to shout at him. Swallowing all the bubbles of soggy, soap-opera hissy-fit. Cos you gotta respect your uncles and aunties. Don't matter which race or religion or city you're from.

That shit's the law.

Ramona had explained it to me at school one time after she'd had a bust-up with her own aunt. She'd told me she'd realised that you couldn't shout your fucking lungs out at someone if they weren't your actual parent. That shit just Wasn't Done. Even if that someone had been the most rock-solid substitute parent, or the world's greatest surrogate parent – even if they rolled like Uncle Phil from *The Fresh Prince*. Because as every kid knows, you gotta respect your granddad/uncle/godfather/the female forms of all of the above. Gotta show em the kind of respect that you wouldn't never show a parent.

"I mean, think about it, Uncle – how the hell can you even begin to have a discussion with someone if they only wanna think what they already think?" There's some caps lock on my voice, though, so I back down with a rapidness. "I mean, just in general, Uncle, just all the aggro and toxicness on social media – I mean the partisan divide."

"I don't know what point it is you're trying to get out of your chest, Dhilan, but it's good you feel you can shout at me. Like a son, not a nephew. I don't want for you to hold these things in. Even though, when you shout, you sound just like your loner loser of a father."

Whenever Mum has pulled that resemblance shit on me it's like flipping on my inbuilt apology switch. When I'm done saying sorry to Uncle Deepak, I try and drop in a drive-by question about my old man – but without sounding too lippy or nothing, so basically without actually questioning anything. In fact, really, it's more like I'm just agreeing with him – about my dad being a loser and so on.

"Exactly, the man was a fool," goes Uncle. "He chose to lose his wife and his son. His problem was he was the work-addict-holic. Always too busy with his busy-busy insurance busy-ness." He reaches for my broken door handle. "You know, if you want I can send you a good locksmith – they'll fix this free of charge as a favour to me. You must have a good lock, Dhilan – you need be safely and soundly when you sleep."

32

CAN'T REMEMBER IF it's bad luck that comes in threes or visitors. Drag my chair to the middle of my room, sit facing the door. Should probly scroll through my fones or something. Flip open my laptop. There are comic-book superheroes who can tap photographic memories, unlimited knowledge and powers of prediction. I just stay staring at my door.

"Did you know your lock is broken?" The botched-Botox man chucks me a bag of chocolate chip cookies. "They're freshly baked. Or are you still not big on breakfast?"

I tell him let's just say some websites still hit me with ads for pregnancy-testing kits.

"Once upon a time, morning sickness would often lead straight to mourning sickness. Yes. It's true. And not just because of high infant mortality rates – also because, under certain pre-Christian laws, newly born newborns weren't considered human until they'd been put to the breast. Can you believe that, Dillon? It's true. Not human until they'd had a proper taste of the titty."

Shoulda been a bit more badass and kept my other chair ready for him – man's gotta shove away my laundry before he can sit.

"Yes. It's true. Did you know this, Dillon? Yes? It was perfectly legal to just delete your child, provided you did so before its first feed. Dump it in a river. Or just leave it on some windswept mountain with its feet bound – they called it 'death by exposure'. Yes. You know this, Dillon. It's known that you know this."

"Look, I didn't take my father's place."

"Come again?"

"You just dropped another one of your neon-lit references to Oedipus. And so I'm telling you that I didn't take my father's place. I left my mum's bedroom. Even left her living room when the living room become her bedroom."

"Strictly speaking, your father hasn't slept in your mother's bedroom either – at least not for several years."

Most people, they get properly creeped out by the thought of their mum and dad getting jiggy with each other. Me, I get kinda tranquilated – like when you swap out your Red Bull for sweet milky tea.

"Come to think of it, Dillon, if your search history once again serves me correctly, you haven't actually overlooked that part of the story. People tend to overlook that part."

Technical term for it is "backstory". We're talking back before Oedipus could even crawl. Oedipus' birth parents had him dumped on some mountainside cos they'd heard the exact same prophecy from the exact same oracle. Only, instead of dying, little dude got rescued. Raised up by some next parents.

Took some proper searching – ebooks and journals and that. Articles by actual psychoanalysers. No clickbait stories. None of that *Recommended for you* bullshit. Didn't hardly even understand most of what I read, but eventually I puzzled out how the real bad deed went down long before Oedipus had marital relations with his mum.

Way before Oedipus killed his dad, even.

Way before Oedipus could even walk.

It was when his father bound his newborn baby's feet.

As if any dad who dumps his son might as well just cut to the chase and dump him in bed with his night-sweating mum.

i.e. it weren't Oedipus' fault.

Problem was, by the time I downloaded this new info, it didn't make no difference. Standard story of Oedipus was hooked too deep inside my head. Technical term for that: "the new information failed to challenge my core beliefs". Like how when know something on some kinda intellect-level but somehow you just can't tell it to your brain.

That's all for today about Oedipus.

Botox man clicks his flabby fingers in my face. "So I've come here to tell you I gotta hand it to you, kid: what you did with your father's stories was almost ingenious. Now they're up there on the online archive but no one will ever even know they're there as they won't register in any search results. You did that the night of the antics that got you fired, I assume? Well, I have to say, it was almost ingenious."

I ask him what he's gonna do. To the stories – what's he gonna do to my dad's stories?

"What the hell do you think I'm going to do? I'm going to get one of the other data-enterers to finish the job, of course. Have them apply metadata and character recognition to each story so that they'll start showing up in keyword searches. Otherwise your whole endeavour will have been about as pointless as wanking without a noose."

"Okay, whatever, I'll play along with this shit – even though you know I don't get it."

"What's not to get? Making the text searchable is often the whole point of digitising things. After all, it's not the searching that's new here – humans have always been hunters and explorers and navel-gazers – what's new is that everything is now so readily searchable. A searchable version of reality. That's always been key to utopian ideals of a universal library. All stories must be searchable just as all archives must be searchable. Then the stories can become indexes of themselves just like every other digitised text. Or book. Or archive. Or person. But you already know this, yes – it's the overblown sales pitch of your own student start-up. Yes. It's known that you know this."

"Yeh, obviously I know what character-recognition software is – what I don't get is why you're okay about what I done. Why ain't you just deleting the stories? Wouldn't even need to piss about with a black marker pen this time."

"And why the fuck shouldn't I be okay about it? Actually, I think what you did was admirable. All the trouble you took to get hold of unredacted copies of his articles . . ."

"Yeh, about that – do you think you could return his cuttings book to me, please? He's really freaking the fuck out about it."

"But here's the thing I don't understand: given all the trouble you took with this – the elaborate exploits you staged in the office as a decoy and so on – why in the hell did you bother *editing* his stories down?"

While I think up some semi-believable bullshit, I realise that I'm once again trying to imagine this guy fully bearded.

"But then, that's the way things worked before the invention of the printing press, right kid? Back when books were reproduced by pen-pushing copyists. You think those monks and scribes didn't rewrite things as they copied them? Tidied up the punctuation a little. Maybe cut to the car chase – or at least the grisly death. It's what they called 'medieval collective texts.'"

I let him carry on trying to sound bearded and brainful. Even rearrange my facial muscles to encourage him.

"The printing press was just an aberration, Dillon. Briefly replacing rewriting and modifying with identical reproduction and copyright and whatnot. But while all those monks may have edited and shortened things as they copied them, I doubt they ever edited things down quite as much as you did. And so I'm inviting you to tell me why."

By now I'm ready to hit him with some premium level beard-stroking bullshit digital jism – I tell him I edited down Dad's stories in order to make them more byte-sized.

"You think I'm that stupid, Dillon? Did your father tell you to omit all the eyewitness quotes? Only, I'm almost certain he doesn't even know what you were up to that night. I mean, do you think I'm stupid?"

My face like permafrost Botox.

"Your father told you that he made them up, didn't he? The quotes – that's why you left them out."

Fuck it – I nod.

"Well, hats off and all that. You did a remarkable job." Starts stroking his stubble. "You've engineered stories that are actually designed to *not* be clicked on – written by a man who can't be googled. I can't tell you what a breath of refreshment that is."

Tell him I'm happy to be of service – that I know how much he hates clickbait stories. That I think maybe he might've mentioned it before.

He holds out his sumo fingers like he's pointing a gun. Starts clicking in my face again. "Okay, fine," he says. "You want to mock me? Then come on, count my click rates. You want to feel the effects of clickbait and clickety click clicks? Then let's do this. Count my clicks."

I flinch my whole head. "What the hell you doing, man?"

"My clicks. My fingers – what other clicking sound could I be talking about? I'm not the one who's obsessed with the sound of women walking in high heels. So, come on, count my finger clicks." Steps up to me again snapping his flabby fingers – once, twice, three times. Each snap releasing some kinda ash cloud – or dandruff or pixels or whatever. "My click-through rates. My swipe-throughs. Shares. Likes. Web hits. Video watch time. Viralness. Engagement levels. Strategic hyperlinks and optimised headlines. Whatever you want to call them, Dillon – whatever propels stories to the top of social media feeds and search engine ranking systems."

Fuck knows whether I'm now ducking my head to dodge his clicking fingers or to take shelter from another incoming Media Studies lecture.

"Of course, the tech companies have a friendly term for all this clickability. They call it 'a relevant user experience'. And as soon as they decided to give it more weight than accuracy – to effectively devalue the currency of truthfulness – well, then it was only a matter of time before the fuckfest commenced." And then another set of three clicks, but with less ash now so the sound is wet and slippery – dirty, meaty echo like smacking up a carcass. "Just a matter of mere time before all their clever digital architecture – the basis of your society – became one great big feedback machine for people's fears, anxieties, prejudice, anger, perversions, righteousness." Now double-clicking his fingers in my face like as if he's double-jointed. Slipping off the beat now and then because of the sweat. "Algorithms curating your own alternate reality. The exclusion of facts that you might find disagreeable. Ethnosupremacists running around thinking that evil is now just a valid partisan position. Facebook feeding you up with—"

"Okay, okay," I go – holding up some textbook to shield me from his clicks – "I get it, okay. So you got some serious beef about bullshit fake news stories. Why you telling me all this again? What exactly is it you trying to tell me?"

"We're not just talking about bullshit, Dillon, we're talking about a cocktail of bovine laxatives. A plague of projectile bull dysentery. The truth becoming whatever the hell a person wants it to be. And a digital infrastructure that couldn't have been better at persuading you to drink up all the bull dysentery. Couldn't have been better if it had been specifically built for that purpose." The man's actually spitting now. Proper convulsating. His botched-Botox like he's got air sacks in his face. I offer to make him a cup of tea or Horlicks, whatever, my mother's morphine. *One lump or two?* Dude just looks like at me like how the fuck is tea gonna fix this?

"The bile and bull diarrhoea have already bolted through the floodgates, kid. Burst right through the banks. It's all very well for those overindulged tech giants to try and clean up their acts and their algorithms now. For Facebook to try and save face by finally taking some responsibility for the junk they've been putting in people's newsfeeds. For the Silicon Valley superpowers to finally wake up to the kinds of accountability and quality control that every other industry has to abide by. Good for them. Give them a medal. But the bile and the bull diarrhoea have already bolted the floodgates. What has happened over the past few years cannot just be undone, Dillon. Certain kinds of demons, you can't just put them back in the bottle. Took the human race decades, if not centuries, to make some types of evil socially or ethically unacceptable. You can't just put them back in the bottle."

And then once again with his finger-clicking. But, again, it ain't hypnotism. It ain't faith healing. Ain't a magician snapping his fingers to signal some break in reality or establish their commanding authority or whatever. Then, finally, he drops his hands by his sides, like as if he knows he's already over-milked the overdramatic effect. Looking like he's about to start crying or someshit. We're talking proper eye saliva. Asks me if I've figured out what he's trying to tell me yet. Takes the mug of Horlicks I give him. When the fuck did I just make Horlicks?

And then he's back on some lecturising. Some stampede of footnotes. Says that obviously all them tech tycoons didn't *intend* for all this bile and bull dysentery to be unleashed. Didn't *mean* for their platforms to get toxic. Problem was, they just never clocked how their giant ad machines that had basically been designed to help advertisers manipulate people could also be used to manipulate people. He says that tech people talk about gaming the system – about Facebook being "weaponised" by dealers of fake news and dodgy foreign agents and political consultants. But, way he sees it, ain't nobody gamed nothing – they just used the system the way it was designed to be used. Cleverly targeted marketing and manipulation of users who are hooked on cleverly targeted content.

Then he asks me again if I've figured out what he's trying to tell me.

Shake my head.

"All in the name of clickability and user relevance and ad revenues. Think of the colossal stupidity of it, Dillon – that these truth-devaluing business models should have come to govern the largest public spaces the world has ever had. In fact, it's proved to be such a catastrofuck that one of my colleagues has even been exploring whether the consequences were in some sense metaphysical. After all, the tech giants basically built a digital archive, library and database of all the world's knowledge, history and likely future intentions. A *divine mind*. If that isn't the Tower of Babel or Library of Babel, then I don't know what the hell is. And, what's more, it explicitly attempts to translate away all our language barriers in real time. Well, what happened with the Tower of Babel?"

I start scrolling through my head but obviously the Botox man is happy to answer his own question: "The fragmentation of society into tribes who couldn't even talk to each other."

Then he asks me again if I've figured out what he's telling me. Downs his Horlicks in one shot. Tells me to mix it with milk instead of water next time. "Speaking of which, you know why the tech giants kept claiming that they couldn't stop every single litre of bull diarrhoea from seeping into their systems? Why for years and years they just refused to take adult responsibility for the problems stoked up by their own products? They said it's because they have too many billions of users uploading billions of pages of content. As if there's some kind of edict from heaven that says they *must* be too big to monitor themselves. And always hiding behind the algorithms that do all the recommending and feeding. As if the algorithms weren't actually the crux of their own corporate strategies – their own actions. As if personalised relevance and clickability *must* be given greater weight than accuracy. Google's algorithm already filtered out pornography so what was to stop them being even more responsible? Likewise, what was to stop Facebook altering its feeds so that users got fed proper reporting over junk stories that go viral? Nobody was asking them to be the arbiters of truth, just to stop devaluing the relative currency of truth. It's as if the tech giants themselves had been warped and distorted by their own tech bubble. Their jacuzzis of profits from monetising your data. Their ridiculous insistence that they aren't really media companies – just neutral tech companies with neutral platforms and neutral algorithms." And then, all sudden-like, he switches his voice back to shouting mode: "Do me a fucking favour! The two largest distributors and gatekeepers of news and information in the history of humankind – that means they aren't just media companies, they're the biggest media companies that the world has ever known. Only, they didn't want the regulations that came with being media companies, they just wanted the readers and the revenues. Didn't want to deal with any thorny editorial decisions – as if the decision to put user relevance before accuracy wasn't the single biggest editorial decision anyone ever made. A fucking ten-year-old could have told them that they're media companies because a ten-year-old gets most of their news and information through Facebook or Google. As you may well remember, Dillon." He watches me weigh all this up. "Now do you understand what I'm trying to tell you?"

I tell him seems like, once again, he's just trying to get me to blame Google and Facebook for the way my shit got so fucked up and twisted. Same as how he always does. Like as if I should rewrite that poem we done in English Lit. – *They fuck you up, Facebook and Google.* I tell him I've listened to all his lecturising and I still ain't gonna blame them. Just like I ain't gonna blame all those predictive Oedipal scare stories. Just like I ain't gonna blame my mother. Ain't even gonna blame all them government cutbacks that deliberately turn kids into district nurses and "intimate care" providers. I tell him that I did all my fuckery. *Me.*

"Oh come on, Dillon. If all I was trying to say is that you should blame Google and Facebook, I would have stepped off my soapbox days ago."

"Then why can't you just tell me what it is?"

"I can't just *tell* you the answer – and that in itself should tell you something." He takes a swig from his empty mug and swallows like as if he's actually drinking. "Look, Dillon, you know that social media and search engines don't just filter the way a person processes the world now, they filter the way a person processes themselves. That means if you want to know what kind of man you really are – I believe the technical term is 'to own your own shit' – then you have to start knowing yourself better than they do. Which means knowing more about the systems that seek to know you and mould you."

"The fuck do I even care? I just wanna know why my dad's stories were blacked out."

"You know your problem, Dillon? You've clearly been misreading Oedipus. You think that truth just magically forces its way to the surface. That the truth will always out, that it has some inherent power to overcome crapfuck falsity. This is a misapprehension shared by both the chronically guilt-ridden and the chronically naïve – and apparently also by media regulators. Oedipus' truth doesn't simply force its way into the open. Oedipus drags it out himself, tooth and toenail. Kicking and shitting."

That's all for today about Oedipus.

"When Oedipus starts searching for the identity of whoever has committed the sins that have brought a curse on his city, he's initially hobbled by all the usual fallibilities of the human mind – all those cognitive biases you've learnt about in Behavioural Economics. He uses reason and logic to reject things that don't conform with his own preconceptions. Only believes those things he already agrees with. Digs his heels in when confronted with counter-evidence and contrary opinions. Accuses his own brother-in-law of plotting against him." The Botox man hands me the empty mug like as if he expects a top up or someshit. Turns out, he just wants to bust out some gesticulationary action. "But then, slowly, Oedipus switches right before our eyes. He stops simply rejecting inconvenient information and grows into someone who actively seeks out the hard facts regardless of how unpalatable they are. He starts to curb his own righteousness. Makes a point of really listening to people who have different views. And why is he able to make this switch – to overcome his natural tendencies towards confirmation bias and so forth?"

"Cos he's heroic and that just happens to be his designated superpower?"

"Because he isn't stuck in some digital echo chamber, Dillon. He's not trapped in a bubble of like-minded opinions and self-reinforcing thoughts. Because the inbuilt fallibilities of his human mind haven't been given external rocket boosters by social media and search engines. Because all the reports and information that he amasses don't appear on the same platform, the same cellphone screen, which means they don't all appear equally credible. Herdsmen, messengers, shepherds, seers, oracles, relatives who beg him to ignore the prophecies, relatives who beg him to quit searching. Oedipus consciously chooses to carry on clicking on the most credible sources and stops clicking on the less credible sources – even though the latter are telling him the things that he'd much rather hear. This is how Oedipus wills the truth to emerge. How he breaks out of his own alternate reality. And not just the truth about having inadvertently married his mother and killed his father, also the truth about the fuck-up that set his whole misadventure in motion."

I finish the rest of the movie for him. It weren't cos of the prophecy. Weren't cos he was just dumb to the true facts about his real mum and dad. It's cos he believed in *false* facts. And cos, after hearing the predictive prophecy, he acted like as if the false facts and misinformation were true.

As the man's Botox finally stops bulging or bubbling or whatever, his face looks a little less botched. *Young Carer's Playbook #498: Sometimes going ape can be good for them.* And, yeh – I hate it how that shit works.

I tell the Botox man that I think maybe he's putting just a bit too much personalised spin on the story of Oedipus, though. That I don't think all them audiences in Ancient Greek theatres were clapping cos the dude didn't just blindly pull out his smartfone and go with the top five Google results. "Anycase, so what is it, then?" I ask him. "What's the false fact?"

Cuts me a look like as if to pretend that now *he's* the one who ain't clued up.

"Come on, man. You keep saying how it's known that I know this and it's known that I know that. So then clearly you also know what I *don't* know. All this time I been thinking you're trying to get me to blame Google and Facebook, but, truth is, you just been trying to make me wise up to how some false fact slipped into my head. Which means what you're really trying to tell me is the fact that there's some false facts in my head."

And again with that look. Longing it out this time, though – full-on stare down. Can even hear him breathing. And munching his cookies. Crunching his cookies – crunching the data. Then, finally, he speaks. "Who says I'm even talking about your mother, Dillon? I was under the impression I was talking about search engines and social media. About the bile and bull dysentery. About swastikas and whooping cough. About the fact that truth doesn't always beat falseness. So why do you have to make everything about you and your mommy?"

"Ain't even saying it's about my mum – obviously it's got someshit to do with my dad. After all, that's why you come here, ain't it? You came here and asked about me digitising his stories. So don't treat me like a fool. Just tell me: what's the false fact? What is it that I don't know?"

"I've given you more than enough metadata, Dillon. Information about information."

"I know what metadata is."

"Yes. Just a shame you didn't apply any metadata to your father's stories so that they'd show up in search results. In fact, you've made them so near-impossible to search for that I now have to ask you something directly – and you may have noticed that I don't normally do directly. But are you absolutely sure you omitted each and every single one of your father's fabricated eyewitnesses and their fabricated quotes?"

I tell him I'm sure.

"For all thirty-six stories?"

I tell him there ain't no names, no quotes.

"Well that's incredibly fortunate. For you and for me. Why do you think your father's panicking so much about his missing clippings book? You know you really had better return it to him."

Before he splits he looks towards my window like as if to ask why the hell I don't just open the curtains.

Door closes behind him; I flip open my laptop.

The newspaper's publishing system. The online archive. My password.

Sorry, my *username* before my password.

Fuck, not *that* username – my Dylan username.

I'm now single-zone focused by the need to make double, triple sure I didn't accidentally let through any of my father's fabrications.

Invalid username. Invalid password.

Of course, I can't log on cos I got my butt kicked off the project. So I try going on their website like as if I was just some casual reader – access the archive from the front end.

Invalid username. Invalid password.

It ain't a pay-for website, but you need to be registered so that they can put you under watch and target the ads.

Invalid username. Invalid password.

This time checking for caps lock and Freudian typos.

Invalid username. Invalid password.

Even sign up from scratch as some brand-new customer – i.e. creating a brand-new email address, a new fake name and so on. But this don't work either. It's like as if the website's specifically blocked off access from my specific laptop.

Next, I just search Google, even though I already know that the stories I digitised won't come up on Google. Don't search for Dad's name, of course – already know for definite that I deffo didn't include his name. Instead, I search for the fake names – the people he'd made up for the eyewitness quotes he'd made up. Don't even need the actual scrapbook to remember some of them – that's how fake they was: John Squirrel, Jack Badger, Ravi Otter. Oh, and let's not forget the other made-up names he'd used: Jack Dylan, Hardip Dylan, John Dylan.

No hits for the newspaper that used to be my client.

But ain't no zero search results, either. Each time I click open a link, it's like I'm clicking down my room's thermostat switch. Turns out that all Dad's made-up eyewitnesses – or at least the ones that I remembered – also show up in stories published by other newspapers. Ditto their word-for-word quotes.

All in, the fake names appear in stories published by four different newspapers under nine different bylines. Fone a couple of switchboards to check if each of these bylines is the name of a real, actual journalist and not some made-up name for my dad.

My room doesn't actually have a thermostat switch.

Turns out the other journalists are real. Can picture all the reporters shoving their dictaphones and microphones in front of the same eyewitness just like they do in films. Cos whichever way you cut it, this can only mean one thing: the eyewitness quotes are actually real and my dad didn't fabricate diddly-fuck. He made up all that shit about making shit up.

33

SEVENTH TIME YOUR mum told you she had the C-bomb, she was trying to tip off prospective burglars. Note stuck to the wall by her bed that she'd typed up in size forty-eight font: *"Please do not steal these tablets. If you are a burglar, there is £100 cash on the kitchen table. Please take it and leave these tablets alone. These pills will not make you feel happy as a kite. These pills are my medicines. I have cancer."*

One good thing about her sleeping in the living room: she no longer set the burglar alarm. You dropped your house keys in another pocket to stop them rattling against the keys to your student halls. Switched your mobile to silent and used it as a makeshift torch. Shoulda invested in a proper flashlight instead of always using your phone to search for stuff.

You pulled up a dining chair beside her bed. Checked she was deffo set to sleep mode. Technically, it was your bed – no point lugging down her Ikea king-size. Noises from her liquid-filled lungs drowning out Masi's snoring from up in your mum's room. All this musical beds fuckery. Back when it first started eating away her bones, you'd looked into getting one of them chair-lift-stair-lift things. But then the council sorted her out with a downstairs disabled-access bathroom. With a bed now in the living room, she could wake up and admire her self-laid patio. The patio eaten away by the bathroom.

You offed the baby monitor that connected her to your masi. Dimples breaking on her cheeks where your lips had just been.

Even in a chemical sleep, your mum hesitated before committing to a smile. Gauntness pronouncing her grin like how your school French teacher used to exaggerate the accents. Beside the bed, a silver bell for minor masi-league emergencies. A blood-red button for ambulance ones. Laptop, plastic kidney bowls and a three-volume alternative guide to some hypno-homeopathic-past-life-regression approach to regaining your positive health. Hand behind her ear like she was listening out for some better dream. Your own recurring dream in which you were an actual appendage of her. Your arm growing out of her hip, your leg coming out of her ankles. Cold sweat, bottle of Volvic, telling yourself it weren't no big deal, that it was just some dream – that she was your mother, not your torso. Apparently when we're babies, we reckon that our mothers are appendages of *us*. You drop your rattle from your high chair, try to reach to pick it up, your mother's arm magically does it for you. Same shit when your nappy needs changing. Same shit when you wanna be fed. Her hands magic-like unbuttoning her blouse. Figuring out that she ain't actually part of you is one of the first things you ever know about yourself. Must be a proper mindfuck for little babies – a mashup of shit-horror and sigh of relief. Maybe that's what it's like even when grown-ups find out who the fuck they really are – when they bust through all the bullshit and the smoky mirrors and finally crash into the truth. That's all for today about Oedipus.

You'd had to go. Had no choice, had to go. Not to keep things going with Ramona or nothing, but cos you couldn't even share the same unaired airspace without having one of your mother–son marital rows. The couples therapist had told you that you had to go. Google had told you that you had go. Not to mention confirmation of the oracle's prophecy from your three bearded aunties. *HE WILL TAKE THE FATHER'S PLACE. Yes, yes, yes – he will take the father's place. He will sleep in his mother's bed.*

You'd told her it was cos of the commute to uni. One hour each way on the Piccadilly line Tube. Dressed it up like minor-level pillow talk. She'd told you to stop bullshitting her. Begged you to just please, just tell her the truth. Then she said something about the bathroom extractor fan not working. Or needing batteries for her MP3 player. *Dhilan, do you remember that time?* Your marriage therapist advised couples to just change the channel whenever their rows started entering the red zone. Just talk about some other subject for two minutes. Apparently this was better than simply counting to ten. Any topic would do.

"Dhilan, do you remember when you started primary school and I picked you up at lunchtimes to bring you home for proper Indian food? Saved you from the moody dinner ladies. You remember?"

Any topic would do.

"But I didn't realise that lunchtime was also a playtime. That all the other children gobbled their school dinners and went outside to play. And so I got so upset with myself. I didn't *want* to be that kind of mother, Dhilan." Dropping some eye saliva as she spoke.

"You've told me all this before, Mummy."

"So then you can see why I want you to be truthful with me. Because if it really is just about the commute then you'll only need to stay in halls from Monday to Friday. But I think the truth is maybe you should be there on weekends as well."

The pillow-talk-tucking-in routine had started way back before her sickness. Those months straight after her divorce when you'd stand in her doorway each night and just talk and talk and talk. Not about any complicated family-related crap – just about school or TV or the universe. You'd time it just before she switched off her lights. Harder to get the timing right now that you no longer lived in the same house. Previous night, you'd turned up too early. A mashup of mixed-up signals – couldn't work out if she was asking you to stay the night. The nightcap, the negligee, the hints about early-morning visits from relatives. You offered to make her a mug of Horlicks instead.

"*Horlicks?* Not even hot chocolate?" One of the living-room walls had just been repaired and redecorated. The paint watching her die. "I see – so now that you're in student halls you only have time to drink with your student halls friends."

You gave her some sancti-sappiness about not being like all them others – the ones who pissed away their opportunities down All Bar One urinals.

"Well then, you'll be okay to have a little tipple with your mummy." And again with the accents on her smile.

Couple of weeks after you'd moved out, she'd made herself believe that it wasn't her, it was just the sight of her in hospital you couldn't stand. The high-tech wiring and the low-tech tubing. The G-clamps, the wax, the leftover forceps. The unsealable disposable gown. And so now that your living room had become a hospital room, she weren't upset that you couldn't stand the sight of her at home. Her pillow talks getting proper rambling not cos of meds or dementia or morphine, but cos she didn't wanna think this through.

She'd suggested the nightcap even before you'd started putting your coat back on cos you hadn't even taken it off yet. Her wearing the negligee you once bought her for Mother's Day. Lilac – satin lilac with a matching below-the-knee nightie. Only three times in the year when a guy can linger in a lingerie department without the sales assistants thinking he's a pervert: Valentine's, Christmas and Mothering Sunday. Weren't even your mum's most lingerie-like nightwear set – that would be her beige one. As she hobbled to the hallway, she reminded you of Yoda. You following but forgetting how to walk so slowly. After all, ain't like you *intended* to knock into her. You grabbed both her shoulders to stop her from toppling, she swivelled round faster and hugged you tighter than shoulda been possible.

"Mum, maybe it's time for you to go to bed."

"Well, it's been a very long time since you told me that, Dhilan. I've already forgotten what it's liked to be tucked in."

"I only moved out like a month ago. Are you sure the doctors said it's okay for you to drink? Like, will you be able to walk?"

"Why – are you offering to carry me?

*

Now in the living-room-cum-bedroom, you tried telling yourself that the fact you wanted to move back home meant that moving out had worked – which meant that you shouldn't move back. Moonlight from the patio like the ghost of a pillow, trying to smother her face.

You'd positioned her bed directly opposite the sofa – your bed, her bed, whatever. *The* bed was opposite the sofa. Headboard in the place of a plasma television. Pakora crumbs and popcorn – the residues of rolling family gatherings. Your mum always texted to warn you before each consignment of complicated family-related relations. Just that week, the fifth carload of relatives from Birmingham since the last time she'd been discharged/ readmitted/ redischarged. All along the M6 to repay or renew their penultimate respects. All the way, all of them saying what a bloody-asshole you were. SICK – ABSOLUTELY, HE MAKES ME THE SICK. THIS THING WOULD BE SICKENING EVEN IF SHE WASN'T WITH THE SICKNESS. *Yes, better now that she doesn't live a long life – otherwise one day that jerk would put her in an old person's home as if he was white.* BUT WHY HE CAN'T DELAY THE STUDIES? *Because she says she wants him to finish his degree quickly – she wants to live to see his graduation photo.* And now she says that he's running his own business – that this is why he's always so busy, busy, busy. BULLSHIT RUBBISH BULLSHIT! HIS MASI TOLD ME HE'S JUST A TYPIST. *Yes – yes, yes, yes. He's become a typist so he can sit with the miniskirt* ladki *secretaries.*

And then the exact same bullshit all the way back to Birmingham. All of them who'd dissed her when she'd got divorced and made out like her cancer was her karma. Rolling their eyes whenever she limped or coughed. All of them who'd been feeding her and holding her and wiping her and hugging her and probly hiring a dehumidifier to cope with her eye saliva ever since you'd fucked off.

34

"DADDY, WE NEED to talk about your stories."

Check my dad landing his tray on the table like some toy aeroplane. Some kinda L'Oréal bounce in his moustache. Check me telling him how thanks to the Happy Meal, McDonald's is the largest toy distributor in the world – though I ain't sure if that's by volume or by revenue.

"Your news stories, Daddy – the ones that are supposedly fake."

Now check me teaching Dad how to Instagram his Big Mac – cos otherwise his food won't exist and he'll starve.

"Thanks very much for returning my cuttings book, Dylan."

Dad's got chocolate today.

Removes the lid from his cup like he's waiting for his milkshake to cool down.

"Look, Dad, if I had it then I'd give it back to you."

"Thank you for finally doing so, son."

"I swear down, if it shows up I'll give it straight back."

"I'm very glad you did, Dylan. But you could have just brought it along with you now – you needn't have biked it over by courier."

"Wait, *what*?"

Steam rises from his milkshake. "You should let me reimburse you for the cycle courier. I know you have your data-entry income, but you should let me help you."

I tell him he knows damn well I didn't bike over diddly nothing.

"That's a good one, son. I like how you use humour to defuse our differences." Check his stripy drinking straw like a punchline into his face. "Just like that library borrowing slip you stuck inside the cuttings book, Dylan – that was a nice touch also."

"Okay, Dad, what fresh-brewed bullshit is this?"

"It was very good of you to return it to me, Dylan. It was the decent thing to do."

I tell him it was no problem.

Tell him it was a pleasure.

Tell him to Instagram his milkshake or supersize cappuccino or whatever, his pint of Horlicks. Otherwise his beverage won't exist and he'll dehydrate. *Young Carer's Playbook #172: Gotta pick your battles cos your parent can't pick theirs.* Anyway, allow all this fuckery. Ain't got enough memory space. And I ain't meaning the voice memo app on my fone – today I'm packing a single-function, top-of-the-range dictaphone. Pop-out USB connection to pin his bullshit straight to my hard drive.

"Daddy, we need to talk about your stories."

"Why all the fiddling with your jacket, Dylan? If you need to check your phone then go ahead."

Tell him I'm just checking I ain't been pickpocketed.

"Well? Has anything gone missing in the last thirty seconds?"

Should've freed up more gigabytes. Erased last term's lectures. Delete a pre-bereavement bereavement session, the secret recording of her crooning while croaking, the sounds of her smiling in her sleep. When Dad had finally shown up, I slipped the dictaphone into my shirt pocket, but like a dumbass I forgot to hit record.

Before it got jacked from my student halls, I'd kept Dad's scrapbook in the drawers beside my bed. His stories, my bedside; the clock saying half-past bedtime. *Get it? Got it?* Good.

"Dad, we need to talk about your stories."

He looks at me like, sure, fire away.

So I start hitting him up with the full download. Everything I've managed to puzzle out about his supposedly fake eyewitness quotes. Even catch myself reckoning myself – *Hey Daddy, look at me riding my bicycle.* That kinda thing. Cos if your daddy doesn't see you, your bike won't actually exist and you'll fall flat on the fucking ground. Graze your elbow and your backbone. Apologising out of nowhere. Your teachers or line manager thinking you're some dumbfuck chump. Every sentence you speak becoming some oil-slick egg-and-spoon race.

But not today.

I tell Dad how instead of googling his name, I been searching online for the names of his supposedly fake eyewitnesses. How I'd spotted them popping up in other stories – stories written by other journalists for other publications. "And here's the thing, Dad: those other stories contained the word-for-word exact same eyewitness quotes that you told me you'd made up."

Wanna just leave it at that. Let my daddy fill in the blanks. *Don't let him see me crash.*

He asks me to please continue.

"Well, I'm just saying that . . . Look, Dad, some of them other websites even posted video footage and audio clips."

For instance: *"'My family and I have been waiting at the airport for eight hours,' said John Smith, a blacksmith from Cheshire."*

For instance: *"'They didn't have any beds so they did the surgery in the corridor,' said Anna Cook, a chef from Croydon."*

"So the others had the same quotes and posted video clips. So what, Dylan?"

"So I was just thinking that, well, you know, clearly you couldn't have just made them up. All them eyewitnesses must've been for real and their quotes must've been genuine."

Now cupping his milkshake to warm up his hands. "I see. So instead of concluding that the whole dishonest news media must've been faking and fabricating things, you instead conclude that I've been lying to you?"

"Well . . . yeh." I sit back and work the logic again – just to be sure my conclusion is the blatantly bloody obvious one. Not too long ago, this shit would be open-and-shut. If everyone's story is basically the same, chances are the story is true. Same shit goes for random eyewitness statements. Same shit goes for answers to random quiz questions. General knowledge, trivia, the facts of the fucking matter. But today this shit don't feel so open-and-shut. Today it feels like open season on shut.

"Look, way I see it, Dad, only way they could've all got the exact same quotes is if they all pulled out their notebooks and dictaphones and microphones in front of the same eyewitnesses – just like how they do in films. So you see, you *couldn't* have just made it all up. Which means your fake stories ain't actually fake." I take a hit of my own milkshake. Emergency protein injection. "They had the exact same quotes," I tell him again. "Word-for-wordbatim. C'mon Dad, work with me here." Like as if I'd rather that he'd lied in all his stories and was therefore telling me the truth.

"Dylan, first of all, I didn't lie to you. Secondly, if I'd told you the truth, you wouldn't have believed me."

"Okay, I don't know even know what that means."

"The only thing that it can mean. That I'm telling you the truth when I say I faked all those quotes. But also that what you've since found out is also true: my fabrications somehow started appearing in other people's stories for other publications. Except that in those other publications they weren't trumped-up fabrications – they were genuine."

"Sorry, is that supposed to clear shit up?"

"Actually, Dylan, I'm a very plain-speaking person. Believe me, I'm probably the plainest speaker you'll ever meet. So let me speak plainly with you, son: what happened with my stories was a major paranormal phenomenon." His face now somehow uplit by the downlights in the ceiling. "Either I was having premonitions of words that would later genuinely be spoken by genuine eyewitnesses. Or, by making things up, I was somehow making it come true – and all the other journalists on other publications were genuinely reporting that truth."

It's like he doesn't even *want* me to believe him. Like he couldn't give two fucks either way.

"Dad, please."

"I was sceptical at first myself, Dylan. I thought perhaps all the others were just copying my stories to generate cheap clicks. After all, some journalists do that – just lazily recycle each other's stories to get maximum web hits. And if the stories turn out to be fabricated, they just churn out another story debunking the first story and then they get even more clicks. Believe me, son, media professionals can be the most dishonest people on earth."

"Don't worry, Dad, I believe you."

He tells me how he then contacted each of those other journalists. Asked them how the hell they could just copy his quotes like that – though obviously he didn't tell them he'd been faking the quotes. "Well, they all flat-out denied it, Dylan – a few of them even played me their dictaphone recordings to prove that their own content was genuine. And then, just for good measure, they posted their audio clips on their websites. As you correctly inferred, they'd all reported the same quotes as each other after descending together on the scene of the incident or stage-managed news event in question and thrusting their microphones and dictaphones in front of the same eyewitnesses or spokespeople. They weren't copying my fake stories. And I wasn't copying their real stories. Rather, as I said, son, it was a major paranormal phenomenon."

There's this cognitive bias called the Bizarreness Effect. We lock onto facts that are strange. Probly explains all them times I've had YouTube on autoplay and each "Up Next" video gets more and more weirdness, keeping me logged on for longer. Maybe even explains why I stay sat here instead of standing up and splitting.

I start counting all the holes in Dad's story. Some of them multiply like cancer cells too fast to even be counted. Some of the smaller holes slowly turn into assholes the size of truck tyres. And some of them start fronting like black holes, sucking in the rest of his story. But other holes seem to fill themselves in as we talk about them so that they ain't no longer holes. Dad dropping actual physical evidence – pulling out his laptop and showing me timestamps that show how all those other stories were published within seconds of each other. Tells me that means the reporters couldn't have been copying each other. Next he pulls out his actual cuttings book and shows me how the publication dates of his fake news stories back up the story that he's just told me. I sneak a peek through the book: all his stories all intact, the pages untorn, spine unscathed, no bruises or redactions in black marker pen. Allow this shit – you wanna know about holes in someone's story? Try talking to an immunocompromised woman with actual holes all over her oral orifice. Broken sound of her words as she tries reassuring you she ain't in pain – that she ain't even hungry anyway.

I ask Dad for extra info. Deleted scenes, director's commentary. Just to show some buy-in or open-mindedness or whatever, obedience. For instance, were all the other journalists as spooked as he was – or at least as spooked as he expects me to be?

"Actually, one or two of them got angry at me – they were worried their own editors might suspect that everyone was just lazily copying everyone else's content. I remember one of the reporters had a lisp and he kept grovelling and begging me, 'Please, please thstop jeopardithing my career.'" As he says this, Dad twists his arm out like he's translating the lisp into sign language or something.

"Wait, Dad, did you just make fun of some other guy's speech impediment?"

"Of course not. I never mocked his speech impediment. I would never do a thing like that, son. I was simply doing a general impression of someone grovelling."

Guess I could play back the audio to prove him wrong. Call my dad out on this specific dollop of bullshit. But most probly he'd still deny it. Probly claim it was just a recording glitch – that my dictaphone had malfunctioned due to the price of fish or something.

Dad tells me how he even did a few experiments, making up more and more ridiculous eyewitness quotes. For instance: *"We never spoke to the last occupant but sometimes we saw her walking her baby elephant."* And yet, each time he did this, all his fake shit ended up actually being spoken by genuine eyewitnesses at random news incidents and then reported in other publications. "By this stage, Dylan, I'm not ashamed to admit that I was in danger of completely losing the plot."

"Tell me about it, Dad."

"I mean, who are you even meant to go to with a thing like that? I didn't trust normal so-called experts, so why the hell would I trust paranormal experts?"

First time me and my dad manage to pull off laughing at the same thing at the same time. Shame we both just pretending to laugh.

"When the man first approached me, Dylan, I thought maybe he was some kind of media regulator. A real one, I mean – one that regulates social media and search engines. He certainly looked the part – aside from the mud on his hands. Whoever the hell he was, he warned me that if I wasn't careful, my increasingly outlandish fake stories could end up killing someone. That's what he said, son: 'Your words are actions and they can kill.'"

One thing I've learned from monitoring my mum's bedtime browsing habits: crazyass conspiracy theories ain't meant to be believable – they're meant to be comfortable. Easier to believe something comfortable than something factual. And having something or someone to blame is way more comfortable than blaming randomness. All those viral health-scare stories spread about on Facebook. *Mummy, please stop reading that stuff.* That "shareable" anti-vaccination crap that actually kills people. *Mummy, please stop reading that stuff.* That *Daily Mail* breast cancer story that didn't reveal until paragraph 19 that the research in question had fuck all to do with breast cancer – just clickbait with caveats to cover their asses. *Mummy, please. Stop clicking on the links.*

Dad's milkshake has finally cooled down or warmed up or whatever. Folds his arms like he's trying to hug himself. "Over the years I've come to believe what that strange man told me: words are definitely actions, Dylan. They can change things. And sometimes fabrications can become the truth."

We shoulda just stuck to small talk. Kinda chat where all we was basically saying beneath all the bants was, *You and me, we're good.*

"I'm not talking about how fake news stories catastrophically altered reality via the ballot box. I'm talking about the fact that if you call me a journalist, Dylan, then at some deep, cellular level I actually become more of a journalist than I would be if you kept calling me an insurance salesman. Likewise, if you call me Dad, I become more of a dad."

Don't matter how many times Dad calls me Dylan, though, I'm still acting like Dhilan – sitting here soaking up whatever crap he needs me to soak up. But why the hell would he make all this up? There's gotta be enough more believeable stories that he could spin if he just wanted to put me on divert.

"So you see the reason for all the secrecy now? Why I never told you I worked as a journalist and why I actually encouraged your mother and her family to tell people I worked in insurance. And of course it now goes without saying that you must never tell these things to anyone else, Dylan. Not even your friends, your girlfriend, Mona – is that her name? Not a word of this to her. She should respect your right to some family privacy." He tells me he doesn't actually care if I don't believe his story. All he cares about is that I leave all these things alone now so that we don't have some kinda throwback to whatever forces were at play all them years ago.

I figure this is a bad time to tell him how I've already gone and digitised all his fake stories. So instead I tell him I buy the idea that words can alter reality. Start hitting him with the example of oracular prophecies in *Oedipus* when he cuts me off – like he doesn't wanna hear about Oedipus.

"You ever heard of something called 'automatic writing,' Dylan? It's similar to what happens with a Ouija board, only instead of a board you just have your pen or your typewriter or laptop. And you just write. Or rather, some other force writes and your mind just takes dictation. And sometimes the things you write down happen in real life. Whether you're predicting it or causing it, I have no idea, but it's my belief that that's what was happening when I was fabricating things in my news stories."

I tell him I don't know nothing about automatic writing but that it sounds kinda similar to—

Again, he cuts me off like a gameshow buzzer: "Come on, son, these days there's no such thing as not knowing something."

I pull out my Dhilan handset. Soon as I start to google the words "automatic writing", Google predicts what I'm typing before I even finish the word "automatic". Tonight, Facebook will hit me with a video about it. Amazon will hit me up with a book. End of the week I'll probly be an expert. Fuck knows whether Google's some oracle or whether I'm writing my future by typing. Or whether I'd be reading about automatic writing right now even if I'd actually been searching for an automatic washing machine. And fuck knows what happens to you when autocomplete and predictive text become as natural for choosing what words you write next as more old-school forms of writing tech – like using spellcheck and cut-and-paste.

Soon as I put away my fone, Dad starts acting all extra and parental, saying he wants to link up on the regular. Finishes his Big Mac and closes out by saying let's meet in McDonald's again tomorrow – like as if he can't find a midpoint between abandonment and smotherment. And I can't bring myself to say no. Don't want him thinking when he's walking past some lonely loser's strip club that he's now also been rejected by his son. Or when he's walking past the top shelf in a newsagent's – clutching some takeaway pizza box like the closest he'll get to feeling the warmth of a woman's arm across his chest.

"Dylan, in the past, I had a number of limitations. Your mother said she didn't need anything from me. And in spite of this, I kept trying to do my maximum for you. But one thing you should do is let me help you now." He asks me if my start-up business happens to have a funding shortfall. Even more specifically, if I need any bucks from him to help me branch out into new businesses. More specifically still, if he can drop, say, five hundred bucks to help me diversify away from digitising. "After all, one day all the newspapers and books and documents will have already been digitised."

I tell him I don't need him to give me any money. Thanks all the same, though – thanks.

"Then think of it as an investment. Bridge financing. If you ever have any cashflow problems, no bank will lend credit to a start-up run by a student. In fact, give me your account details and I can transfer five hundred pounds right now – or even one thousand if you prefer."

I have to lock eyes with him just to stop mine from rolling. The fuck is he keep offering me money for? Man's being way too obvious for it to be bribery or divertory tactics. Best-case scenario, it's just something to do with his tax return – offsetting his liabilities or someshit. "This is to stop me asking questions about your fake news stories?"

"I've already answered all your questions, Dylan. I'm offering you money because I don't want for you to have any additional worries and stress while you complete your studies. You must believe me when I tell you that I was denied the opportunity of helping you in a variety of ways in the early period. With all the limitations, whenever I could, I did my best for you."

Fuck's sake. Now I gotta reach back into my pocket to hit record on my dictaphone again. Or swipe open the voice memo app on my fone. Or pull out a pad and take old-school notes. Or just take a stool sample from this latest bout of bullshit and stick it in a jar of formaldehyde.

"If you don't want to branch out and diversify, then that's fine – I'm not trying to dictate anything, son. But then at least use my financial assistance to rebrand – give your company a proper name, something you can put on LinkedIn. See what you can do with this little start-up of yours – you don't want to be a typist for the rest of your life."

If Mum had called me that shit, I'd get proper man-menstrual with her. Tell her I ain't a bloody typist, I'm a digitiser/data-enterer/data temp. Why is it that I'd shout at the parent who took care of me but not at the parent who didn't? Surely should be the other way round. Ditto calling him out on his bullshit. Ditto calling him out on my bullshit. Best I can manage right now is to just say things that *sound* like they should be shouted – or at least thrown up in a raised-up voice. For instance: *"I never needed your money, etc."* Only I say it all on the down-low – like we're a couple of actors quietly reading rather than rehearsing some loud and angry showdown scene. For instance, all them showdowns in those films set in newsrooms – when reporters and editors start arguing about sources and truth. Or deadlines and truth. Or truth, justice and truth. Trouble is, we ain't in a film – we ain't in a film where the journalist is a sleazeball, we ain't in a film where the journalist is a superhero; we ain't in a film. Cos the dialogue's already recorded in a film. You don't need no fucking dictaphone to play his bullshit back to him, you just hit rewind on your remote.

35

EIGHTH TIME YOUR mum told you she had the C-bomb, she told you via an intermediary. And, no – we still ain't talking the spirit-medium kind.

Even though it was daytime, they'd closed the living-room curtains. Sunset oozing through green fabric, turning it from emerald to the colour of baby shit. We're talking intermediaries plural. Like you'd walked into the opposite of a surprise birthday party. Where instead of jumping up and shouting, "Surprise!" everyone falls down and starts crying, "She's dying!"

"Welcome home, Dhilan," said your Uncle Deepak. "Please – have a sit." He gestured at a kitchen stool cos the sofa, dining chairs and latest prospective deathbed were occupied by your masi and, like, nine other various assorted aunties and uncles – mostly aunties. Weren't sure if you were actually related to them all, or even if you even knew them all, but they were definitely aunties.

"Where's Mama?" you said to some general blur of coiled opinions. "I want to see my mum."

"Just, please, just have the seat."

The stool had been placed against the nearside wall, beneath the LED picture light your mum had rewired. More framed fotos from weekend wellness breaks. The sunsets, the moonlit-candlelit dinners, the arguments about you being too sissy to slow-dance with her, the breathing exercises by the indoor rehab pool with the tropical-themed drinks, those breakfast-buffet bikinis and swimsuits of hers with the pouches for her plastic prostheses, her with her travel spanner for tightening the bolts of your honeymoon suite bed. You dreaded school holidays. Couldn't wait for them to end. Then you'd dread the start of term in case something happened to her while you were stuck in some bullshit Biology lesson.

In among the various assorted aunties and non-aunties and uncles and non-uncles, you spotted your cousin Ravi – rocking chinos and regulation Ralph Polo logo. "Rav-man? I thought you was in New York?"

"I was meant to be, Dhilan. But I cancelled my trip because I love my aunty."

Cutting through the all-round silence of approval came the sound of your mum's accessible downstairs shower. Spurting and gurgling and groaning in sync. *But wait a sec* – even if some Macmillan nurse was in there helping her, you were for cert your mummy could only be washed in bed. (Or maybe that was a month or two later.) (Or could be a month or two earlier.)

Next, one of your aunties or non-aunties asked you if you'd like a cup of tea. Like some dipshit gimp you almost said yes. Checked yourself, though – somehow you mustered your mother's bollocks. "How about if I place the teacup on my head – maybe you could all aim at that instead?"

"Don't try to be clever," said Aunty Number Five.

"Fine, I'll try and be stupid."

"You are bloody stupid!" Uncle Deepak at max volume. "When my own mother had the heart attack I never had this chance that you have now. But you, instead, you do the gallivanting and the studying and the partying and the typing and the laughing and the studying."

"And also the gallivanting with the girlfriend," Aunty Number Four jumped in.

"Look, if you're referring to Ramona, I was actually lying when I told Mum she was my girlfriend."

"Bullshit rubbish bullshit," said Aunty Number Six. "You think we're all the fools or what? Boys tell their mothers they don't have the girlfriend only when they *do* have it – they don't say they have the girlfriend when they don't."

You didn't know whether to tell them that Ramona was more like your best-friend-with-benefits or just someone who settled for you and your weirdness, whatever, your dirty fucked-up foot fetish. Truth is, this shit weren't even about Ramona, it was about the fact that, back then, even *you* reckoned the worst thing you could've done to your mum was to split. Bail. Walk. Wash your hands of her metaphorically as well as literally. Looking back, it was actually kinda sweet. Maybe one or two of your aunts had heard about euthanasia and reckoned *that* was the worst thing you could do – in which case that would've been kinda sweet too.

"Dhilan, why are you moving your mouth like a horse?" asked Aunty Number Four. "Are you chewing the bubblegum while talking to us?"

You told her you were sucking a mouth ulcer. Mouth ulcers plural.

"You think *you've* got the mouth ulcers," replied Aunty Number Six. "Wait you see your mother's mouth. In my life I never see such a horrible thing."

"I'm familiar with her methotrexate-induced ulceration," you shot back. "Have you tried giving her pineapples?"

"For what pineapples?"

"It stimulates saliva. Though obviously she shouldn't lick the skin."

"Bloody asshole idiot," shouted Aunty Number Five – you reckoned her name was Aunty Chamlesh, though you weren't for definitely sure. "You think this is some game or what?"

The assembled aunties and uncles all started murmuring. And nodding – lots of nodding. Giving signals to each other.

"No. I don't think that this is a game. That's the whole point. That's why there ain't any rules as to how I should be reacting."

Snorting from somewhere. Biscuits and rice cakes. Lonely low-fat crackers like the edges of burnt birthday cards. Relatives and non-relatives. Random elderly men with turbans and long white beards even though your family weren't even Sikh. Only thing missing was your mummy as a wig-wearing judge.

"Listen, young man," Aunty Number Six tagged herself in. "Only reason we tolerate all this crap of yours is because your mother keeps begging us not to shout at you. She's so used to you bloody selfish shitting on her, she doesn't even to complain."

"Exactly," said another unidentified aunty. "Exactly, exactly. She lives for you, she lives for you and all you can do is your bloody selfishness."

You knew from your mother–son couples counselling that the reason their bullshit boiled your blood was cos part of you probly agreed with them – i.e. it weren't actually bullshit. After all, if they were just sitting there calling you a crack dealer or something, it wouldn't have meant shit to you cos you knew for sure that you weren't one. You figured that even if only 2 per cent of your mind agreed with them, that'd still mean you against 2 per cent of yourself. You'd watched your mum fight against 2 per cent of her body and so you knew how much that fight could fuck you up. As if Aunty Number Five could read your mind, she then started dissing the couples therapist who'd told you all this. "All this Westernised wanting-your-space nonsense of yours is all because of the counselling." Then she turned to Uncle Deepak. "Isn't it? Tell him what it is I told you."

"Dhilan, why you don't tell *us* what we can do for you?" said Uncle Deepak. "Is there something more you need from us? To help you start acting like the responsible grown-up? I've told to your mother many times, the two of you should have never gone to see all those counsellors and bouncellors. This is what family's for. All your problems will be resolved if you keep it in the family."

In the corner of the living-room-cum-bedroom-cum-hospital-room-cum-courtroom, a man leaned forward from the sofa and you could've sworn down he was your old headmaster – the one who'd died while shouting at some kid for wearing trainers to school. Except this man here was wearing a turban. And with a long white beard and so on.

"You wanna know what I think?" said your fucking same-generation cousin Ravi. You sucked on your mouth ulcers while he waited for everyone's attention. Then, as if he'd just discovered the concept earlier that same week, he declared, "Dhilan, I think you're in . . . *denial*."

You counted to ten. Fifteen. Fuck it, twenty. Then you told him, on the calm, that being in denial would imply you didn't think she was really dying, whereas, in actualtruth, you'd been thinking she was dying since you started high school – back when Ravi reckoned you was just being a goth.

"Okay, tell me something," Aunty Number Four or Five sounding sweet as her own *jalebi*. "Do you feel your mother's a *burden* on you?"

Oh. Fuck.

What the hell were you s'posed to say to that? She knew full well that if you said *No* you'd be contradicting all your behaviour and digital data and so on. But if you said *Yes* then you'd be full-on fucked cos your aunts and uncles probly defined the word "burden" as something a person doesn't want. Figured if you was a nurse or a social worker or something then you could just say the technical term was "burnout". But seeing as how you weren't a nurse, you didn't know what word to call it. And so you just stuck with the dictionary definition – the definitions you'd spent the past nine years defining: "Well, *obviously* she's a burden."

The sound of everyone drawing a collective breath through their collectively clenched teeth. Kinda sound you might hear if time flipped into reverse. Straight away, you wanted to scroll back and elaborate. But what could you have told them? That, technically speaking, *you'd* been a burden on your mum back when you were a baby/toddler/infant/boy? Or should you have tried to explain that part of the "burden" here was the fact that you'd already lost her? Lost her years back.

Instead, you just decided to complete the general stun-gun effect – reached into your pocket and pulled out a pack of cigarettes, like some kinda clown-town-fucko-drama-queen. An ad for lung cancer on the back of the box. Next, as if you weren't being enough of a ridicu-dickless cliché, you reached across and tried using one of your mum's sick bowls or bedpans as an ashtray. Problem was, it was one of them disposable cardboard ones so pretty soon the ash was burning right through into your lap. Aunty Number Six jumped up to douse out the bedpan with her glass of lassi – we're talking an ice-cold lassi cum-stain all over your fucking crotch. While you dabbed your general dick area dry, she handed you your mum's pink plastic kidney bowl. "Here. Take it. The cigarette won't burn through this one."

And so you swallowed your dipshit pretentiousness and started fretting about the cigarette smoke. "How long does Mama usually take in the shower? If you open the curtains, we could open the windows. How long before she gets out of the shower?"

"Well, let's see," said Aunty Number Seven. "It takes her a little longer than normal these days because of the plaster cast on her broken femur. Sometimes she has to stick it outside the shower to stop it getting wet, other times we wrap it for her in a plastic bin liner."

"You see," said Aunty Number Fifty-Four as your scowl dropped into the kidney bowl, "it's high time you came back to reality."

Big fucking surprise: Uncle Number Twenty-Nine agreed with his wife. "Do you know why it is your mother's making such a *tamasha* about showering today? It's because she's so much excited that you're coming to see her during the daytime instead of ten rush-rush minutes in the night. Such a small, simple little thing has made her smile more than I've seen her smile in two weeks. Why the hell you couldn't just do this for her before? Every day you could have been bringing her the joy."

Could feel some kinda carbon-copy jury take their seats up in your head. We're talking permanent residency. All of them thinking what they already thought. All of them having the same opinion. Taking each other to some next level of the same opinion.

"And then when you do come and see her, she tells us you do the bloody miserable moodiness," said Aunty Number Three. "Even on her birthday you were sulking and bringing her down."

"Sulking?" You weren't asking whether you'd been on some sulk cos you knew for definite that it was true. Instead, you were asking whether they were seriously being serious that your sulking was even an issue. Your mum's last birthday – her forty-eighth – had been widely billed as her *last* last birthday.

Once again, Aunty Number Fifty-Four read your mind and hit you with another truth bullet: "You don't think we didn't find it difficult also? Heh? Huh? Eh? But we all of us just put on the brave and happy face for her sake. You should have done the same – after all, it was *her* birthday, not your birthday. All the times she's put on the brave face for your birthday."

In the corner, your old headmaster started nodding and pouring himself a scotch. Poured one for one of the bearded Sikh men too.

"Here, look, why not I show you," said Aunty Number Twenty-Seven as she pulled some brand-new iPhone on you. Started playing back the video she'd filmed during your mum's last Last Birthday. "See?" she said. "See how you're not even trying to smile."

You started weighing up whether you'd be still crying on your mum's birthday thirty years after she'd actually died. Or would the tears dry out after twenty years? Ain't like there was some law that said you'd ever have to stop – like as if mourning could ever actually have an end date, even if it even had a proper start date.

Aunty Number Forty-Five was trying to watch the fone footage with you but kept having her small-screen squint-fits. No problemo – your cousin Ravi was at the ready with an adapter and cable to connect the iPhone to the 33-inch plasma TV. Dude probly even had boxes of popcorn in his bag. Nachos, even. (Though no hot dogs obviously cos the cinema ones are usually made of beef.) "See, Dhilan?" he said as he kicked off the special red-carpet screening.

"See how while everyone else is trying to lift your dear mother's spirits, you're just sitting at the end of the table and sulking?" He grabbed Aunty Number Fifteen's iPhone from your hand and started scrolling forward. "And here – look – you look like you're at a funeral." Before you could tell him that he ain't never had to mourn someone every time they tried to smile, he scrolled forward again. "See? And see there? You see that? And even when she cut her cake – see what kind of atmosphere you're creating."

You backed off instead of punching your cousin in his always clean-shaven face. Because the worst thing about your mum's birthday video weren't the way you were sulking like some spoiled little emo-brat with semen-tinted teardrops. It was the sight of how scared of you she was. Like she was more afraid of your hi-def stubble than she was of her own prognosis. Like as if, in that one split second, you'd switched from curing her nightmares to causing them. Like she already knew back then the shitfest that was coming next.

You shoulda just hit the pause button. Cos you knew straight away that you were always gonna be paused there. Bang in the middle of that pre-bereavement bereavement mindfuckery. But, of course, all this digital footage meant you could still drill deeper and deeper into all the Bigfuckingdeal-Data. Not just pause, rewind and playback, but pinch-to-zoom, screenshot, crop, filter, auto-enhance, timestamp, geolocate, metadata, higher-def, 3D effect, combine the footage with other eyewitness footage, Google Image Search, remove red eye, make yourself an eternally eternal gif. Each time you moved closer to your mum and her birthday cake, her leaning the fuck further away. And each time the others forced her to lean in for another mother–son foto, she'd freak out – her left shoulder actually rising up against you on some sorta self-defence-type shit. You didn't even take a slice of her birthday cake – the iPhone footage actually caught you telling her that your hands were too dirty to eat with cos you'd been holding the handrails on some fictitiously delayed Tube train. But no one else in the room seemed to notice the worst-worst thing about her last-

last birthday: how after you told her that shit about not wanting a piece of her cake, your mum stopped eating her own slice. Spat it out into her napkin like a radioactive dollop of chemo vomit.

"And to top it all off, Dhilan, you turned up an hour late," said Ravi. "Look, let me rewind and show you. All of us trying to make awkward small talk. Nobody wanting to be the one who asks where the hell you are and why your mobile was clearly switched to airplane mode."

"Enough." Your masi stood up outta nowhere and did some snatch-and-grab action with the iPhone. "Whose idiot idea was it to show this video? You want the poor boy to stick pins into his eyes or what?" And then turning to you: "Dhilan, I don't want you to ever watch this video again. There are happier videos – many, many much, much happier videos. And I will make sure Ravi emails them to you. Because we're not trying to make you feel the guilt, we're just trying to make these days happy for her."

Your mum and the Macmillan nurse entered the living-room-cum-bedroom just in time to see your masi hugging you – hugging you tighter than actual Huggies. Uncle Deepak's attaboy arm around your shoulder. Her bath-towel-turban as if she had hair drying underneath it. Fronting like the whole committee hearing had just been some impro-freestyle coincid-fluke.

36

WORD IS RAMONA was laughing right before it happened. Word is you couldn't really tell when the laughing stopped and the screaming started. I try walking like I don't know where I'm going. There's sobbing in the corridor and no fone signal. No energy drinks in the vending machines. There's always sobbing in this corridor. Should be a word for getting lost on purpose.

Turn right after minor family dramas. Hang a left after full-on family throwdowns. Mama told me not to worry about her. Told me I could go and light up her whole life later – *"But please this time, Dhilan, don't forget the visiting hours end at eight."*

I've brought Ramona's toothbrush and underwear just in case she needs them. Her six-inch stilettos to avoid confusion. *Sorry it took me so long – a dog ate my travel pass. I was stopped by the police for crying in the street. I got here quicker than I could.* Now another blood-soaked corridor – it's like finding your way around disability claims forms. I walked in here through this sneaky shortcut back entrance and I'm making my way to the main entrance. Know my way around a tax return backwards too. *Well, good for me, yeh.* I told you this shit's been good for me. That homesick smell of disinfectant – just gulp it down your nostrils. The lullaby sound of sirens. Snort it up your ears. All them times I hear alarm bells in my head and reckon it's just a ringtone – that shit ain't my fault. Or when I clock the beat of the countdown and reckon it's just the beep of an alarm. Ain't my dirty dumbfuck fault. Same shit goes for global warming and Islamist and alt-right terrorism. Same shit goes for all the good shit. Ain't my fault if her sickness has been good for me.

When I step into the beeping, flickering A&E department, it's like going back to school. The plastic chairs, the shouting, the whole fucking hospital thing. Ain't no sign of Ramona but I clock her friend Naliah. Right before she stands up and slaps me. It's fine, though – I'm like some cross-wired emergency services provider; always putting out fires in ambulance mode. I tell Naliah all that entry-level antshit about needing to stay calm. That I know this is all my fault – don't matter that I weren't even with Ramona when it happened. I tell her to shout at *me*, not the nurses. Fuck it, I even got stopped by the police for crying in the street. Then I tell her, yes, I'm an asshole. A dickhole, even – a dirty, infected dickhole. A peephole cigarette burn in a lump of fungified faeces. First time I ever lit a cigarette was in this exact same waiting area after they said it had spread to Mum's lungs – that's the kind of dipshit drama queen I can be.

You're supposed to ask the doctors and nurses lots of questions. It demonstrably demonstrates just how much you care. I learnt this from watching my masi in action. I learnt this from watching flashbacks of my snot-nosed nine-year-old self. Best to avoid asking female nurses, though – no sense in making Mummy jealous. And it's easier to do all that Q&A bullshit when there ain't no doctors actually around – you just keep asking nurses to please call a doctor so that you can ask said doctor some questions. Trouble kicks in when all your bleeding-heart queries start running dry or scabbing up. That's when you'll ask anyone in a white coat anyshit just to show her that you're doing something. *Is it environmentally friendly to cremate prosthetic breasts? Do you reckon Spurs will win the Ashes?*

Today, Naliah shoots down my questions with answers before I can even ask them. 1) Turns out Ramona hasn't been crying

– ain't even shed a grain of salt. Screaming and grunting and convulsing, probly, but not crying. 2) Turns out she's been taken away for tests and X-rays – i.e. my lame ass must've walked right past her. Whenever I've walked past Mum in the X-ray unit, all the lead-lined concrete in the world can't block the vibes between us – doesn't even block our fone signal. 3) Turns out she ain't dying – either of injuries or embarrassment. The paramedics assured her it weren't the weirdest accident they'd ever handled.

Naliah facepalms while she waits for my non-response. Truth is, neither of us is ready to talk details yet – the liquids, the tendons; the actual incident. Or whether Ramona did it by herself or if she was somehow twisted by yours truly.

We start trying to out-care each other. Ask the doctors even more pressing questions, express even deeper concerns, decline offers of tea and coffee even more strongly. But that shit has a safety switch – you can't escalate all the way and offer to do the actual surgery. So eventually Naliah clicks back to the other Ramona-related topic – specifically the sub-thread about my "swollen-asshole behaviour". All that torment and torture that, until today, she'd assumed was just emotional. Even asks me if my dad knows how much of a wank-flannel I've been, like as if I'd actually fess up my sins to my father.

I tell her my dad ain't to blame for this shit. Fuck it, my mum ain't even to blame for this. I could try blaming my fone, of course. All them social networks and search engines that reinforce our perversions/persuasions/general-fucked-upness.

But once again I don't. Cos I did this. *Me.*

It was through the mortuary. Only reason I knew that short-cut back entrance I took here is cos you gotta walk through the hospital mortuary. The mortuary corridor is where I used to fone Ramona from whenever Mum was an inpatient up on the eighth floor. Proper dead silence down there – could pretend I was just foning from home.

"Hey Dillon, what's up? How come you took so long to phone me back?"

"Nothing's up. Just chillin in my crib, innit."

In order to properly lie about where you're foning from, it ain't enough to just find a silent spot, though. You also need a spot that gives maximum forward visibility of any incoming noise. The mortuary corridor is divided by these big-ass fire doors spaced every ten or so metres apart. Each set of fire doors has those little glass portholes so you can scope all the way down to the top of corridor in case some trolley-pushing hospital porter is headed in your direction. Then you could micromanage the fone convo – steer Ramona into some kinda rant or monologue just as the porter approached and then just hit the mute button. As for the porter with the corpse or whatever, I'd just pretend I was grieving until they passed.

A nurse heads towards us holding a hypodermic needle and jabs the waiting-area television back to life. Random scroll of end credits – some daytime Oprah/Springer/soap opera coming up next. Naliah doesn't change the channel, though – more like the opposite. Starts using the whole daytime TV vibe like a surgical tool to scrape out more intel on me and my dad. Yeh – *I know*. This ain't even a leap, it's more some intergalactic belly flop. Like she reckons I'll be caught off guard or someshit. But just ask your adrenal glands: medical emergencies are when we're at our sharpest. And, besides, I already got me a gameplan for this. Don't even need to tell her I know she ain't being on the level with me, that she's blatantly working another angle here, that she can quit snooping about on behalf of the Botox man. You see, something in my daddy's latest scare story about his fake stories must've had the intentioned effect: I'd decided there and then in McDonald's how to patch the whole Botox-man-and-Naliah problem.

First, the deflection: "What the fucking fuck, Naliah? A woman we both care about is undergoing a major medical crisis here and you wanna turn it into some drama about my dad? What kind of backasswards bullshit is that?"

Naliah smiles but works hard not to say nothing.

After throwing down this deflection, I then switch to diversion. Instead of claiming I don't know jack about my dad's fake news stories, I'm gonna create me a story of my own. Distraction rather than denial – just like how all them dirtbag politicians do. But here's the badass part: you know how they say the best place to hide a book is in a library? Or how the smartest place to bury a dead body is in an actual graveyard? Well, I'm gonna distract Naliah from the topic of my father by telling her all about my father. That's right – I'ma throw her off his scent by pumping his stink straight up her nostrils. Only, we're talking his *life*, not his *work*. I want Naliah to report back to the Botox man that I don't give two flying shits about my father's fake news stories, that my interest in him is purely personal, not professional – i.e. it's private, i.e. it's got fuck all to do with journalism. That my brain ain't scratching at the black scabs of his bullshit blacked-out scare stories.

Here's the problem with my plan, though: I actually know fuck all about my dad. Best I can do is roll out some recap action of some small talk we did in McDonald's. Pro tip: don't even bother trying to have a compelling conversation about a conversation about the weather. Or about energy tariffs. Or root vegetables. Or sports. Next thing, I'm telling Naliah how I don't even know my dad, like some whining pustulating pussy-fart. Only time I manage to keep some cred intact is when I tell her my dad cut contact with me when I was "I dunno, like, maybe about seven or eight years old" – as opposed to the actualtruth, which is that I was seven years old, nine months and five days.

"Dillon, why are you saying all this to me?"

"Just trying to be topical. Apparently Father's Day is coming up soon – like, sometime in the next twelve months."

"You're telling me these things about your dad because you can't discuss it with Ramona – she wouldn't understand it properly because she still doesn't know anything about your mother."

"Oh for fuck's sake, Naliah, ain't you bored of this already? Of my mum, I mean. It's dull. Wanna know why cancer battles are usually just a background subplot? It's cos long drawn-out deaths are so fucking boring they're considered too cruel for animals. And, anyway, this has fuck all to do with my mother – my dad cut off contact with me long before she got sick."

"Sure, but nonetheless you're implying that he continued to keep himself cut off in spite of the fact your mum got sick."

"But he didn't completely cut contact with me – like I just told you, he sent me a couple of birthday cards and he foned me on Diwali once."

There's this payphone stuck up on the waiting-area wall like some ancientquated museum artefact. And fuck me if it ain't the exact same payphone I once tried dialling my dad from. Must've been back when I was in Year Nine or Ten. I guess at some point they just stop upgrading old-school tech.

"So it wasn't a big bust-up situation with you and your dad – it was just gradual?"

"Yup – same as it was with him and Mum. Apparently they just gradually grew apart."

Could've just used my mobile to call him back then instead of the payphone. But I was worried he'd recognise the number. Or save it or delete it or rename it. Change Mum into me or me into Mum. He might've just changed Dhilan into Dylan.

"Look, Dillon, sometimes dads leave – there's no need to be a pussy about it . . . I think that's actually a line from *Iron Man* or *Man of Steel*. One of the superhero films."

"I ain't being a pussy, Naliah – *you're* the one who keeps asking me about him." And then I carry on trying to throw her off his scent by being a pussy about it. We're now talking Maroon 5 levels of whining whingery. How, over the years, the man just gradually washed his hands of me.

"Washed his hands of you?"

"It's a figure of speech. I don't mean he literally washed my bodily fluids off his hands."

I did actually ask my mum and dad which one of them "just gradually grew apart" from the other one first. They told me they both did. Standing either side of me. Both of them holding me – one hand each. Me letting go of both their hands so as not to upset one or the other. Later, Mum making me sit on her lap so she could download the detailed footnotes: *"Neither of us intended to grow apart, Dhilan. Both of us were just trying to make things better. But people have different ideas of what better means. What's best for one person isn't always what's best for the other person. What I called better might have been what your father called silly. What your father called better might have been what I called boring. At first when you're married you're not trying to make things better – you're just busy being married. Then later, when you start trying to make things better, if you both have different ideas of what better means, then that's when you start growing apart."*

And here's Dad when I asked him a day or so ago as part of our ongoing death by small talk: *"But you already know why your mother and I got divorced. We just grew apart. What does it matter now, anyway, Dylan? It was eleven years ago."*

"Actually, it was twelve years ago."

"The point is, we just grew apart. I'm not even sure whether your mother ended it or if I ended it – whether she kicked me out or I walked out or whether she kicked me out while I was walking out. At certain times in my life I'd have given you one answer, and at other times I'd have given you another answer. So telling you that I don't know is the most honest answer I can give you. We just sort of grew apart."

And here's one of my quick-fix therapists: *"All infants and young children believe that the divorce is somehow because of them because all infants and young children still think the world revolves around them. That's how humans develop. Very young kids just can't compute that something is happening for reasons that are unrelated to them. That's why these things are so traumatic. Because very young kids are still at the centre of their own little personalised bubble."*

And here's Naliah in the hospital waiting area: "You didn't express a preference to live with one or the other? Or try to corroborate what they told you?"

"I was seven years old. I thought custody arrangements had got something to do with custard. And, anycase, I already made a point of asking both of them, so why would I corroborate things when I'd already corroborated them – otherwise when do you stop corroborating your corroborations?"

"I was just thinking about the way it is in journalism: apparently you can only rely on two sources to stand up a story if both those sources are unrelated. If not, you need a third, separate source. And, whether they like it or not, divorced parents are still related."

"Naliah, don't be treating me like I'm some dumbfuck dipshit idiot. I see how you just spun this whole convo back to my dad's journalism. But here's the thing: I don't know jack shit about it. That's cos I ain't even interested in my father's news stories. Okay? You can report that back word-for-wordbatim."

Some guy sitting across from us has been eaveswatching our whole convo. I feel like I should buy him some nachos to complete his whole movie-going experience – though that'd actually be stupid seeing as his jaw has been blown off, probly in some sort of international espionage incident.

Turns out the reason Ramona's taken so long in A&E is cos her injury is so minor. The doctor comes over, tells us that nothing is broken and nothing is torn – despite what they first thought. The doctor is a woman and let's just say she ain't exactly impressed when she clocks the pair of six-inch stilettos that I've brought along in Ramona's night bag. Looks me square in the soul. "Is *that* what was responsible for this?"

"Damn right," goes Naliah. "Oh wait – you mean in the *bag*? Hell no – those things are plimsolls in comparison. The shoes that did this aren't even meant to be worn. Well, actually, tell a lie: they *are* meant to be worn. Just not while standing up."

Only reason I brought this stupid pair of stilettos with me is so that Ramona wouldn't think that I'd got preoccupied picking out her underwear or anything. That I was just being standard and only perving over her shoes.

The doc does some kinda eyeroll/side-eyes combo. Says Ramona definitely won't be wearing "those things", but neither will she need crutches; she'll just need to lean on me for support.

37

HERE'S A MANUAL for sons who wake up one morning and find that they've morphed into sickly pus-filled pussies with daddy issues:

- After a decade or so of being estranged, don't try too quick to become buddies.
- 'Absent Fathers' and 'Abandoned Sons' should first slide into more old-school roles – with the father firmly asserting his seniority, laying down the lines of paternal authority and just generally hogging the remote control.
- Only when you been rocking a while in these old-school roles can you then move on and do all that best-mates-buddy-movie bullshit.
- Without first installing this basic ass-whupping operating system, you'll just get a mashup of angst/anger/anarchism.

This ain't some download from a therapy session.

I know all this shit from asking Google.

I know this from letting Google predict what I'm gonna ask.

In fact, fuck it – maybe that's why I been acting like such a patsy. Busting my balls to be all respectful and non-confrontational. Tongue-biting, ten-counting, allow it – as if the shitstains between us didn't exist. Gotta be a reason for it. Ain't like I just decided one day to be dickless.

Or maybe somehow, on some deep-down down-low, I already knew where all this bullshit with my dad was headed.

Again a McDonald's. The office-like strip lighting. Again the plastic furniture. Dad didn't have time for no milkshake or dead cow today. *Daddy has to catch a choo-choo train.*

"What the hell do you think you're doing, Dylan?" His grip on my arm twisting his words into italics or someshit.

The coffee. The milkshake. The little plastic coffee stirrers. We sit at the plastic furniture. He has to free my arm so we can sit. Glossy mag and thermos flask peeping out his raincoat like swag from some lonely loser's sex shop.

"Please just tell me, son: why the hell would you do this?"

The seats. The milkshake. The tubs of ketchup that came with the milkshake.

We sit.

Uneaten family meal on the table beside us, like we scared them all away.

"Okay, okay," I go. "*Okay.*" You know that thing where you try and find the right words to say "No" but you end up saying "Okay"? That shit ain't dicklessness or politeness – it's cos part of you actually *wants* to say okay. "Just forget what I said in my email, Dad. If you really want to invest in my start-up then, okay, that'd be great. You can be my majority stakeholder."

He looks at me like, *Do you think I'm bloody stupid?*

I'd turned down Dad's offer to invest in my start-up the night before last. Kept my email short. Three sentences – though it coulda been a thesis. Matterfact, fuck it, here's all the cocksucker crap I cut out:

Because I want a father, not a shareholder.

Head of the table, etc., not chairman of the board.

Because I'd feel like I'd been bankrolled by my daddy and therefore badly in need of a bath.

Because, just because. Because I ain't some beige-trouser-wearing public-school ponce with foppy pubes that they probly have to perm or something just to keep it real.

Because it's a little fucking late in the day for your fucking support.

Because Mum got really sad that Saturday you dropped me home late after taking me to Toys R Us.

The red. The yellow. The tubs of ketchup. The non-toxic colouring crayons.

"In fact, if you like, Dad, you can even be the chairman . . . or the senior non-exec on the board of directors . . . or the boss."

The crayons that came with the tubs of ketchup.

"What bloody board of directors, Dylan? You're just a freelance data temp. So stop all your nonsense. And you know damn well this isn't about my offer of investment. If you don't want my money, fine – I understand when I'm not wanted. But just explain to me, please, what the hell do you mean by feeding her all that bullshit?"

"I know it's fucked up, Dad, but there's a reason why I always have to bullshit and lie to Ramona . . ." You know them times you just find yourself fessing up? Admitting random bad deeds just for bants? Do people actually fess up to their actual fathers? Is that like a thing, or just something you see on TV? "Dad, the reason I keep shit hidden from Ramona is because . . ."

"Why the hell are you talking about Ramona?" he cuts me off. "You know damn fucking well that I'm referring to Naliah."

Over the next few minutes, my dad actually does a pretty good impression of Naliah:

"I always knew there were fishy skeletons in your closet."

"How can we believe anything you say when all this time you've been lying about why you've had no contact with Dylan?"

"How can I trust you to take care of my mum when you couldn't even be bothered to keep in touch with your own son?"

Then Dad goes back to doing an impression of himself:

"Don't pretend you didn't know who she was, Dylan."

"Oh, please, don't insult my intelligence. As if you hadn't worked it out weeks ago."

"Don't take me for a fool, Dylan. Even if you didn't guess it, your masi or one of your other Facebook-addicted aunties must've long-ago told you about me and my . . . my companion."

"I even asked you point blank that evening you turned up at my flat – I asked you what she'd been telling you about me. And even back then you pretended to play dumb."

"And now apparently I'm guilty of abandoning you and washing my hands of you. Either you're very good making up stories, son, or being in denial is just your default setting."

This new turn of eventualities is actually pretty straight: Naliah's basically been doing a more full-on version of what Ramona once did back when her own mum's boyfriend was running for the role of husband. Due diligence, auditing, investigative reporting – i.e. what all good children should do for their mums. *And then to give away her clammy hand.* Proper old-school analogue snooping. Had been threatening to track me down for months. Dig up some deep, dark-winded secret about why my dad had less than zero contact with his son.

Again the plastic furniture. The windows. The strip lights flickering. The windows that look out into the train station.

This thing about my dad and Naliah's mum should be a bolt from a breaking newsflash. So then why does it feel like just some standard-issue bog standardness? Just another one of them updates to my dad app – a patch to fix our latest father–son mindfucks. Like as if all our earlier technical hitches and screen-freezes were actually moments of lucidness. Glitches of clarity.

The windows. The people, the passengers. Check them all standing on the concourse like bowling pins beneath the large information board. Staring down the lanes of train platforms. The gutters of empty tracks. Strike; Delay; Cancellation; Emergency Engineering Works – all of my all-purpose cover stories.

Dad's got a theory. His mind is made up. Reckons I been acting outta spite and malice and malignantness cos I don't like it that he's "finally found a life companion" in Naliah's mum. Tells me it ain't fair me behaving like as if his companion is some kinda villain. Fuck knows which platform he got this from – which website or app or channel. Ain't no need to be digital, even – stepmums are easy villains in pantomimes. Nursery rhymes, even. Daddy's told himself the easiest story in the book.

I try hitting him with denials.

Dad sticks to his easy story.

I hit him with evidence to the contrary.

Dad sticks to his easy story.

Even hit him with random stats – all the times I ain't dissed him or fucked up his shit even when I probly should've. All the times I been respectful and non-confrontational and just generally gluten-free. Tell him that he ain't even on Facebook, meaning even my aunties couldn't have even known.

Again, Dad doubles down, digs in, lashes out. The more counter-evidence I hit him with, more strongly he buys his own bullshit. In our Behavioural Economics module, they call this shit the Backfire Effect – happens when people feel threatened by facts that they don't like. Also the Continued Influence Effect – the way people still believe misinformation even after it's been corrected. Dad either carries on just excluding things that don't fit with his easy story, or he adapts to my facts but somehow still clings onto his original conclusion: "Okay, son, so maybe you didn't know about my partner. But clearly you were still trying to spite it."

"C'mon, Dad, surely you can see your story's full of holes."

"All these things you're saying, they do not represent holes in my story. Don't dismiss my very solid argument as just some 'story', son. It's not just a story, it's true information."

"Well, where the hell did you get this information?"

"I was given that information, Dylan – I've seen that information around. I have very good gut feelings about these kinds of things."

I tell him his guts must be from Krypton or something if his gut feeling beats down my actual factual evidence.

Dad says that, actually, I'm the one ignoring *his* evidence.

We long out this back-and-forth for a few more minutes. Everything I say just reinforcing his already made-up mind. Ain't even sure we can meet each other halfway here. Halfway along *what* way? He won't even see my set of facts and I sure as fuck don't recognise anything factual in his bullshit. Then finally it daybreaks on me: I don't actually even *need* to prove my facts – not if my feelings are as equally valid as facts. Cos I can't have been fucking up his relationship with Naliah's mum outta spite if I don't actually feel any spite. And I don't – don't even feel upset by it. Actualtruth, it's more like the opposite.

Exhibit A: First time your mum asked you how you felt about her and your dad splitting up, you told her you just wanted them both to be happy. Told her you were worried they'd both be really unhappy if they divorced and really unhappy if they didn't. Back then it just sounded like something you *should* say – just some stock-standard Australian soap opera crap. Weren't till a year or so later that you realised just how much you actually meant it.

Exhibit B: Ain't even know what Naliah's mum even looks like, but I can already picture her smiling. Daddy smiling back. Plus picnics and barbecues and dinner parties. Do parents actually have dinner parties, or is that just something you see on TV? (BTW, for the purposes of picturing all this, I'm just assuming Naliah's mum is the spitting image of her daughter.) Next thing I know, there's some party time going on up in my head. We're talking canapés and party poppers. Cartwheels and pom-pom routines. I tell Dad let's forget Maccy D's and milkshakes – we should be hitting Carluccio's or something, get us some lobster lasagne and

Dom Perignon. Balloons, even. Presents. A *Congratulations On Your Actual Relationship* card. What I don't tell him is that inside this card (which is blank for your own message), I'd elaborate:

"Dear Daddy, congrats on not being the useless lonely loser that everyone thinks you are – nor the pathetic, pizza-eating porn-addict that I was starting to think you were. Love, Dhilan."

As if he can read this card on my forehead, Dad scrunches up his own. "Please stop being sarcastic, Dylan. It's only been just over a year. My relationship with Naliah's mother is still tentative – and thanks to your silly sob stories, it's now becoming tenuous." His hand starts doing this opening and closing thing, like maybe he's got repetitive strain injury. Then, half open, he slams down on the plastic table. "I mean, what the bloody fuck is your problem, Dylan? You know, when Naliah first threatened to come looking for you, I was actually very relaxed. After all, what did I have to hide in that regard? A son who stopped phoning me when he turned ten and didn't want to know me."

"Wait, but, Dad, that isn't—"

"That isn't the point?"

"No, I mean it isn't even—"

"You're right, Dylan, it isn't worth retreading. And I wouldn't have had to if you hadn't told her all that whining woe-is-me bullshit. I'm supposed to be moving in with her, son – I've got everything packed away in cardboard boxes and crates. She already has my coffee table and my favourite rug. But now suddenly she wants to tread carefully because she thinks I'm some shyster who abandoned his son."

Should probly go get him a cup of Maccy D's tea – help him swallow his beef with me. Or maybe that'd be dickless when he's sitting there with some thermos flask poking out his coat pocket.

"I thought things were going well between us, son. You even agreed to meet with me that first afternoon in McDonald's. And so not only do I finally get to have a proper life companion in Naliah's mother, I also finally get my longed-for relationship with my son."

The look that scrolls up on Dad's face is the exact same look he'd rock during the first few months after the divorce. Like he'd slipped over in public and wanted everyone to know it weren't his fault. *Floor was wet. There was an uneven step.* It was like there'd be a fight on his face between embarrassment and anger and he'd be putting all his muscle into backing anger. *Why's this fucking floor wet? Stupid fucking uneven step.* Right now, the fights on his face are minor compared with the even bigger fights in his body. Juddering knee, closing fist, opening fist, diaphragm doing self-CPR. Can't even steady his hands to stop his thermos flask slipping out his raincoat. I catch it and stand it on the table – where it carries on wobbling a few secs as if his shakes are contagious.

Daddy doesn't even notice my catching skills.

"I don't know why Naliah seems to have it in for me, Dylan. I try – I *really* try. But then she tells me I'm being creepy and too nice. So then I try to keep my distance and she tells her mum I'm full of secrets and hiding things. She just refuses to trust a single word that comes out of my mouth."

"No shit, Dad."

Next, I'm telling him that if I'd been in his shoes, I'd have probly told Naliah and her mum the exact same thing. I tell him I'll help him to clean up his mess – help him keep his Trusted Seller status. "For instance, Dad, if you like, I can help you strategise. Show you how to keep all your stories vague so Naliah and her mum can't catch you on the details. Also, you can use mnemonics to keep track of what you have and haven't told her. Key thing is don't put all your bullshit in one basket."

"What?"

"Or I could just say to Naliah that I only told her all that stuff cos I was trying to impress her or something – some pulled-myself-up-by-my-own-bootstraps bullshit. Seriously, Dad, I can patch this for you. I mean, so you been lying to Naliah's mum cos you're afraid of losing her. So what? I guess that's just what men do, right? Doesn't matter who gets hurt so long as you don't feel the pain of being dumped or rejected. So I'm totally down with lying for you."

He smacks the table again. "I'm not asking you to lie to her, Dylan, I'm asking you tell her the truth. It's bad enough the way you've apparently been lying to Ramona about your mother all these years. Do you realise how badly that reflects on me? Naliah keeps saying, 'Like son, like father . . .'"

Okay, fuck being respectful.

Fuck being non-confrontational.

"They're not bloody lies, you silly man!" The other McDonald's diners start eaveswatching. "Dhilan hasn't been lying, he's been telling the truth."

The diners. The plastic tables. The colouring crayons.

"Okay, why are you referring to yourself in the third person, Dylan?"

"Don't try and change the subject, Prakash. Just because you and I got divorced, that doesn't mean that you had to cut off contact with our son. I couldn't stay married to you, but why to punish him?"

"What the hell?"

The milkshake. The thermos flask. The ketchup that came with the milkshake.

"He's just a boy, Prakash."

Dad probly thinks I'm fucked in the head. Truth is, I don't know how else to stand up for myself. The Norman Bates routine just came to me – another little glitch of clarity. Only problem is my laughing keeps giving me away.

Dad starts pulling some rapid-fire small-talk action. Five minutes of the weather, five minutes about root vegetables, five minutes about sports. "And how are your studies going, son? How's your little business doing?"

I tell him how I've finally decided on a name for my student start-up instead of just calling it Company A. "I've decided to just use my name."

"Your name?"

"Yes. D-Gital."

"If you check your passport and birth certificate, you'll find that your surname is Deckardas. Or are you just naming it after your mother's family to carry on making a fool of me?"

"Come on, Daddy, don't be like that. D-Gital is clearly a perfect name for a digital business. I wouldn't exactly be communicating my core deliverable client capabilities if I called the company D-Deckardas."

"Well, in view of this, I think I need to consider taking my investment off the table."

"What are you talking about? It's already off the table. Anyway, don't get in a strop about this too – it's just a name."

"Names are important, Dylan. You can't just pick and choose your name."

I start listing random corporate names just to prove their randomness: Google, Yahoo!, Amazon – even Microsoft is pretty meaningless when you really stop to think about it. Truth is, I never really thought about the big-dealness of names until one time when I was googling stuff about Oedipus and I read how the dude got his own name wrong. He thought it meant "know foot" – and this spin that he put on his own name probly even gave him the confidence/self-belief to solve something called the Riddle of the Sphinx, which was this big deal brainteaser about feet.

Dad starts strangling the neck of his thermos flask. "Dylan, I hope you're just joking about calling it D-Gital. Think about the message it will communicate to Naliah and her mother if you take my money and give your mother's family all the kudos. They'll think I'm a fool after the way you've treated me over the years."

"Come on, Dad. This is getting long and boring. Now, look, I admit that when I was eight or nine maybe I cancelled a bunch of our Saturday lunches. But I was probly too scared to leave Mum or something."

"Or more like you were too busy being brainwashed against me by your uncles and aunts."

"What the hell is wrong with you, Dad?"

But, of course, I already know what's wrong. I know that even though we clearly got some personal beef between us, that ain't the reason why we're getting dragged apart here. It's cos of the Backfire Effect, Confirmation Bias, Motivated Reasoning and all them other mental fallibilities that have been supercharged by social media and search engines. A drop of my eye saliva splashes into my milkshake and I realise that if didn't know all this Behavioural Economics stuff, I'd probly start losing my shit with him right here in Maccy D's – and, of course, Dad would just take that as proof I was upset about him and Naliah's mum. Instead, I try telling him how we're just getting polarised by inbuilt mental processes that make us intolerant of people who view things differently.

"This isn't about a different point of view, Dylan. From the way Naliah tells it, anyone would think that I'd just dumped you in a doorway or left you crying in a bundle on some windswept mountain. When, in fact, all I've ever been doing is trying to help you. I was – I wanted to try to help. After your mother fell ill. I could be giving you so much help and advice."

"The hell kind of advice could you give? You got any nursing tips? Know how to insert things?"

"I could have told you many things, son. There are many things I could be telling you. For instance, not to search online for her symptoms – it could affect your health-insurance premiums. Even your chances of getting a mortgage."

"What the hell?"

"Even the kind of people you have as friends on Facebook can affect your insurance premiums. The food you buy. Do you know how many insurance headaches are created by data and predictions and DNA and genetics? My own father, he kept things simple and just called these things destiny or fate."

Clean my fone with an antibac wipe. Now a story about getting through it. An article about coping. An ad for a way out.

"So you see how I could be of help with the insurance, Dylan. And it's all the more galling given that *I'm* the one who's tried to re-establish our relationship by getting back in touch with you after all those years that *you* cut contact with *me*. So we need to get something straight, son: I didn't abandon you or wash my hands of you. I was there for you – whenever you needed me. It was *you* who washed your hands of *me*."

"Excuse me, sir," comes a woman's voice from behind me. "I'm very sorry, but you can only consume food and beverages bought on the premises at these tables."

Yup – we're saved from our latest father–son screen-freeze by the intervention of McDonald's.

"I'm not drinking from this flask," Dad goes to her, "I'm just standing it on this table so it doesn't slip out of my coat."

"Yes, but your flask creates the impression to other people that drinking their own drinks here is permitted."

"Look, it was slipping out of my coat."

After a little more back-and-forth, I grab the flask and tell them I'll keep it out of view in my rucksack.

"There's no need for that." Dad table-dives to snatch it. Next thing, the two of us are kicking it slapstick, fighting over the flask like we're battling to pay the restaurant bill. And in accordance with the generic slapstick conventions, the thermos flask goes flying. Slams against a wall, lid comes off; grey ash everywhere.

"Oh my gosh, I'm so, so sorry," says the McDonald's woman. "I didn't realise it was an urn."

"Dad, who is it?" I ask.

"What?"

"The ash. Whose ash is it? I mean, who died? Who gave it to you? And why the hell are they in a thermos flask and not a proper urn?"

"Of course," Dad says. "You think I've killed someone, right? You're now going to go and tell Naliah that I'm a murderer too?" My just-drunk milkshake bubbling in the corners of his mouth – like that time Mum and me seemed to puke out each other's food. His whole body shuddering out of his raincoat now the same way his flask had done. Fighting to fling himself free from its sleeves.

"Dad, calm it, yeh. It's okay. Everything's gonna be okay."

"No, I will not fucking calm it," he shouts.

"Sir, I'm really so sorry about your urn," says Ms McDonald's. "I'll go and get some wipes and a dustpan and brush – no need to use your coat like that."

Dad doesn't wait for her. Just drags his raincoat across the floor and starts stagger-styling towards the exit.

I block his path. "Wait, Dad. Wait up. Let's just say for argument's sake that you're right. That everything you say is true – that I've somehow been brainwashed against you and that I been fucking up your shit outta spite."

"That *is* the truth, Dylan."

"Yeh, I'm saying let's say it's the truth. And, better still, let's just say, just for argument's sake, that I even got violent or something – punched you in the face or whatever."

"Do you want to punch me in the face, Dylan?"

"No. But even if all those things were true . . . well, it still wouldn't be a reason for you to cut off contact with me now, would it?"

King's College. Later that afternoon.

"Dillon, this is a student chemistry lab not *CSI*," says Anjali. Or Anna or Aekta. "I won't be able tell you whose ash it is."

All the same, I twist open the lid. She looks inside the flask and laughs. "Is this a joke? That's not human ash."

I tell her I know – that I just wanted to be sure.

Turns out it's just paper.

Specifically, newspaper.

Even more specifically, newspaper that has been pasted to thicker paper, as if in some kind of scrapbook or cuttings book.

38

NINTH TIME YOUR mum told you she had the C-bomb, she told your ass via telepathy. Not cos the sickness had spread to her mouth or her throat or her tongue or her tooth-fillings, but cos the two of you couldn't get even a minute to shoot the shit together. Even though you'd been texting each other like teenagers the previous evening. Even though you'd been the first visitor to show up that morning. Problem was, you hadn't counted on how many aunties and uncles were actually living with her by then.

And then friends, neighbours, strangers, random respect-payers – the doorbell like a boxing ring, the kettle jeering and hissing. You used to pray for house guests. Even pollsters or meter readers. Anything to bring about a tiny change in air density. All them years you hated the way your mum and you practically had to shower and shit and shave together, but now only thing you wanted was a one-to-one in a room with a door with a lock. Probly the nearest you got to being alone with her that morning was when she spotted some foto of you that had been boosted from its frame and then folded or scrunched or, whatever, deformed. She started massaging away all your crumples and creases. Scanning the living room to puzzle out who the culprit was. The living-room-cum-bedroom-cum-hospital-cum-hospice-cum-heaven's-waiting-room.

In the middle of all the tea-drinking and praying and respect-paying and TV-watching, you jacked one of your various assorted uncles' various assorted digital devices. Some fone or single-function camera or camcorder – fuck it, maybe even a top-of-the-range torch with video capture functionality. *Over here, Mama, look this way. Come on, one last final close-up.* Gaunt pale majestical bulimic-chic imprint of partial-rebreather oxygen mask. A forty-nine-year-old woman sculpted in a velvet-lined wind tunnel. The Macmillan nurse had helped her into that baggy peach dress, but by that stage, your mum was only allowing your masi to bathe her.

Over here, Mummy – look over here. At me – at the camera across the room. I've maxed out on zooming in. You figured that's what all these toys were basically for. From old-school Polaroids and camcorders to all them places that'd print your fotos onto mouse-mats and cushion covers. Or chatbots that can mimic their emails and texts. Cos digital data doesn't die, etc. *Over here, Mummy – I'm sitting over here.* Everyone overpaying compliments about her dress while you carried on like one of them front-row fuckwits who watches the gig through their fone. As she pretended to smile at someone who was pretending to laugh. As she flinched at the sight of some food smell. As she slipped the foto of you back in its frame. (You wondered if they'd found the fotos you'd slipped beneath your bed slats.) (Christmas fotos, mostly.) (Her with her cans of silly string and the semi-automatic party poppers.) (Wearing a surgical mask just for jokes while she carved the turkey.) *Come on, Mama, don't be shy. Look over here and smile for the camera. Can't you see how hard I'm trying to smile behind it?* Next, she started fixing up all the other framed pictures. The fuck did you keep hating all those fotos for? What's wrong with having happy memories? *And who the hell are all these people, Mum? All these friends and relatives and neighbours and relatives? How come they all know you so well? And how come they know this house so well? I don't even know where you keep the sugar these days.* The Macmillan nurse making like her personal bodyguard, though by that stage she was way past warning visitors about the risks of giving your mum an infection. The whole living-room set-up suddenly looking ridiculous. Surely if you enter life in a hospital, you should exit in a hospital? Or an ambulance. Something that says you kept trying. And again with the frigging foto frames – even though she tagged more shit on Instagram than you did. *You hear that, Mum? Stop fucking around with the fotos and smile for the camera. Please.*

You thought of the time you'd chucked all them fotos in a bin liner. She'd been admitted overnight with another low white blood count and you figured, fuck it, if Ramona really wanted to see where you lived, that evening would be as good a shot as you'd ever get. *No, Mum, look this way – over here. I'm way over here.* Hadn't planned on hiding away the framed fotos – to begin with, you just wanted to clear away all her C-bomb stuff. The pills, the wigs, the kidney bowls, the cannula, the tubing, the pills to counteract the pills, the crutches, the Caucasian-coloured prostheses, the pills, the Asian-coloured prostheses. Then you figured that, while you were at it, you might as well chuck in all her chintzy kitschness. The porcelain ballerinas. The embroidered proverbs. The long-distance lace table runners. All those romantic weekend wellness break fotos. Her with her tunics and telltale headscarves. Ramona texted to say she was on her way. You looked at the clock: six minutes – *shit.* Cleared away your mum's kitsch and cancer pap like some maniac burglar-impersonator. First, taking fotos with your fone of how everything was arranged so you could put it all back perfect whenever she got discharged. You looked back at the clock: six minutes – *shit.* And then the doorbell rang and you unloaded half a can of aftershave in your hair. And then the doorbell rang again and you dabbed your mum's foundation on your zits. And then the door opened by itself and your mum hobbled in. "Guess who's still got the fight in her."

"Mum?"

"I don't need to block a hospital bed – I don't need to get in the way."

This way, Mama. Look towards the lens. Over here on the sofa. Stop slumping by your deathbed-to-be and come and sit here next to me. Just allow all those anonymous aunties who are leaning on your dressing-table-cum-sideboard – what the hell is your dressing table doing down here anyway? And who the hell bought you that Get Well Soon calendar shaped like a flower? The one where you tear off a fucking petal after each month.

Soon as your Mum limped into the living room, you texted Ramona to tell her she couldn't come over cos you suddenly had to go out or someshit. Next up: how to douse out your aftershave.

"Er, Dhilan . . ." The words from your mum like some worm too scared to leave the nest. "Dhilan, where is everything?"

You told her you were in the middle of tidying up for her. Nothing drastic, just dusting – "I was gonna surprise you, Mum. Make everything nice."

"Don't bullshit me, Dhilan. One good thing about dying young is I'll die before I go senile."

"You ain't gonna die young, Mum."

"Clearly not young enough for you. Better make sure you save some of that aftershave for my funeral. You can talk to all the girls you like then – believe me, they'll all want to be your special friend."

"It's deodorant." Ramona still hadn't texted you back. You looked again at the clock: six minutes – *shit.*

"You can even kiss them on the lips if you want to, Dhilan. They won't bite you with the mouth ulcers. So, tell me, then, what time is she coming here . . . wait – you put away all the photos because you're embarrassed of me? You're ashamed of my swollen face."

Look up, Mama. I'm over here. The camera's over this way. Stop talking to Uncle Kushil and come and sit with me. After all, I'm still your BBF and soulmate and so on. And I ain't just saying that shit just cos everyone wants to be the dying person's best friend.

Two minutes after she'd noticed the framed fotos were missing, she realised the rest. "Dhilan, where are all my medicines? And my wig?"

You nearly told her: "In a bin bag." Instead you told her: "It's just a game, Mum."

"Bloody, what game?"

And still Ramona hadn't texted you back. You looked once again at the clock: six minutes – *shit.* "I was so upset about you being readmitted that when I got back from school I decided to play a game. The game's called 'Mummy's Been Completely Cured'. That's why I had to clear away all the traces of your illness."

Then, like some special kinda bullshit buzzer, Ramona finally texted you back.

"I suppose that's her, is it? Your little girlio. But I *want* you to have girlfriends, Dhilan. I don't want to be that kind of a mother."

"Nah. It's just some girl called Ramona. Actually, she wants to come over and borrow an essay." This much was actually true: Ramona's text message said that even if you had to head out, she still needed to borrow your Thursday night Economics homework. You looked at the clock on your fone: six minutes – *shit.*

Anyway, fuck the bin-bag incident, Mama. Remember how I used to bring you flowers, Mummy – all those battered bunches. I know everyone buys flowers for people in hospital, but didn't I get you that bunch after my first day at uni? I wrote in your blog that it was the happiest moment of your life. Just turn to the camera and come and sit with me.

"I'm not a bloody idiot, Dhilan."

"It isn't what you think, Mum. The thing is, Ramona – this girl – she doesn't know you're sick. I never told her cos you told me not to tell anyone."

"But I told you it was fine to start telling people after it spread to my hip."

"Yeh, but it was too late for me to tell her then. I'd already lied to her too much."

"But I don't understand why you needed to hide all my medicines. Just tell her I've only recently fallen sick."

"Don't you understand? She thinks you're alive."

"What? Are you on drugs, Dhilan? I *am* alive."

"You know what I mean."

Then you looked once again at the clock: six minutes – *shit.*

It was that whole cancer-props-in-bin-bag routine that first gave you the idea: what if you slowly started stealing her hats and stuff? Little by little. Wrap them up in cling film. So that if by some miracle she was mortal after all, then five years or so later, after she finally checked out, at least you'd know you'd kept the scent of her scalp alive.

"Please don't be upset, Mum. How about a cup of tea – would you like a cup of tea? I can bring it up to your bedroom." Six minutes – *shit.* "I can bring you one of your wigs, even." Six minutes – *shit.* "She'll be here in six minutes, Mum. Don't you understand? She'll think I'm a liar. She thinks you're alive."

"Dhilan, I *am* alive."

"You know what I mean." Six minutes – *shit.*

And why not cling-film her shower caps and hooded anoraks too? And if by some miracle she was mortal after all, maybe you could frame her shopping lists and Post-it notes along with the fotos – just to preserve her handwriting and that.

"No, actually I don't know what you mean, Dhilan. I *am* alive. I can see quite clearly from all your little home improvements that you can't wait for me to hurry up and die, but I'm afraid I'm still very much alive."

"They ain't home improvements, Mum, I'm just customising the house to realign the facts with Ramona's alternate reality. In fact, I think the era of mass-customisation as opposed to mass-production actually started with customised home furniture."

"What?"

"*Ramona's* alternate reality – the one I basically bullshitted into existence. Mum, please. She'll be here any minute." You checked your watch. Six minutes – *shit.*

Then the doorbell started ringing. "Mum, *please.* Otherwise there'll be a catastructive context collapse – like when you see fotos of your teachers getting drunk on Facebook."

"But I'm not going to collapse, Dhilan."

The doorbell rang again. You looked again at the clock: six minutes – *shit.* "Mum, *please,* I'm begging you. She doesn't know you're sick. She doesn't know how much I've lied. She won't speak to me again if she finds out. She thinks you're still alive."

"Dhilan, I *am* alive."

"You know what I mean."

Or maybe you'd be better off converting all those fotos of her into personalised mouse-mats and T-shirts and coffee mugs. Useful, functional crap. Cos if by some miracle she was mortal after all, there'd be no point simply staring at framed fotographs of her like as if she was somehow trapped within them. No point dicklessly talking to them – or even talking to the sky or the sunset or the ceiling.

"You want me to go and hide in my bedroom in my own house, Dhilan?"

The doorbell rang again as if confirming this on your behalf. "Mum – she's already here." You looked at the clock. Six minutes – *shit.*

And how about Perspex cases for her plastic prostheses? The old pair she'd chucked by her feet at the foot of her bed. Still warm even though they'd been lying on the floor for a month – as if you could just mould the shape of a breast out of Blu-Tac or Plasticine or pizza dough and it would just miraculously generate heat. Allow it – technically, it ain't foreplay if you just endlessly fondle.

So fuck it, why not just put your mum in the Perspex case and put the prostheses in the coffin. If you mummified your own mummy, would her corpse still have the C-bomb? And, anycase, how the fuck would you lug around a cling-film-covered bed?

"You really want me to go and hide in my room, Dhilan? Because you're embarrassed of my bald head and swollen face?"

You looked at the clock. Six minutes – *shit.* And so, for reasons you'll never really understand, your precise words in response were: "Yeh, Mum. *Yes.*"

Okay fine, Mum, even if you won't leave all them other people to come and sit here with me, it doesn't change the fact that you're still my BFF. Why does there have to be a reason, anyway? Why can't we just say I fucked shit up and leave it there? Can't we just say that I shouldn't have? And why did you have to keep telling me all that crap about being your soulmate, Mum? I'd have been your soulmate anyway, but why did you keep on telling me I was? Come and sit with me, Mum. Fuck you – you ain't dying; fuck you.

39

RAMONA ASKS HOW many more Tube stops till Acton Town. I list all six stations like a time-stretched audio file. As if saying their names in slow-mo will somehow long out the distances between them.

See, I finally found me a way to stop lying to her about my mum but without having to tell her the truth: I'm gonna *show* her the truth. Just show it. See what happens. As if the lying-ass part of my brain is now maxed out and busted. *Like father, like son*, my bony brown butt. No more bullshitting my girlfriend just cos I'm scared of losing her.

"But it was six stops last time I asked."

"Didn't you notice that time stood still while we was kissing?" And then I lean in again. Try and buy us some more time.

"Er, simmer down, Dillon." Ramona disconnects me from her mouth. "We're in a Tube carriage."

Didn't even use tongue out of chivalry and hygiene and general rules of engagement. She's been blocking Public Displays of Affection ever since we accidentally went full-penetration in that kitchenette in my client's office. New access restrictions suit me too – less risk of physical escalation, less risk of cross-contaminating, less risk of being spotted round London by one of my aunty-informing cousins. But today, I figure, fuck it. Today, I ain't got nothing to lose.

"Oh, don't look so wounded. I just don't want to have to redo my lipstick. Do you think I should've worn a cardigan? Not for modesty, obviously. I mean in case it gets chilly."

One last lie, though – just for old time's sake. Before I gotta watch her face as she works out just how many other lies there've been. I'd told her we was headed to my house for a barbecue to celebrate my mummy's fiftieth birthday. *Get it? Got it?* Good.

The props are all in position. The paraphernalia, the souvenirs, the disposable paperboard pap. The pills, the bedpans, the kidney bowls, the sick bowls. The pills, the syringes, the tubing, the dressings, the ointments, the Caucasian-coloured prostheses, the Asian-coloured prostheses, the breast in formaldehyde, the breasts in glass museum cabinets, the backlit framed sickness certificates, the dummy pre-death death certificates, the wigs on velvet mannequin busts that have had their actual busts sawn off.

Oh – and one last lie told to Naliah, too. Just to draw a line under that whole father–son thing with my father. Told her I'd been fucking up my dad's shit on purpose. Not cos I resented her or her mother or nothing – and deffo not cos he'd cut contact with me/washed his hands of me/abandoned me/poor, poor me, etc. Nope – instead, I'd told Naliah this brand-new blend of bullshit: that I was afraid my new-found father–son thing weren't gonna last, seeing as how I didn't deserve it, and so I'd been subconsciously sabotaging shit on purpose. Like a wrecking ball for removing uncertainty. A crystal wrecking ball.

Tube train's now on some red signal hold-up. Driver dropping surround-sound apologies. Delay ain't a licence to bail or wuss out, though. More like the opposite: the hold-up is telling me to tell her. Not just *show* Ramona the truth, but sit her down on one of these puke-stained Tube seats and fess the fuck up, right now. Cos showing her instead of telling her would be gutless. Showing instead of telling would be too clever. And I ain't wanting to be clever about this shit.

Then, *"Please stand clear of the closing doors."* And we carry on rolling towards Acton Town. Pulling Ramona towards me. Telling her I'm only doing it so she ain't gotta touch no flu-infected handrail. Tucking the tulips under my armpit, even though today's bunch ain't mine to crush. She'd even asked if my mum and me had the same pollen allergies.

"Okay – but this time please try and resist your urge to kiss me."

"It's a westbound Piccadilly line. People will just think one of us is dropping off the other at Heathrow – that we ain't gonna be seeing each other for weeks. Maybe months. Maybe even ever again."

Hold her tighter; the train speeds up.

"Doubtful, Dillon – we don't have any baggage."

Tighter than any handrail has ever been held in the history of public transport.

"This train is now ready to depart."

"Please stand clear of the closing doors."

Anyway, allow it – kissing is proper wrongness now. Not just in our own fucked-up situation, but also kissing in general. Don't need no postgrad degree in biology to see there's maybe some link between kissing and breastfeeding. Clue: humans didn't develop lips in order to make out in nightclubs.

"Due to essential maintenance work, escalators at the next station are not in service."

Obviously there was an in-between stage – people didn't just jump from suckling to tongue tennis. Before human evolution developed Heinz baby food, mothers used to beef up their breast milk by chewing mouthfuls of actual beef and other iron-rich meats and then, instead of swallowing, they'd basically French kiss their babies. Technical term for this is premasticating. Birds and apes still do this. Why the fuck did both Google and Facebook decide I wanted to know this shit?

"Please stand clear of the closing doors."

Not all experts agree that kissing evolved from premasticating. Some say it's a pre-loaded program, like breathing and blinking. Experts also don't agree on whether premasticating is good or bad for a baby's health – they reckon most probly it depends on the mother's health – her oral abscesses and mouth ulcers and so on. Don't ask me why people always blame mothers when it comes to this stuff. Ain't like you need breasts to premasticate.

Honestly, Naliah, my dad's a really good guy. Kind of man a son can look up to and then stand tall. I'd even set him up with my own mum, but obviously that'd be ridiculous.

Dad had foned last night to tell me that the ashes that had spilled out of his thermos flask weren't human. Didn't admit that it was his cuttings book, though – just told me it was some clever alternative to document shredding. Bank statements, bills – copies of tax return, probly. Hit the bullshit right out the park. "After all, Dylan, these days identity thieves can use software to piece together shredded paper. So I give all my old bank statements and confidential papers to a man in the City who runs a special document crematorium. But for health and safety reasons you have to dispose of the ashes yourself. That's why I had to use a thermos flask."

No lie, Naliah – he's a really great, straight-hitting man.

Cos, fuck it, man's just dealing with his shit. Having gone and told Naliah and her mum some CGI story about why he had no contact with his son, he ain't got no choice now but to keep pushing that story. Not cos he's gotta cover up the truth but cos he's gotta cover up the bullshit.

Ramona lets go of my arm. "Dillon, are you chewing bubblegum?"

"Nope."

"All this time – even while you were trying to kiss me?"

Shit – should I be warning her about the side effects the same way I'd once warned my cousins? My famously backfiring email: *"Please be advised that your aunty has broken out in mouth ulcers that look like bullet holes and upside-down insects. Not suitable for viewers of a squeamish disposition."*

"A breath mint, then?"

"Nope."

"Then why do you keep sucking the inside of your mouth?"

"Nope. No. I don't."

According to my mum, all mouth-ulcer treatments are a waste of bucks – best way to treat a mouth ulcer is to swab it with salt. It hurts – she said it hurts like you're trying to remove them with a hybrid vibrator-cheesegrater, but if you can man up and brace against the pain, you can cure mouth ulcers with salt.

"Dillon, don't. Stop sucking like that – you look like you're trying to imitate a horse."

"Dhilan, stop sucking your mouth ulcers – you sound like you're having oral sex."

"What's oral sex, Mummy?"

"It's when you love someone with your mouth."

It's just three or four small sores today. Broke out inside my face this morning. Ramona kisses me on my cheek – dead centre of each kiss somehow hitting dead centre behind each ulcer. She does this even when I got a toothache or headache – even when my fingers cramp from typing or my kidneys twinge from ODing on energy drinks. Seems to know about the pain before it starts paining – same way she knows me so well even though she knows nothing about my mum. Gets me even better than anyone who does know. And why the hell not, yeh? Some people know the whole Tube map by heart even though they ain't got a clue how London's roads are arranged. Meanwhile taxi drivers know bugger all about the Tube map. Point is, both sets of people still know London way better than most people do. And Ramona knows her way around 'Dillon' better than anyone else does, has done or ever will.

"Okay, fuck it," goes Ramona. "Let's just embrace the fact that we're finally becoming slightly less dysfunctional. I don't care that we're on the Tube, Dillon. Kiss me again – but properly."

"What?"

"Let's just pretend that we're heading to Heathrow – all the way to the end of the line."

I tell Ramona I can't kiss her properly – with tongue and mouth and so on – cos I got mouth ulcers. Oral abscesses. Tell her I don't wanna infect her. Tell her that we're on a Tube train. Then *she* kisses *me* for being considerate. Says she'll give me some medicated mouth gel when we get back to her student halls. Behind her, I clock an ad for Bonjela above the carriage doors. Beside it, an ad for a search engine. Then an ad for some dating app that says: *"Don't search for love, let love search for you."*

Start praying for another signal failure. A points failure. Emergency engineering works. I know some guys are apparently so manly they're strong enough to dump women before the woman in question dumps them. Technical term for that is a "pre-emptive break-up". But I ain't one of them guys. This whole thing's such a neon-lit fuck-up it's like as if I actually *wanted* to fuck it up. Get my ass punished or whupped, whatever, redempted. Except how the hell does that even begin to make sense? – That I'd prefer guilt over happiness cos being happy makes me feel guilty. Allow that bullshit.

I suck on my mouth ulcers just to calm myself. Sucking and chewing in time with the beat of the Tube tracks. At first, Mum only got mouth ulcers when her cocktail of chemo contained anthracyclines or methotrexate. Then, at some stage, salt sachets became a permanent part of her morning make-up-and-meds routine.

Ramona comes closer to kiss away my soreness. Gives me no choice but to step away from her. To leave her no choice but to hold the handrail. Cos, like I said, kissing her is wrongness now. Your tongue don't belong inside another person's mouth. Fucking might be functional, but kissing don't do shit – even licking a woman's feet clean has got more purposeness than kissing. We ain't birds who chew each other's food and feed it back to them, we're people who crunch up each other's feelings and feed it back.

Ramona pulls out her fone with her free hand.

"You ain't gonna get no signal – we're still underground."

"I'm not phoning anyone, I'm deleting someone. Still can't believe how she lied to us."

I tell Ramona that, technically, Naliah didn't lie – she just didn't give us the whole story. I tell her she was only looking out for her mum. That Emotional Sincerity Is More Important Than Being Truthful.

"Look, I realise she might one day be your stepsister or whatever – and you should totally forgive her if you want to. But she lied to me too and I just can't ever forgive that crap. You know how I feel about liars, Dillon. But, look, that's my own problem and I'm sorry to burden you with it."

Now we're on the overground part of the Underground. Somewhere between Earl's Court and Baron's Court station. Don't notice this cos of the daylight, I notice it cos the signal-strength indicator reappears on Ramona's fone. When she's done binning all Naliah's texts and messages, Ramona starts unfollowing, unfriending and blocking – and we're talking with proper violenceness.

I try meditating and mindfulating. My school lunchbreak mantra for dealing with pre-bereavement bereavement: *Losing someone who you've already lost ain't no loss at all. Losing someone who you've already lost ain't no loss at all.*

"Stand clear of the closing doors. The next station is Hammersmith" – aka the stop for Charing Cross Hospital. Meanwhile, Hammersmith Hospital is in Acton. All them times I used that shit as an excuse to turn up too late for visiting hours. All them times I used to try and pick a Tube carriage that contained at least one prettyful woman – someone, *anyone*, nearly as prettyful as Ramona. That shit weren't lechery, it was just rehearsals for whenever I lost her. Because "eventually", "inevitably", "deservedly" all meant the exact same thing. Pre-bereavement bereavement strategies for dealing with one day getting dumped.

But ain't nobody ever comes close.

A magazine with Rihanna on the cover looks ridiculous in comparison. Ekta, Emily, Nicole, Nina, Nadine, Anjali, Amelia,

Amy, even Ramona, yes, even Ramona, even Beyoncé, even the actress Eva Green – they all look ridiculous in comparison. Cos I ain't some bodily objectifising masculinity asshole. Cos I don't just mean prettyful in terms of looks, I mean the prettyful that stays there even if they become bald and breastless. Kind of prettyful that perfumises the scent of their puke. Because my mummy is the most prettyful woman in the world. Just like that other mantra I told myself every morning on the bus to school. *My mummy is the most prettyful woman in the world. My mummy is the most prettyful woman in the world. My mummy – the woman who made my packed lunch this morning – the world's most prettyful lady.* We're talking the best of the best of the best. And then a few years later, just like Daniel Day-Lewis at the Oscars or Roger fucking Federer, my mummy was *still* the best. Only, this time, with the sweet smell of her scalp where her hair shoulda been. The mess of scars on her chest where her breasts used to be. The sweetshop stench of her regurgitated meals. The soaking-wet night sweats. That fine film of her hair whenever she re-entered remission, like the scalp of a newborn baby. Her howling like a baby, staring at her disfigured self in the dressing-table mirror that I kept on re-repairing for her. Screaming at the irradiated B-movie zombie alien. The mirror itself howling back. Louder and madder and more piercingly. Later, just smashing her own fone screen. Crying herself to sleep in the bed that she and me way-too-often shared. Me not leaving her side in case she woke up dead. Cuddling the safe zone above her tummy but beneath her scarring. The positions she collapsed into beside our non-slip bathtub. Her madly fluctuating body heat. The toxic medicine in and out of every orifice. Mopping it off the bathroom floor; the exact same squelching sounds all day, on the daily, still inside my brain. The chemo sweat on her inner thighs brought to the boil by my hydrochloric tears. Me screaming at her in my own sleep like some silly, soap-opera drama queen: *Please, Mum, please don't fucking leave.*

When our train pulls up at Hammersmith station, I know it's a no-need-to-google-no-brainer. There really ain't no other choice for me. "Come on, Ramona, this is us."

"What are you talking about – your mum's house is in Acton."

"Nope. No. We get off here."

"Please stand clear of the closing doors."

Next we're on the platform at Hammersmith station and Ramona has no idea what the fuck's going on – thinks maybe my mother's *moved.*

"Listen, Ramona, I don't really have any mouth ulcers."

"Then why did you say that you did?"

"Cos I was lying."

"But . . . why?"

"I just didn't wanna kiss you. Only reason I was forcing myself on you in the Tube carriage is cos I was basically forcing myself. Cos I don't like kissing you. Any more or ever again. I think you should cross over to the eastbound platform and go back to your student halls. I'm very sorry."

And another mantra – the one I once thought Mum was actually actioning: *The more that they hate me, the easier for them to move on.*

Ramona doesn't argue. Doesn't say a word. Just turns around and walks. The pre-birth heartbeat of her footsteps beneath her elevated heels.

40

PREFERRED THIS BACK when I was a boy. When the only way to do this was to sit at my desk or the kitchen table. Laptop instead of a fone. First laptop Mama and me owned was called a ThinkPad. Me tapping to the sound of her tinkering with something. Just being busy being okay. We bought that laptop for ourselves for Christmas. Don't remember why we decided to share the same user profile.

I pull out my fone, my fones, my other fone – my "Dhilan" fone. Head to my home screen while all these other people here head back to their homes and that. Feeding themselves into the Tube station. Tutting cos I'm in their way. But I need to do this. Need to scroll and search like all these commuters need food and warmth. Their fones giving their faces their own glows.

Now an ad for junk food. An article about low blood sugar. A story about acid reflux. Turns out there's a McDonald's right here in Hammersmith Tube station.

"Sugar's behind you," says the man behind the counter.

"No, I said *salt*. I asked if you had any salt sachets."

"For your milkshake?"

I tell him I got these mouth ulcers – that I know I should probly buy some Bonjela, but my mummy told me to just put salt on them.

Cool my ulcers with my salty milkshake. Warm my chest with my overheating fone. And then, when I'm ready, I start asking the database/library/archive/oracle.

What happens when you lose someone you love?

How do you carry on when they're gone?

How will I cope when I see her in lectures laughing at some other guy's jokes?

Back when I was a boy – back before all the full-on custom-tailorising – sometimes search engines could take shit too literally and their psychic insights got twisted. *How to be a better man?* Here are some healthy-living tips and adult education courses. *How to run out on her?* Here are some stories about pre-running stretching exercises and ads for Nike trainers. Then search engines got smarter – a lot smarter. Ads, articles, answers – they basically became correct if people clicked on them; bumped up their algorithmic accuracy or something.

How did my shit get so twisted?

(No, this ain't a query about braided bowel movements.)

Okay, my heart, then? The way that I been treating her.

And is there any point in even having a "Dillon" fone without Ramona?

Do I shut Dillon down now?

Should I just leave him rotting on some external hard drive or USB storage device?

(Even though Dillon was the only one with any spark.) (The only one who'd bounce his ass outta bed soon as he woke up.)

I want Dillon's customised ads and articles and answers. I know that the Botox man keeps beating up on Google and that, but how the fuck would I even know anything without Google? *What would Dillon do? What would Dylan do?*

So, yes, right now I want all them custom-tailored answers. The targeted ads and articles. The familiar pattern of stories. The warmth of the sick feelings. The recommended products and YouTube videos. The homeliness of the search bar set to auto-complete. I *wanna* be dependent on the recommended. The premasticated. I *wanna* swallow my own feedback and soak up my own night sweats.

Anycase, I know that sometimes in life there ain't no standard-issue answers no more – that you gotta make your own sense of shit, your own decisions about what shit means, your own calls about what's right and what's wrong. But maybe, by custom-tailorising my search results, Google gives me a hit of both these things in one reassuring single dose. Standard-looking answers and my own answers – and they don't contradict each other cos they the same fucking thing.

So I *want* the custom-tailorised. Cos I wanna have my say in the truth that Google tells me. My future clicks determined by my search history. All my unknown data crunched from the known. My new data crunched from the old. Cos all them stories and that about Oedipus – it weren't no specific story that fucked with my head and twisted my shit. Weren't any particular media outlet. My shit got twisted by me – not cos of what I done to her, but cos of all my decisions to press click.

Guess maybe this means all them counsellors and therapists I bailed on, they weren't actually wrong when they kept saying how your feelings are as valid as reality. That emotions got the same weight as facts. Ain't nothing wrong with there being a shit-ton of different realities, different readings, different filters, different truths. Problem is when your clicks start locking you in. Lock you so far into whatever you already think that you start believing it's the only truth.

Down some more milkshake before it gets warm and start scoping out the commuters. Some of them on Red Bull, some of them on fruit smoothies and that. End of the day, *we're* the ones who partly select what stories and info we're actually shown – even partly select the selection we get given.

And so I swipe my fone and start searching about Oedipus. All the exact same ads, articles and answers I've read fuckteen times before.

Oedipus didn't mean *to cause so much suffering.*

Dude didn't intend *to cause people pain.*

Oedipus can be corrupted and crooked without being guilty.

A person can be wrong without being at fault.

A person can be wrong without being at fault.

That's all for today about Oedipus.

Apparently the oracle in the story of Oedipus had this sign in the temple forecourt that said "Know thyself" – i.e. Ancient Greek for *know your own shit.* Botox man was right, though: only way to know yourself now is to school yourself up about social media and search engines – know more about the systems that try to know you better than you know yourself. This means you gotta know yourself better than your own data. School yourself up about your own twistedness. Wise up to your own toxicness.

The problem isn't Oedipus' ignorance or foolishness, it's that he has the wrong facts – about his parents and about himself.

Oedipus misjudges reality by using reason and logic instead of checking out the actual factual accuracy of things.

i.e. making calculations based on his past experience.

Predicting the future by crunching data about previous outcomes and behaviours. Inferring the new from the old.

Oedipus learns that no amount of clever calculation can ever be as good as really, truly knowing.

Especially if you don't even know what it is you wanna know.

That's all for today about Oedipus.

And so, finally, this is when it hits me.

This is when I put away my fone, my other fones, I put away all my fones.

Actually, I disable my Google app and then put away my fone.

(Actually, first, I google how to disable Google, then I disable Google, then I put away my fone.)

Cos what if the best thing for you to do next has fuck all to do with your existing data and previous search history? What if the right thing to do in the future has fuck all to do with your previous clicks? What if you shouldn't be locked into who you already are? If you gotta just move the fuck on?

41

THE LOCK ON your room door busted again. Can tell from ten metres away as you walk up the corridor. Every door in between holding in sounds of laughter or message alerts or intercourse. Sudden gust of louder bassline. Your wide-open doorway silent. Your daddy's raincoat lying like a corpse on your bleach-stained carpet. You stop in the corridor and consider turning and splitting. *You didn't want your daddy, you wanted Ramona.* You stop in your doorway and knock on your own open door. *Please can I come in, Daddy? It's cold out here indoors.*

Your daddy is sitting on the edge of your bed, watching his crumpled carcass of raincoat. Plastic bag by his feet is puking up its replacement – a brand-new leather biker jacket. Battered cowhide, double-breasted, zipper in need of a dentist. Also his briefcase and newspapers – only thing of his not mashed or crumpled is his moustache. "I'm here because I need your help, son." He says this without looking up. "Oh, and the door was already open."

In your hand, a one litre-bag of table salt you'd bought when the local late-night Tesco had closed even later than usual. No table in your dorm room so you dump it on your desk. "Would you like some salt, Daddy?"

"What?"

"I've decided to call my start-up whatever you want me to. If you like, I'll even name it after *you*, Daddy – and I'll stick a pop-up billboard for it right outside Naliah's bedroom window."

Turns out his visit has fuck all to do with Naliah and her mother and fuck all to do with you and your start-up. Your daddy just needs your help lifting stuff. "I need to borrow your brawn," he says – still talking to the carpet. "My back's been giving me problems. I can't believe I'm now having back issues." Finally, his bloated eyeballs on you. "But we need to do it now, son."

Here's the problem with the thin-walled student hall sounds of intercourse: you only ever hear the blokes – as if the guys turn it up and the girls turn it down. Your dad keeps pretending not to notice, which just makes the sounds even louder. "Actually, it isn't just because of my back, Dylan. To be honest, right now I don't trust anyone else enough to ask."

"But it's nearly midnight," you tell him. "What the hell do you need to lift at nearly midnight? A bed?"

"Of course it's not a bloody bed!" he shouts down someone's breakbeat grunting. "Why the hell would I need to move a bed?"

"I dunno, Daddy, sometimes a person just needs to move a bed. Say, from upstairs to downstairs. For assistive access."

"But, Dylan, I live in flat."

Your daddy didn't even need to cut you a deal. All the same, the man almost bent his knee joints to offer the following sweetener: "If you do this for me, Dylan, then I promise I'll explain things that until now I've been unable to explain."

Next thing, you're in an underground car park near your student halls that you didn't even know existed. Strip lighting and a line-up of luxury poser's cars. "I didn't know you had a car," you call out as you try closing your dad's ten-pace lead.

"I don't," he says, not slowing down. "I used to – with a BMX rack and child locks. But it transpired that I didn't need it."

You let that slide. But then, in a dumbass effort to make father–son convo, you ask your daddy what car he had.

"A blue one, Dylan."

Jump-start of some big-ass ventilation fan muffles a revving engine. Your daddy ignores it, walks straight towards the ticket barrier, ducks underneath, then carries on up the exit ramp in the direction of outside. You catch up before he reaches outside and for a moment it's like you're both in a wind tunnel. His brand-new biker jacket flapping like a raincoat. His newspapers all fucked up like a broken umbrella. And then the real umbrella from his briefcase as he dumps the crumpled newspapers. And then the rain on your faces like a slap from your mum.

"Come on, son, keep up." He looks over his shoulder. And so you look over your own. Nothing – just rain and the realisation he'd led you out the car park entrance, not the exit. Exit must be on another road.

"Daddy, you gonna tell me why we just randomly walked through a car-park?"

"You'll soon find out, son."

"Daddy, you gonna tell me where you're taking me?"

"You'll soon find out, son."

"Daddy, you gonna tell me why you need my help lifting stuff at one o'clock in the morning?"

"You'll soon find out, son."

Daddy, why is the grass green?

I don't know, son.

Daddy, why is the sky blue?

I don't know, son.

Daddy, why are you and Mummy shouting at each other?

I don't know, son.

Daddy, you don't mind me asking you all these questions, do you?

Of course not, son. If you don't ask, then how will you ever learn anything.

Soon as your shoulders are finally level, you realise he's smoking a cigarette. Pass up politely when he offers you a hit. Ain't a health thing – you'd be down for sharing a pain-relieving spliff with him. But sharing a cigarette would just feel weird, like you was indirectly kissing or something.

Daddy, is it okay to get her stoned to signal-boost her morphine?

Daddy, just to smooth out the screaming? Just one little toke of hashish?

Daddy, do you think she could OD on caffeine? Do you think I could lace her pills with Pro-Plus, Red Bull, whatever, speed?

Daddy, what the hellfuck did they mean? What did my three bearded aunties mean that night they prophesised that I would take my daddy's place? And what the hell did Google mean?

Daddy, please don't tell me to just ask Google.

You could've asked him all these questions by fone, you suppose. Just called him up and introduced yourself. Could've easily got a number for him, but you didn't want to fone him, you wanted to bump into him; you wanted to know what *he* would want. Deffo nothing deep or emotional. No woe-is-me drama-queenery. Deffo no need to have heard him say, *Together we'll both get through this.* Or the sound of the rhythm of the Tube to school. *Whatever she needs, son, whatever it takes. Whatever she needs, son, whatever it takes.*

"Come on, Dad, if you ain't gonna answer them other questions then at least just tell me where we're headed."

"We're going to a twenty-four-hour storage facility."

Then you shut up and stop asking stuff.

As he hails a taxi, you tell him you know a direct bus to Stockwell.

"Dylan, how did you know that the storage place is in Stockwell?"

Then he shuts up and stops asking stuff.

Windscreen wipers like another of them cure-for-cancer mantras. *You didn't want your daddy, you wanted Ramona.* In her blue raincoat and randomly matching hardback and headphones – not footwear, *headphones.* Cos she's more than just a pair of feet. Telling you that although she no longer gives a shit about Dillon, she might have time for this Dhilan person.

"Incidentally, Dylan" – your dad staring out his backseat window as he speaks – "I wanted to thank you for finally being honest with Naliah. Things have become a lot easier with her now – and therefore also easier with her mother. Actually, I was thinking it would be good for you to meet her. And I want you to know that there are no hard feelings on my side. I understand why you told Naliah what you did – it makes sense that you didn't want her to think badly of you and the way that you just washed your hands of me."

Allow it – maybe the best way for him to keep pushing his story is if he actually believes it to be true. Can't just *pretend* to be all hurt and cut up, he needs to genuinely *feel* it.

Your taxi pulls up at the Stockwell Deep-Level Shelter and you notice while paying the fare that your driver has been weeping through her mascara. At the entrance, another woman makes a note of the time and then hands your daddy a torch. She ain't fronting like some security guard, though – more like them women who stand with the guest list outside places where fun-having people go to have fun. No bag check or nothing. Just lets your asses in.

"You'd better lead the way," your daddy says. Switches positions with you and hands you the flashlight. A sticker on the handle says, *Only switch on if you cannot read this.*

The cage lift is now lined with some padded pink plastic – like yoga mats made of premasticated bubblegum. Soon as the doors close, you start scoping for the Door Open button. *You didn't want your daddy, you wanted Ramona.* Nothing – not even an alarm. You lean against the sticky walls and start hitting him with more questions. "Daddy, why didn't you just tell me we were coming to this place in the first place?"

"Because then we'd talk about it and I'd probably lose my resolve, son."

"Daddy, how the hell did you get security clearance? I thought this place had been closed off."

"Not for the subcontractors working on strengthening and renovating the tunnels, son."

"Daddy, why the hell are we hauling out all the boxes of back issues when we don't have a van to load them into?"

"We're not taking them away, son."

Daddy, I've fucked things up with her. So now what's there for me to do? How will I cope every time I hear her laughing at some other guy's jokes?

This time, the lighting down in the tunnels looks different. Brighter but less white. Louder cos of portable power generators. A draught and various assorted dead rodents. *Daddy, do we really have to do this? Whatever the fuck this even is.* Behind you, your dad's breathing starts sounding more sad than anxious. Kinda sadness people turn into anger to make it easier to handle. He lays his hands on your shoulders as if he's blind and you understand it's now too late to back out.

Along the tunnel, some of the metal bed-frames-cum-shelving-units have been cordoned off and wrapped in plastic. Hard to tell if the sheeting is clear or tinted because of reams of actual red tape. That evening your mummy looked up and swore down that it weren't just a reflection – that even the rain from the clouds was pink. You look up at the tunnel's ribbed steel walls and realise it ain't just the lightning that's different, it's the glistening. Some water leak or sewage or something – special storage facility slime. The drone of portable generators is the sound of pumps and dehumidifiers.

"Dylan, what the hell is that noise?"

You tell him pumps and dehumidifiers.

"No, I mean the noise *you're* making. You sound like you're gargling."

You tell him it's the echo. You tell him you're just sucking the inside of your mouth.

As of tonight, your total number of mouth ulcers is nine. Or eight, depending on how you count two that have merged into one. You reach into your pocket, make sure you got your self-made salt sachets – sealed up in Ziploc bags.

"Well would you mind not doing that, son? It doesn't sound nice."

"Sorry, Daddy, I have many mouth ulcers." Man's got a point, though. The more that you suck on mouth ulcers, the more you like sucking them – their fatty feel, the metallic taste – and, therefore, the more that you suck on them. You shoulda bought a medicated gel or a mouthwash. Did I mention you can cure ulcers with salt?

"Apparently when all this renovating is finished, these tunnels will be turned into a nightclub." Your daddy now whispering into the back of your neck like as if he's your mum or something. "I can't really understand how that will work, but I suppose you'd know better than me – do young people these days dance in single file?"

When you don't answer, your daddy tries again: "And do you youngsters still do all those student drinking society initiations? All those mind-altering substances and forcing yourselves to vomit?"

Next, your daddy stops to check out a stack of leather-bound files. You tell him you ain't there yet – that this ain't your section of the tunnel. Then onwards through the largest filing cabinet in London. The tap of his handmade Italian shoes on the cold steel floor like Ramona in high heels in her shower cubicle. Allow it, whatever, fuck his footsteps – anycase, high heels were originally for men. To keep the feet of Ancient Egyptian butchers free from guts and brains and other throwaway organs. To help Persian horseback soldiers sit better in their stirrups so they could fire arrows with more force. Then white men started wearing them just to look more macho and cos of the general hipness of all things Persian. Then women started wearing them to look masculine. As if he knows you're listening to his footsteps, your daddy stops making them.

When you arrive at the right beds, your trousers are torn and you stink of sweat. One of your salt sachets has split and spilt all down your leg. Your dad starts checking out the boxes and stacks of back issues like as if he'd been expecting more of them. "These will all still exist online, right?"

"You gonna tell me what we're doing here then?"

"Why are you even asking, Dylan? Surely you can smell it?"

How the fuck is it that you failed to pick up on the scent? Either your mouth ulcers have jumped from your gums to your nostrils or something else has been blocking out the now-obvious odour of an underground bonfire.

"One of the ventilation shafts has been rigged to double as a chimney for an incinerator," your daddy explains. "It saves them having to needlessly carry things up that don't need to be carried up. Though given that most of this stuff is paper, you'd think they'd at least have one of those big green recycling bins."

"Wait, what?" Then sniffing your hands, the sleeve of your jacket, your hood – all of it stinking like you been flipping burgers and newspapers on some plebby fun-having family barbecue. "How the fuck are we doing this, Dad? How do we even have access or permission?"

"We're doing it because it needs to be done." He tries maxing out the mystery by leaving it at that, but he can't. "You remember those ashes that were in my thermos flask? The ones I said were bank statements and bills that I'd burnt as an alternative to shredding them? Well, they weren't really bank statements and bills."

I tell him I already know that was his cuttings book – that I ain't a fucking idiot. "But, Dad, this is different. For starters, the back issues down here don't belong to you; for another, all your stories in these editions have already been deleted with marker pen – which means there ain't no need for this." You start ripping at the newspaper stacks to show him. "See? Your stories are totally unreadable. Can't even be skimmed or even semi-skimmed."

"Maybe they're unreadable today," he goes, "but who knows what technology will come out in the future. They might invent some chemical that removes marker pen without erasing the printed ink beneath it – like the way that cheque forgers use toenail-varnish remover. Or maybe they might invent some kind of highly discerning high-tech scanner. That's why this needs to be done, Dylan. And it needs to be done tonight – while we have this whole place to ourselves."

The sound of the storage facility creaking as if the tunnels are growing or spreading or growing. You sit on a stack of back issues. "Okay, well I ain't barbecuing nothing until you tell me once and for all what the fuck this is really actually about."

"Dylan, don't wuss out on me – we need to do this. And then afterwards, when we're out of here, I'll tell you what we've done."

"You know what, I wish I'd just leveraged this shit the other day – I shoulda demanded to know the truth about your stories in return for lying to Naliah for you."

"Oh for the hundredth bloody time, son, I never asked you to lie to Naliah, I simply asked you to speak the truth. And, please, stop moving your mouth like a deranged horse." The sound of the underground Tube trains above you even though the trains stopped running two hours ago. "Let's just do this, Dylan. Let's just do this and leave. And then, after we've done this, I'll tell you everything."

There's a flat trolley for loading stuff onto. You get to work but then stop.

"*Now* what's wrong, son?"

There are other people down here.

Your sudden certainty of it.

Dealing with other back issues in other parts of the tunnel.

You can't actually see any of them – guess they're all just quietly lifting and hunching and lifting in the dark spaces between the different rows of bed frames. But you're aware that they there, though – same way you can be aware of people popping up in your dreams even if you don't actually dream their faces.

"Dylan?" your daddy asks. "What's wrong?"

"You sure we got this place to ourselves?"

"Trust me, I wouldn't be doing this if we didn't."

"Well, there are definitely other people down here, Dad."

42

FUCK KNOWS HOW you got there and fuck knows how you left. **Tenth time your mum told you she had the C-bomb.** Whether she knew by telepathy you wanted some one-on-one time with her or whether all your aunts and uncles and cousins were busy. Her voicemail like some kinda formal invite. Darth Gruffness, official summons. *"Dhilan, I'm just phoning to let you know I'll be alone tomorrow at one."*

However the fuck you got there, on the way there you started pretending you'd be able to take her out to a restaurant. Both of you together again at a candlelit table for two. Obviously nowhere too swanky-and-knickers-off but also nowhere skanky like McDonald's. *How about a pub lunch, Mum? By some posh stretch of the river near Hammersmith.* Last time you'd taken her outta the house for lunch, it was to the Costa in Charing Cross Hospital.

From the front gate to the front door, some satnav in your head said you were walking in the wrong direction. *Turn around, turn around. Don't wait for the next exit, just turn the fuck around.* Pretend you got held up at uni or in a meeting with one of your clients. Maybe the reason your mum's voicemail sounded proper forced and formal was cos she knew as well as you did that you should no longer be left alone together.

Once inside, you realised that, technically, the two of you weren't even alone. District nurse by her deathbed-to-be in the living room, Aunties Number Three and Four rearranging the cutlery drawer in the kitchen. All those part-time and full-time occupants probly didn't even know they were preventing you from doing whatever it was you were gonna do . . . No, not *you. Me.*

I did what happens next.

Aunties Number Three and Four try and blank me but they're too polite to pull it off. Forks and spoons all mixed up. Watery meat in the blender meant for beetroot juice. And since when did we have a set of steak knives? Anyway, forget the cutlery-fest in the kitchen, go to the living room. *Go on* – the living-room-cum-bedroom-cum-hospice. The tightly drawn curtains. The sunlight. Your shared-ownership bed but now with a brand-new mattress. The sunlight screaming behind the curtains. Your mum splayed on her brand-new mattress like as if her body might get upgraded with it instead of rotting on the old one. Snoring some morphine mantra babble. Like she'd just been assaulted by death itself – like the Grim Reaper had got busy with the wrong end of his scythe and afterwards decided to leave her living.

"I'll leave you two alone, then," the district nurse said as she put on her coat and helped your mum sort of sit up. "Don't worry, I'll call back in a couple of hours."

Your entering the room flipped a switch that changed your mum from spaced-out to totally on it. "Dhilan, sweetheart – you're staying for lunch?"

"What – can she – eat?" you asked. But the district nurse had already left. Her car pulling outta the accessible-access driveway.

"Of course I can eat," croaked your mum. "So long as it isn't solids, son – I'm afraid I'm not doing very well with solids again."

By then, her body wouldn't have made it out to the back garden, never mind out to a restaurant. You started wondering what the home-cum-hospice equivalent of five-star hotel room service would be. Your cousin Ravi would've probly organised that shit a whole month in advance. Hired a Michelin-starred chef to come home and make carrot-and-beetroot-chemo-superfood soup-du-jour. The kinda service where they roll it into the room with flowers on a ready-laid table. Balloons, even – all that golden-boy grandchild-bearing bollocks. Allow that bullshit – best you could manage for her today would be a simple, slapdash pub lunch. A riverside gastropub-cum-restaurant. Because restaurants, like hospitals and romantic holidays, would now always feel like portals pulling you back to her. All them brochures and itineraries and today's specials. Soup of boiling bodily fluids. Swollen meat soaked through you.

You pulled up a chair from the dining table and placed it at her deathbedside – apologising to the other diners in the gastropub for nearly spilling their drinks. "Mummy," you kicked off while she tried to hide a stain on her duvet, "Mummy, you said you wanted to talk about something?"

"I felt we should have a talk, sweetheart."

"Sure, Mum. But about what?"

"Stuff, my darling. Just stuff. How's your school? How's your uni going?"

So this was it then, you thought. *That* talk. The talk – the talk she's spent ten years prepping. The talk nearly every cancer-patient parent eventually has with their children. You gave up rehearsing hearing it about six years into her illness, but deep down you always knew the end would begin with a talk. That it wouldn't really end with sirens. No 999 on speed-dial – probly wouldn't even end in hospital. No vending-machine coffee in the waiting-room, no string-orchestra soundtrack, no nurses looking at you like maybe they just might snog you outta sympathy. Just aunties and aunties and chutney and the bogey-green curtains and carpet in the living room. The talk that begins with: *"Son, I'm really sorry, but it looks like the treatment isn't working."*

Her curtains, her carpet. The sunlight. The sunlight shouting behind her curtains. Her inner-supermum strength from which would probly spit forth a totally different version of That Talk: *"Son, I'm really sorry, but it looks like the treatment's actually been working. They think it was a delayed reaction. I'm heading back into remission – I'll probably be around forever."*

You helped her to pull a cardigan over one of the nighties you'd bought her. That band of sequins across the cardigan like the ghost of a belt – like even *she* wanted to pretend you were dining out somewhere special. Both of you too numbed by your mouth ulcers to order anything but soup and soup and then more soup to replace the spilt soup. Her chewing her soup so intently as if she knew she wouldn't be able to hold it down. You suddenly feeling like your taste buds were dead, another dipshit synced-up side effect. Random splodge of sequins across her chest. No hat or headscarf, though – just the baby baldness of your mummy reduced to snivelling infant, stringy incontinent toddler's drool. You like some kinda paedo trying not to trace the outline of her body. Ramona had kept all these sick thoughts of yours away – she did, she does, she must've done. Kept all these thoughts tucked deep in the pits of her toe cleavage. Were you really some asshole afraid of her body or just afraid of being afraid of it? And did fear always have to lead to hatred?

"You know, sweetheart, this could still go on," your mum said to the mug of freshly brewed Cup-a-Soup that you'd somehow poured and stirred and placed in her stringy-cheese hands. Tomato liquid runny lipstick. "What I mean, darling, is that nothing bad has happened. I was dying the last you came to see me and now I'm dying again – that's all it is. Same story for years. I wonder how many times the doctors can say I'm dying before even their words become dead."

Your mum probly knew what she was trying to say. You were trying not to know.

"Why should I go to the hospice?" she pressed on. "They say I could become completely bedridden and then get a bit better again and then become bedridden again, so tell me, why should I go?"

"Mummy, where have you gone? How much morphine did the district nurse give you?"

"Don't be silly, Dhilan – she wouldn't have left if she'd given me morphine. I'm perfectly lucid. I'm always lucid at lunchtime. Too bloody lucid for my liking. I'm trying to tell you that I could become completely bedridden and then get up again or I could become completely bedridden and then never get up again. Who knows? It could be months, weeks or days. The only thing the doctors know for certain is I've got cancer."

"Come on, Mummy," you spoke into the scalp you were suddenly stroking and sniffing and stroking. "Don't talk about weeks or days. You gotta think positive. That's what you always say. And, anyway, if it's really just a matter of weeks or days, then what the hell am I doing still staying in student halls?"

Your mum just looked around the living-room-cum-bedroom-cum-hospice as if looking at all the other people in this gastro-pub-cum-restaurant. Even though the tables were donning napkin rings, it weren't one of them moonlit, candlelit, teeth-lit places. More like the pub she took you to on your sixteenth birthday for your first ever pint of shandy. "*You* know why you're still staying in student halls, Dhilan."

Next, she tried placing her mug on her bedside table, turning to look at the couple kissing at the table to our left as if telling them to get a room – as if this pub was one of them countryside pubs with upstairs shagging quarters. When you leaned over to steady her arm, her left leg slid out from beneath the duvet. Or maybe it was the duvet that slid. Either way, you tried not to look. You always tried not to look. Hating how her various assorted medicines always made her feet swollen. Hating how the word for "swollen foot" in Ancient Greek was "oedipus". The living-room-cum-bedroom the exact same living-room-come-coven they'd all been talking in. All them years back when Aunties Number One, Two and Three had assumed you were keeping your end of the babysitting deal and sleeping. *But how she can divorce her own husband? If my daughter did a thing like this I would* thapar *her one.* Me, I feel sorry for her son. One hard slap across her face. *The son will take the father's place.* ALWAYS THIS IS WHAT HAPPENS

– THE GOOGLY-ENGINE IT SAYS THIS. THE FACEBOOK STORY SAYS HE WILL GO OFF THE RUFFIAN RAILS. *Yes. Yes, yes, yes. He will become the weirdo and take the father's place . . .* And so on and so forth, the television laughing, the light fixtures flickering, all three aunties' voices amplified and distorted by the living room's future furniture-cum-electrical-medical-equipment.

You laid your head gently against your mummy's scalp. Your elbow on the edge of her pillow. Two gastropub tables to the right of the bed, you clocked two of your old school teachers. Everyone at school had known they was a couple – the clue was in the fact they was married to each other. Mr Forest taught drama; Mrs Levis taught art. It still messed with your head when you saw teachers outside school – even though you no longer went to school. Even more so to be seeing them in your mum's favourite gastropub by the most romantic stretch of the Thames. They didn't belong in there, *nobody* did – just you and your mummy. And they deffo didn't belong in your living room.

"Whatever happens, sweetheart, you must remain strong," your mum said – then getting annoyed with herself for sounding cringe. "No," she tried again, "if you feel sad then, okay, then be it – be sad. But please try not be so angry, son. Even right now I can see it in your face."

You looked at your reflection in the butter knife that had been placed beside the napkin ring. But all you could see was your acne – like some inverted counterparts of your mouth ulcers. Put the knife back down, spilt soup on her duvet – *your* duvet, *the* duvet, *our* duvet, whatever. One of the waiters rushed from behind the bar to help you wipe it off the table and hand you a brand-new menu. While he did so, you spotted Aunties Number Three and Four peering through the crack in the living-room doorway. Without moving from her bedside, you reached for your mum's walking stick and shut the door in your aunties' collective face. They snorted, all shocked and offended, then sighed, then knocked. "We're just going to Tesco," they said in sync.

"Your mother needs some things," said Aunty Number Three.

"We'll leave the two of you to talk alone," said Aunty Number Four.

"Dhilan, can we get anything for you?"

When your voice answered, "No thank you," you didn't speak towards the door but to your mother's swollen feet. Scent of salt from her feet – how the fuck had her eye saliva dribbled down her thighs to her feet? "Actually, wait," you called out. "Don't go. *Please.* Stay in the house. Come inside the room, even. I'll go Tesco myself when Mummy takes a nap, but for now just please stay in the house with us."

They pushed open the door, but just by a centimetre.

"No, Dhilan," said Aunty Number Three – her teeth a sliver of yellow through the gap in the doorway. "You be alone with your mother."

"Yes, you be on your own with your mother," agreed Aunty Number Four. "After all, this is it, what you want."

And so you listened to the keys and the latch and the storm porch as you just sat there and let them leave . . . No, not *you. Me.* *I* did what happens next.

My mum restarted from where she'd left off before we got interruptured. "It's just that on Saturday, Dhilan, when everyone came here to the house, they all said you looked so angry. So angry that it scared them. Other people noticed it too, not just me – other people said you looked angry. Always hiding your handsome face behind the phone camera."

You wanted to ask her how the hell they saw your face if it was always behind the camera, but you didn't cos you didn't wanna sound angry.

"Because anyone can be angry, sweetheart. It's much easier to feel anger against people than it is to feel sad within yourself. Just look at me and your masi – whenever one of us feels sad about something, we suddenly find some reason to fight with someone else. I know this without you needing to tell me. But I don't want *you* to be like that, sweetheart. That's why I'm telling you not to be so angry. Be as sad as you like, sweetheart, but please don't be so angry."

You wanted to tell her: *What the fuck? Surely not you as well, Mum? The others I can understand, but not you. How can you seriously say all that when you came to all them couples therapy sessions with me?*

But you didn't tell her this cos you didn't wanna sound angry.

"Or actually maybe what I mean is please don't hate me, darling – you don't have to keep looking at me like you hate me. Try to remember me better than I am. Maybe this is why it was a good thing when you moved to the student halls. But, still, even on Saturday you *still* hated me."

You wanted to tell her: *Of course I don't hate you, I hate your fucking illness,* and so on. But you didn't tell her this cos you didn't wanna sound angry. Or because, even if you said it, you knew she didn't even have the strength to change her mind. Unless she was just fishing for you to tell her again that you loved her. How to convince her, though? How to slap her back to her senses – one hard slap across her face. *Fuck you, you ain't dying, fuck you.* Instead, you started giving her your usual reassurances: I love you, I love you, I love you and so on. Forget about Ramona and Beyoncé and Eva Green, etc. – sometimes I think maybe they're just there to keep just how much I love you in check. *A boy's best friend is his mother,* and so on. *You're my one and only BFF. But, Mum, that don't mean we're eternal hermaphrodite Siamese soulmates or something. We ain't gonna be together in another lifetime and I weren't your husband in some previous life. We're just mother and son and what we got is here. I been thinking about it ever since I was eight and I ain't angry with you or even with God, I'm just angry with the clock.*

"Because I'm sorry, Dhilan." Sudden curve of her normally square jaw. "I'm really, really sorry that it's taking so long. That's why I called you over today – to tell you that this could still go on and on. Now they're saying they think there's a chance I might even respond to a new type of treatment. So, sweetheart, I want you to tell me truthfully . . ." Your mum looked round the gastro-pub-cum-restaurant to make sure ain't no one else was listening.

Switched her mobile to silent, yanked the living-room landline from the phone socket. Put down her fork, pulled at the duvet. Smiled at your two teachers – the ones who'd once told her during parents' evening that they wished she'd brought up all their pupils. ". . . Just please, just tell me truthfully, Dhilan: would you prefer it if I just gave up the fight?"

Your mum didn't ask you this in some angryfied Anti-Oestrogen way, she just laid it on the table like it was some kinda for-serious question. The gastropub-table-cum-living-room-bedside-table. Didn't even use the word "dead" or "die", just "give up the fight". All her whole life's battery power diverted into sounding dignified. And maybe it was cos of her businesslike lack of melodrama. Or maybe it was cos the question obviously didn't need no answer given that, treatment or no treatment, things now seemed so close to the end-of-the-story end. But, either way, you didn't reply. After all, if you'd said the words "Please don't give up the fight" you'd sound like *you* were the one being melodramatic. Like you was kneeling over her wounded and bloodied body sprawled on the floor of some random gastropub-cum-restaurant, begging her to keep breathing, keep her eyes open. Begging her not to leave you – like those kids who get lost from their mummies in shopping malls and start howling in front of total strangers and sniffling and dribbling and shitting in their no-longer-nappies. Or maybe you just didn't know how to reply. Either way, your dumb ass didn't reply. And when your mum's face started liquefying like you were back in some Groupon-deal mother–son sauna where her eye saliva sliced through her sweat – there and then in the gastropub-cum-restaurant, right in front of total strangers – it felt too fucking late for you to reply. It'd just sound like you was lying – same way everyone lies when someone they love starts crying. She didn't even wipe away a layer of eye saliva – as if she didn't want to draw it to your attention. Just stayed sitting there like some over-oiled wooden statue, varnish and various assorted bodily fluids dribbling down her chin, into her lap, down her legs. Ditto you just carried on sitting there watching her as she carried on sitting there liquefying. All the other gastropub diners staring at her, waiting for you to just get up and hold her and help her and wipe her – if only to prove that her jawline wasn't actually made of syrup or something. If you could have moved a muscle in your own jaw, you'd have told them all that they were watching the most courage-ful woman any of them would ever see. But you didn't even try cos they weren't really there, and cos the two of you never left the living room, you understood that you'd both always be in that gastropub-cum-restaurant wherever either of you now went. Unless, of course, you managed to . . . No, not *you. Me.*

I did what happens next.

43

SO NOW YOU'VE ditched all your sob stories and your daddy's ditched all his scare stories. Only shit left is the stories you came down here for in the first place.

"Are you sitting comfortably, son?"

You're still squat-sulking on top of the first stack of back issues. Your daddy leaning on the trolley for carting them to the underground furnace.

"I swear there are other people down here, Dad."

"No, Dylan. There isn't anyone. They're not here. You're mistaken."

"But then why . . ."

"There isn't. You're mistaken. I promise. There isn't. Just rats and shadows. Nothing to be scared of, son."

"But . . ."

"Be brave, son. Be brave."

Allow this bullshit – next he'll be telling you little boys shouldn't be afraid of the fucking dark. Except it ain't even that dark in here. There wouldn't be no shadows if it was *that* dark. Anycase, you ain't even afraid of the dark – you used to stream horror movies just to kill the sadness. Being stressed or scared shitless the only break from all the pre-bereavement bereavement.

"But then what about at the other end of the tunnel?" you ask. "Someone must be operating the incinerator? Surely we ain't meant to just shovel all these papers straight into the flames like they did with all those diseased cows?"

Reason it ain't dark in here is cos of the pink neon strip lighting. And the clear plastic sheets that somehow seem tinted. And the puddles beneath the shelving. And the slime on the surface of the ribbed steel walls.

"I mean, it's just basic workplace health and safety, Daddy. You can't have a self-service incinerator. *Under the fucking ground*."

Your daddy just asks once again if you're sitting comfortably. And then he nods on your behalf. "Well then, let me begin, son. Once upon a time in a city called London, there was a jaded young journalist who was recruited by a colour-by-numbers crime syndicate to plant coded messages in newspaper stories. These coded messages took the form of fake eyewitness quotes. And then they all lived happily ever after. The end."

You tell your daddy: "Thank you for telling me." And then: "Well, let's do this and then we can go."

The crusty stickiness of the newspapers. One stack at a time. Put your non-existent backbone into it. No biceps to speak of either – you eat more caffeine than protein. Doesn't count as carrying her over the threshold if she's in a stretcher.

"Dylan, I'm telling you the truth."

"I know, Daddy."

You knew straight from jump that this time he was going for full factual accuracy. That this weren't another one of his fake news stories. That maybe this was always gonna be the deal between you: your daddy ditching his scare stories and you ditching your sob stories. Ain't even whining about your mouth ulcers no more – told him the blood was just from shaving cuts. Acne scars or something. Shit, *wait* – could shaving cuts be seen as a sob story?

Two minutes later, your daddy starts throwing down some extra footage. Deleted scenes he'd cut for length. Tells you they couldn't just plant the coded messages in the newspaper's classified or personal ads cos that shit's already been done to death and so the cops are always checking for it.

You tell him you don't care. You load up the trolley with another stack of back issues.

"Dylan, look, I appreciate it's a bit of a nothing burger. Maybe the only surprising fact is that you hadn't already guessed all this yourself. But nonetheless it's still serious. These people are dangerous and not to be trusted and they mean business. That's why I told you all those other stories – to protect you. To stop you nosing around. I realise telling you that thing about it being a paranormal phenomenon was perhaps a bit far-fetched – though no more outlandish than that woe-is-me tale you told Naliah about me abandoning you."

The scent drifting through the tunnel from the furnace no longer smelling like a bonfire or barbecue. More like an engine – or an overheating electrical appliance.

"So how much they pay you then, Daddy? To plant all them secret messages."

"You really want all those details? I'm happy to give them to you. Give you my tax returns too. I'm not hiding anything. Not any more. But surely all that really matters is that some sort of illegal activity was committed. People were doing things they shouldn't have been doing. Some people got away with it and the people who got away with it got away. Some people were punished and the people who were punished for it were punished. End of story, son. Everything else is just padding."

For some reason, this bit of his story fucks you off something serious. The way he tries to own it. Sure, the whole thing might've been minor and boring, but ain't no need to front about that. It's like as if, all sudden-like, your daddy now reckons himself. Like all them cocksure student start-up founders. Or those posh boys who just shoulder shrug whenever they fuck up.

Hey, Daddy, you don't have to be remorseful or nothing, but try not to act so manly and matter-of-factly.

It don't suit you, Daddy.

Don't suit you one bit.

Let's face it, you ain't exactly Vin Diesel.

In fact, you're *the one who should've been popping anti-oestrogen pills, you lonely fucking loser of a man.*

This is when you realise you've accidentally unmuted all this.

Your daddy slam-shoves the half-loaded trolley outta the space between you. Barely even rolls three feet, though. "How dare you, Dylan? After all your crap these past few days, how dare you? You know what, let me tell you something about journalism, son: it isn't the *who, what, when* or *where* that makes a story, it's the *why* that matters most. I didn't plant those fake eyewitness quotes for money, you fool, I planted them for a woman."

Cliché #1: Turns out the woman in question was a PR woman. Or at least she'd fronted like she was a PR woman.

Cliché #2: Your daddy says the important thing to remember is that, technically, he didn't have an extramarital affair with her cos he didn't actually do the deed.

Cliché #3: So basically he's claiming he ain't some lonely loser of a man cos he once managed to have an affair, but, at the same time, he ain't some pathetic piece-of-shit of a man cos it weren't technically an affair.

Turns out it started as just some little game they played – he calls it "the logical extension of the usual game played out between journalists and spin doctors". This woman would persuade him to insert random shit into his news stories – bits of song lyrics, for instance, or properly obscure words that they'd sit down and choose together by scoping through the dictionary. He tells you he did all this just to humour her/impress her/game her. And when they were done inserting song lyrics into his stories, they then started inserting cheeky references to places he and her had had lunch together. You figure he basically means places they'd fucked each other, but you don't call him out on it – better he saves today's truth quota for more important bits of his story. Anycase, *emotional truth is just as important as factual accuracy.* Your daddy tells you that, next thing, this woman started to choose the obscure words all by herself and their publication became a precondition for "meeting for lunch". Then the words became whole sentences in the form of fictional eyewitness quotes. Only reason your dad started getting sus was because even though she was a PR person, she didn't ask him to insert any spin into his stories when he was writing about one of her clients. And that's when he realised he'd been played. Pretty soon, he clocked how the same fake eyewitness quotes had been planted in other stories in other publications. Apparently the pattern of duplication was part of the code.

Cliché #4: He clarifies with a quickness that all this went down many years before him and your mum divorced. Apparently your mummy ain't never found out – never even suspected. *No harm, no foul.* Oh, and of course, technically, he weren't even cheating (see **Cliché #2**).

Your daddy carries on busting out clarifications and qualifications, but you already know you ain't in no position to judge. And not just cos of all them afternoons with Ramona – also your school lessons, your library books, your A-level essays, your daydreams, your class detentions, your Eva Green posters. All your thoughts of life without her. But for some reason, you start weighing up whether maybe you could judge him anyway? Or if not judge him, then at least cross-examinate him? Or if not cross-examinate, then at least interview him?

"So, there you have it, Dylan. A honeypot. A femme fatale" – aka your daddy's late entry for **Cliché #5**. "But once again, son, I cannot stress this enough: all those lunches and dinners were the nearest I ever got to attempting to cheat on your mother. I never did anything like that again and the whole episode had nothing to do with our divorce – it happened many, many years before our divorce." Your daddy no longer leaning on the trolley now. "In fact, if anything, it actually helped our marriage because afterwards I realised what I stood to lose and I put all of my energies into our marriage – your mother and I grew a lot closer as a result of all this." Ding! **Cliché #6**.

And this is when it finally hits you. "Have you been trying to keep all this hidden cos you didn't want Naliah to find out? *Daddy?* You're worried she won't give you her mother's hand in marriage if she knew that, once upon a time, you tried to cheat on your first wife."

"Please, Dylan, I already told you: I've been trying to keep this hidden because these people are dangerous and not to be trusted and they mean business." He turns to face the bed-frames-cum-shelving. "Though now that you mention it, son, I would very much prefer it if Naliah and her mother never found out about this. Not a word of it – you understand? After all, you know what people say: if you marry a man who cheats on his wife then you're marrying a man who cheats on his wife."

After that, just the sound of portable power generators buzzing and crackling – like them special lights for killing insects. But despite all this crackling and glitching, the lighting in the tunnel stays steady – like it's being powered by something else and the generators are there just for sound.

The light means you don't need the flashlight.

So why the fuck are you picking up the flashlight?

Why switch the thing on and shine it onto your daddy's pulsating face?

"But *why,* Daddy?" you ask.

"You mean why should you keep this a secret from Naliah? What more reason do you want, Dylan? Do you want me to give you some money? Is that it?"

"Ain't gonna tell Naliah nothing, okay – I told you before, I've got zero interest in fucking up your shit. Far as I'm concerned, your relationship with Naliah's mum is the best thing about you. When I asked you why, Daddy, I meant *why* – as in, *why* did you do this?" You shine the torch onto the newspaper lying open at one of his blacked-out stories. "*This*, Daddy – *why this*?"

"But I just told you why. My stories were redacted as they contained fake content because some honeypot PR person used me to plant secret messages in them. Messages for bog-standard illegal activities."

"But *why*, Daddy?"

"You mean why did I attempt to have an extramarital affair?"

Truth is, you actually ain't got no idea why you keep asking why, like some whining five-year-old. Next, the torch shines onto his throat and you end up asking why again – like as if the reason you keep asking him shit has got something to do with the torch.

"But *why*, Daddy?"

"How the hell do I know? How does any man really know exactly why these things happen – why they have an affair or they attempt to have an attempted affair or whatnot. There are always so many different factors involved."

"But *why*, Daddy?"

Now a lecture on all the complicated factors that push men to have extramarital affairs. The fucker even tries blame-shifting onto the women. You figure you should spit in disgustment or someshit, but the pink neon lights would probly make it look like you was just spitting out some premasticated bubblegum.

"But *why*, Daddy?"

Or maybe you're just saving your spitting for later? Maybe you know on some deep down down-low that there's way more messed-up shit still to come.

"I keep telling you I don't know why, because affairs are complicated and so I genuinely don't know, Dylan."

"But *why*, Daddy?"

Stop beating around the bullshit, Daddy.

Just cos you covered it up in extramarital ejaculate, Daddy, it's still basically whitewashing.

"Oh come on, son. This is getting tiresome. Or, wait a second – are you asking me why your mother and I got *divorced*? Because if so, then I've told you before and I can tell you again with certainty that we just gradually grew apart. It had nothing to do with my attempt to have an attempted affair – as I've already said, that whole episode happened many years before the divorce." He picks up the newspaper lying open at one of his blacked-out stories. "Why don't you just shine your torch on the date of this paper. See? That proves beyond a doubt – to both of us – that my attempted affair was many, many years before the divorce. And, as I said earlier, if anything, it actually helped our marriage . . ."

The portable power generators start making a powering-down sound before suddenly booting up again. And, once again, their sounds and their struggles make fuck all difference to the neon strip lights – i.e. you don't even need this stupid torch. And you deffo don't need to be pointing it back at your dad. Flicking it up and down across different parts of his body.

"But *why*, Daddy?"

"For fuck's sake, I don't know, son. Maybe it just felt like that other woman and I had some kind of special chemistry. Or maybe I just liked who I was better whenever I was with her. Maybe I felt less alone, less bored. Or maybe it was just something to do with her face. Or maybe it was her hair. Or her legs or her backside or her breasts . . ."

"Her *breasts*?"

"Or her backside. Or her hips. Or her personality, Dylan. I keep telling you I don't know. I can't remember. I don't know."

"But then why even mention this other woman's breasts?"

"Because. Just because. Look, Dylan, some men get turned on by a woman's legs, other men get turned on by her breasts or by the back of her neck or her backside or buttocks. Others get turned on by her face, her eyes, or her shoulders, or her midriff, her hips, or her hair . . ."

"Daddy, I think you and I need to have a really long father–son chat about the objectification of women's bodies."

"Or even her personality, Dylan – her inner beauty. Equally, some men will get turned on by other men – by another man's pectorals, or his jawline, or maybe even his penis. And other men get turned on by a woman's smell. Apparently some sick perverts even get turned on by feet. But I suppose if you're going to put me on the spot like this and force me to play pin the donkey, then I'd have to say I've always been into women's breasts. And, yes, the woman I attempted to have an affair with, she happened to have nice breasts. But, hey, that's just me, Dylan. So sue me – I hear from Naliah that you're one of those people who are into feet."

This time when the portable power generators go down, they take the lights with them. You point the flashlight at the neon strip lights like as if you're trying to give them some kinda transfusion. By the time you point the thing back at your old man again, your daddy lets out a high-pitched groan. Just a short burst – almost like a laugh. But it ain't no laugh.

It deffo ain't no laugh.

"Dylan," he goes, "I think maybe there's something I need say to you." Your daddy sits his butt down on a stack of newspapers. "But I need to try and think clearly here, son. So, please, just help me by not confusing me. Don't confuse the chronology of things by continually bringing up my affair and my fake stories. It doesn't help me think clearly if you keep bringing up things that have nothing to do with this."

"To do with what, Daddy?"

"You know what I'm talking about, Dylan."

"Actually, I don't have a fucking clue."

He facepalms, but not in a gif way. "Oh no. No, no, no, Dylan – you really don't know, do you? Your mother never told you. I just assumed that eventually she would have." Your daddy busts out a handkerchief. Doesn't wipe his nose or his eyes, though, just holds it against his chest. "Dylan, do you remember when you were six years old and we drove you to Birmingham one summer to stay with your cousins and your Uncle Deepak? You remember? This was about two years before our divorce and a good few years after my attempted affair. And yet do you remember what we told you?"

"You told me it was cos you and mum were having arguments with each other."

"And didn't you ever think it strange that we'd burden you by even telling you that much? After all, you were just a little boy."

Looking back on it now, only thing that seemed strange to you was how little they argued when you got back to Acton. As if by some marriage guidance miracle all their beef with each other had been eaten up.

"The fact is our marriage was better than ever in those days. If anything, the only thing we were arguing about was whether or not to send you to Birmingham. I wanted that we should tell you what was really happening. But, you see, your mother didn't want to upset you – you used to get so clingy and worried about her dying in an accident or whatnot. You'd come crying to our bedroom in the middle of the night sometimes. Said you'd had a nightmare that Mummy had died. You were just five – you were still wetting the bed and she didn't want to make things worse. So she didn't want to tell you that she'd got sick."

"What sick? How sick?"

This time your daddy facepalms with his handkerchief, like he's hiding from the flashlight.

"What sort of sickness was it, Dad?"

"Come on. Take a guess."

"What are you talking about? Mummy got sick when I was nine. That's two years *after* you and she divorced. Not two years *before*. Two years *after*." Your daddy waits for you to finish. "Dad, I was *nine*. Not five. Nine. No way I could forget how old I was when my mum died."

"Died? *What?* We're talking about when she first got sick."

You tell him he knows what you mean. You tell him again that you were nine.

"Listen to me, Dylan. That isn't true. Don't you see? The first time your mummy told you she had cancer was actually the second time she had cancer. Likewise, the second time she told you she had it was actually the third time, the third the fourth, the fourth the fifth, and so on. Do you follow me, son?"

"But then where was it? The first one. Which bit of her body was it? *Hey?* Was it her legs? Her hips? Her shoulders? Back of her neck? Her feet? Her hair? Tell me, Daddy, which bit of her body?"

"Come on, Dylan. It was her breast, of course."

"Well then that's obviously bullshit, Daddy. Cos I was with her through both her breast cancers – both her mastectomies. And, anyway, I shouldn't even be talking to you about her breasts."

"For her first surgery she just had the lump removed – a lumpectomy, not a full mastectomy. We even thought it might be benign. Oh, damn me even more – maybe limiting it to a lumpectomy was just for my benefit? Either way, the point is she didn't want to tell you. And then she decided that she didn't even want to tell your masi or any of your other aunties and uncles. As I understand, you're also very good at not telling people about her illness. Anyway, she had a course of radiotherapy while you were staying in Birmingham. We thought she was cured. But clearly it came back again two years after we divorced. Which is why the first time your mother told you she was sick was actually the second time she was sick, the second was the third, the third the fourth and so on."

You scroll through your memories – your thoughts, your messages, videos, fotos. First comes the *how*, then the *why*. How she'd always let you go with her for her scans, chemo and physio appointments, but never ever to the routine annual one-on-ones with her consulting oncologist. How she sent you away from her hospital bedside whenever anyone with a clipboard started talking about her histology. How she came back from work that time just to get a login password she'd scribbled on the back of her medical records instead of just phoning and asking you to read it out to her.

But why keep it on the hush? Why hadn't she just clued you in herself when you was old enough to hear it – say, when you were eleven or twelve? You lost count of her tumours after tumour number seven anyway, so what the hell difference would one more have made?

You realise you already know why.

Knew it almost straight away.

No need to guess when it comes to your mum – never no need to ask, "But *why*, Mummy?" You've always known why with her, and she's always known the why of it with you. She'd kept it hush to protect you – cos delaying her sickness's start date would basically lengthen her life expectancy. Cos even when you been her full-on carer, she still be helping you change your own sheets whenever you drenched the bed with your own cold sweats.

Or maybe – oh, shitfuck, no, please, no – maybe she'd kept it hush cos she didn't wanna admit the dirty stinking mess that your daddy had done?

"But . . . *why*, Daddy?"

"You mean why didn't your mother tell you all this herself?"

"No, why did *you* tell me, Daddy? Why tell me all of this? I only asked about your fake news stories. But your news stories had nothing to do with all this."

"Oh, wake up, Dylan. Just please, just wake up, son . . ."

If you woke up with me, Dhilan, I wouldn't have to face the sunrise by myself.

But I am awake at daybreak, Mummy. I do my homework at five in the morning.

". . . After all, now that you've awoken me to all of this, the least you can do is see it with me, Dylan." Your daddy speaking through the fabric of his handkerchief now. "Because, yes, I think that maybe that's the reason why. Yes. I really think maybe it is. It isn't what I've always *thought* happened – I always *thought* that your mother and I just generically grew apart. But now that you and I are talking, son, I'm no longer so sure." Your daddy just whispering behind his hanky now. Ain't no need for vocal projection when mostly talking to yourself. ". . .Or at the very least, if we did grow apart, then I think that maybe I grew apart from your mother first. And I think perhaps it had nothing to do with our incompatible personalities or my workaholism. *Dylan? Are you listening?* I'm saying I think it was because after her operation I think maybe

I couldn't stand it. But what exactly am I saying? *What* couldn't I stand, son? *It.* I couldn't stand *it* – I couldn't stand the sight of it. But it wasn't repulsion or anything, Dylan – I never said it was repulsion. It was more like an anxiety that I had. Irrational fearfulness. *Okay? Happy* now are you, Dylan? I couldn't stand the sight." Wet patches in his handkerchief. Sniffle, sniffle – various assorted bodily fluids. "Anxiety, Dylan, not repulsion. After all, why do you think all those redneck American congressmen want to regulate women's bodies even more than hardline mullahs do? Why they're all so obsessed with purity and menstruation. It's because they're anxious and afraid of women's bodies too. But because they're too macho to admit they're afraid, their anxiety gets distorted and turns into domination or disgust or abuse or hatred. So, you see, it's not just me, son – men have always had these issues."

"The fuck, Dad? Is that seriously supposed to be your defence?"

You realise that with him it's the other way round: you can handle all the eye saliva, just can't deal with all these noxious secretions coming outta his mouth.

"Dylan, you have to remember that when we split up, she was two years into remission. We thought that original lump was probably benign. I mean, I didn't think of it as divorcing a cancer patient, Dylan. We thought she was cured. And it wasn't as if I didn't try, son. I tried to be more positive. More responsive. I tried. I tried very, very hard. Nobody in the world could have tried harder than I did."

You wanna tell him, *What the fuck, Daddy? Are you having some kinda internal competition with yourself to see how low you can make my opinion of you freefall?*

But you don't tell him this.

You just tell him, "But *why*, Daddy?"

Or, actually, maybe this time you don't ask him why. Maybe don't say nothing at all. You just cut him a look and then watch that old familiar fight on his face – the one between embarrassment and angryness.

"Oh, don't sit there and judge me like that, Dylan. Or rather, *Dhilan.* Anyway, this isn't about her scarring – I never even said it had anything to do with her scarring. As a matter of fact, this happened even before she got sick. I mean, do you even realise that you didn't just get the Good Morning kiss, Dhilan, you got the Welcome Home kiss even when *I* was the one who'd come home from work – working harder than any man in the world works. And eating from the same plate, even – she used to say, 'So what if we share the same plate and cutlery? Dhilan would never be disgusted with me.' In any case, she wouldn't have been able to spend time with me even if she wanted to because every time she was out of your sight, you'd start crying. It was as if you were afraid of her disappearing or something. You cried when the two of you played peek-a-boo. And then running to our room every night to make sure she was still there. And, anyway, do you have any idea how long you were breastfeeding for, Dhilan? Until you were four years old. *Four years old!* All that suckling and soreness, Dhilan. That's four years of no access for me. Just staying up till five in the morning and getting stuck in a rabbit hole of online pornography – do you have any idea how the web takes hold of your minor fixations and then warps your whole mind with them? And during all that time I stayed with her – my one attempted indiscretion with that other woman notwithstanding, I stayed with your mother. But then that horrible operation and I'm sorry, Dhilan, I'm really sorry, but I'm now beginning to realise that maybe that's the real reason I started growing apart from her. In fact, why the hell am I still qualifying and couching – why don't we just embrace the certainty of it now. Because now that I'm thinking about it, son, I remember that, one day, I even physically retched. And your mother pretended she didn't notice me retch. And no, not just at her post-surgical scars, but even before that – my retching in repulsion at the thought of you suckling on them. So I'm sorry but fuck it, Dhilan, her breasts belonged to you anyway – maybe I thought you'd look after what remained of them better than I ever could."

"Good," a voice rolls in from further up the tunnel. "Absolutely fucking contemptible, but good." The botched-Botox man steps out of the blackness into the beam of the flashlight. He nods at you, then pats your weeping father on the back. "Good that you've said it, Deckardas. It's a pity that it came to it, but given that it came to it, it's good that you've said it."

Something about the botched-Botox man is different now. Different down here. His biker jacket is now a long grey raincoat. His stubble now firmly heading towards full-beard. He kicks the trolley gently into your daddy's knees. "Now both of you can get on with deleting all these wilting newspapers."

He reaches into his raincoat and busts out a bag of mint chocolate chip cookies. Offers you the bag, says it'll help boost your energy. But this time you wise up. This time you don't accept his cookies. "Aw, Dillon, I thought you liked mint chocolate chip."

"What's going on here?" goes your daddy. "Do you two already know each other? You sent my own son to snoop on me?"

The Botox man eye-rolls till his eyes meet yours. "Don't look so angry, Dillon. I know your father's beyond the pale, but don't look so angry. After all, you and I both know that you're going to forgive your dear little daddy, don't we? And we both know *why* you'll forgive him." When you don't respond, he shouts at you, "Come on, Dillon, don't be afraid of this. Don't be like your pitiful old man over there – the kind of man who keeps flipping his fears into hatred. That's too easy, Dillon. It's too easy to feel repelled by the things you fear, and it's too easy to be hating and demonising the things that repel you. *Yes*, this is going to feel uncomfortable. *Yes*, it will hurt you and may even mutilate you. *So let it.* Why do you people always have so much trouble accepting things that cause you discomfort and pain?"

You tell him you don't know what he's talking about.

"Well, that's a very disappointing start, Dillon. Haven't I told you many times before about all the terabytes of data? The search histories, the messages, the seamless recording and uploading? Which means pretending you don't remember something is like claiming you don't know something. But you already know this, yes – you don't even need a search engine to tell you it." He places a hand on each of your shoulders. Pats twice and then smiles. Then he lets go and steps back. Clicks the neon strip lighting back on, relieves you of your flashlight, then heads down the tunnel in the direction of the exit.

When he's gone, your daddy finally grows the balls to step closer. "Dylan? Son?"

He looks for a chair. There ain't no chair.

"Dhilan? Dylan? What's wrong? Do you want me to call a doctor?"

You mean an ambulance, Mummy. An ambulance.

"Dylan, what's happening to your face?"

Apparently you can cure ulcers and other oral infections with salt.

"Son, what the hell is happening to your face?"

44

AND THEN YOU were back in your mother's hallway. Opening the front door in one last attempt to persuade Aunties Number Three and Four not to leave your ass alone with her. To tell them you'd go Tesco yourself later – you'd get whatever Mummy needed. But they'd gone, were long gone, you already knew they was gone. Been gone for thirty minutes. And then your mum started complaining about the door being open, about the draft slicing through into the living-room-cum-bedroom-cum-crematorium-anteroom. "I can feel it under my blanket," she moaned, *the breeze is making my down-below cold.* Like she was fine to suffocate on some tumour or choke on her own vomit just so long as she didn't catch a chill.

You slammed the front door as if slamming it shut behind you. Framed photographs falling. And then you – no, not *you. Me.*

I did what happens next.

Because at some point that afternoon – in that house-cum-fucking-hospice – you realised that this was all just gonna end in sadness. Heartstrings, violins, handkerchiefs. Teardrops and snot – *I'm very sorry for your loss.* Pandemic dribble of your mummy's liquefying jaw. Big group hug and then everyone cuddle whoever cries the most. You'd seen that shit in movies and oncology wards all across west London: *sadness always leads to consolation.* But after all the fuckugly shit she'd been through and fought through and all the things she'd done for you – after all her battles, all her muscles to smile through all the pain, all the selfless angelic sacrifices she'd made – surely sadness and consolation would be an insult? *What for all the bubbles of vomit and shit and blood if all we're gonna do is cuddle and sniffle and comfort each other with cups of sweet milky tea?* So, you see, that's how it finally hit you: this couldn't just end in standard-issue sadness. This shit had to be proper horrible.

When you stepped back into the living-room-cum-bedroom, the gastropub-cum-restaurant still hadn't full-on dissolved. The bed, the oxygen cylinder, the tables, the waiters, the diners. Your mum still dribbling eye saliva down her thighs – through the table cover, through the duvet, down her thighs. "I thought you'd gone away," she whimpered and snivelled and whimpered, "Dhilan, my sweetheart, when I heard the door slam I thought you'd gone away."

The smack of your hand on the wall like the sound of a knock on the door – not the front door, though, instead *that* knock on *that* door. The one where your student hall security guard bangs on your student hall door, tells you to stop sucking so-and-so's feet and get the hell outta bed, get your coat, get your keys. There's been an accident, a fatal side effect – the final fatal side effect. The chemo-induced pulmonary embolism and so on. All over the internet, minicab with sirens, what the hell is wrong with you, you weren't answering your fone. Culmination of ten years' hormonal action-hero fantasies about various assorted emergency scenarios, and now finally you understood why: cos this couldn't just end in standard-issue sadness – it had to be horrible.

"Why do you keep slamming the door and slapping the wall, Dhilan?"

"I don't keep doing it, Mummy, I only did it once."

"You did it twice."

"No I didn't. I did both things once. Two things, one time each."

"Two things once is the same as twice. Anyway, why even do it once, Dhilan? What is it? *Tell me.* You want to smash up the house? You want to break all the walls just because I asked you to close the front door? What is it you want from me? I'm bedridden. What do you want me to do?" And so on – as if she realised you now needed a row as a ruse to turn around and walk outta the home-cum-house-cum-hospice. That only by bailing on her could you make sure this shit wouldn't end horribly.

"I have to go now, Mum."

"But – where? Why? Why do you have to go?"

"Nowhere. Just the newsagent's. Just to get some stuff. Some milk." *Do you need anything, Mummy? Any asprin or vitamins or sanitary napkins?*

"But, Dhilan, we *have* milk. And – but you *hate* milk. And, anyway, what are you talking about, sweetheart? You just saw that your aunties have gone to Tesco – they'll get the milk and all my things. They always get for me all my things. So, no, Dhilan, no. You're here now, so now you stay here. Right here. With me – you and me. Like how we always used to. How we're meant to."

You smiled at a couple now kissing two tables to your left. The menus, the cutlery, the moody waiters. It would've been wrong to just leave your mother there by herself. All by herself in the afternoon. On a Tuesday afternoon. Not as shitty as leaving her by herself on weekend evenings and mornings and evenings and afternoons and mornings and evenings and weekends, but, nonethefuck, still wrong.

i.e. you shouldn't leave her, Dillon.

Dylan, you mustn't leave her.

After all, *Dhilan* would never have even moved out to student halls – *Dhilan* would've probly got himself homeschooled. So just stay put, stay here, stay and learn some lessons from Dhilan.

Do what Dhilan would do.

What Dhilan would've done.

For instance, if you weren't allowed to head to the newsagent's, you could always go chill in your bedroom – *her* bedroom, *your* bedroom, whatever. Count to ten. Think about the way she used to smile back when she was still herself. Or, better still, just go hang out in the toilet. Not her pantry of multi-buy bedpans, her actual downstairs accessible toilet. Bog-standard lid-free toilet seat; step-free, curtain-free shower cubicle. Handrails and handles everywhere like as if the tiles had contracted some kinda towel-rail disease. Dampness cos both the window and extractor fan were bust. If you smell a puddle of blood for long enough without it drying up, you'll notice it starts to smell a little sweet. Same with vomit. Same with excrement. Same with horrible.

You looked around the gastropub-cum-restaurant for the door or the stairs to the men's room. *Just go to the men's room and be done with it.* Cos there really weren't no other choice for you. For serious – what were your other options? Bog-standard hugging? Bog-standard cuddling? That bog-standard sadness fuckery? Bog-standard sadness-followed-by-consolation-followed-by-time-heals-everything? Or how about bog-standard compassion-fatigue followed by visions of euthanasia? Bog-standard accidental matricidal overdose? Bog-standard mother–son smothering flipped 180 into literal smothering combined with compressive asphyxia? But surely that shit just leads to sadness too – still bog-standard sadness. Well then, how about a bit of bog-standard Oedipal incest? Bog-standard bathtub awkwardness? Only it couldn't be bog-standard cos it had to be horrible. When you was a little boy, you used to be so, so scared of your mummy dying in some accident – so fixated by the fear of it that you kept wetting your bed. So what the fuck happened? What the fucking cuntfuck has happened here that you stopped being allergic to the thought of it? Did you start mourning her sooner than you actually needed to? How do you fix the bereavement equivalent of peaking too early? And if you can't stop grieving for someone while they're alive, how the fuck you gonna stop grieving for them when they actually dead? Cos she was dying and dead and dying. *Your mum is dead, your mum is dead, your mum is dying and dead and basically all but oven-ready dead.* Cos how to make that sentence less awful? Delete the word "dead" and replace it with "dying"? Delete the word "dying" and replace it with "not dying"? And when that no longer works? Could you then delete the word "mum"?

"Mum?"

"Yes, son?"

"Mum?"

"*Yes, Dhilan?*"

"Nothing. I won't go newsagent's. I'll stay." *I'll stay. And watch. And wait. See what happens. Let things bubble up to the surface.* "I'll stay."

And so you just sat there and sucked your mouth ulcers. Your Dylan, Dillon and Dhilan fones all switched to silent then laid out and surrendered on the dining-cum-dressing-table. Just plastic rectangles now that no longer spoke, no longer glowed, no longer corroborated your own dirty distortions, no longer foretold.

"Why do you keep chewing your cheeks, Dhilan? Is it the mouth ulcers again? Stop sucking them, sweetheart, just put some salt on them."

You told her you'd already put salt on them. That you'd gargled with salt water while heating her soup. You'd even drunk some of the salt water, like the closest you'd ever get to downing a fun-filled shot of tequila.

And then you slammed the empty shot glass on her dressing-table-cum-dining-table-cum-bar.

"WHAT IS IT, DHILAN?" she screamed. "WHAT IS IT, WHAT IS IT, *WHAT THE BLOODY FUCKING HELL IS IT*? WHY DO YOU KEEP SMACKING THE TABLE AND THE DOORS AND THE WALL?"

Breathe. Count to ten.

Another ten.

Delete the word "dying".

Delete the word "dead".

Delete the word "mum".

"Daddy?"

"*What?*"

Not knowing why the fuckness you was suddenly bringing your dad into it – back then you didn't even *know* your dad, hadn't even seen the man in years. Couldn't seriously be pining after your father like some sappy, emo-listening sixth-former – and yet you went and said it again: "Daddy".

"You want to go live with your father? Is that it? Is that what this is? Give me my phone, then, Dhilan. Go on, give me my phone, maybe I still have a number to call him. Though why in the hell you can't just wait till I'm dead . . ."

You can't be dead, you ain't even dying.

You can't be dying, you ain't even dead.

This ain't some plain-vanilla state of denial, this is just crunching the data from all the other times you been dying. Predictions based on your previous behaviour.

". . . and please, Dhilan, stop sucking your mouth ulcers – just leave it to the salt to heal them. *How many times do I have to tell you?* I won't always be here to tell you – can't you see that I'm dying?"

Then swallowing the sudden rush of vomit but only tasting the salt water. *Oh, fuck you, you ain't dying, fuck you.*

You ain't dying, you're making it up.

You ain't dying cos you're only forty-nine and you got breast cancer when you was thirty-nine.

You can't just end when you're thirty-nine.

I'm only nine years old back then – you haven't even taught me how to shave yet. Haven't taught me how ride a bike, tie a necktie, untie the necktie, you haven't taught me how to walk away. So, no. No, you ain't dying and you ain't my mum, you're making it all up.

"I'm sorry, sweetheart. I'm so sorry that I keep telling you I'm dying. It isn't fair for me to keep saying it to you – I know it isn't fair. Everything about this illness isn't fair. But I just . . . it's just . . . sometimes I wonder if you think I'm making it all up."

The first time your mum told you she had cancer you wanted to ask her to show you her tumour. Not just the pictures from her mammogram, you meant her actual-fact tumour. And not for the purposes of proof – more a souvenir. No, a *specimen*. A sample so that you could personally try and find a cure. Couldn't they stick her tumour in a jar or something? Or in a mother–son Valentine's jewellery box. A pillbox, a velvet cushion, a jar. With pickle so her Sweetheart Son could eat it. Just eat it and chew it and swallow it and make it magically disappear. "Fuck you, woman, you ain't dying, *fuck you!*"

"Dhilan?" she sniffled. "What are you talking about?" Now full-on sobbing. "What is it that you want from me? I'm going, son. Sweetheart, I promise I'll soon be gone."

She must've thought you was gonna smack her or someshit. To stop her chatting all that nonsense about dying. To smack her back to her senses. *I tell you, if my daughter did a thing like this I would* thapar *her – one hard slap across her face.* And when she raised her right arm in self-defence, the left shoulder strap of her nightie slipped off. You didn't notice it at first – you was too busy reassuring her that you wouldn't never ever hit her. Or maybe you just didn't notice it cos you'd seen it all before. All them accidental sightings while changing her dressings and unzipping her dresses and petticoats and that. Body-scrub, towel-dry, moisturise, rub iodine into her underarm scars. Allow it – ain't nothing to feel embarrassed about. Men were allowed to flex some pride in their battle scars, so why the fuck shouldn't women? Men displayed them on their arms and their pecs – their own little slits of superheroism. So, no – no need for her to feel awkward or shamed of the mess of scars on her chest where her breasts used to be. Or the scars on her hips or the scars on her stomach or the scars on her soul. And ain't no need for you to feel embarrassed by her lack of embarrassment. Don't get all soppy and chivalrous though – no need for this to end in sadness when it could still honour her by being horrible. Like the promise of an oracle or the prophecy of an algorithm – everything in accordance with the horribleness of her disease. Here – look, here – right in front of you. The most pornofied part of a woman's body and the reason humans evolved lips in the first place. The reason we're called "mammals". Reason babies can afford to be born so weak.

"Do you understand what I'm saying, woman?" This time you spoke directly to her exposed spaghetti of post-surgical scarring – "You ain't my mummy."

Scar tissue is harder for a reason. Everything stronger at the seams. Your mother–son love like two lumps of meat soldered together instead of sewn – fused by fever and chemo and screaming. Cos this shit couldn't just end in sadness – it *had* to be horrible.

"What the hell nonsense are you talking, Dhilan? If I'm not your mother, then who the hell *is* your mother?"

"You are, of course."

"*Please,* Dhilan, what the bloody hell are you talking?"

"I mean your Facebook page is. Your blog is, your Instagram is." *Because digital content doesn't die, etc. And cos, online or offline, women don't actually have to be defined by their bodies.*

You carried on staring at her scars just to prove you wasn't afraid of them – of the caverns and indents and nodules within them.

Don't even have to be defined by their body odours. Or by their various assorted bodily fluids.

The rigid scar tissue and the squishy. The bone dry and the clammy. Cos this couldn't just end in sadness – it had to be proper horrible.

Ain't no lymph glands online either. No sweat glands, no nostrils, no arsehole, no armpits.

Every tiny little bump and lump and dimple. Beneath them and between them. The fungal terrain of some kinda psycho-psoriasis battleground. Cos this couldn't just end in sadness – it had to be horrible.

And why am I always so hung up about your bodily fluids, Mum? Why do they make me so upset? After all, weren't I born in them? And before I was born, didn't I basically used to be them? Didn't I used to be liquid fucking bodily fluid?

Every little blister-like bunion and abscess and every ulcerated contusion. Because, for both of you, it had to be horrible. No, not *you. Me.*

I did what happens next.

Cos you ain't my mum, you're just her body. Your liquids ain't her spirit and your stench is not her soul. I mean your scent – your scent is not her soul. All your fluids and your illness and your liquids, all of those things mean that I don't even know where your body begins and where your body ends, Mummy. It's just like what I told you when I was nine and I couldn't yet calibrate my cuddling: how the hell can I hold you properly if I don't know which bits of you to hold and which bits of you to let go?

"And do you wanna know the reason you ain't my mummy?" I asked her – though now just staring at and stroking her swimming-cap scalp. Wondering if it was horrible that I'd miss her scalp more than I'd miss her hair and I'd miss her scarring more than I'd miss her scalp. "It's cos you're too mashed up to be my mother. Too gross and disgusting and . . ."

When, right on cue, my stomach started retching, I tried telling Mum that it was only cos I'd swallowed all that salt water to cure my mouth ulcers. Next, I tried telling her I was retching with guilt over all the sick horrible shit I'd just said to her – *that I wasn't really retching at the sight of her.* But I couldn't say these things properly cos I was too busy retching. Then I tried telling her that I'd seen her body probly thousands of times before and I'd never felt nauseous once. But I couldn't say this properly cos I was so nauseous. Her tears making it seem like as if the scarring had now spread to her face. The pre-bereavement counsellor had warned me that even my mourning would be deformed, but they didn't say jack about this part – the part where it can't just end in sadness, so it has to be horrible.

The drool from your mouth like some brand-new blend of gastric acid. Like the liquid itself was ulcerated. To melt away this moment or maybe to mark it, imprint it, to motherfucking milk it. To sulphurise any lingering sweetness. Until finally, fucking finally, you were in sync once again – mother and son crying and retching in sync. Her whole face squelching while sniffling. Skin tone draining from cancer-patient pale to public-toilet porcelain. And before you could move away from her, your puke came, projectile-style – off-white McDonald's vanilla milkshake. Blanket coverage all over her bed, but – oh shitfuck – maybe her bedding was waterproof or someshit, non-absorbent, mercy-resistant. Because no need to spell out where your vanilla milkshake vomit should choose to pool and puddle. Flowing back towards the place like rainwater is drawn into drains. Her reaching for one of her wigs to frantically wipe it away. Howling out to her own dead mum for help.

You remember trying to back away or swallow it – to swallow any follow-up.

You remember being drawn to it. Some kinda duty to stay with it.

Watching it to see if it would melt her or mark her or contaminate her. Maybe even make things even more horrible by infecting her mammary scar tissue so you could drink the pus and pretend you was once again suckling. Cos it couldn't just end in sadness.

Later, you remember wondering why your feet were boiling. The soles of your trainers.

Like the carpet was sweating gastric acid. Or underground radiation. A bonfire beneath the floorboards.

The burning of possessions and refuse and shit that should really be recycled or donated.

A dirty old man incinerating secrets and a stash of topless pornography.

A boy disposing of stolen headscarves and dresses and other flammable items.

Note to Norman Bates: do not store your mother in the heat of the cellar.

Note to businessmen: do not hide your data servers in the basement.

Note to Oedipus: stay the fuck away from oracles and smartfones and search engines.

Note to men in general: we all got our liquids and fluids so do not diss her and don't be horrible.

Be an adult, focus on the positives.

Pay her compliments. Buy fucking flowers.

Be careful which stories you choose to click on.

Or else you'll never even get close to deserving her love.

And you'll never be able to bury her or burn her or both.

Your mother gave up with the sopping-wet wig. Just gazed down at her chest like as if she was looking at you – all your private unseen thoughts forced outta your stomach and now visible. Like the puddle of your puke was part of you, the same way part of your mummy sometimes seeped into the bathmat. But, truth is, right then the puke seemed more like someone else – a third person right there in the room with you. A witness. She'd told you one time that she felt shame when she was alone and embarrassment when with you. Well, now your vomit was the stranger that made her feel total humiliation.

You looked towards her bedside table – as if you could somehow divert her attention from your soaking sticky foulness. More framed fotos, stack of kidney bowls, bouquets of clichés in plastic vases. *Didn't I used to buy you flowers, Mummy? All those battered bunches. Everyone buys flowers for people in hospital, but I got you that bunch after my first day at uni, even though you were back in remission. You wrote in your blog that it was the happiest moment of your life.*

Didn't you?

Didn't you?

You started remembering that the bouquet in question had actually been meant for Ramona – but you figured, fuck it, that detail no longer mattered now. Maybe it never did.

And you blogged about my exam results, didn't you? Didn't you? Fuck my A levels and GCSEs. I wish I could just give them all back. If I'd just settled for grade Bs instead of As that coulda given us an extra three months together. Or if I'd aimed for Ds and Es we could've had another nine months. You made me in nine months, Mummy. Made me out of your body and bodily fluids. Fuck it, if I'd just failed everything we could've had another two years together. Just fail everything and take better care of you. I hate my fucking exam results, Mummy. I don't wanna be some golden-escalator graduate trainee. I wanna flip burgers in Maccy D's. I want us to have had another two years. Or how about I just fuck up now at uni just to even things out? I'll never be able to say I did my best but maybe I could fuck up everything else just to even shit out?

Then, as quickly as it had happened, the clean-up. The mopping and scrubbing and cleansing. Nearly new sheets, nearly new nightie, nearly new wig. And throughout this, she didn't say diddly-jack. Your somehow-still-prettyful mum didn't say a single word. Knew straight away for definite that she'd never ever speak of this to no one else – that your aunties and uncles and aunties would always think the worst thing you ever done was just walk out on her. And she didn't even seem disgusted by it: as if cleaning up your bodily fluids was part of the dictionary definition of motherhood. Just gave you a blister-pack of her high-strength anti-vomiting tablets. Well, what did you expect? That she'd rip the cannula from her arm and use the needle to poke out her eyes? Fuck's sake, haven't you read the story, Dillon? It's Oedipus who gouges out his eyes, not his mother. So no – no drama, no cannula, no hypodermic needle, no knitting needle, not even a pair of her blindfolds to shield you from the sight of her. Just a pack of her anti-vomiting pills. And a box of Imodium. As if to reassure you it was probly just food poisoning. As if she'd already rehearsed every possible scenario too often to let any of them be horrible.

Or maybe she'd just rehearsed that specific scenario.

Maybe she knew that the retching hadn't really come from you; it had come from someone else.

45

WE DON'T BOTHER incinerating the newspapers. Dad and I don't speak about it, don't speak about anything. We just reach some agreement not to do it. Like he's taken on my mummy's mind-reading techniques. Still, we walk through the tunnel to the furnace. To go through the motions. To say that we came. The incinerator itself more like some rubbish bin – the steel kind, the kind that homeless men light fires in. Abandoned trolleys and tracks on the floor where people have dragged their files and dropped them in.

Dad says he's been clearing out his flat for the benefit of Naliah and her mum. Reaches into his briefcase and chucks in a collection of topless porn mags. I reach into my breast pocket and throw in my mother's lilac headscarf. And also flowers – why can't I conjure up some bunch of flowers? Don't matter who I'd bought them for. Don't matter that every time I'd magicked them into existence, Mum would tell me I deserved a better mum. Or that I've never actually told her that she couldn't possibly be better.

"Son, there's something I've wanted to tell you ever since we got back in touch with each other." Dad speaks as if I'm standing in front of him instead of beside him. Heat slapping up against our faces. "That first time we met in McDonald's – when you thought I was an insurance salesman. Well, it reminded me of something I learnt from my colleagues in the insurance company. You see, when insurers do all their predictive modelling to work out a customer's health premium or life premium or whatnot, they only look at the hard data. The evidence. They don't look for stories – for cause and effect and whatnot. This is because correlations in the data are not the same thing as causation. Over the years I found it very helpful to know this. And I think maybe it's important you know this too."

When Dad tries laying his hand on my shoulder, I throw it off. "Then why the hell tell me everything you just told me?" I ask him. "All that stuff about your stories – about why you turned away from her. Why did you tell me all that? Why didn't you just carry on keeping it hidden?"

Dad says that he hadn't been hiding it – that how could he have been hiding it when he didn't even know it himself. He says that over the years he's told himself many reasons why he and my mum had got divorced, but never *ever* not once the reason he'd told me tonight. He swears he honestly didn't know it till now – not until I started searching for him.

When he tries again to lay his hand on my shoulder, he brushes my face and I turn my head. For some reason, this makes him flex some smile. "You know, you used to do that all the time when you were a baby, Dhilan. You'd turn your head whenever we touched your face."

I tell him that all babies do that. That it's a reflex, a pre-loaded program. Like breathing and grasping and suckling. In fact, it's the reflex that leads on to the suckling reflex. I tell him there's a technical term for it, but I don't know what it is.

"Yes you do, Dhilan – there's WiFi down here so it's in your pocket. It's in my pocket too." He pulls out his smartfone. "With all the knowledge we carry in our pockets these days, it's a wonder we don't need industrial-strength belts and braces."

He googles the words "babies turning heads before suckling".

Turns out the technical term is a rooting reflex. Turns out there's also another technical name for it: the searching reflex.

Epilogue

LEFT MY OLD man in the external storage facility. Told him I'd got me some 5am breakfast lecture/seminar/business meeting bullshit. Figured it was okay to lie to him so long as the lie was obvious. Besides, if I'd stuck around we'd have had all that single-file weirdness while I followed him out, and I'm done with following him. Don't matter that it was me who led the way in. Me who'd been holding the torch.

Wait around in the middle of the street like I'm scoping for a taxi. Botox man takes his time showing up. We stroll badass-style in silence, then duck indoors when it starts to rain or turn cold or snow or whatever. First time I ever been first in line for a freshly laid Egg McMuffin.

"Your father, he wasn't lying to you back there, Dhilan. But as you already know, his story requires a small clarification. Or an update. Old-fashioned word is correction."

We got the pick of every freshly disinfected plastic table. I choose some maximum privacy setting by the window.

"We told your father that story about being a crime syndicate for the same reason he's spent the past few days telling stories to you. Stop him seeking out the truth. At first, we tried not to tell him anything. But you yourself know how difficult that strategy can be. So then we simply tried to create endless confusion and debate. That's how things work these days: censorship through distraction, too much information, trivialism, continuously contesting the basic facts."

He chucks a sachet of sugar into his coffee. Without actually opening the sachet.

"You know, Dhilan, this food chain has really started to grow on me. Milkshake on tap. Flesh patties on tap. All that clever industrial pipework inserted into bleeding udders. The wonders of American technology bequeathed to the whole wide world. Remind me, how old were you when your mother forbade you from eating McDonald's?"

I tell him seven.

"Horseshit. You'd just turned eight. Imagine if she knew the crapfuck you fuel yourself with these days. Then again, our bodies are hardwired to gorge on sugars and fats because those things used to be so scarce. That's why junk food's so addictive, Dhilan. *Hardwiring.* And, as you surely know in your bone marrow by now, the same goes for junk information and junk stories."

I tell him it'd be a bit of a dick move to bust out more media sermonising after the shit I just been through. Thing is, though, I already got me some generalised idea what he's gonna fess up – like as if my brain is switched to autocomplete. Cos it ain't about your data, it's about what your data does to you when it's crunched up and processed and fed back to you. And cos, sometimes, how you wind up knowing something can change what you wind up knowing. Cos some answers, they shouldn't come instant-style at the click of some button. Sometimes you gotta layer it – gotta know enough to know it.

"You were almost correct the first time we met, Dhilan. I *have* been trying to stop a student start-up. But your snivelling solipsism meant you thought it was your own start-up. You're so accustomed to being at the centre of your own mother–son drama – your own personalised little snot bubble."

He tells me the made-up eyewitness quotes that he'd got planted all them years back in a bunch of English-language newspapers contained special triggers: "A series of coded mathematical triggers rendered as letters of the Roman alphabet. They would be activated by the simple process of being digitised and put up on the web. And the purpose of these triggers was to subvert an algorithm that had been devised as part of a PhD thesis undertaken by two enterprising students at Stanford University. But unlike today's student start-ups, they didn't use their clever algorithm to establish some sillyfuck restaurant reservation app. They used it to create the mother of all search engines."

He scans me for some response. Only newsflash for me here is this guy's sudden brand-new skillset for getting straight to the point.

"Understand that I have no beef with Google, Dhilan. They had the best of intentions. Give people the most relevant answers to their questions as quickly as possible. Simple. Noble. *Yes* – even noble. Our beef had more to do with the way we expected that original search algorithm to evolve – specifically the idea of relevance that lay right at the algorithm's heart."

I catch myself once again fronting with geekness: "Because relevancy means clickbait?"

"Because relevance means relevance, Dhilan. We wanted to stop you people from being conditioned to expect to find relevance in the stories that you're reading. Equally, we wanted to stop stories from aspiring to relevance."

That's all for today about Oedipus.

Ain't fully for sure what he means by relevance, though. Start scrolling through the dropdowns in my head. Could mean it links in with the subject you been searching for. Or could be it links in with some topic in the news. Could be it links in with your own personal shit – or with your family or your friends or your neighbours or whoever. Fuck it, could even be it's relevant to someone who you hate. The dropdown options keep on dropping.

"When you look back on today's shitshow, Dhilan, whose answers to your question will prove most relevant – your father's revelations or my revelations right now? Or maybe even someone else's revelations still to come? Surely this is something that you alone will be best placed to judge. And, ideally, *after* you've taken in whatever we've told you."

Botox man's now on some proper solids for breakfast. Can't tell if it's just an Egg McMuffin, though. Supersize hands and munching it without removing the wrapper. Carries on talking with paper wrapping in his mouth. Telling me how, back in the day, relevance was mainly about the quality of the webpages thrown up by Google's search engine. It meant cutting through all the spam and second-rate crap on the web. Filtering out the shit and the sex. Says that the whole fixationship with relevancy then spread to other tech platforms, other digital businesses – till one day it dominated how the digital world works.

Now an ad for custom-tailorised advertising.

An article about surveillance capitalism.

"But at the end of the day, kid, these algorithms are designed to serve business models. Businesses that are obliged to keep growing. My associates and I therefore feared that, for many tech firms, ad-funded revenue models and targeted personalisation would wind up limiting the concept of relevance to popularity and personal resonance . . ."

Now an ad for a recommended story.

". . . And, of course, those same business models would mean that these conceptions of relevancy would be valued higher than factual accuracy. How useful and glueful the information is for the user becomes more important than how truthful it is." He says it wasn't difficult for them to predict the fuckfest that would follow.

See also: the well-known history of humankind.

See also: all those well-known cognitive biases of the human mind.

"I mean, you didn't exactly need the oracle from Oedipus to tell you what was likely to happen, Dhilan – just a basic Humanities degree would do." He puts down his food like it can't help him no more. Still ain't sure if this is just some Egg McMuffin. "You know the rest of the story, kid. What happened to the world. People deciding to only believe stories and information that they agree with. The monetisation of misinformation and hatred. Polarisation.

The source of unlimited information serving to limit so many people's understanding. Knowledge itself becoming ignorance. And, of course, everything now both true and false. Every fact like that famous cat that gets locked in a box with poison – the one that's both alive and dead at the same time. Dying and dead and dying – they should call them Schrödinger's facts."

Then he switches to talking about the practical stuff. Says the task of cleaning up the algorithms couldn't be left to dickless governments and media regulators. He explains that if their trigger codes had worked, they'd have kept on fucking up Google's early search results so that people would've got used to different ideas of what counts as relevant info – would've got into the habit of deciding it for themselves. Search engines would've then evolutioned on some different path, steering the rest of the digital world away from the fields of bullshit. Maybe something closer to old-school surfing instead of searching. Or selecting your own multiple definitions of relevance for each individual search query. Or some kind of built-in randomness, serendipity, diversity, alternate perspectives. Whatever would make it physically impossible for people to just swallow whatever knowledge and info they got fed with. Whatever would save the facts from hand-to-hand combat with relevance. Whatever would stop the truth from becoming irrelevant.

Then he throws out a For Example. Tells me to imagine searching for images linked to the keyword "beauty". Only, this time, forget being hit with answers dominated by the beauty industry's definition, and forget being hit by my own personalised foot fetish. Instead, I'd get images of sunsets or baby elephants or something – or, fuck it, why not even distorted faces and other deformations. Flexing his botched Botox as he says this.

And now for today's lesson about Oedipus.

"Better still, Dhilan, think back to your first few childhood searches for knowledge about Oedipus. Now imagine that, instead of receiving stories dominated by the standard Greek tragedy or Freudian incest nightmares, your top search results also contained the American rock band named Oedipus. Or, at the very least, completely different viewpoints – contrary viewpoints, counter-theories, diametrically distinct perspectives. Or how about the perspective of Oedipus's mother and wife? After all, she was the smarter one who managed to understand it all before he did. And the first recorded version of the myth focuses on *her*, not him."

That's all for today about Oedipus.

I scroll back with a quickness: "So wait a sec. Your big badass plan with the trigger codes and the made-up eyewitnesses quotes – you're basically saying you were planting fake news stories in order to save the world from fake news stories?"

"Well at least the cure would have gone viral, kid."

But, of course, their big badass plan got trashed when my dad rumbled himself and his stories never got digitised. The trigger codes they spent so long planting, calibrating and sequencing remained incomplete.

"Your father's fuck-up gave us pause for thought. Rather than simply plant the missing bits of code in someone else's stories, we decided to wait a few years – to wait and watch what actually happened. More fool us. And then along came Facebook with their own algorithmic models of what's relevant – though I understand these days they prefer the term 'personally informative'. None of us back then could have even imagined the power Facebook would have to decide what kinds of stories and information people are fed. And our methods were simply inadequate for dealing with their levels of diaperless toddler chaos. Best we can do for now is just keep those original trigger codes hidden in order that we might keep ourselves hidden while we figure out what can be done."

Now he starts straight-up eating the remaining sugar sachets. Swallowing them with his coffee like as if they're capsules. "Dhilan, how come you haven't asked me who we are – my associates and me? I've finally told you what I've been doing and yet you don't even ask who I am."

I tell him ain't no point in having knowledge without understanding.

Anycase, fuck knows if he's even been telling me the truth here. Could be, I guess. But I do know he's for definite speaking truthfully when he tells me I should never have given away my attention so easy to all them custom-tailored scare stories. Those algorithmic recommendations and prophecies about Oedipal relations. That predictive tech is basically just another kind of narrowband relevancy. That Google and Facebook ain't actually the oracle; if anything they were more like Oedipus himself – tripped up by misinformation and false facts. That I shoulda been flexing more carefulness and judgement – not just about what stories I chose to click on, but also what stories I chose to accept as relevant and what definitions of relevance I chose to accept. In fact, fuck Oedipus. What the hell has Oedipus got to do with the shit between me and Mum?

The Botox man starts getting ready to split but then stops. His jumbo-sized hand stuck in some holding pattern – as if it can't figure out if it'd be cringe to land on my shoulder. "You know, it's idiotic enough to be authoring your own reality with your search history and so forth, but how could you possibly expect to get a sense of your mother's world that way? Obsessing over the most virulent imagery and information. Autoplaying more and more extreme versions of the same scenes in your head. Writing off her rage and bodily expulsions as just simple side effects of her treatment. Fixating only on what you're shown and told. What kind of relationship can someone have if they can't enter a shared reality? And even beyond your mother's perspective, what about that of other people in your life? Because once you let go of relevance, you'd be surprised at the things that turn out to be much more relevant."

Then finally, after all his lecturising and sermonising, he drops one final data download like a footnote – an afterthought to a side-convo. The info I ain't puzzled out yet, the false fact, the thing that made me misunderstand the algorithmic predictions and prophecies: when they said I'd "take the father's place", turns out they weren't actually talking about *my* father. They were talking about my mummy's father.

Follow her into Holborn station. Piccadilly line – a straight line. Tube map turns everything into straight lines. Ramona ain't headed nowhere, though – just buys a newspaper and then steps back outta the Tube station. Rocking a grey woollen cardigan that's basically a coat. Ain't actually rehearsed how I'm gonna apologise for dumping her. Or how I'm gonna fess up about all my lies. Or tell her how she's been living in some alternate reality that I bullshitted into existence.

I just lame-like call out her name.

"So you've finally come to apologise."

Even though I've just basically jumped her, Ramona's like the polarised opposite of surprised.

"Only exactly what part do you want to apologise for, Dhilan? For ditching me? For treating me like a sack of shit? Or for lying to me for longer than I can even fucking remember?"

"Lying to you?" The denial in my mouth on autocomplete, sent before I can delete it.

"You seriously can't stop yourself, can you?"

I know I should probly be angstipating now, but it's like that shit's all been used up. My panic button worn down and busted. "So Naliah finally told you about my mum, then?"

"Oh, wake up, Dhilan. I knew long before Naliah showed up."

She says: why the fuck do I think she put up with the way I treated her all them years?

She says: sure, she might not have known all the details, but every time I let her down, she had a generalised idea why. Every time I kept secrets.

"I mean, seriously, Dhilan, how do you suppose I coped with all your nonsense? How do you think I did all those things that I did? Never mind how did I convince myself you weren't really cheating on me. And why the hell do you think I kept bringing you breakfast from Starbucks after every night you suddenly bailed on me in the middle of a date? I'm not a doormat, Dhilan. Maybe my feelings for you could rise above all the fictions and the facts, but my brain still had to operate at some level of reality."

I don't ask her how she found out. Or even when she found out. Seem like stupidass questions right now – questions more about me than her. Ramona now with full-on eye saliva, telling me she did all them things cos she wanted to help me. Says she could see that, even when we was together, I was always worrying about my mummy. And, anycase, given the nature of my bullshit, she didn't see no choice but to keep forgiving me. "I mean, otherwise I'd basically be labelling myself a heartless bitch, wouldn't I? And even right now, right here, I can't even have this conversation that we're having without putting to one side all the questions I desperately want to ask about your poor mum – I can't even imagine how horrible things have been. And so, once again, I feel like I'm being heartless for not asking. Well, I'm not bloody heartless, Dhilan. But, at the same time, I can't keep treading on eggshells around you."

I ask her why she let me keep on lying to her all them times. Lying for nothing for years.

"Because I wanted you to come clean, Dhilan. I wanted to know that you *would* come clean. I wasn't letting you lie, you dumbass, I was letting you tell me the truth."

Ramona looks down at the floor. Some midpoint between leaning towards me and leaving. "Look, you always seemed on the verge of telling me. But then another week would go by. Another month, another year. You know, for a while I even thought maybe your start-up was just a cover story."

She watches me fiddle with my Oyster card. *The fuck am I pulling out my Oyster card for?*

Because I can walk through the ticket turnstiles now.

The Piccadilly line – a straight line. Today an even straighter line.

Cos I'm ready to go back to Acton now.

Step closer to Ramona and hold her. But, again, I'm doing that thing where I'm only hugging as tight as I calculate a woman in this state should be hugged. And so I tell her that I can do better now – I mean *properly*. I tell her I can do this properly now. Tell her, "Everything can be okay now."

She kisses me on the forehead. Smiles. And, still smiling, she scrunches her nose. Tries to free herself from my hug but doesn't even need to cos my arms ain't no longer hugging her. Doesn't wanna say nothing, but her words come out anyway. "Except I guess we both know that's obviously bullshit, don't we, Dhilan?"

And I'm thinking, maybe it was meant to be obvious?

Cos, fact is, I don't need to bullshit her no more. Don't need to bullshit anyone ever again.

Acknowledgements

THANK YOU SO much to everyone at Unbound for turning my manuscript into a book, particularly my editor Rachael Kerr for your invaluable suggestions, advice and endless moral support; DeAndra Lupu for masterminding the publication and for all your patience and understanding; John Mitchinson for rescuing both myself and the manuscript from the scrapheap and also for suggesting the perfect title; Georgia Odd and Jimmy Leach for all your crowdfunding advice; Amy Winchester for your tireless championing of this project; Lauren Fulbright for your work behind the scenes; and Anna Simpson for all your encouragement.

Thanks also to Mark Ecob for a literally cracking cover; Justine Taylor for copy-editing; Kate Quarry for proofreading; Mark Bowsher for the fundraising video; Peter Straus, Matthew Turner, Mohsen Shah and everyone at Rogers Coleridge & White.

And thank you, thank you, thank you to each and every single person listed in the back for crowdfunding the book's publication. This book simply wouldn't exist without your incredible generosity and faith.

As for writing the manuscript, it wouldn't have been doable without the support, guidance, patience/forbearance of so many people, inspirations, Gods and deities. I hope all those to whom I owe thanks will forgive my failure here to mention individuals by name. You shall always have my deepest gratitude. A shout-out to all those young carers and former young carers who took precious time out to speak with me, or whose testimonies I read.

Thank you to Shri Hanuman and to the Bhagavad Gita.

Thank you to our mother, Meena, for all the wondrous things she's done for us. You came before names, before language.

Thank you to Maria for keeping the faith – I couldn't have nailed this book without you.

And, finally, thank you to you for reading this book.

About the Author

Gautam Malkani's first novel *Londonstani* was published in 2006. His journalism has appeared in the *Financial Times*, the *Guardian* and the *New York Times*. He lives in London.